"Callahan transports us back to postwar America, nailing the politics, fashion, cars, and social mores. As real as this story of Betty's brief and scandalous reign is, it's the best kind of fiction; so believable that I was wondering about its authenticity until the author's note." —*Star-Ledger*

"Truth plus fiction equals an entertaining read."
—*Philadelphia* magazine

"Callahan nimbly guides the reader from the rounds of the Miss America competition to Times Square to a climax on a seaside cliff during a masquerade ball. *The Night She Won Miss America* is a delightfully dramatic and fast-paced summer read, with just the right amount of darkness to balance out the fluff."
—*BookPage*

"Callahan clearly enjoys the camp, loading his book with period details and midcentury slang." —*New York Times Book Review*

"A wild tale . . . Early in her pageant experience, Betty muses that 'Miss America does odd things to people.' Clearly, she had no idea. Callahan creates a story that is brisk-paced and fluid."
—*Kirkus Reviews*

"A heady whirl of gowns, gloves, chaperones, lipstick, escorts, cocktails, and romance. This engaging tale paints an evocative picture of a bygone era and the postwar ideal of young American womanhood."

—Helen Bryan, author of the international bestseller *War Brides*

"Callahan has crafted an intriguing suspense story marrying the frothy, fashion-fueled pageant world with the secrets people have to live with." —*Booklist*

"This plot-driven story blends aspects of romance, mystery, and thriller . . . Fans of midcentury drama, beauty queens, and gripping romance will enjoy this adventurous read."

—*School Library Journal*

"I can't remember the last time I got so caught up in a novel. Michael Callahan's gorgeous prose brings to life an intoxicating world of beauty queens and thwarted dreams that will sweep you away in a whirlwind of intrigue, passion, and secrets."

—Matthew Pearl, best-selling author of
The Dante Club and *The Last Bookaneer*

"A page-turner." —*New Jersey Monthly*

the
Night She Won
Miss America

the
Night She Won
Miss America

Michael Callahan

Mariner Books
Houghton Mifflin Harcourt
BOSTON   NEW YORK

For information about permission to reproduce selections
from this book, write to trade.permissions@hmhco.com
or to Permissions, Houghton Mifflin Harcourt Publishing
Company, 3 Park Avenue, 19th Floor, New York,
New York 10016.

hmhco.com

Library of Congress Cataloging-in-Publication Data
Names: Callahan, Michael, 1963- author.
Title: The night she won Miss America : a novel / Michael Callahan.
Description: Boston : Houghton Mifflin Harcourt, 2017.
Identifiers: LCCN 2016045994 (print) | LCCN 2016054728 (ebook) |
ISBN 9780544809970 (hardcover) | ISBN 9781328915832 (paperback) |
ISBN 9780544810013 (ebook)
Subjects: | BISAC: FICTION / Historical. | FICTION / General. |
GSAFD: Love stories. | Romantic suspense fiction.
Classification: LCC PS3603.A44336 N54 2017 (print) |
LCC PS3603.A44336 (ebook) | DDC 813/.6 — dc23
LC record available at https://lccn.loc.gov/2016045994

Book design by Rachel Newborn

Printed in the United States of America
DOC 10 9 8 7 6 5 4 3 2 1

"(There She Is) Miss America," words and music by
Bernie Wayne. Copyright © 1954, 1955 (Renewed)
by Bernie Wayne Music Co. All rights controlled and
administered by Spirit One Music (BMI). International
copyright secured. All rights reserved. Used by
permission of Alfred Music.

For Matt and Sean,
"The Boys"

The dream of a million girls who are more than pretty
Can come true in Atlantic City.

—from the song "(There She Is) Miss America,"
by Bernie Wayne

Prologue

Don't pick up don't pick up don't pick up.

Two rings, three rings. Only one more and the office voicemail kicks in, and he's off the hook. He has his message already rehearsed.

He hears the click of the receiver being retrieved, silently curses to himself. He thinks about hanging up, but Caller ID makes that impossible.

Fuck.

"Where are you?" she says. No hello. Not that he can blame her. Half of her job is spent trying to figure out where he is at any given moment.

"I finally got the break I was looking for on the Miss America story," he replies with as much gravitas as he can muster. "I shook out an address."

She sighs, the way every managing editor he's ever worked with has sighed. The job of a managing editor is to enforce deadlines and discipline, and he is abjectly terrible with both. But he is talented, the most talented writer at *Philadelphia* magazine, and his boss knows it and he knows it and even stern managing editor Emily Lawrence knows it, so he is cut more slack than everyone else. Which has only ensured that he is hated by everyone else.

"You knew that the monthly staff meeting was this morning at eleven," Emily says, the ice creeping into his ear. "Everyone needs to bring two ideas for the Shore Guide. You already missed the Best Things for Kids meeting last month."

He exhales wearily. "Em, we both know I suck at the service stuff, which is why I don't write it. So why would anyone want my ideas? This is a great story—"

"That's always your excuse for not pulling your weight. 'This is a great story.'"

"And they always are."

"Hold on. He just walked by. I'm transferring you. And don't dare hang up. He knows you're on the line. Good luck."

She says these last two words with enough sarcasm to fuel a late-night television monologue. It's justified, of course. He is aware that he makes her life more difficult. But he also knows he makes the magazine better, and in the end that is the only thing that should matter, especially in an age where print is dying quicker than a carnival goldfish. He wonders if this is how it felt to be working for a company that produced vinyl records in the 1980s. Or to have been a blacksmith, and then watched Henry Ford putter by in his Model T.

Fletcher clicks on. "Where are you?"

"On my way to Gladwyne. I finally tracked down an address for Betty Welch. Turns out she's been here for the past few years, hiding in plain sight. I told you my source said she was local again. Her husband died about five years ago, and she moved here from Colorado to be closer to her son and grandkids."

"For a guy who has written pieces uncovering payoffs in the judicial system and a toxic waste dump in the middle of Bucks County, you seem oddly fixated on an old Miss America. I hope this story is going to prove to be worth all of the energy you're putting into it."

"Not a doubt. Look, she's never talked about what happened. Ever. She's been dodging the press for decades—she even stopped using her first name. She's gone by Jane since it all happened. She's in her mid-eighties now. If ever she was going to say, 'Oh, what the hell,' it's going to be now, when she's near the end of her own road. It's a fascinating tale and she's never told it. This could be like the Philly version of having gotten Jackie Kennedy to tell the whole story of what it was like in Dealey Plaza."

Fletcher snorts. "Gee, I'm glad you're not overselling this."

"Look, Fletch, will you just trust me on this? I know everyone thinks I am a total pain in the ass—"

"You *are* a total pain in the ass."

"Yes, but I am a pain in the ass who delivers. Trust me here. My instincts are good. We know she has an amazing story to share. It's just a matter of getting her to open up and actually share it."

A deep sigh on the other end of the line. Sometimes Bron pictures the entire staff sighing in unison when his name comes up, one gigantic, weary whiffle. The same one he has heard from his parents, his grammar school teachers, every one of his girlfriends. The wordless expression of *What are we going to do about Bronwyn?*

"Well, you're halfway there, so okay, fine, go see if she'll talk," Fletcher says. "But when you get back into the office, we are having a serious sit-down about your lax attitude about staff meetings, idea generation, writing for the Web, everything. Whether you like it or not, you are part of a team here, Bron. It's time you start acting like it. You are not irreplaceable. Are you hearing me?"

"Loud and clear," Bron replies. "Talk later."

Team my ass, he thinks, shaking his head as he continues up the

Schuylkill Expressway. *What you need me to do is to get great stories. And that is exactly what I am going to do.*

❧

The center-hall Colonial is Main Line standard issue, white with pine-green trim, matching shutters, side garage, and a nicely mani-cured lawn sloping down to the street to a ye olde black lamppost. Bron checks the address again, flips his notebook closed. He grabs a ballpoint pen from the cup holder and steps out of the car. The road curves up from Route 23, transforming from busy highway to bucolic street in mere seconds. Bron wonders how many dough-nuts have been consumed on this block by cops sitting in their se-dans, speed-trapping driver after driver making the exit at 60 only to suddenly find themselves in a 25 with almost no warning. But what the hell—someone has to pay for the fancy public schools.

In journalism circles, it's called "doorstepping." You eschew call-ing someone because you know they won't talk, or you leave five hundred messages and then figure you have nothing left to lose, so you just show up on their doorstep. The power of the element of surprise. Bron has done it before many times. But in those cases it was someone who was running from the law, or at least ethics charges. Here was someone who had been running from her past for decades.

Bron pulls at the lapels of his wrinkled tan corduroy blazer with the elbow patches—he wears it when he wants to look writerly— and strolls across the street. Instinctively he tries to tamp down his hair, a pouf of competing angles that is always messy despite the amounts of goo he glops on to tame it. No matter. He's confident. He's good with old women. Actually, he's good with all women. Another reason his coworkers hate him.

He squares his shoulders, rings the bell.

Minutes pass, and he is about to ring it again when it opens.

And, like the song, there she is. It has been more than sixty years since anyone has taken a picture of her for public consumption, but Bron knows it's her. The hair is shocking white and Barbara Bush–like, but the eyes are a dead giveaway. Exactly the same, hazel and piercing. She wears a knit top, navy slacks, and sensible flats, the uniform of the retired affluent housewife.

"Mrs. Proctor?"

The eyes narrow. "What do you want?"

He bends over, places a hand on his chest, his wan demonstration of warmth and sincerity. "My name is Bronwyn McCall. I'm a writer at *Philadelphia* magazine. I wanted to know if I could ask you a few questions about your time as Miss America."

She stiffens visibly. "There is no Miss America here."

"I understand. Mrs. Proctor, please. I know you haven't spoken to the press in a long time, but if I could just—"

She begins to close the door. "You're mistaken. Now please go. And don't come back." He goes to say something, but it's too late. The door shuts. He hears the thud of the deadbolt, the sound of her eighty-six-year-old footsteps slowly retreating. There is a television on somewhere in the house. He hears frenzied bidding on *The Price Is Right*.

He stands still for a moment, weighing his options, none of them good. He'd known this was likely. He recalled the story of another reporter, maybe twenty years ago, who'd tracked her down when she was still living in Boulder and who had been given the exact same response: *There's no Miss America here.*

The thought of going back to Fletch empty-handed turns on a spigot of dread. He'll be lucky not to have to write the whole damned Shore Guide by himself. But he'll figure it out. He always does. One way or another, he's going to get the story of Betty Jane Welch.

He walks slowly down the driveway, plotting his next move,

spins around to take one last look at the house. *What is she doing now? Is she calling someone, nervous that a news van will pull up next? Is she peering from behind the curtains, making sure he's going?*

What is it like to spend your whole life denying the one thing that defined it?

These are the questions running through his mind as he backs off of the curb into the street, still studying the house. He never sees the car rounding the corner from Route 23 until just before it hits him.

the
Night She Won
Miss America

One

June 1949

Lemon cake, her favorite. The smell she would recognize anywhere, but especially here, in the front foyer, hanging up her jacket. It is the aroma that tells her it is her birthday, or that she has just done something very special to make her parents proud, or that Aunt Edith is coming to visit and *Betty, I need you to be nice to her,* because Aunt Edith is trying even on her sunniest days, and those are infrequent at best.

For Simon, it is double-fudge chocolate cake with cream-cheese icing, served with a tall, chilly glass of milk. He once pruned not only their rosebushes but the Webbers' next door for one, and Simon is rarely vertical when gardening or any other form of household chore needs to be done. For Ricky, it is ice cream, vanilla and strawberry, in equal portions, which does not carry a scent but whose presence is signified by her mother's sly smile and singsong chant, "Somebody's got something special in the icebox!"

But the lemon cake is Betty's and Betty's alone. Her mind scrambles, hoping to locate a recent achievement, a cause for honor temporarily forgotten, but she knows that this is in vain. Her mother wants something. Aunt Edith is coming, or worse.

She walks casually into the kitchen. "Hi," she says, as her mother turns around from the stove. The scent of the lemon cake is even more pungent, intoxicating. It couldn't have come out of the oven more than fifteen minutes ago.

"Hello, darling!" her mother replies, a tad too cheerily, and the verdict is confirmed. "I didn't hear you come in. How was Abbotts?"

It is summer, the summer between her freshman and sophomore semesters, and Betty is working at one of the most fashionable dress shops in Delaware, Abbotts on Main, earning spending money. Her father's idea. Idle hands, the devil's workshop, all of it. Her father is big on axioms. Especially when he is foreclosing on someone's house. Betty thinks platitudes help him shove the truth about what he does, the misery he inflicts on other people, out of his mind. She wonders where he hides it.

"Mrs. Summerhays was in again. She keeps insisting she's a ten, and it wreaks havoc every time. Patsy keeps threatening to quit if she has to wait on her." Patsy is Betty's best friend, the one who got her the job. No college for Patsy. She's biding her time until the husband and kids show up, hopefully in that order, but with Patsy one never knows. Betty drops onto a chair at the kitchen table, inhaling deep whiffs of the lemon cake without letting on. She takes a furtive glance around, spies the covered cake dish on top of the icebox. "I think we're going to have to put aside some size twelves, rip out the labels and sew in tens, and then just keep them for her when she comes in. 'Vanity working on a weak head, produces every sort of mischief.'"

"Who said that?" Her mother, showing she is listening attentively. She prides herself on her active listening.

"Jane Austen. Perhaps she knew Mrs. Summerhays." They laugh. Her mother turns back to sprinkling something on the meat cakes she is preparing, and Betty is struck by an odd thought, for she is forever having odd thoughts. She wonders if her mother ever gets angry. Not cross or silent—she has seen both of those, most recently after Daddy had too much brandy at the Webbers' Christmas party—but truly, outrageously, screaming angry. Try as she might, she can't picture it. She wonders if her mother, in her starched collars and crisp white aprons and two-inch heels, will one day simply erupt, like a long-dormant volcano, after some minor infraction perpetrated by her or Ricky or Simon, and send dishes and glasses flying all over the house. Betty cannot imagine always being this composed, this restrained. It seems like it would take unimaginable effort.

"I smell lemon cake." Enough preliminaries.

Her mother does not turn around. "Just took a notion," she says, the way you tell a police officer you had no idea you were speeding.

"Moooommm."

Her mother grabs a dish towel, wipes her hand on it a bit too aggressively as she sits across the kitchen table. "Well, there is something I was hoping to discuss with you."

Here it is. Aunt Edith, due on the morning train.

"I bumped into Elizabeth Howell the other day at Peggy Claiborne's. We were there for cards and a few cocktails. Don't tell your father. Anyway, we got to talking about something she's very involved in . . ."

Definitely worse than Aunt Edith. Elizabeth Howell is the president of the Junior League of Delaware, which Betty's mother has been desperate to join since, oh, who knows how long. On more than one occasion, Betty has asked her mother why she simply doesn't ask one of the women she knows in the League if she can join, and the query is always met with the same response: *That's not how it's done.* It is somehow preferable to suffer for years, your face pressed to the window like a small child yearning to be allowed

3

into the kids' birthday party every other schoolmate was invited to, rather than simply assert yourself and pose a simple question. Betty thinks it explains how her mother ended up with her father. He was merely the first to ask.

She tunes back in to her mother's soliloquy but finds she has evidently missed key information. ". . . and I told her I was, of course, extremely flattered that she would inquire about such a thing, and that of course I couldn't commit for you, but that I would certainly discuss it with you."

"Discuss what?" Betty blurts it out, a bald admission that *she* has not been actively listening.

"The pageant."

"The pageant?"

"Betty Jane Welch—I swear sometimes I wonder if you hear a word I say!" Cross, but not angry. Calm quickly descends, like the beam of a summer sun that had been momentarily eclipsed by a drifting cloud. "I said that Mrs. Howell is on the committee for the revived Miss Delaware scholarship pageant, and she's seeking entrants, and she asked if you would be interested. You know, it's been five years since they've sent a contestant from Delaware to Miss America. It's a very great honor to be asked."

Betty can no longer detect even a faint whiff of the lemon cake. "You want me to enter a beauty pageant?"

Her mother places her dishrag on the table, begins wiping a stain that's been there at least two years. "It's about more than *beauty,* Betty," she says. The table surface squeaks under the rag. *Wipe, wipe, wipe.* "The girls who are already entered are some of the most achieved young ladies in the state. Athletes, scholars, performers. It's a great honor to be asked."

Betty wants to point out that her mother has already made this questionable assertion, but lets it go. She wonders if girls who enter pageants are even allowed to eat cake. She doubts it. Mulling over this is better than considering the dilemma before her now. Agreeing to enter a ridiculous bathing beauty pageant will surely get her mother into the Junior League. *That's the can-do spirit we're looking for!* Declining will surely kill her chances. She pictures her mother, sentenced to a lifetime of exclusion, sitting silently at games of bridge and dinners at the Wilmington Country Club and listening to the women chirp on about all of their good works and the committees and *Oh, that speaker last month was just divine!,* and *Yes, he was. And so good-looking!* Titter-titter. She has no interest in a pageant whatsoever but ponders whether she has it in her to deny her mother. She remembers their trip to see the Miss America Pageant seven or eight years ago: all of the lights, the pretty girls, the electric moment when the winner was announced. *Miss California, Rosemary LaPlanche!* Funny how she can recall the name so clearly. If she had any flicker of desire to be on the stage herself, it has been long extinguished. The mere thought of appearing in a swimsuit in front of an auditorium leaves her paralyzed.

She needs to buy time, find an excuse that her mother cannot refute.

"You need a talent to enter something like that," she offers.

"Darling, you play beautifully!" comes the rapid reply. Her mother has anticipated every objection. Betty can see this is going to be more difficult than she anticipated. She has gone into battle impulsively, against a foe bearing far heavier artillery. The fact is that Betty plays adequately. The harp, a lavish gift from her grandmother. Exceedingly challenging to learn, but Betty was both precocious and determined as a child. How many years of lessons? Six? Seven? Her performance at the high school talent show was a raging success, but in truth it was her trio partners, a violinist and a cellist, who did Vivaldi's heavy lifting. Betty is hardly ready for the Kay Kyser Orchestra. But to argue such logic is pointless. They'll get her another tutor. Fly in Harpo Marx if they have to. She pictures herself in a flowing evening gown, harp tilted to her chin, thrumming "A Tree in the Meadow" in front of an auditorium in some musty hotel in Wilmington. A chill zips down her back.

"Mother, I know this is important to you, but I just—"

"Of course, dear. I understand. It's a lot to ask. If you would really rather not, I'll simply call Mrs. Howell and tell her you decline. Simple as pie."

Or cake.

Betty sighs audibly. The humble understanding, the faux posture of *I support whatever you decide,* underneath which lies *I will be bitterly disappointed if you do not do this for me—I ask so little of you.* Betty closes her eyes, wills the entire conversation away, knowing she has already been defeated.

"I'll think about it."

"Delightful," her mother says, almost in a squeal, and for a moment Betty is gratified that she has done this, made her mother so happy. Because *I'll think about it* always means yes. How many people say, "I'll think about it," and then decide in the negative?

But . . . oh. A beauty pageant. Betty stares down at the hulking slab of lemon cake her mother has sliced for her—on the nice china, how subtle!—and, picking up her fork, wonders if she can gain twenty pounds before the contest. Disqualified for girth! But as she chews the moist, delicious cake, she knows this is folly. She will enter Miss Delaware; she will play her harp; she will come home with a nice ribbon for entering. Her mother will join the Junior League. All will be well. It's one day, for goodness' sake.

After all, Betty thinks, *it isn't like I can actually win.*

❧

"*I still cannot believe* you are doing this."

Patsy is lying on her stomach on Betty's bed, which Betty now realizes is too pink, too juvenile for a young woman of nineteen. It's

6

almost as if her mother is trying to keep her a girl, frozen at eleven years old. A sense of foreboding she has been fighting for weeks descends again, threatens to compromise the feigned look of disinterest she now wears like a mask. She is scared to death. None of it makes any sense, so she has stopped trying to make sense of it. Instead she simply flits through the days, like a butterfly fluttering through the garden. It's easier.

"*I* can't believe how much I have to pack," Betty says. "You'd think I was going away for a year. And speaking of which, I thought you were coming over to help."

"You've been shopping for weeks. Didn't your evening gown require, I don't know, ten fittings?"

"Which one?"

"The important one."

"Six."

"Six. Six! My sister didn't need that many for her *wedding* gown, and she got married at the Hotel du Pont, I remind you. I just can't believe you are doing this."

"It would be helpful if you would stop saying that. I would think by now your disbelief would be over. I believe it should be very clear that I am indeed doing this." She has to.

She has won Miss Delaware.

She closes her eyes. *Deep breath,* she commands internally, feeling the air fill her lungs, slowly seep out of her nostrils.

This is the hidden cost of being the good daughter, the good student, the good girl. People take advantage: with flattery, with emotional manipulation, one slice of lemon cake at a time. Sometimes she feels like more of a receptacle than a real living person. Someone other people project their aspirations, goals, ideas, and tasks onto. And she simply accepts them, like a bank teller taking deposits, perfunctorily fulfilling one request after another: *Watch your brother. Practice your harp. Set the table. Stay away from* him.

Get smart. Go and change—that's not appropriate. Watch your tone. Do your homework. Get the mail. Do it all over again.

But then, it is her own fault, is it not? You cannot play the good girl, relish the rave reviews and metaphorical standing ovations from the critics—your parents, your teachers, your neighbors, your boss at the dress shop—and then complain that everyone only sees you as dutiful and earnest, with no thoughts or real depth of your own. And so she endures: the dull lectures at the college her parents chose; the wallpaper in her bedroom her grandmother chose; the expectations, or lack thereof, that society has chosen, not only for her but for every girl like her. And who would feel sorry for her, decree she has been cheated or slighted? She has had advantages most other girls would kill for.

And yet.

She cannot tamp down the disquiet, the small knot of adrenaline that continually sloshes around her stomach like a peach pit. She has dismissed it as nerves, attributed exclusively to the fact that she must now subject herself to an entire week of something far worse than a sociology lecture or overly floral decor. But in her most solitary moments—in this moment, folding clothes as Patsy idly flips through the pages of *Glamour* and spouts girlish nonsense lying on the bed—Betty knows better. She *knows*. And the knowing is the worst of it.

She realized, with all due horror, that she was going to win Miss Delaware as soon as she walked into the hotel in Wilmington. Betty had expected a girl from every county and charitable organization, and had instead found just seven others like herself, a solid half of whom failed to disguise the feeling that they'd had no idea how they'd gotten roped into this.

Clearly there had been more than one lemon cake baked.

One by one, like dominoes, they fell. One girl's voice

cracked like a shattering ice cube as she attempted Verdi; another's evening gown looked like it been made before the war, perhaps for a maiden aunt, and then been hemmed and tucked and sewed into something passable. During the question-and-answer portion, another girl couldn't explain what Truman's Fair Deal was but did somehow manage to relay the story of Grady the cow, a 1,200-pound Hereford that had made national headlines a few months earlier when it got wedged in a silo door in Oklahoma. It was hardly surprising when Betty's harp solo —Salzedo's "Chanson dans la Nuit"—and answer to the question "Do you feel there is a divide between today's youth and adults in American life?"—she'd answered that throughout history there have always been divides between generations, but rather than cause alarm, we should be encouraged, because this is how new ideas are formed and progress is made—left her with the crown. Her mother—and, to her surprise, her father and brothers—had overflowed with pride. It had all been something of an unexpected lark. Until Betty realized what was coming next.

Atlantic City.

"Stop, stop, stop!" Patsy is saying, stretching out from the bed and grabbing her forearm as Betty shoehorns a nightgown and slippers into her case. "You're packing like you're going off to prison. Come over here for a minute. Stop being a crazy beauty queen. Good golly! It's me, remember? Talk to me."

Betty plops beside her on the bed. "It's all pretty silly, isn't it?" she says. "Look at this." She reaches over, retrieves the Miss America Pageant yearbook she has been sent. Bios and pictures of fifty-two young women, some from cities—Miss Chicago, Miss New York City—most from states, all vying for the storied title of Miss America 1950.

Patsy is still on her elbows, flipping through. "Wow. Some of these girls are really pretty."

"You sound surprised. Are you worried people will think I simply wandered in?"

Patsy rolls her eyes. "Horse feathers. You're a dish and you know it . . . Holy cow! Miss Michigan is a dead ringer for Lizabeth Scott."

"I just never stopped to think that this whole thing could get this far."

"Eh, you did it for your mom. That's not a bad reason."

"It's not a particularly good one, either." Betty gets up, resumes packing. She stops in front of the dresser mirror. She has been doing this incessantly as September has crept closer. It's bad enough she is missing a week of classes for this, but what really bothers her is the constant self-examination, the picking apart of her cheekbones and hair and lips and eyes and brows. Weighing herself against the competition, when she has sworn to herself, more times than she can count, that she doesn't care about any of this. Except that it's evident that in fact she does, which is the most annoying thing of all.

"This is a great picture of you," Patsy remarks from the bed. Patsy begins reading aloud. "'Betty Jane Welch was born on May 12, 1930, in Dover, Delaware, and is the first titleholder in five years from the nation's first state, winning over a formidable field. About to enter her sophomore year at Maryland State Teachers College at Towson, she is an A student and will be exhibiting her talent as a harpist. She is 5'6" and weighs 118 pounds, with strawberry blond hair and hazel eyes. Her interests include tennis, swimming, and crafts.'" Patsy crinkles her nose. "Crafts?"

"I had to put something. It was as good as any. After all, I *can* be crafty." Meant as humor, comes off as pathos. Patsy is the one person who can always see behind any façade she puts up.

Patsy scoots off the bed to stand next to her, her arms reaching over, hands interlocking to pull Betty closer. Betty recalls a day long ago, both of them barely tall enough to see over this dresser, when they had looked into this same mirror, weighed down in her mother's jewelry, their tiny mouths sloppily smudged with lipstick. Dress-up never ends.

"You act like you're going off to the guillotine," Patsy says, tilting her head onto Betty's shoulder, addressing their joint reflection. "You are Miss Delaware! You get to spend a week in Atlantic City, getting your picture taken and feeling like a princess. You'll be on the radio, for God's sake! And you could win some terrific scholarship money. And I'll be there Saturday with your family to root you on. And don't forget the best part."

Betty smiles in spite of herself. Patsy can always manage to make her smile, even in the sorriest of circumstances. "Well, don't keep me in suspense," Betty says back to their reflection. "What's the best part?"

"The escorts," Patsy says, winking. "Every contestant gets one of the local college boys as an escort for the week. Your future husband could be standing in front of his own mirror right now, wondering what it will be like to meet you."

"Wonderful," Betty replies, reaching up to place a hand atop Patsy's arm. "Some awful rum pot who's probably six inches shorter than me and perspires profusely, and will spend the week stepping on my toes during every dance."

"C'mon, Bett," Patsy says, in a soft, gentle voice she does not use all that often. Her mouth turns up into a crooked smile. "Look at this as a wonderful caper. What's the worst that could happen?"

Two

Atlantic City is marvelous. Certainly not elegant or refined or couth. But it is most certainly, unequivocally, crazily marvelous.

It has never been a weeklong destination for the Welches. For them, every summer brings the rental of a lovely beach cottage in Rehoboth, save for four years ago, when they packed up to visit her grandparents in Morristown, New Jersey. A four-hour drive, Simon and Ricky fighting the entire way.

Atlantic City, she thinks, must be a fun place to be a child. But after only a night here, Betty can see it is far more fun to be an adult. She is, of course, deeply enamored with the flashing lights and marquees of Steel Pier and Steeplechase Pier and Heinz Pier, their myriad distractions and amusements and shows and thrill rides. Last night she simply strolled the length of the Boardwalk, inhaling the smell of sea air mixed with fresh popcorn, sawdust, fudge, and eau de toilette splashed on by giggling girls trying to attract the attention of swaggering boys.

But it is the nightclub marquees and restaurant signs and

beckoning awnings that have left her enraptured. Marty Magee's Guardsmen in the Mayfair Lounge at the Claridge; the Irving Fields Trio at the Senator; the sign above Tony Baratta's Escort Bar at the corner of Atlantic and Missouri, tantalizingly asking, "Wouldn't You Rather Have the Best?" She fantasizes not about being Miss America, but of sitting at a table at the 500 Club or dancing all night at the Hialeah. She forlornly reminds herself that a week's worth of pageanteering will surely preclude any of it.

Like all of the hotels that line the Boardwalk, the Traymore — located in the heart of town on the Boardwalk at Illinois Avenue — is enormous, a dusk-colored sand castle capped by two tiled golden domes in its center that glint in the late morning sun, and which looms like a mythic Xanadu above the beach. The bathtubs here are legendary; each has four faucets, one each for hot and cold water, one each for hot and cold ocean water.

Betty cannot understand why anyone would want to bathe in ocean water.

Breathe. Breathe.

It is Labor Day, and there is a bustling hum in the art deco lobby that contrasts with the stately accoutrement of the space — its huge semicircular windows that face the ocean, the dramatic sheer drapes, green velvet chaises, and tasteful Oriental rugs. A sign at the far end advertises Lenny Herman appearing in the Submarine Room, "the mightiest little band in the land, with Nancy Niland." Chagrined visitors check out, mark the official end of their summers, going back to their lives and the approaching coolness of autumn. An ebullient din emanates from those arriving, a tossed-together sorority of girls here to register for the pageant in the Rose Room by six p.m., the official deadline. Betty conjures an image of a harried girl scurrying in at 5:57, frantically trying to scribble her name in before her sash is discarded into the nearest bin for tardiness. She laughs out loud at the thought.

"Please, share the joke! I could use a laugh right about now."

Betty glances up just as a girl sits down next to her on the sofa, artfully crossing her legs. She must be a pageant contestant as well, but at first glance she seems incongruous as a Miss Anything. She is dark and beautiful in a femme fatale type of way, the kind of mysterious siren who lurks in the shadows in gangster movies, secretly in love with the informant. Her chestnut hair is done up in a top reverse roll, the center peak arching up into an almost perfect question mark, the sides big fluffy rings that frame her angular face. She wears a plain gray dress with short melon sleeves and black single-sole pumps, and clutches a small polished silver case in her right hand. She extracts a cigarette, proffers the case to Betty, who demurs. "You sure?" the girl says. "Last chance before we enter the convent. From here on out, it's the rules of Mother Abbess over there."

Betty follows the girl's sightline, spies a matronly woman in enormous pearls with curly, prematurely graying hair in the corner, holding court with four other contestants. "That's Lenora Slaughter," the girl says. "She's the boss lady. Runs the whole show. Trust me, you don't want to get on her bad side. She can make sure every judge hates you before you even put on your first pair of stockings."

Betty looks back to her new companion, now taking an artful drag on her cigarette. "You're a contestant?" She says it with unintended incredulity.

The girl laughs. "Hard to believe, I know. But yes, you are looking at Miss Rhode Island, in the flesh. Don't worry. You're not the only one who's shocked. Practically everyone's wondering how I slipped into this thing." She takes another puff of her cigarette, looks at Betty appraisingly. "Now don't tell me: You're too wiry and athletic to be from a New England state, but no tan, so not from warm weather. You also don't have that annoying midwestern accent. My God, they all sound like pirates. So I'm going to guess . . . Mid-Atlantic. Am I close?"

Betty laughs. "Yes."

"Ah! See? This should be my talent. I could just come out with a crystal ball and a head scarf. I'd certainly probably score higher than I will belting out show tunes. Let's see . . . Maryland?"

Betty chuckles. It is the first time she has felt somewhat at ease since arriving in Atlantic City. "So close! Delaware."

"*Delaware!* Oh, killer-diller, we would have been here all day if I'd had to guess that. I didn't even know Delaware sent anyone."

Betty spreads her hands in "ta-da" fashion. "The first in five years."

"Well, isn't that the cat's meow," the girl says, grinning. "We're the two smallest states here!" She extends a hand. "Catherine Grace Moore, of the Newport Moores. Though call me Ciji. It's pronounced C period G period, but I spell it C-i-j-i. It's a better name for a movie marquee, I think. I came up with it myself."

Betty shakes her hand. "Betty Jane Welch, of the Nowhere Welches," she replies, smiling. Perhaps this week won't be so bad if the girls are like this. Though Betty very strongly suspects the rest of the girls are nothing like this. "So you're going into pictures, then?"

"No other reason to be here, cookie. My wants are very simple: my name on a movie screen and Eve Arden's apartment in *The Unfaithful*," Ciji says, stubbing out the cigarette. "They give the winner a screen test. And I figure if a Jew like Bess Myerson can become a celebrity, then so can I." She takes in Betty's slight look of shock. "Oh, don't be so soft, Delaware. You should hear some of the mouths on these girls when they think no one's listening. And make no mistake. I can put on my gloves and be as dainty and moony as any of them. And I sing a hell of a 'My Happiness.'"

"How y'all doin' today?" Another voice, breathy and viscose, above them.

MISS ALABAMA, the black sash, perfectly angled from top left shoulder to right hip, blares in white block letters. The girl has skin so pale, so flawless, that for a moment Betty wonders if she's wearing cold cream. Her hair is jet black, swept up in a tight updo that matches her meticulously arched brows, hovering over her eyes like two perfect half-moons. The eyes, a chocolate brown, seem a little too small for her face, but her mouth—full and pouty and accented by dark ruby lipstick—is sublime. Betty takes in her efficient two-piece rose suit with a cloverleaf collar, the barrel sleeves and trumpet skirt.

Ciji scoots over, waves the girl onto the settee. She is Mary Barbara Adair, from Monroeville, Alabama, "the hometown of Mr. Truman Capote, the famous writer," though Mary Barbara quickly confides that she doesn't know a single person in Monroeville who's read a thing he's written. In the space of ten minutes, she has relayed her entire life story—her father is a vice president at the Vanity Fair textile mill, her momma's a housewife, she has four siblings, she's majoring in English at Birmingham-Southern College, and she is grateful to be attending there, because if you live in Monroeville and you want to do something exciting, you need to travel more than two hours away to Montgomery, "'cause Monroeville is mighty pretty, but there is absolutely *nothing* to do." Then come the questions: where they're from, their talents, their state pageant experiences, the hotels they're staying at. Ciji behaves, perhaps to prove to Betty that she can back up her claims of pageant propriety.

"Sooo," Mary Barbara says in a conspiratorial whisper, "do you have any guesses about who all you'll get?"

Betty and Ciji look briefly at each other in puzzlement, then back to her. "'Who we'll get'?" Ciji asks.

"The *escorts,* of course," Mary Barbara says, an "I shouldn't be talking about this, but it's too fun not to" look planted squarely on her porcelain face. Betty flashes back to Patsy, how excited she was fantasizing about Betty's pageant escort, how much she would adore this absurd conversation.

"Tonight we get introduced to the young men who are going to be our dates for the week," Mary Barbara continues. "All of the local college boys fall all over each other to be one of the fifty-two selected. Although I am sure they all want Miss California or Miss New York. Because they're probably, well . . . *you know.*"

"Tall?" Ciji quips. She winks at Betty.

"Fast," Mary Barbara whispers. "I mean, I enjoy a nice-looking boy's time as much as the next girl, but if he thinks he's getting a look at anything under here, he's got another thought comin'."

Romance. Betty admits that it would certainly make the week pass more quickly. She has not dated much her first year at college. She is afraid going steady will take too much energy, too much focus. A thought flickers into her head that perhaps she is simply afraid of too much, too much of the time. Her thoughts return to Patsy. She is now convinced that there is some awful fraternity boy awaiting her.

Mary Barbara spies two other states, hurriedly pops up from the settee with an airy "So nice to meet you girls," and dashes off. Betty turns, takes a quick glance around. More contestants meander in. Miss Slaughter has shifted into army general mode, herding entrants toward the Rose Room to register as she answers nervous questions. Betty glances at her watch. Two o'clock. "Well, I guess it's now or never. Are you coming?"

"Okay, Delaware, let's go," Ciji says, standing and dropping her cigarette case into her clutch. She threads their arms together. "The runway has no idea what's coming."

❧

17

Don't do anything. This, Betty decides, is the one general rule to emerge from the grueling, almost-two-hour orientation at Convention Hall that she has just endured. No alcohol, no swearing, no exposed shoulders during daytime except for pageant-sanctioned beach excursions, no padding of swimsuits, no skirts above the knee, no smoking (Ciji delivering a side-eye), no male guests — not even dads or brothers — in their rooms at any time, no gum chewing, no nightclubs (there was audible moaning), and no going to official pageant events without proudly wearing your sash. "During this exciting week, we want to remind you that all of you have been selected as ambassadors, here to serve not only as contestants in a spirited competition but also to project a beacon of youthful vigor, optimistic spirit, and refined femininity to the world," Miss Slaughter said in her best Eleanor Roosevelt.

Miss Slaughter had greeted Betty warmly at registration, handing over her sash and then calmly directing her upstairs for her bathing suit fitting and then on to her photography session. Catching snippets of the pageant hostesses' gossiping, Betty knows that Miss Slaughter has a reputation for being very feminine, stern, and demanding, not always in that order. She instituted the scholarship program; when it came to talent, she was said to favor musicians. (Miss Montana's talent, horse jumping, will be shown on a projected screen; ditto for Miss Indiana's alacrity at diving. After an afternoon culling whispers, Betty has quickly ascertained that no one is particularly hopeful about the chances of either.) Miss Slaughter single-handedly changed the "bathing suit" competition to the "swimsuit" competition to promote an image of health and vitality rather than one of a pinup, though there is healthy skepticism that it has made any such difference to the general public. She hates the color black — eyeing one girl's evening gown selection two years ago, she is said to have witheringly snapped, "This is a pageant, not a state funeral, Miss Iowa" — and does not encour-

18

age as much as insist on as many pastels, taffeta ball skirts, and elbow gloves as can be displayed. She has no time for Negroes and makes little secret of her intent to keep them from ever competing. She isn't too fond of the Catholics, either, but tolerates them.

Betty listens to the band inside the ballroom of the Hotel Dennis, watches Miss Slaughter greeting contestants at the door. She sips a ginger ale that she's asked the bartender to pour into a champagne coupe, so she can pretend she is interesting and dangerous.

The Miss America Contestants Reception is where the pageant's organizers and sponsors get to mingle with—and covertly leer at—the girls. Betty has changed into a green brocaded empire dress accented by a smart gold bracelet. She recalls Mary Barbara mentioning their escorts appearing, but so far the only men she sees are Park Haverstick, the jowly, bespectacled president of the pageant, and similar fogeys she suspects are the sponsors and husbands of the pageant hostesses. Betty spies Ciji wandering over in drapey fire-engine red, replete with shoulder pads—that *girl!* She silently curses herself for not wearing something more daring, even if Ciji's ensemble does make her look a bit like an able Grable.

"Did Miss Slaughter hand you a demerit for that dress?" Betty asks, taking a sip of her not-champagne.

"Well, well! Look who's coming out of her shell," Ciji says, sidling up to her at the bar. "I will take some credit for that."

"I'm not surprised."

Ciji has arranged to be Betty's roommate at the Chalfonte-Haddon Hall. ("Strength in numbers," she remarked when broaching the idea.) There are now large poster-size photographs of the two of them on display in the Chalfonte lobby, along with those of several other contestants who are staying there. All of the girls have been sprinkled among the hotels, like fairy dust.

"I met Missouri on the way in. Seems nice enough. Not quite as smiley as some of the rest of them," Ciji is saying. "We were both asking why Miss Canada is here. Is Canada now part of the United States? And have you met Mississippi? She's a card, that one. I didn't know you could make your hair *do* that. One thing's for certain: she has no intention of obeying the 'no nightclubs' rule. Neither do any of the others, from what I can tell. And here I thought I'd be the only one making trouble. Old Lenora is going to have her hands full." She orders a soda water with lime. "God, I wish I could have something in this. Met anyone interesting?"

"Not really. After the orientation I took a walk. My Lord, the aroma coming out of that White House Sub Shop! I was positively salivating for a hero. Which I am happy to say I did not have."

Ciji scans the room, her shiny gold button declaring RHODE ISLAND catching the light. Tonight the sashes are put away; each girl has been given a button that declares her home state. Some of the other contestants have been querying each other about the change, with various theories for answers. Betty wishes she could muster enough curiosity to want to hear them.

"Ladies, may I have your attention, please," Miss Slaughter states from a podium at the top of the dance floor. It takes a few minutes for the talking to subside, hostesses fanning out like theater ushers and shushing in every direction. "Thank you. We are all so delighted to have you with us and to be here at the Hotel Dennis to officially begin the Miss America Pageant."

Polite applause. "Some of you may have been wondering why you are wearing buttons with your home states tonight rather than your sashes," she continues, "and it is because we wanted you to enjoy your dancing without worrying about them. We are to have a little fun. In a moment, the fifty-two young men who have been selected as your escorts for the week will be coming through here" —she waves a gloved hand over to two doors to her left— "and each of them will be wearing an identical button on his lapel to your own. It is up to you to find your matching state beau!"

From the reaction, one might have thought Tyrone Power had walked in. Betty wonders how many of these girls will be crushed when the doors swing open and they find themselves approached by a boy with buck teeth and bad breath whose father owns a local peanut shop. And yet her heart speeds up a beat or two, and she feels self-conscious, as if the other girls can see her nerves. She is going to be with this young man for the entire week. It's only natural to be a tad jittery, isn't it? Every girl here is. Though Ciji projects an air of apathy worthy of her ambitions as an actress.

The hostesses quickly disperse the girls around the ballroom, including the two of them ("Come now, ladies, no young man wants to meet his date slouched over the bar"), and Betty and Ciji find themselves separated. Betty is standing in a small cluster with Nevada, Maine, and Louisiana when the doors whoosh open.

The room, bathed in golden light and soft music, is hushed, the contestants holding their collective breath. At first there is nothing but the partial view of a hallway, and then they come in—rush in —tall and short and lanky and lean and stocky and broad, every sort of boy in every sort of packaging. They wear suits, almost all of them double-breasted, with ties and matching pocket squares and shoes that have been buffed to a waxy shine. The first wave is smiling, laughing, shouting the occasional cheer—*"Where's my beautiful Miss Minnesota?!"*—while the second group walks in more casually, circumspect, confident, not wanting to appear too eager. Betty freezes. The young women around her slowly peel away, gliding onto the ballroom floor like swans. There are friendly handshakes and the occasional hug (quickly admonished by the hostesses), and Betty cranes to discern the locales on the buttons pinned to the boys' lapels: New Jersey, Texas, Chicago, Nebraska. She smells the boys' peppermint aftershave and oily hair cream, her eyes scanning, scanning, noting the dwindling number of un-attached bachelors. For a fleeting moment, she is stricken by the thought that hers has decided not to come. She feels conspicuous, already a loser with the pageant barely begun. She pictures Miss Slaughter walking over, gently placing a hand around her shoulder, saying, "Don't worry, dear, we'll find you someone."

Her palms are slicked in sweat. She craves something stronger than ginger ale.

And then she sees him, walking toward her.

Three

*H*er own hair color has often been described, including in the Miss America program book, as strawberry blond, but the only thing Betty can think of as he approaches is that men's hair color is never described this way. And yet his, with its perfect left part and symmetrical razor lines cascading across his forehead, is the closest thing she has ever seen to her own on a man. She wonders if the Miss America matchmakers have done their duty based on hair.

He is in a soft navy pinstriped suit with a starched white shirt and a pale blue tie. His face is square and perfectly symmetrical; he has haunting pale gray eyes the color of ice water. As they hold each other's gaze, his face breaks into a smile that is pleasant if a bit forced. "Were you afraid I wasn't coming?" he says.

"I had faith."

He extends his hand, shakes hers as if he is meeting her father to discuss a loan. "I'm John Griffin McAllister, though my friends call me Griff."

"What do your enemies call you?" An attempt to be flirtatious. *Awful.*

He laughs tepidly, the kind of laugh you give a child who has just performed a card trick. "A girl with spirit. That's great." She suppresses a groan and concentrates on how crackerjack handsome he is instead. She stares at his lapel button, which clearly states: DELAWARE. Confirmed. This is her guy. He has the fine, square jaw of an athlete. Quarterback, if she was guessing. Her disbelief at her luck is palpable. She has planned for Peter Lorre and landed Guy Madison. *Hubba-hubba.* She will not win the Miss America contest, but she'd bet her grandmother's pearls that she has just won the Miss America escort derby.

She scans the room, trying to spy Ciji's and Mary Barbara's dates. She wants a witness, someone to envy her good fortune. "Am I boring you already?" he asks, the edge in his voice unmistakable. A stifling awkwardness blooms, like a moat bubbling up, separating a castle from the fields.

"No, no, I'm sorry. I was just trying to see who my friends ended up with, to be honest. There was a lot of speculation about all of this before you fellas showed up."

She catches his dismissive look. "I bet," he replies. Every time she makes eye contact with him, all she can think of is how many girls have probably thrown themselves at him, how many unopened love letters are sitting in the chest of drawers in his bedroom. She tries to wish away how utterly bored he looks.

"So how did you get coerced into this?" she asks.

"I was volunteered," he says, now casually scanning the room behind her. "My mother is one of the muckety-mucks on the hostess committee. Said it would look bad if her son wasn't an escort. I was kind of dreading it, to be honest." He looks at her, catches the momentary fall of her face. "Though, of course, now I'm glad I came."

No, you're not.

She asks a few rote questions, and he tells her all about himself, because, as Betty learned early on, boys love nothing as much as telling you about themselves. He flatly recites that the McAllisters own the largest nursery in the region, which provides flowers to almost every major hotel in Atlantic City. The family lives down in Longport, at the southernmost end of Absecon Island, evidently not far from a six-story cement elephant. "They call it the Irish Riviera," he says of the town, not the elephant, "because all of the lawyers and high-falutins live there." He attended New York University for a year but dropped out. He does not elaborate.

They stand in silence for several minutes, each looking out onto the ballroom floor, where several new couples have begun to dance. At one point Betty turns to say something and swears she can see his lips moving, as if he's whispering urgently to himself.

Inside she deflates, even as the mannequin she has quickly become for this terrible week remains perfectly intact, beaming synthetic gaiety. She wants him to be provocative, exciting, suave. Most of all, she wants him to be *interested.* But he is gorgeous and surface, like a glittery piece of jewelry. She catches him looking at his watch and reaches for her clutch. "I need to go to the powder room," she says.

He promises to order her another ginger ale. She wonders if he will still be here to watch her drink it.

The band is playing "Ole Buttermilk Sky," and she finds Ciji in the middle of the dance floor—her date is nominally attractive, save for a large, distracting mole under his right eye—and Betty quickly makes apologies to him as she hustles Ciji off toward the ladies' lounge, though of course she has no intention of actually entering the ladies' lounge. Inside it will be a herd of other states, already comparing notes, awarding points like judges at the Olympics.

They come to a stop near the phone bank at the end of the hall. "So?" Ciji asks. "What's the deal with Mr. Handsome? *You* certainly hit the jackpot."

"He has as much interest in me as he does in Miss Slaughter."

"Don't expect sympathy. You didn't get the guy with the big mole on his face."

"I'm just . . . I don't know, annoyed. I know I shouldn't be. I mean, we're all just thrown together like this. It's crazy. But he just looks like he's run out of gas or something." Betty sighs. "I think I caught him talking to himself."

"Oh, stop. My uncle Joe talks to himself all the time. And he's a doll."

"I just want to go home."

"What's the matter with you? It's been, what, ten minutes, and you're already carrying a torch? You're being a crackup. And anyway, who cares if he's a stick in the mud who mutters? He's still a dreamboat. You could've gotten a juvie. You'll hardly see him this week, anyway. Tomorrow morning we have to line up like fish in a barrel in our bathing suits for that big photo. Then there's the Boardwalk parade in the afternoon. Geez. You'll see him maybe a couple of times, for like fifteen minutes each, you'll get through it, and if you're lucky, you'll walk away from all of this with some scholarship money and a nice photo of you and Monty Clift there that you can paste into your scrapbook." She smiles, puts a reassuring hand on Betty's arm. "And at least you'll have a new friend you can come visit in Rhode Island."

"Or Hollywood," Betty says, smiling.

"Oh, let's hope, sister." Ciji pivots them around, guides them back to the ballroom.

Betty threads her way across the thicket on the ballroom floor, where the hostesses hover like a flock of well-dressed crows, ready to strike at the first sign of the improperly placed hand or, God forbid, lip. John Griffin McAllister still waits by the bar. Her eyes narrow. *Are his lips still moving?*

He spies her and steps forward, and as he does, she notices something changed in his disposition, a look on his face that is both devilish and sheepish. She has no idea what has transpired while she has been gossiping with Ciji, but clearly something has. He's more squared in the shoulders now. Different.

"So, I have a question for you," he says.

A dance. Well, that will be nice.

Then he unleashes a smile that almost knocks her over. A huge, bright, blazing flash that sends a boozy warmth rushing through her body, right down to her toes. She hates that a man who looked at his watch immediately after meeting her can elicit this kind of visceral reaction with one smile. She also cannot deny it. He leans in a bit closer. "Whaddya say we get out of here?"

❧

Captain Starn's is a sprawling shack that's actually more like a compound, plopped in the middle of a marina. A tiny fishing boat façade leads into a big white clapboard restaurant with cloth awnings that flap and flutter in the salty bay breezes. Betty puts down her menu and looks out at the twilight sky, streaked in dusky purples, oranges, and pinks. These are the kind of places she loves, ramshackle and unfancy, authentic and long-loved, the kind where people come to order messy crabs and corn on the cob drizzled with melted butter.

"They make a great chiffon pie here," Griff says. He has loosened his tie, unbuttoned the top of his shirt, which has only helped make him look even more rakish. Patsy would dub him "Trouble, with a capital T."

"Unfortunately I have to be in a bathing suit on the Boardwalk tomorrow morning to get my picture taken," Betty says. "So no pie for me."

A waitress in a starched uniform and matching cap ambles over. She looks like a grouchy nurse, with a demeanor to match. Betty orders a shrimp cocktail and a tomato juice, while Griff orders the Captain Starn's Special: baked stuffed lobster with clam filling, mashed potatoes, coleslaw, and biscuits, with a dry martini to wash it all down. He asks again if she won't join him in a cocktail, and she reminds him that the rules forbid it. "Yeah, we'll see how long you hold out," he says with a laugh. "Every year the girls say, 'Oh, I can't drink! They'll kick me out!' and every year they end up sitting at a table at the Torch Club with a brandy alexander." He lights a cigarette.

"I didn't know you've had so much experience. Just how many states have you squired?"

"You're my very first. But as I told you, my mother's a hostess."

They sit in silence for a minute, the only sound his fingers flicking open his lighter, then closing it, over and over. *Flick, flick, flick, flick, flick.*

"Are you dying to light something or just preoccupied?" Betty asks.

He appears momentarily startled, like a child caught taking money out of his mother's purse. "Oh, sorry," he says, shoving the lighter into his pocket. "That's annoying. No, I'm not preoccupied. Actually, that's not true. I am a little preoccupied. I feel like I am making a terrible impression, and here you are, at the pageant, a real cookie, and I am the 'escort' supposed to show you a grand time, and I'm failing miserably."

"Well, at least you've stopped muttering to yourself."

She can almost see the blood drain from his face. She has no idea what nerve she has touched on, but she knows she has done just that. "I'm . . . I'm sorry. I was only kidding. My . . . my uncle Joe talks to himself all the time. And he's a doll!"

His eyes betray a look of fleeting panic. "Old college habit, I'm afraid," he finally says airily. "I used to memorize answers and then recite them over and over before tests as I was walking around the campus. It's really rather embarrassing."

Betty begins to apologize again, but he cuts her off. "Anyway, I feel bad that I said that thing about dreading it. You know, my mother . . ." He says it in a way that Betty interprets as *If you only knew.* "Is *your* mother here?"

Mothers. Safe ground. "Not yet. Thankfully my brother broke his wrist playing baseball, and that derailed her plans to come and hover over me the entire week." Ricky, always ending up in some sort of fix. What was it with boys? "She feels terrible she's missing the parade tomorrow. She'll be here with my father and brothers for the weekend. So your mother is one of the hostesses?"

"Yes." He takes a graceful sip of his just-delivered martini. "I take it you haven't met her yet."

"No."

"Lucky you."

His face fades back to impassivity, like a curtain has just dropped over it. *Not again.* Now he seems positively morose. She can't figure him out. One minute, disinterested and bored; the next, charming and attentive. One minute, funny and clever; the next, bitter and miserable. It's like he's some sort of Atlantic City Jekyll and Hyde. At least *they* split the day and the night. She doesn't know which one she is speaking with from minute to minute. She wonders if she just should have gone back to the hotel, spent the evening in her nightgown laughing with Ciji about Mary Barbara's ridiculous dress.

"You're wishing you had just gone back to the hotel, aren't you?"
Oh my God.

She startles for just a second, adjusts the napkin on her lap. "Of course not."

He leans back in his chair. He proceeds to button the top of his shirt again, adjust the knot back up. "Tell you what," he says. "Let's start all of this over." He extends a hand across the table. "Griff McAllister. Nice to meet you."

She shakes his hand. "Betty Jane Welch, Miss Delaware. Likewise."

The food arrives and they talk—or mainly she talks, because his meal is enormous and hers consists of five shrimp in a cocktail glass teeming with shaved ice—and they cover broad territory, from her uneventful upbringing to her mother's longing for the Junior League (she's since gotten in), the lemon cake that led her here, her brothers, her studies, her best friend Patsy, things to do in Delaware. He is dutifully impressed she is a harpist but seems more thrilled by the fact that she roots for the Philadelphia Eagles. She had the athletic identity correct but the wrong sport: no football. He was a rower through junior year of high school. She doesn't ask why he didn't row his senior year, and he doesn't offer an explanation. In fact, other than the fact that he has a younger sister named Martha, he offers very little about himself at all. She doesn't know whether he is shy, or mysterious, or simply not very interesting. She does know he is the best-looking boy she's ever laid eyes on.

On his second martini, he finally wears her down to take a sip. She pictures a buzzer going off, a mob of hostesses led by a grim Mrs. McAllister swarming in with handcuffs, stripping off her sash. Though, of course, she is not wearing her sash.

"So your family supplies the flowers to all the hotels in Atlantic City?"

"More or less."

"You must send flowers to every girl you meet."

He laughs. "Is that a hint?"

She flushes. "No, of course not."

"Any schmo can give a girl roses. I never do."

"You own a nursery and you never send flowers?"

"I didn't say that. I said I never send roses."

"I see. And what do you send, when you are inclined to send?"

"Variety of things. But for very special girls, I send sunflowers."

"Sunflowers? That's unusual."

"I think they're just beautiful. Those big brown circles, surrounded by the yellow, orange, tangerine buds sprouting outward. And they're hearty. They last. They're a message that sticks around." He winks. "But like I said, I only send those to very special girls."

The dinner flies by.

She notes things, files them away for dissection with Ciji later. The way his gray eyes disappear into matching crinkles when he laughs. The fullness of his mouth, soft like a woman's. His hands, large and masculine but smooth to the touch. His ability to not talk, to enjoy moments of silence during a dinner conversation, and his artful use of them as bridges to new topics.

By the time he has paid the check, she feels both deeply smitten and deeply inadequate. His mood has whiplashed throughout the entire evening, but she discounts it, overwhelmed by the skein of butterflies fluttering about her stomach. He is a college dropout but clearly an urbane young man of taste, style, discernment. For the first time since forking into her mother's lemon cake, she is happy about her decision to enter Miss Delaware.

He places his hand lightly on the small of her back as they leave the restaurant, and a current rips through her. She has never been on a date like this, never been with a boy like this, never felt . . . this. Her head swims, and the feeling is delightful. She wonders if it is not she, rather than he, who has had the two martinis. She senses a nonstop stream of laughter surfacing, fights to stave it off. Her face is hot.

On the pier in front of the restaurant is a wishing well surrounded by a white wooden fence. Griff digs into his trouser pocket, extracts a penny, hands it to her. "Make a wish," he whispers.

Betty closes her eyes, sends the shiny penny flipping into the water with a gentle plunk.

Throughout the ensuing years, on those rare occasions when her Herculean efforts to keep this chapter in her life locked away from her consciousness fail her, it is always this memory that she recalls most vividly. For she knows it is the moment where she lost everything.

Four

A few more minutes and I am going to wilt out here."

Betty doesn't know who says it—Connecticut? Colorado? Definitely one of the C's—but she cannot agree more. The calendar says September 6, but the weather says mid-August. It is ten a.m. and the thermometer is already approaching eighty. She has powdered herself silly in an effort to stay dry but is quickly losing the battle. They're all going to look like dishrags if this photograph isn't taken soon.

They have gathered—all fifty-two of them, including the just-arrived new Miss Idaho (the first was disqualified when officials found out she had entered two local pageants in the same year)—under the band shell across from Convention Hall, to pose for the annual contestants photo. They wear identical navy panel bathing suits trimmed in white. Betty and Ciji have spent fifteen minutes in their hotel room this morning trying on heels to match, but it doesn't really matter: who wears a swimsuit with heels? Betty finally went with a white wedge-heeled sandal and hoped for the best. And now here they all are, lined up like the Rockettes behind the opening curtain.

As the photographer continues to fiddle with his camera, urging patience and uttering more than one "Just a minute, ladies," the girls cordon off into clusters, seeking shade. Ciji has had the foresight to bring a newspaper and is now providing commentary on today's headlines as they wait. Actually, they are yesterday's headlines; with the heels crisis, there was no time to stop for today's paper.

"Listen to this," Ciji announces to a half dozen girls near her. "Rudy Vallee got married to his fourth wife, who is twenty-one—"

"Oh my God!" pipes in Miss Florida. "Isn't he seventy or something?"

"He's forty-eight. Listen, listen. They're getting married, and she stands too close to a candle, and her veil catches on fire! Says here Rudy rubbed out the flames with his bare hands. But not before his bride's hair got completely singed."

"Serves him right, the geezer. And her, too. What a hussy." Betty recognizes the milky drawl without having to look over. Mary Barbara, Alabama. Of course.

"Did you catch that picture of the girl in the bikini? They're all the rage now," comes a voice from the left.

"I wouldn't count on seeing one on Miss America anytime soon," Ciji responds, to appropriate laughter.

"Ladies, places, please!" the photographer shouts.

The girls scurry to their assigned spots, twenty-six on the top row, twenty-six on the bottom, as Miss Slaughter stands in a straw cartwheel hat behind the photographer, eyes hidden behind dark oval sunglasses. Betty smiles, the girls smile, Miss Slaughter most noticeably does not smile. The camera begins to click.

Betty must admit it: she is enjoying herself. Yes, there are the difficult girls, and snobbish girls, and overly competitive girls, and two-faced girls, and one or two ridiculously stupid girls. But overall the whole thing is like a Girl Scout jamboree with makeup and gowns.

And there is Griff. She spent last night thinking of him as she settled down onto her pillow and struggled to shut off her mind, watching Ciji, her closed eyes recently ministered to with witch hazel ("It de-puffies," she'd said) across the room, fast asleep. Betty had played the night over in her head like a favorite record, lingering on each moment, from his walk across the Dennis ballroom to the penny tumbling into the wishing well. She still feels the butterflies. He has promised to come to the parade this afternoon. It cannot get here fast enough.

"Hey, Delaware!" Ciji yells up. "I hate to interrupt your nice daydream, though I don't need to guess what it's about. The pictures are over. Come down. There's someone I want you to meet."

❧

Eddie Tate is a reporter for the *Atlantic City Press,* part of an army of men in fedoras and sweat-stained dress shirts walking up and down the Boardwalk this week chronicling every step, word, and wave of the Miss America delegation. Betty squirms in the heat, uncomfortable and self-conscious, sitting on a bench while still in her swimsuit, sash, and too-tight wedges. She is pretty certain she is not supposed to talk to a reporter without a hostess present; wasn't that one of the thousand rules rolled out yesterday? But in his little round spectacles and too-big fedora, Eddie Tate seems nice and affable, almost gentle, less like a reporter out for a story than a young medical intern about to dispense aspirin. He's short —maybe five-seven?—and wiry. His blond hair makes him appear even younger. He can't be older than twenty-four.

"So how did a nice girl from Delaware end up in a crazy whirlwind like this?" he asks. She bristles. She's not even sure why. The gumshoe phrasing seems crass, demeaning. She wonders if he's putting on a wise guy act, or whether her first impression is mistaken.

"How do you know I'm a nice girl?" she asks. She gets a mental picture of an invisible hostess next to her, fainting right onto the Boardwalk.

His eyes register due surprise. *A live one,* they seem to say. "I've met the people who judge this stuff," he says, smiling. "It's pretty hard for a bad apple to get out of the orchard and make it all the way here."

She nods. "Well, to answer your question, it's very simple, really. Like all the other girls, I entered a state pageant, and by sheer luck I won." She tries to remember her bullet points, the sheet the Delaware pageant folks gave her. "You know, it has been five years since Delaware sent a delegate here. I am just so honored to have been chosen."

Betty catches his eye roll, watches him scribble some random words into his notebook. "Well, thanks," he says, standing up.

She hoods her eyes, squints up at him in the blazing sun. "I take it I am not a very interesting interview."

His face clouds. "You've just got nothing to tell me. None of you do. It's all the same, with these canned answers of how wonderful it feels to be here." He makes no attempt to hide his contempt. Though he seems too young to be this jaded.

"I've got news for you, Mr. Tate," she says, a trace of snap in her voice. "It *does* feel wonderful to be here. Maybe the problem is that you're too much of a skeptic. Or maybe you're just not asking the right questions."

He arches an eyebrow, shrugs. He plops back down, flips the notebook back open. "Okay, Miss Delaware, go ahead, please, by all means: tell me what I should be asking."

For a moment she says nothing, instead gazes directly into his blue eyes, watches a trickle of sweat travel from his matted hairline down his left cheek. She should be focusing on what to say, but the only thing she can think of is how hot he must be in his suit and tie, sitting out here roasting in the midday heat. She is in a swimsuit and feels like she's on a barbecue spit. Somewhere in the distance, a young boy is yelling, "Get your tickets now to see the beauties on parade! Bleacher seats twenty-five cents cheaper than last year!"

"What do you think your readers want to know?" she asks finally.

"I think they want to know how girls end up in this crazy circus," he says. "Which you have already told me is not the right question."

"The problem is that you have already decided what the answer is. You think we've all been roped into this by domineering mothers." She does not mention the fact that her own mother, in fact, did rope her into this.

"You're making assumptions about me," he says.

"No, you're making assumptions about *me*."

He leans back, appraising her. "You're not like the other girls," he says, as a smile creeps onto his lips.

"Well, I'll give you this, Mr. Tate," she says, as she stands up and begins to walk back to the hotel. "That's one assumption you've gotten correct."

❧

Like her state, her float is small and unassuming, at least compared to some of the other Tournament of Roses–worthy contraptions gliding down the Boardwalk. It is anchored at the front by two massive papier-mâché blue hens, the mascot of the state university, and festooned with various blue, yellow, and white flowers and ribbons that flutter in the balmy afternoon breeze. She is sandwiched on the parade route in between the St. Joseph Cadets in front of her and Miss District of Columbia's float behind her, and the marching band's glistening instruments send both the dazzling sun and their brassy music into her eyes and ears, obliterating her senses. And the crowds! Thousands of people lined up on both sides, cheering and screaming and waving, as if it were a ticker tape parade for General Eisenhower on V-E Day.

She is in yet another gown, this one mercifully sleeveless, though her palms have already sweated through her lace wrist gloves. Her mouth hurts from the relentless Cheshire cat smiling, her arm on fire from the incessant waving, and yet the parade is only twenty minutes old. There is an endless supply of floats: from the hotels, from the American Legion, from the local banks, the electric company, the taffy shop, the trades union. One spotlights Hercules in a chariot; another is made completely of seashells. The Steel Pier float features a live trapeze artist, a seal, and a mechanical elephant. The band from the Baltimore Colts marches, as does the U.S. Naval Air Station color guard and rifle platoon. Even amid the din, she can make out the faint sounds of catcalling and wolfish whistling a block behind her, what she is sure is a standard reception for the Catalina Swimwear float.

Behind her sunny mask, Betty is recalling Eddie Tate's query: *How did I end up in a crazy circus like this?* The dreams of so many girls are coming true. Though she cannot deny the steady stream of adrenaline traveling through her body, she knows this has never been *her* dream.

She has always wanted—or at least thought she wanted—a life like her mother's: a nice home, a nice husband, nice children. A life fueled by her future husband's steadiness and her maternal love. She has been brought up with the firm expectation that she will fulfill this vision, and when she's pictured it she has never rebelled against it, or wished to alter it, or thought of it as anything but a happy dream, like a bedtime story.

But will it be enough? Such a question would have never flown into her head before she came to Atlantic City. This is the first time her life has taken any kind of unexpected turn. She thinks she likes it. She does not need all of this—the hoopla, the tinny glamour, the sensory overload—and she is smart enough to know that it is theater, a giant game of charades that will end Saturday night and be forgotten by Monday morning. But something inside of her has been sparked, nudged, a larger question suddenly emerging. About whether her vision for her life is big enough, ambitious enough. She will have a family as a measure of her own worth, of her life's work. But what will she have accomplished for herself? A sash, some pictures atop a float?

How will I know what's enough?

She switches to her left arm for the waving. She should have been alternating the entire time, admonishes herself for not thinking of it sooner. The cadets' brigade has started up a rousing version of "When the Saints Come Marching In," and in an attempt to give the crowd something, she begins to sway in time with the music while sitting atop her perch, under a curving blue banner that says: THE FIRST STATE.

"Incoming!"

She hears it clear as day, remarkable considering the cacophony. In the corner of her eye, she has seen something flying toward the float, landing somewhere, but she is still smiling, still waving, still turning, to the right, to the left, so she cannot see what it is or where it has landed. She hopes it is not something vulgar, a dead fish or filthy diaper or, her brothers springing to mind, a trapped mouse, flung onto the float by a group of mischievous boys.

It is another block and half before some clouds overhead momentarily block the blaze of the sun, and in the brief window of shade Betty darts her eyes around the float to try to see what it was that was tossed up from the crowd. She smiles when she spies the massive sunflower, its big brown face staring up at the sky.

Five

*T*he Shelburne is yet another towering hotel dotting the Atlantic City Boardwalk, and the din in the restaurant at eight in the morning hurts her ears. So many girls saying so much about so little. It looks like a WAC convention, a sea of young women in white and navy, with only the occasional yellow or pink, all wearing their gloves and hats and pearls—who wears pearls at eight in the morning?—and Betty looks down at her own outfit, a gingham two-piece suit with bow-pleat skirt. A mistake to sport such a bold pattern?

Oh, why do you care?

"I don't know about y'all, but I am soooo nervous right now!" Mary Barbara yelps from across the round table. The six other contestants seated with them nod and murmur ascent. The rotating preliminary contests start tonight, the fifty-two of them divided into three groups. Betty's group will compete in swimsuit, then evening gown tomorrow, and finish with talent on Friday. But the truth is the preliminaries really start now, at the first of the two Miss America breakfasts, where judges will go from table to table to "interview" the girls for several minutes and, one presumes, covertly identify their early favorites. Park Haverstick has laid out the rules at the lectern. There is the tinkling of a bell, and the room falls to a hush as the judges fan out.

Vyvyan Donner pulls out the available chair at their table and sits. She is the women's editor of Twentieth Century-Fox Movietone News, and in her lavender skirt-suit and matching hat, she looks every inch the iron butterfly that her reputation commands. Pulling off her gloves one finger at a time, she already seems weary from the whole exercise. "Good morning, ladies," she says, making eye contact with nothing but her gloves. "How are we all this morning?"

And off they go. Predictably, Mary Barbara dives into the conversation headfirst, vomiting her biography and thoughts on everything from Walt Disney (there was a story in the paper this morning about how he conceived his vision for *Cinderella*) to saltwater taffy. Vyvyan Donner takes no notes but rather simply sits back in her chair, seemingly content to wait for the jingling bell telling her to move on. A few other girls attempt to offer commentary—Miss Illinois gamely expounds on the future of television as a medium —but Betty says nothing. She comes to realize that she is the only one actually eating.

"You're rather taciturn this morning, Miss Delaware," Vyvyan says out of nowhere, staring at the folded place card in front of Betty. Vyvyan lights a cigarette, holds it artfully in two fingers in the same hand in which she now rests her chin.

The rest of the table turns its collective gaze to Betty, who chews a mouthful of her fruit cup. She feels like she's just been caught sleeping in the back of class.

She gulps down the fruit. "I . . . I suppose I was waiting for the right moment to join the conversation," she says. *Could I have said anything worse?*

"No time like the present. What's on your mind this morning?"

For a moment Betty hears nothing but a whooshing in her ears. But then she accesses something, a little voice that reminds her that none of this matters, that she didn't even want to enter Miss Delaware, never mind Miss America, that she owes none of these people anything. That she doesn't need to be anyone other than who she is.

"Home" is all she says. And with that, she scoops up another spoonful of fruit, begins chewing thoughtfully.

Vyvyan Donner looks bemused. She leans back into her chair, arms crossed. "Please," she says, "do elaborate."

Out of the corner of her eye, Betty can see Mary Barbara's vicious glare, her face wordlessly expressing, *Hijacked! By Delaware, no less!* Betty takes her time, swallows the fruit, then gingerly takes a sip from her water goblet. "Well, I suppose I am thinking that I miss home. Which no doubt might sound odd to people, since my home is less than a hundred miles away. But I like my life in Delaware, I like the routine, I like my friends and my studies and even my brothers, though of course they drive me crazy." There is polite chuckling from several girls.

"I know!" Mary Barbara interjects. "Monroeville at this time of year is so—"

Vyvyan Donner holds up her hand in Mary Barbara's direction, cutting her off without a word. Her eyes never leave Betty's. "You're here in this exciting place with a chance to change your life, and the only thing you're thinking about is being back in the kitchen with your mother, baking pies? How . . . quaint," Vyvyan says. She takes a long drag on her cigarette. Mary Barbara shoots over a smug look of triumph.

"Hmm. I would use the word 'genuine,'" Betty replies, holding the eye contact. "It is the mothers who baked for us and dressed us and prayed for us and took care of us and worried about us who

42

built the American family. Who, I might argue, built the country. Without them, none of us would be here. Without my mother, I can most certainly declare I would not be sitting here. You're indeed correct, Miss Donner. It is exciting to be in Atlantic City. But yes, I am thinking of home. I find it comforting. And grounding. It keeps me aware of who I am, so I don't get lost in the noise."

Vyvyan stubs out her cigarette, exhales a cloud of smoke right over Mary Barbara's untouched eggs. "Well. Well said, Miss Delaware. I can see why you've captured the attention of the press," she says.

The bell rings. Vyvyan Donner grabs her purse and gloves. "Thank you, ladies," is all she says before she gathers her breakfast tray and travels over to the adjoining table.

Captured the attention of the press?

What does that *mean?*

There is no time to ruminate. Singer Conrad Thibault plops down, his dashing appearance setting more than a few of the hearts at the table aflutter. He is no Vyvyan Donner. He flirts, laughs, tells jokes (one of them a tad off-color . . . a test to see who laughs?), and then the bell rings again, and it's former Miss America Barbara Jo Walker, then artist Coby Whitmore, and Clifford Cooper and Vincent Trotta and Earl Wilson, the latter the syndicated columnist who engages them in an odd game of riddles that no one seems to be able to unravel except him. Ten judges, an hour and a half, and the breakfast is mercifully over. The girls are instructed to rest this afternoon before the preliminaries and are dismissed.

Ciji gallops up beside her as the girls begin filing out. "That was completely nerve-racking!" she exclaims. "But fun. I have no idea what I said. How did your table do?"

Betty laughs. "Mary Barbara Adair was at my table. What more do you need to know?"

"Oh my God. Did anyone even get a word in?"

Betty is about to respond when she feels a hand on her forearm. A pageant hostess. "Miss Delaware," the bony woman says officiously, "Miss Slaughter would like a word."

❧

Lenora Slaughter gets right to the point.

"I am rather distressed," she says to Betty, slowly and carefully, enunciating every syllable, "at this breach of the rules."

They are sitting in the lobby of the Shelburne, in view of, well, everyone, but especially the other contestants, many of whom are still here, window-shopping in some of the boutiques. Betty strongly suspects that Miss Slaughter has done this deliberately. How are scoldings effective if not displayed for all to see? Betty looks about the room, catches Miss South Carolina and Miss Mississippi in a corner, meeting her gaze as they whisper conspiratorially. Betty burns slightly at Mississippi's judgment, given the reputation *she* already has. And that hair!

On the table between Betty and Miss Slaughter is today's edition of the *Atlantic City Press*. Predictably, it is smothered in stories about the pageant, but Miss Slaughter has circled a particular one, under the headline EARLY FAVORITES EMERGE FOR BIG NIGHT, which mentions several contestants, including her. The problem appears to be that while the others are touted for their talent or appearance, she is mentioned for an entirely different reason.

> . . . Miss Delaware, one Betty Jane Welch, dazzled this reporter with her charm, wit, and general confident demeanor. She's a terrific girl, who isn't afraid to speak her mind. And she looks like a baby doll, too. She may have made this guy feel like a meatball when he asked a dumb question, but she's gravy for the finals, we're sure. Good things do come in small packages—and states.

Betty doesn't even have to glance at the byline. *Eddie Tate.*

"It is precisely this kind of vulgar prose we do not wish to have associated with the Miss America Pageant," Miss Slaughter is saying crisply, "and is also precisely why we do not allow contestants to be interviewed except in the presence of an official pageant hostess. Something which is clearly spelled out in the rules, Miss Welch."

And Vyvyan Donner wondered why I was thinking about home. Betty briefly considers speaking her mind right now, telling Miss Slaughter what she really thinks, about how absurd all of this is, how she only did this because she is a good daughter who wanted her mother to get into the Junior League. But she knows she will not. She will take her lecture, the rap with the ruler to the hand, and she will fall in line along with the rest of the girls.

Stupid Ciji. This is all her fault, anyway. Funny how she isn't mentioned in this article.

"Of course, I understand," Betty responds contritely. "The truth is I didn't really know who he was until it was too late. And we only exchanged a few brief words. He has taken severe liberties here. But it doesn't excuse the fact that I was lax in paying appropriate attention to my own conduct. I do apologize, Miss Slaughter. I promise you it won't be repeated."

Miss Slaughter spends ten more minutes on admonishments, making sure to get in all twenty lashes before dismissing Betty, who walks out, cheeks aflame, amid the torrid whispers of the various other Misses. She walks in broad strides on the Boardwalk toward her hotel, making eye contact with no one. She is torn between wanting to see Eddie Tate to give him a piece of her mind and not wanting to see Eddie Tate for fear of being disqualified for slugging a reporter.

She is still churned up when she walks into the Chalfonte lobby. And then, in an instant, it dissipates: the anger, the frustration, the doubt, the apathy, the resentment toward her mother. Because leaning against the registration desk is Griff McAllister, in a knit T-shirt, pleated trousers, and a pair of brown-and-white spectators, a crafty grin on his face. He swipes a package wrapped in paper off of the desk, offers it to her.

A whole bouquet of sunflowers.

"A little birdie told me all you girls had the afternoon free," he says. "Can I entice you to spend it with me?"

Six

"Oh *Lord, now she's humming*," Ciji says to no one in particular, because no one else is in the hotel room except her and Betty.

Betty smiles from her seat at the dressing table. She admits it: she has, in fact, been humming. She cannot remember the last time she felt this happy, filled with a feeling that is unfamiliar but thrilling, as intoxicating as any stimulant could hope to be. It has been one of the best days of her entire life. Is that not deserving of some musical accompaniment?

"You're simply jealous," Betty says.

"You're darned tootin' right I'm jealous!" Ciji answers. She sits on her bed, snaking a fresh pair of stockings up her legs, forcefully clasping them. She is wearing nothing but a body corset. Ciji thinks nothing of nudity, of showing her body to Betty inside the room. She leaves the door to the bathroom unlocked. For Betty, modesty is almost a second skin. She has twice now undressed in front of Ciji, mortified each time. But she senses something inside of herself that is becoming unchained, freed. She feels like a colt just out of the gate, running its first race. *Quite a terrible metaphor,* she thinks, giggling. *What would Eddie Tate think?*

Ciji looks over at the dressing table, where Betty has finished brushing her hair out from the underside and is now sweeping the left back in place with a sparkly barrette. "I can't believe I even agreed to this. You're gonna owe me, Delaware. I mean it."

"You were going to have to see the Mole anyway," Betty says with a shrug. "At least now you'll have company."

"I could have told him I was sick."

"He just saw you sing in front of ten thousand people. He knows you are not sick."

The Boys, as Ciji and Betty have come to call their escorts, were in the audience tonight at Convention Hall, the first night of the preliminary competition. Betty was so on edge, standing in the wings in her swimsuit—thank *God* for Lastex—that she thought she might actually be physically ill, right there on the stage. She was hardly alone. Girls paced, shook out their hands—Mary Barbara led an actual prayer circle, on their knees. The tension bubbled from every corner of the amphitheater. More than a few girls were crying from all of the nerves. This was it, the first night, the chance to make their second impression before the judges, and either cement a place in the Top Fifteen on Saturday night or fade into the background for good, relegated to Miss America wallpaper. But then Betty had thought of Griff, sitting out there in the audience, waiting for her to appear, and the memories of their afternoon together had flooded back to her, and a spontaneous smile had blazed across her face. She couldn't have wiped it off if she'd tried.

It had been a spectacularly normal few hours, and that was what had made the whole day so special. They'd gone shopping on

Atlantic Avenue, stopped in at the Bayless Pharmacy to buy film for Griff's camera, then to Ella Packer, where he'd bought her a small bottle of perfume. They'd had lunch at Huyler's Tea Room (actually, Griff had lunch; Betty was once again too daunted at the prospect of being in swimwear in front of thousands of people to manage a bite), and then gone to the movies, to the Capitol to see Dan Dailey and Anne Baxter in *You're My Everything*. Betty had originally wanted to see Joan Crawford in *Flamingo Road*, until Griff pointed out—correctly, no doubt—that being seen coming out of such a racy picture could possibly engender even further ire from Miss Slaughter. And besides, this movie seemed more fitting somehow: Griff was, rather quickly, becoming her everything.

Betty gets up and plops down on the bed next to Ciji. "I didn't get a chance to tell you," she says quietly, "but your song tonight . . . It was just . . . breathtaking. I can't even imagine being able to sing like that." Neither of them won their preliminaries. But Betty is being true; Ciji's vibrato—full of vulnerability and light with a palpable sense of yearning—brought a piercing fragility to "Some Enchanted Evening" that could have made anyone forget that Perry Como ever sang it. Betty thinks of the odd assortment of judges, dour and intense, sitting in the front row like a college admissions board, and wonders how they could not have heard what she did. To Betty, no one else's talent even came close, no offense to the night's winner, Miss Oregon, and her lively tap dancing.

Ciji smiles wryly. "Too late to butter me up now, kid," she says. "You're still gonna owe me. But we'll make the best of it. At least the boys are taking us someplace swell."

Betty's brow furrows as Ciji slips into her dress. "You don't think we're going to get into any sort of trouble, do you?" she asks. "I mean, Miss Slaughter already has it in for me. I don't need to make any more headlines."

"Relax," Ciji says. "It's dinner. I mean, they gave us *escorts*, right? Which means we are supposed to be escorted."

"We still have to be in by curfew."

"We will be. Stop worrying." She opens her compact. "You looked like a peach in that swimsuit and you spent the day moony-eyed over your new boyfriend and now you get to see him again. And I'll be there to make sure nothing goes wrong. God knows I won't be occupied with *my* date."

"I think you're being very unfair to Jerry. I mean, if you took away the mole—"

"Oh, for cryin' out loud, Delaware! Just be happy, will ya? You have the dreamboat! It's fine. Besides, I didn't come here for romance."

"Neither did I."

"That may be," Ciji says, snapping the compact shut. "But you got it."

❧

It looks like any of the other captain's houses in Atlantic City, a white, stately mansion with multiple gables and striped awnings over the downstairs windows, the shrubbery in front of the wide wraparound porch immaculately pruned. They might have been going to a fashionable lawn party. But the house on Iowa Avenue, across from the Ambassador Hotel, is anything but a typical seashore vacation home. Inside it lays the famed Bath & Turf Club, where the continental of Atlantic City come under the cover of night to play. Quite literally.

On the surface it is a restaurant and cocktail bar offering "famous Chinese cuisine." But Betty can see no one is coming here for the food. She takes in the heavy gold drapes crisscrossing the high-paned windows, the plushness of the carpet underneath her new narrow-heeled shoes, the tuxes on powerful men, the dresses on slinky women. Griff orders a scotch neat for himself and Jerry, and two sidecars for her and Ciji.

"Oh, I can't drink that," Betty protests. "It's against the rules."

"Look around, Betty," Griff says with a chuckle. "*Being* here is against the rules. Relax. I've been coming here for two years and have never once seen a pageant hostess in here."

"Including your mother?"

"God forbid. C'mon."

He takes her hand, and they walk through the parlor into a larger second room, dotted with gambling tables. She hears the clink of ice in glasses, the satisfied exhale of Cuban cigar smoke, the click of the dice tumbling down the felt craps table. She imagines her mother's pained visage, how her parents would kill her if they knew she was here. A panicked thought creeps into her brain. She turns to Griff. "Don't places like this get raided all the time?" A new image comes to mind: her picture on the front page, shielding her eyes as police lead her to a squad car, Eddie Tate spilling all of the scandalous details with his gum-cracking prose.

"This place hasn't been raided since 'Two-Gun Tommy' Taggart was the mayor," Griff replies. "That was five years ago. Honey, you have to learn to relax a little bit. You're only in Atlantic City for a week. Live a little."

Now, another image. It's like a photo album turning pages inside her head. This one is of her packing, of never being with Griff again. Is that what is coming to pass? Never mind being arrested, being talked about.

What if I never see Griff again?

A low whistle from Ciji interrupts her thoughts as the four move toward a blackjack table. Jerry and Griff sit down. "Dang! Have you ever seen a place like this in your life?" Ciji whispers. "I've heard of some spots like this back in Newport, but I've never actually been in one. This place is absolutely lulu."

"Miss Slaughter will have me on the first bus to Delaware and you on your way back to New England if she finds out we were here."

"How is she going to find out we were here? Oh, for Pete's sake, Delaware, what's eating you? For a girl, you're a total fuddy-duddy. It's okay to slip out of the pew once in a while. Lightning ain't gonna come and strike you down, I promise. And neither is Slaughter. I'm sure she's busy right now having dinner at the Chamber of Commerce, eating goulash and criticizing some contestant's shoes." She takes Betty by the shoulders. "Listen: I put on a nice dress and am going to spend my night rooting for the Mole to make some moolah so we can go out after this and have some real fun. The least you can do is get into the swing of things."

Betty takes a look around. Ciji is absolutely right. This is an adventure. Wasn't this whole week supposed to be an adventure? She takes in a deep breath, lets it out, resets her psyche. Half of the girls in the pageant are out on the town tonight, their arms in those of their escorts, watching movies or sharing dinners or walking along the beach. It's time to stop worrying and start living.

Betty turns to Ciji. "We need to get the boys to give us some money," she whispers. "I want to play roulette."

Ciji smiles. "Atta girl," she says.

❧

Where am I? she wonders.

The room is blurry at the edges, like a memory, and Betty blinks and blinks and blinks, fighting to find her faculties. She has not had that many drinks, but however many it's been, it's been too many. She cannot recall the last time she had alcohol. A glass of champagne at that sorority party? Her parents drink—not infrequently—but it has never occurred to her that this is something passed down, like war bonds or diamonds. At some point you just begin.

They are in the Submarine Room. No, no, no, they were *going* to the Submarine Room, but there was a last-minute switch. The Mole knew one of the bartenders at the Brighton, who would serve the girls the famous Brighton Punch and not ask too many questions, like, for example, how old they were. It's coming back to her now. They are in the Brighton, just off the Boardwalk, mercifully in walking distance of the Chalfonte, where she should be right now, safely tucked into bed. *What time is it?* She lacks the courage to ask. She gets her eighty-eighth image of the night of Miss Slaughter, standing sentry at her hotel, waiting by the lobby doors, slapping a rolling pin into her palm.

Betty takes a gulp of ice water, joggles her head, as if shaking off a cold. She needs to eat.

"Can I order something off the menu?" she asks Griff.

"Of course, doll!" he says. It is the most jovial she has seen him since they've met. The orchestra is playing Porter. What tune? Betty recognizes the melody but has to wait for the chorus to come around to identify it. "'Night and Day,'" she says to no one in particular.

Griff cozies up, puts an arm around her. He smells delicious, like vanilla cake. "I'd rather they played 'Let's Misbehave.'"

Betty faintly swats him away, not meaning it. She swigs more ice water. The waiter comes and she orders a bowl of snapper soup, with extra crackers, while Griff orders another round for the table. Betty starts to protest but stops. Let it come. She doesn't have to drink it.

A half hour later Betty has spooned up the last of her soup, her head beginning to clear. Ciji and the Mole arrive back from the dance floor. "Where's Griff?" Ciji asks.

She's unsure. He went to the men's room, but it seems like he's been gone awhile. Now that she thinks about it, a good while, actually. "He'll be back any minute," Betty says, trying to appear indifferent and failing.

"Ladies and gentlemen! Can I have your attention for a moment, please?" It's the bandleader, a tall, angular man with thinning slicked-back hair and a devilish mustache, the kind villains sport in silent movies. "We hope you are enjoying your evening here in the fabulous Brighton. Tonight we have a surprise performance for you. One of our patrons has a very special dedication for a very special lady. Ladies and gentlemen, please extend a warm welcome to Mr. John Griffin McAllister!"

Ciji clamps down forcefully on Betty's forearm. There he is, Griff, her beau, strutting across the stage, taking his place behind the mic. Betty's head swims: with excitement, with alcohol, with embarrassment, with anticipation and pride and . . . love.

"Like many of you fine fellows," Griff is saying, "I am here tonight with a very lovely girl. I have not known her very long, but I *hope* to know her very long indeed. And so I wanted to tell her that, in a little song I wrote just for her. Betty Jane, this is for you."

A little song I wrote.

He wrote her a song.

Betty places her hand atop Ciji's, and her heart swells, so big, so quickly, that she actually pictures it like a water balloon being filled by a garden hose. No one has ever done anything like this for her. She tries not to blink, because she doesn't want to miss a second of it, of this gift. This awe-inspiring, romantic gift. A handsome boy, singing a love song he wrote just for her, in front of a room of all of these fancy people in all of their best bib and tucker.

The orchestra strikes up a jaunty melody, something you might hear behind the Andrews Sisters. Griff starts snapping his fingers, shoulders moving, smile beaming, as he begins to croon. His voice is surprisingly deep and melodious.

> *I was searching, for so long*
> *Though I kinda didn't really even know it*
> *For a girl, and a song*
> *The kinds you find in the words of the poet.*
> *Then came you, by surprise*
> *A dream from which I never will wake*
> *Because you, I realize*
> *Are my love, my life, and my fate!*
> *Baby, I'll treasure the day we met*
> *So dance with me my honey, my lady, my pet*
> *You're my girl, and I'm your beau*
> *And I'm never, ever, ever lettin' you go*
> *Yes, I'm never, ever, ever lettin' you go.*

It's corny. Ridiculous, even.

Betty worships it.

He wrote this for me. He wrote this for me, and dedicated it to me, and sang it to me backed by a full orchestra, in a room full of people.

Even jaded Ciji is impressed. "Forget Miss America, honey," she remarks afterward, lighting a cigarette. "You're walking away with the real prize in Atlantic City."

❧

The Boardwalk is deserted by the time they reach the doors of the Chalfonte. A few showers have passed through; the air smells of rain and wet wood.

It is well, well past curfew, but Betty doesn't care. Ciji has dispatched the Mole quickly and efficiently with a kiss on the cheek and a wan thank-you and then scooted upstairs, no one the wiser, but Betty cannot bear for this night to end. She has the preliminary evening gown competition tomorrow, and she cannot even remember what she brought to wear for it. She only knows what is here, right now, which is the brine in her hair and the piercing eyes now staring down at her and how they make her feel.

"Did you have fun?" Griff asks, mischievously. Because he knows. He *knows*.

"I've had the most marvelous time—" She wants to say, ". . . of my life," but she stops herself. There is still something inside of her that is telling her to hold some control, to not show every one of her cards, even as her emotions roil through her like a tempest. The sidecars and the punch have largely worn off, but just enough residue remains to leave her with the most scandalous and shameful thoughts. "I won fifteen dollars at roulette!"

He laughs. "So you did. Next date, you pay."

"Gladly."

"You're a special girl, baby doll," he says in a heavy whisper. "I know it's only been a little over forty-eight hours, but you have to know by now I'm mad for you. I mean, I've never written a song in my life. I know it was kinda mawkish to get up there and—"

She puts a finger to his lips. "It was the sweetest thing anyone has ever done for me. I was just . . . astonished," she says. She means it.

"Dad-blamed," he whispers, leaning in just a little bit closer, their faces almost touching. "I never thought a girl like you would come along like this. I mean, to be honest, I only did this whole pageant thing because my mother made me. But I'm so glad she did."

"You are?"

He smiles, his lips now mere inches from hers. "I am."

And then the kiss comes, and it is so unlike what has come

before, a series of polite pecks delivered for all to see. Here, in the long after-midnight shadows of the Boardwalk, this kiss is singular —long, wet, languid, at one point ferocious. Betty feels like she might crumple from the sheer force of it. He tastes of bourbon and smoke. She has heard more than one girl at college, and even Patsy, talk about feeling as if their bodies were "on fire," describe a kind of passion she has read about in romance magazines but never experienced. He takes her in his arms, and she holds on to him tightly, gloriously surrendering to all of it.

A few moments later she drifts upstairs on a cloud, lost in her thoughts. She does not see the patrons leaving the bar, or the man moving the sweeper back and forth over the lobby carpet, or the doorman wishing people a good night. And she does not see Mary Barbara Adair, Miss Alabama, who has come down to the front desk to request some aspirin and then proceeded to watch every ardent minute of her long goodbye through the front hotel windows. And she will most certainly not see Mary Barbara at the lobby pay phone the following morning, gently placing a coin in the slot to make the call she is certain will eliminate the girl she has identified as her most unlikely competition, Betty Jane Welch of Delaware, from the Miss America Pageant.

Seven

Betty spots him sitting in the back of the restaurant, reading a copy of his own newspaper over a plate of bacon and eggs. He looks more polished this time, better groomed. But then again, this time he's not sitting on a bench in ninety-degree heat, trying to get pageant girls to talk to him for a story.

His note, delivered to her hotel room just twenty minutes ago, was terse and foreboding:

> IN HOTEL RESTAURANT. COME MEET ME NOW.
> IF NOT, I GO TO PRESS WITH A STORY YOU ARE
> NOT GOING TO LIKE. YOU HAVE 30 MINUTES.
> EDDIE TATE

The maître d' escorts her through the dining room to his table. He rises, waves her into the chair across from him. "Can I get you something?" he asks, overly solicitous. She orders some Brazil mate tea, and the maître d' scurries off.

Betty takes a peek around the room. "I could be disqualified just for being seen with you," she says icily. "Do you know how much trouble I got into for that item you wrote about me?"

"Relax," Eddie Tate says, refilling his coffee cup from the silver pot. "Nobody's going to bust your chops. All of the judges and the big mahoffs are having breakfast at the Claridge this morning. Evidently there was some kind of mix-up in the evening gown scoring last night, and they have to straighten it out. Besides, if anybody sees us together, you can just tell them you were telling me to get lost."

"Which, by the way, I would very much like to do."

He laughs. "You've got spunk, I'll give you that."

"What's all this cloak and dagger about? I got your threatening note."

"It wasn't a threat."

"Then we have very different definitions of the word 'threat.' Out with it: what's this story I wouldn't like?"

"I got a telephone call at the paper this morning. About you and Griffin McAllister last night."

The tea comes and she ignores it. Her heart thumps, like a bell tolling the hour. She remembers almost everything about last evening—particularly the end—but there is a good half hour at the Brighton that's fuzzy, like a photograph that's been left out in the sun. Did someone see her, report her? No. Ciji was with her, as was another contestant—Miss Tennessee?—she glimpsed as they left. No, this is about her and her alone. Did she do something, say something, that someone saw or heard?

She opts to thrust rather than parry. "I'm sure you're aware that Mr. McAllister is my escort this week. All of us were assigned one. Hardly cause for stopping the presses."

"No, but the two of you groping each other like two high-schoolers in the back of a Packard in front of the hotel, after curfew, might be."

The heat rises from the base of her neck, flaring up to her cheeks. She can only imagine how she appears in this moment, red as a summer tomato. It takes every bit of resolve to remain calm. "I understand that the newspaper business is competitive," she says, slowly and deliberately. "But I judged you to be smarter than to listen to such trash."

"Are you denying it?"

"It's not worth a denial. It's not worth anything. It's idle gossip, and if you print a word of it, I'll—"

"You'll what?" His eyes are shining, taunting. She has not noticed until this very second how much he seems to be enjoying this.

She swipes her bag off the table, pushes the chair back. "Let me tell you something, Mr. Tate," she says, a bit too glibly, as she stands. "This grizzled reporter act may impress the girls in the typing pool down at the paper, but it has no effect whatsoever on me. Print whatever you like. It's your reputation that will suffer far more than mine."

"Sit down, Miss Delaware." It's not a request.

She considers this for a good five seconds before slowly retaking her seat. A few eyes cast glances over. Betty can't risk making a scene, and he knows it.

"I have no intention of printing this. I can smell a bum rap when I get one. I came here to warn you."

"About Griffin McAllister?"

"About the girls in this pageant. You may think this is all a lark, but a lot of these girls live for this thing. It's been their dream their whole lives, since they were little girls. And if they see an opportunity to eliminate a competitor, they'll take it."

"I am hardly competition."

"If you really believe that, then you're also naïve."

She cocks her head. "This pageant has been going on since

1921. Everyone knows they never give the crown to the girls from the small states."

"Marian Bergeron was from Connecticut. They gave it to her."

"More than fifteen years ago."

"Everyone also used to say they'd never give the crown to a Jew. But they did."

"Are you telling me that one of the other contestants Ameched to report this ridiculous story?"

"I am telling you that you are bad business to some of these girls."

"That's ridiculous. It's not like I can win Miss America."

"Holy mackerel," he says. "You're awful pretty to be a fathead."

"I beg your pardon?"

He leans over the table, and instinctively she leans forward, as if she's about to hear a secret or a particularly serious medical diagnosis. "Let me tell *you* something, Betty Jane Welch. You're dynamite. You're smart, you're quick, you look like June Haver with Grable's legs, and I don't know what your talent is, but I'm sure it's tops. You could absolutely be the next Miss America." He looks across her shoulder. "Now you better skedaddle. And go through the kitchen. Old Lady Slaughter just walked into the lobby."

❧

She feels like a prize steer out at the cattle auction, waiting for the highest bidder. Betty stands in her swimsuit and a pair of slingback sandals, her hair done up in perfect victory rolls, her mouth beginning to ache from all of the happy grinning. *My God, is this what it's like to actually be Miss America?* she wonders. The parade had been bad enough, but now she feels like her face is about to crack in half. But she stands, still as a floor lamp, her arms around the waists of contestants on either side of her, and shows off her pearly teeth as Al Gold, the ever-rumpled official photographer of Atlantic City, clicks his camera.

"Thanks, girls!" Al says, nodding and gathering up his many photographic accoutrements. It's the middle of the afternoon, and the sun is again beating down, another unseasonably hot day. Many of the tourists here for the pageant are indoors, sipping iced teas or more potent libations. But Betty—along with Daisy Haggis, Miss South Dakota, and Adelaide Carson, Miss Virginia—have no shade in their future. They are taking their turn on "ambassador duty," as it is called within the Miss America Pageant, or "the Meat and Greet," as the contestants call it among themselves. Every day Lenora Slaughter dispatches a few groups of three, in swimsuits and sashes, up and down the Boardwalk, a few in the morning, a few in the afternoon, to pose for pictures and wave to passersby and sign autographs. They started at Illinois Avenue and must make it all the way up to the Inlet, at New Hampshire Avenue, before they can turn around and walk back down the Boardwalk again. And they must not be quick about it. A delegation yesterday returned too early and was given a thrashing by two of the hostesses that was so virulent one might have thought the trio had been caught skinny-dipping with Mr. Haverstick.

"I'd give my left arm for a lemonade right now," Daisy says as the three stroll up the Boardwalk.

"I'd give your left arm for something with a lot more kick," Adelaide answers. "I can't believe I am in this swimsuit all day and then I have to wear it again tonight in front of an auditorium full of people. I'm going to have to wash it out in the room, and then I'll never get it dry in time."

"You will in this heat. What do you have tonight, Betty?" Daisy asks.

"Evening gown."

"Uh! I had evening gown last night. I might as well have worn a paper sack. Did you see that number Texas pulled out? She looked like Scarlett O'Hara at Twelve Oaks."

"It looked so heavy," Betty says. "I bet her shoulders ached something awful after she took it off."

"I thought Nevada's dress was divine," Adelaide says.

"It was!" Daisy answers. "But did you see Maine? Good golly! Did her grandmother make that out of old curtains?"

"Ha! Another Scarlett O'Hara dress!" The two devolve into chortling. "That's why those poor New England girls never win," Adelaide says.

Betty has heard Texas mentioned much in the last few days. The smart money is on her for at least a Top Five. Though she's also heard a lot of chatter about Ohio and California as well. Betty is piqued by the horse-race nature of all of this, how the girls are constantly handicapping the competition, trying to see who's galloping ahead. It's exhausting.

She smiles some more, waves to an elderly couple, winks at a group of young men whistling as they pass. She is rather amazed at how adept she's become at all of this in just a few days. She was counting the minutes, and now wants nothing but to slow everything down. Because now there is Griff. She replays their kiss last night for the hundredth time.

"Mmmm-mmm-mmm, there's that Betty smile again," Daisy says. She is a dark brunette, with a skinny body and flat chest and a nose that is too prominent on her face. Someone said she was only named Miss South Dakota because no one else would take it. It goes that way in some states. *Like Delaware*, Betty thinks. "I heard all about your moonlight kiss with Mr. Gorgeous last night."

"Beat me daddy, eight to the bar! How come this is the first I am hearing this?" Adelaide interjects. Adelaide is shorter, with toned arms and legs from years as a competitive swimmer. She has flaxen chestnut hair and the most beautiful green eyes. "I want the dope! It's bad enough you got the best-looking guy of the lot. Now you're going cuckoo for him, too? Sheesh! Are you rationed?"

I'd like to be, Betty thinks, swatting away their line of inquiry with a benign smirk and a turn of the head to wave to more tourists. A small girl runs up to them with a pencil and paper, temporarily halting the inquisition. But the answer Betty desperately wants to give Daisy and Adelaide is *Yes, I am most definitely rationed. Griff and I are madly in love.* But she cannot. Not here, in the middle of the pageant. She can't give Miss Slaughter any more ammunition. Or Eddie Tate. Or the mystery girl who telephoned him. *Was it Daisy?* No. The more she's considered this, the more she thinks it had to be Mary Barbara Adair, the queen of the dirty look. So much for southern hospitality.

Betty has not told a soul about the small notebook in the bottom of her trunk, where she doodled "Mrs. John Griffin McAllister" several times this morning as Ciji sat, extolling the wonders of her new talcum powder. But Betty can tell Ciji suspects. Even if nothing is said, some girls just seem to have a gift for always knowing other girls' secrets.

Adelaide grabs her arm. "C'mon, Delaware! Are you crazy about him?"

A new smile, this one spontaneous and gorgeous, not perfunctory and rehearsed, creeps onto Betty's face and beams out all over the Boardwalk. The two girls break out into near hysteria.

"I knew it!" Daisy says, pointing. "We've all been going along, putting up with our dates and their stinky cologne and wise guy attitudes, and you end up with Adonis! And not only that, but now it turns out he's a gem, too. It's not fair."

"I'm from the smallest state in the union," Betty utters in mock protest. "Isn't it right that I get some sort of consolation prize?" Never mind that this isn't true: Rhode Island is actually smaller.

64

But Ciji isn't here, thank God. She suspects neither of these girls is a geography major.

Adelaide and Daisy glance at each other, then begin laughing together. "No!" they say in almost perfect unison.

They press for details and Betty, despite herself, relents, just a bit. She leaves out the Bath & Turf Club and most definitely leaves out the cocktails she had there, but cannot help but tell the story of Griff's original song, written and sung just for her. The girls swoon and sigh and chuckle in all of the appropriate places. They spend the next hour and a half strolling up and then back down the Boardwalk, receiving looks of pert approval from wives and looks of a far different nature from those wives' husbands. By the time Betty walks back into the lobby of the Chalfonte, she is almost giddy, as if she has once again spent hours imbibing alcohol and kissing under the stars. She glances at the clock and sees she is late; Griff will already be here, waiting for her for their afternoon date to Huyler's Tea Room for ice cream sodas. He made her promise she'd go once the preliminary swimsuit competition was over. Not that she cares. She'd eat a gallon of ice cream right out of the carton if it meant she got to spend another afternoon with him.

Only Griff is not here.

She scans the spacious lobby once, twice, thrice. No sign of him anywhere. Has he been delayed? Betty walks up the desk, asks if there is a message for her. Or perhaps, she thinks fleetingly, a bouquet of sunflowers, along with a note of apology and a pledge to make it up to her after tonight's preliminary.

But there is no bouquet, no note.

There is nothing.

❧

"*And the winner of* the preliminary swimsuit competition is . . ."

Betty stands in her evening gown with all of the other contestants onstage, waiting for the verdict. There is no preliminary award given for evening gown, only each night for swimsuit and talent. But now, as emcee Bob Russell draws out a pause and the hushed audience waits for the announcement, she feels the electricity of the moment as if she herself had competed.

". . . Miss Rhode Island, Catherine Grace Moore!"

A whoop rises up from the audience, the tiny Rhode Island delegation frantically waving hand-painted signs in the rafters, as Ciji walks calmly to the center of the stage in her swimsuit to accept her trophy and pose for photographs. Betty cannot whoop and holler with the crowd—such exhibitions by the contestants are positively prohibited—but inside, she is doing cartwheels. Ciji has won swimsuit!

Fifteen minutes later backstage, there is noise, dominated by the screeching, howling, exclaiming, musing, and shrieking of the contestants. Such clatter! Sometimes Betty can't hear herself think because of all of it. The incessant chattering of the other girls, the cackling of their hovering mothers, the equally incessant chattering of the hostesses, the barking of the stage managers, the fretting of the state pageant directors (luckily for her, Delaware's is a sleepy insurance agent), the tuning up of the orchestra instruments, the secretaries rushing through the auditorium telling someone that someone has an urgent phone call from someone. Hours and hours and hours of noise, from the very beginning of rehearsal to the nerve-racking announcement every night of the winners of that day's preliminaries.

But noise is not really the issue. She slept-walked through the evening gown preliminary. She is thankful the scoring is not released publicly, like box scores in baseball. For tonight, she struck out. Tomorrow night is the last night of preliminaries: Betty has talent, just in time for her family's arrival. She thinks of the harp, how difficult a thing it is to play, to keep one's fingers thrumming correctly as they gambol across the colored wires. Her head throbs. But it is the feeling in her stomach that bothers her the most: this dull, deep ache, like someone has just carved a hole inside of her and she will never be able to fill it.

She cannot think about that now. She dashes through the throng of assorted contestants, scanning the crowd, until she finds Ciji, just back from her session with the press. Betty wonders what Eddie Tate will write tomorrow.

"Oh my gosh!" Betty exclaims, throwing her arms around her. "Congratulations! I am so thrilled for you!"

Ciji's face carries a mix of triumph and embarrassment. "I may not know as much as some of these other girls," Ciji says, laughing, "but I sure as hell know how to show a little leg."

"Or a lot of leg."

In seconds they are besieged by other girls, all of them complimenting Ciji on her win, at least half not meaning a word of it. Betty slowly extracts herself from the growing throng, goes over to wait and take her turn congratulating Miss New York State on her talent win—in Miss America, exhibiting good sportsmanship is everything—and then drifts toward the dressing room. But before she leaves the backstage area, she feels a hand on her arm. Ciji, still holding her swimsuit trophy.

"You don't get away that easy, Delaware. Something's bugging you, and don't lie and tell me it's not. You don't live with a girl and not know her moods."

"We've lived together for three days."

"I'm a quick study."

And so Betty tells her: about her kiss goodbye last night, about the mystery phone caller she suspects was Mary Barbara, about Eddie Tate, about Griff ditching her today.

"Buck up, Delaware. So he doesn't show for one date," Ciji says. "Look, you can't blame the guy for pulling back a little. He's been coming on awful strong. He wrote *a song* for you. And sang it! In public! Maybe he doesn't want to appear too bonkers for you. Or maybe he and the boys went on a bender. Who knows? He's not ditching you."

Betty pulls her into a backstage corner away from the rest of the girls, behind the heavy stage curtains, near a cascade of ropes and cables from the ceiling. She has to tell someone. She has to, or she's going to die.

"Ciji, I . . . I . . . I've never felt this way about a boy before." She blurts it out, like a confession, which it is. She wants to tell all of this to Patsy, moony Patsy who knows her so well, but Patsy will not be here until Saturday, and she cannot wait until Saturday. By Saturday this hole inside of her may swallow her completely, leave her a pile of smoking rubble in a black sash. "I keep going over it again and again. I mean, he was supposed to meet me. And then he doesn't show, doesn't call, doesn't leave a message?" Briefly, this afternoon, the thought had struck her: *Something terrible has happened. An accident. He's in the hospital.* But she has seen his mother, performing her hostess duties with cool aplomb. Honor McAllister would not be here if something untoward had happened to Griff.

Ciji tilts her head, delivers a crooked smile so condescending, so insincere, that Betty wants to slap her. "First love is a tough thing, honey," she says, and Betty feels the blood again rising, her hurt and anguish frothing into anger. She doesn't need this now. She needs to be outside, to get some air.

"I have to go," Betty says, and rushes away, out toward the dressing area. She looks at herself in the mirror, studies her evening gown as she inches the gloves down her arms. Ciji's gown, by contrast, is like Ciji herself: sleek, sensual, daring, a satin form-fitting green backless dress with a gathered crossover sash in the rear with flounces on the front right. The kind of dress a siren would wear to sing in a supper club. Betty's evening gown is sleeveless—that's daring enough for her—made of white English net with a tiered skirt over a crinoline pleated ruff. She worries that, paired with the triple-strand choker of pearls tonight, it made her look too expectant, too bridal, as if she were waiting for her prince to arrive.

Wasn't she?

She sinks down onto a padded stool, reaches back to undo the necklace clasp. *What is the matter with you, Betty Jane Welch? We came here to have fun. We were supposed to simply fall in line, get it all done with, and go back to college. When did all of . . . this happen? Why did he have to happen?*

She tosses the pearls onto the dressing table, begins unzipping the back of the dress. *Okay. It's all going to be okay. We have two more nights here, and then we go home on Sunday. Who cares what happens with Griff McAllister? A week ago you didn't even know Mr. John Griffin McAllister. Your family will be here tomorrow. Patsy will be here Saturday. You'll have support. After the Top Fifteen is announced on Saturday night, it'll all be over. Take a deep breath. You're fine. You're fine. Let's just get back to the hotel and into bed.*

She is lying to herself, and she knows it. Because even if she were never to see Griff again—a thought so painful she cannot even consider it—she knows that something larger is happening here. Has happened here. She is different. She is becoming someone, something, else. No matter what girl returns to Delaware, she knows it will not be the same one who arrived in Atlantic City.

Fifteen minutes later, dressed in a red suit and hat, Betty threads her way through the other contestants in various states of dress and undress, gabbing and giggling. She craves an aspirin and bed.

She is almost to the doors of Convention Hall, out onto the Boardwalk, when she hears her name.

"Betty! Betty, could you wait just a moment, please?"

The diction is formal, precise, like a grammarian, or Katharine

Hepburn. Betty turns to see Honor McAllister making her way toward her.

In the five days she has been in Atlantic City, Betty has never been formally introduced to Griff's mother. Each hostess has a group of several contestants for whom she is responsible, mainly to ensure that each girl is where she is supposed to be at any given moment. But Betty is not in Honor McAllister's group. She has spied her across various ballrooms and stages but has lacked the temerity to make herself known. And she has found it slightly peculiar that Honor has not approached *her*, has not been curious about the girl her son has been squiring. It has left her with an impression of Honor McAllister as cold and forbidding, the harridan convinced that no girl is good enough for her son.

Up close, Honor is beautiful in the way wealthy older women tend to be, with slicing cheekbones and a long, narrow face that seems faintly equine. She places a bony hand atop Betty's forearm, guides her away from the doors.

"Betty. I do so very much apologize for not introducing myself earlier," she says, her smile bright and gleaming, like an overly sparkly Christmas ornament. She is tall, at least five-ten, Betty thinks, and has a coiffure of chestnut hair the texture of cotton candy that crests right to left over her head in a dramatic wave. Her skin—shiny, uncreased, delicate—indicates mid-forties at best. She has the dramatic eyebrows of a mannequin. "This is my first year acting as the vice president of the hostess committee, and I confess it's been a bit overwhelming. But I do hope to get to know you better, and to meet your wonderful family, of course. My Griffin has been telling me the most lovely things about you."

"He's not here," Betty replies flatly. She meant to say, "It's so nice to meet you." Or "How nice to make your acquaintance." But her defenses are down. Not just down. Destroyed. Stood up one day and she is already unraveling.

I hate love.

Honor pats her on the hand, like a wealthier Mary Worth. How pathetic and mousy Betty must look, pining for the boy who isn't here, a boy she's just met but about whom she's acting as if he were her fiancé. A few girls nearby throw themselves into the arms of their respective escorts. Even Ciji has a date tonight with the Mole. Off to the Saratoga Room. Betty just wants to leave. *Why won't they just let me leave?*

"I know that you and Griffin had plans today, dear," Honor says, and Betty wants to die. Did he really send his mother to ditch her? "But he fell terribly ill this morning. Some sort of stomach bug, I think. He didn't even go to the nursery, and we had a huge delivery come in. He would never have missed that if he weren't genuinely unwell." She looks into Betty's eyes. "He feels terrible that he disappointed you today. But I assure you he'll be better tomorrow. In fact, I was hoping you would come out to the house and be our guest for luncheon."

Betty's eyes narrow. She is momentarily baffled. *Lunch? To-morrow?*

"I . . . Of course. Of course. Yes, that would be lovely," Betty says. "How very kind of you."

"Not at all. I'll have a car pick you up at your hotel at noon. Oh!" She turns, scans the lobby, looking for something. "I almost forgot. Come with me, dear."

And they're off, hustling through the cavernous lobby of Board-walk Hall, until they arrive at a table strewn with flyers, posters, badges, and other assorted Miss America ephemera. Honor picks up a big bouquet, delicately wrapped in brown paper. "These are for you. An apology from Griffin."

Roses. A dozen blooms, yellow, expertly arranged. Betty is not certain of much in this moment, but she knows this: this bouquet was selected by the mother, not the son. *Any schmo can give a girl*

71

roses. She thinks of the sunflowers still sitting on the dresser in her hotel room. She wonders if they're still alive.

⚜

He lies on the mattress in his childhood bedroom, and the silence is everywhere and nowhere. Longport is a low-humming town even in the midst of the hubbub of summer, but now, after Labor Day, it is somnolent and still. And yet he cannot quiet them, these voices in his head, which scream at him, in various tones and accents and sometimes even strange languages. They come and stay, swirling through his brain for hours, sometimes days, and then leave just as quickly—once for several years. But he knows they will come back.

They always come back.

And now they are here, chanting like Trappist monks, loud, angry, virulent, urgent. And so he wonders. He wonders if by chance he was to listen to them, to try to act on their warnings, protestations, and outcries, would they then leave him for good? Would they be satisfied, move on to someone else's brain, go on to torment another soul someplace else?

Griffin McAllister feels the sweat coating his body, looks toward the window and the moon above, searching for answers that never materialize. He tries once again to do his breathing exercises, to clear his mind as the doctors have taught him, but the voices are too powerful tonight, too insistent. *Stop. Stop!*

But the voices continue.

She doesn't love you. Nobody loves you, says the angry woman.

I don't understand you. Why can't you see them? They're everywhere, spying on you. They can see you through that lamp on the table. They're watching you, waiting for you to make a mistake, and then they're going to send you away forever and you'll never see anyone again. The gruff voice, the one that sounds like his late grandfather.

Betty is a harlot. It would be better if she drowned in the ocean, shrieks the one that's always screaming, always pitched.

God wants you to suffer. It is your duty to suffer. Voltaire. He didn't speak for years but has recently returned.

Kill yourself. It's better than living like this.

This last the worst voice of all.

His own.

Eight

The pine-green Cadillac glides down Atlantic Avenue, through southern Atlantic City, then the tiny beach towns of Ventnor and Margate, before coasting into Longport, at the very end of Absecon Island. The driver—a buttoned-up, hulking man with the pug nose of a boxer—has picked her up at the hotel promptly at noon and now deposits her in front of a grand sea captain's house that faces the bay. He opens the rear passenger door, and Betty gives a gracious nod as she exits, carrying the box with the cheesecake she bought this morning at Kornblau's.

She got up an hour early simply so she would not have to rush the decision on what to wear. Ciji refused to help, finding all of the fretting ridiculous and, Betty suspects, not a little bit irritating. In the end Betty mentally used her mother as a guide. What would one wear to a lunch with the Junior League? The answer was evidently a printed crepe day dress with a small white, straw, side-swept hat. The thought enters Betty's mind that her parents and brothers are no doubt already in the car, on their way to Atlantic City. Oh, the endless, overly bubbly inquiries, especially about

Griff, that are sure to surface. She dreads them almost as much as tonight's last preliminary contest: talent. It is one thing to have walked down a runway in a swimsuit, and the next to have walked down the runway in an evening gown. But the biggest group for which Betty has ever played her harp was during the Miss Delaware contest, and that was fewer than two hundred people.

Tonight there will be twelve thousand.

I'm not going to think about that, she says to herself as the driver opens the front door of the house and waves her inside.

The living room is formal, wide and expansive, all the better to take advantage of the views of the bay. It features a floral-patterned Bigelow carpet and a standard selection of hand-painted porcelain lamps and mahogany and cherrywood furniture. There is a slender secretary in the corner, where Betty imagines Honor McAllister sits and composes lovely notes on her personal stationery, all penned in a perfect loping script. The fireplace mantel is a pleasing off-white, and above it hangs a portrait of a Colonial-era gentleman in tailored clothing, no doubt some formidable McAllister forefather, his full sideburns gray and bushy. A small cabinet to the left of the mantel is closed but, Betty suspects, contains a television. A television! This is one of the few areas where she and her brothers have agreed, collectively begging their parents to buy one. It is one of the many in which they have been collectively unsuccessful.

Betty wanders about the room, inspecting the bookshelves and occasionally glancing out to the sunlight shimmering on the water, and wonders where everyone is. She picks up a Chinese vase, tries to make sense of the random markings on the bottom, gently places it back. A check of her watch. Is she early? No. She writhes her hands together, feels suddenly antsy and self-conscious, as if somewhere in the house an argument is in full bore on who is to blame for inviting her.

Roaming around, she spies a small box with a speaker attached to the wall by the window. A radio built into the wall? But there is no dial, just a switch. In an act of nervous curiosity, she flips it on.

The speaker crackles to life, and Betty instantly makes out two voices speaking in hushed but exigent tones.

Not a radio. An intercom. Connected to some other room in the house.

". . . downstairs, darling. Now we mustn't keep her waiting any longer. We are being rude, and I know you would not want her to think you rude." *Honor.*

"I can't. I can't. You know I can't." Griff, barely audible, clearly upset. He and Honor are talking. About her. Betty knows this is wrong, that she's eavesdropping, that she has no right to hear any of this. But she cannot bring herself to turn off the intercom.

"Now, dearest," Honor is saying, "she's come all the way from Atlantic City. And we cannot simply send her back. It will be good for you to see her, to be around someone you like so much. You know what the doctors have always told us, that you need to not isolate during your episodes."

"Stop! Stop it!" Griff says. He sounds petulant, like a four-year-old who doesn't wish to take his nap. Honor shushes him in soothing, babyish tones. Betty can almost picture them, sitting on Griff's bed, Honor gently stroking his hair, telling him it's all going to be all right.

Episodes? Episodes of what?

"She'll know. She'll look at me and she'll know. Just like that reporter—"

"I told you that you had to forget all about that silly reporter. It's clear he fancies Betty and that he only telephoned in order to upset you. But Betty is here. To see you. She cares for you. I know she does."

Eddie Tate? Eddie called Griff? Why?

"Only because she doesn't know the truth," Griff is saying. "Everyone is against me. You're against me, too!" Betty believes she catches a sob in his voice. Is he crying? What truth does she not know?

There is more arguing done in indecipherable whispers, until Honor convinces Griff to take "your medicine"; Betty can make out the pouring of water, the handing over of a glass. Several minutes later it appears Griff has calmed down; Betty can hear movement in the room, the opening of a drawer, the brushing of pants. Hastily, Betty snaps off the intercom and takes a furtive view around. What if the driver had come in, caught her listening?

Why is there an intercom between the parlor and Griff's bedroom?

"You must be Betty," a voice interjects.

Betty spins around to see a girl several years younger than she, maybe fourteen or fifteen, standing by the living room arch. She's delicate, with fine alabaster skin and a sprinkle of freckles on her nose; her long hair, pulled into a loose chignon at the back, is almost identical in color to Betty's own. She wears a playsuit with bright vertical stripes.

"I'm Martha," the girl says, walking into the room and extending her hand. "Griffin's sister."

"Of course," Betty says. "It's lovely to meet you. I've heard so much about you."

"And I you. You're even prettier than Griffin said."

"He's very generous with his compliments."

"Please," the girl says, guiding Betty back into the room, "sit."

Betty sinks down onto the edge of a blue-and-white wingback chair. She poses, crossing her ankles behind her, places her lace-gloved hands one atop the other on the bag on her lap, ensures that her expression is one of pleasant expectancy. As Martha talks, Betty's mind drifts elsewhere: whirling with doubts, with anxiety, with concern for the young man who has so quickly stolen her heart. And with one loud, demanding question.

What's wrong with him?

❧

They walk out onto the jetty that juts into the ocean at Eleventh Street, where the ocean melds into the bay. The breeze is up but warm. The lunch went well; when he finally walked into the living room, Griff seemed himself, with nary a trace of the panicked, churlish boy on whom she'd eavesdropped. He was playful and sardonic with Martha, the quintessential loving big brother. He's wearing a linen oxford and vest with a pair of canvas pants, his feet bare. He puts an arm around her, pulls her closer, and kisses her head.

"Did you notice when we turned up? This is Eleventh Street, not First Street. Even though the island ends here."

"How odd," she says. "What happened to the first ten streets?"

"Legend has it that there was a great hurricane that came and swept the first ten blocks of Longport out to sea. You occasionally still get divers out here, trying to find this Atlantis of the Jersey Shore."

"You mean to say there are ten blocks lying at the bottom of the ocean?"

He laughs. For the first time today, he laughs like he did two nights ago at the Brighton. It's her first glimpse today of the young man she has grown to know. To love. "That's why it's a legend. And like most legends, it's absolutely untrue. Old Man McCullough sold off the first ten blocks across the Inlet. Over there"—he points to houses across the water—"is what's now known as the Gardens section of Ocean City. But they used to be the first ten blocks of Longport. Unfortunately, that's not quite as thrilling a tale as that of an underwater city."

They stand for a few more minutes in silence. A skiff sails by. "Your mother didn't seem to want to let us take a walk alone," Betty says finally. The lunch was, like Honor McAllister herself, elegant and brisk. Cold baked ham and potato salad with iced tea, Betty's cheesecake with coffee brought in on a beautiful white tray for dessert. Honor practically commanded Martha to join them for their walk on the beach, but—bless her heart—Griff's sister resisted the entreaty.

"My mother worries too much."

"About what?"

"About everything."

"Is there something to be worried about?"

He gives her a look of studied sobriety, as if he's trying to discern how much to tell her. Or perhaps what to tell her. "Well, this is a bit embarrassing to confess to a girl, but you're special, Betty. I think you know that." He looks back out toward the water. "I can have trouble handling too much stress, and it takes a toll on me physically," he says, spooning out each word. "It's why I . . . I had to leave college. It's mortifying to talk about, truly. Jeepers, I already said that. The point is, I take medicine for it, and I'm fine. It's just that I have to be careful not to let myself get run-down. Like yesterday. I was just done for. I hated not seeing you. And I feel like a jackass for not calling the hotel and leaving you a message myself. It's off the cob, to have your own mother give your girl flowers for you. And not even the right ones. So I want you to know I'm sorry."

She turns to him, places her hand on the side of his face. "You don't have anything to be sorry for, John Griffin McAllister. You . . . you're the most wonderful boy I've ever known."

"So you're not sore?"

She smiles. "No, I'm not sore."

This kiss is even better than the one on the Boardwalk, dreamy and romantic rather than primal, with just the right degree of longing. Standing tiptoe on the windswept jetty, folded into his arms, Betty has never felt more secure in her entire life. Learning about his condition has made him seem more real, more vulnerable and open.

"Honey," he says quietly after a few minutes, "there is something else I need to talk to you about." He fishes in his pocket, extracts a piece of newspaper that's been torn and hands it to her. "Did you see this?"

Her heart sinks. Not another one. The clipping is from today's *Atlantic City Press*. A column titled "Around the Pageant," with small dispatches about various contestants and goings-on. Betty begins reading an item about Miss Hawaii giving hula lessons to some of the other girls.

"Third item down," Griff says.

> Pageant bigwigs try their best to keep their fillies in line, but that doesn't stop a few from sneaking out every year to explore the wonders of Atlantic City nightlife. Our spies tell us that on Wednesday night a few pretty state-holders were seen at the Brighton, where one particular Miss got a special serenade in the form of a personal song from her pageant escort, which the ga-ga hepcat wrote himself! We're told the crowd went bananas for this fine fella's crooning to his lady, and more than a few gals were jealous he hadn't been selected as their date this week. But does a song dedication help put a girl in the rhinestone tiara? We'll have to wait till Saturday night to find out.

"Hot dog!" Betty exclaims. "How did they know we were there?"

"These reporters have eyes everywhere," Griff says, taking the clipping out of Betty's hands and shoving it back in his pocket.

"Waiters, busboys, maids. They're always looking for the skinny on you girls."

Betty's mind reels. At least she wasn't named this time. But does Miss Slaughter know it was her?

"Don't worry," Griff says, intuiting her thoughts. "If Miss Slaughter knew it was you, you would have had a visit first thing this morning before you ever left the hotel. Publicly they may wag their fingers at this stuff, but deep down they know it's good publicity for them to have you girls seen around town. It fuels interest in the pageant."

Betty squints up at him through the midday sun. "Does it bother you?"

"A bit, I suppose," he says, his eyes again focused on the water. "I come off like a chump."

"Hey, look at me," she says, grabbing his arms. "Talk to me. What's really eating you about this? I mean, it was a beautiful song. You should be proud people were talking about it."

"It's not that."

"Then what?"

"You must know how I feel about you."

"I think I'm beginning to. The song helped."

He laughs. "The thing is . . . I . . . I don't want to be in gossip columns. I don't want to be known as 'Mr. Miss America.'"

"Well, then you're in luck. I'm not Miss America."

"But you might be. Your entire life could be turned upside down by tomorrow night."

"You're being silly. Girls like me are just the filler, the background for the real contestants, the girls like Mary Barbara Adair. You're worrying about nothing. I'm not going to win. I'm not."

"You can't be certain of that. I just need you to understand that if you do win, I can't . . . It pains me to say this out loud. But we can't be together, Betty. You can't be my girl if you win. It'd be too much for me."

And here she'd thought it was something serious. "You know what the good news is?" she asks.

He pulls her back into his arms. "Sure. Tell me: what's the good news?"

"You just confessed you want me to be your girl."

"You *are* my girl. I thought you already knew that."

"Not out loud."

"I sang you a song about it in front of a roomful of people! A song I wrote! How romantic does a guy have to get?" His smile is fulsome, brilliant. He's back.

"Sing it to me again."

"Right here?"

"Right here."

And so he does.

❧

By the time the Cadillac is rolling back up Atlantic Avenue, it is past two thirty. Betty's family is no doubt already at the hotel, wondering where she is, and she admonishes herself for not leaving them a note at the front desk. She has promised Ricky a walk on the Boardwalk this afternoon, before the final preliminary tonight, and now, with this unexpected stop she is about to make, that is out of the question. She is disappointing everyone. It feels strange and oddly liberating.

She is the girl who lives to please, now solely focused on her own pleasures.

The car pulls over at the corner of Mediterranean and Virginia Avenues, and Betty climbs out, asks Honor McAllister's driver to wait. She won't be long.

Minutes later she is striding down an aisle of desks in the hectic newsroom of the *Atlantic City Press,* coming to a stop at his. His shirtsleeves are rolled up, and his hair flops into his eyes. He is hunched over his typewriter, fiddling with the ribbon, which appears stuck. A half-written story peeks out from the top of the roller, a carbon underneath. She wonders if she's in this one, too. She can feel the eyes of the other reporters on her, catches the odd word of a whispered comment here and there. She suspects she is the first Miss America contestant to ever barge into the paper like this, and it thrills her. She likes this side of herself, this hidden layer she has now discovered, bold and brassy, like Kitty Foyle.

Eddie Tate startles. "Betty! My. Hello. This is a . . . surprise," he stammers, banging his knee against the desk as he awkwardly rises from his swivel chair, attempting to smooth back his hair in the process. He reaches for his coat on the back of the chair, wriggles into it as he halfheartedly organizes the messy papers all over his desk, smudging them with the messy typewriter ribbon ink now on his fingers. "What . . . what can I do for you? May I offer you a cup of coffee?"

His fumbling nerves only feed her confidence. She has a memory of her father at the dinner table, quoting the Roman historian Titus Livius Patavinus—he is always tossing out obscure quotes, because they make him appear well-read and, more important, leave him a device for issuing sage pronouncements: "There is always more spirit in attack than in defense."

"No thank you," Betty says, scanning around for a chair. "May I sit for a moment?"

"Allow me," says a voice from the left, wheeling another chair in. A reporter, considerably more disheveled, with a long, rubbery face and a wide nose that is two sizes too large for it. "Chick Kaisinger, at your service."

"Yeah, okay, thanks, Chick. I'll take it from here," Eddie says.

"I bet you will," Chick says, still leering at Betty as he moseys back to his desk.

Examining his flushed face, Betty cannot help but wonder whether Eddie is always jumpy or whether it is she who makes him so. She suspects the former but hopes the latter. Maybe her father is right: it's the effect of the surprise attack. She only knows that Eddie now appears a far different young man than the cocky reporter on the Boardwalk and in the hotel dining room yesterday morning. He looks as if he's about to jump out of his skin.

"So, I don't expect this is a social call. What can I do for you, Miss Welch?"

She crosses her legs, studies him. "I'm here to ask if I have done anything to offend you. And to apologize if I have."

For a moment he says nothing, just stares at her with those icy blue eyes. Every time she sees him, he appears more handsome, and it bothers her that she notices. He is not Griff, of course. But he has . . . something. The blond hair, the freckles, the tiny oval glasses. He's the cute smart boy whose layers you want to peel back, see what's lying underneath.

She blushes at her own thoughts. What has gotten into her today?

"What would make you feel that you've done something like that?" he says finally.

"I don't know. But you seem to be focused on me more than the other girls competing. I confess I find it all rather curious."

"I've mentioned you in one story, Betty. Along with plenty of the other girls."

"Two. You're not counting the item about the unnamed boy serenading the girl at the Brighton the other night."

The *click-clack* of myriad typewriters, a tinny symphony when Betty first walked onto the newsroom floor, has been reduced to a few random strokes here and there; there is almost a stillness about the place, as if everyone is trying to eavesdrop without appearing to do so. Betty can hear the steady hum of the teletype, spewing its curling ribbon of bulletins somewhere nearby. Reporters shuffle papers, walk back and forth, but it's clear her visit is the day's biggest headline.

"I don't write the blind items," Eddie says, frowning. His jitters seem to have been vanquished by annoyance. "If you feel you've been treated unfairly, you can always write a letter to the editor. I'd be glad to pass it on."

"Why did you call Griffin McAllister?" The sentence comes out brusquely, with an edge she did not intend.

He cocks his head, assessing her. "It's a sad day when a sugar daddy has to send his dame over to do his dirty work," he says. "If your precious Griff is too scared to talk to a reporter, he doesn't have to. But don't flatter yourself, sweetheart. It's Pageant Week. This is the *Atlantic City Press*. We cover everything and everybody to do with it, including the mooks who squire you girls around. I called a bunch of guys."

"Really? Who else?"

Eddie stands up, staring down at her. "I don't have to explain how I do my job to you."

"Maybe what you do need to explain is why you're so interested in me."

He says nothing for several seconds. His face is hard, his jaw clenched. But the eyes—soft, yearning—expose him. For several more seconds, they say nothing, simply stare at each other, exchanging wordless acknowledgment.

Betty slowly stands. "I see. Griff has been unwell lately. He is under a tremendous amount of strain due to his responsibilities in his family's business. I would appreciate your consideration in not bothering him further. I'd consider it a personal favor."

"I got your message, Miss Welch. Now if you'll excuse me, I'm on deadline."

"I thank you for your time, Mr. Tate. I'm sure I'll be seeing you tonight at the last of the preliminaries?"

He chuckles briefly and artificially, a laugh laced with a noticeable trace of sarcasm. "Wouldn't miss it."

Nine

"*Did you date at all* in high school?" Ciji asks as she plucks out the last of her pin curls. She begins to separate sections of her hair by hand. "Because it sounds to me like you have absolutely no idea how to handle men." She bends over, shakes out her locks while coating them in a cyclone of mist.

"What *is* that?" Betty asks, waving her hands in front of her face.

"The future of beauty, honey," Ciji says, straightening up and flipping her hair back. She picks up a hairbrush, begins softening the curls. "A miracle. Brand-new. It's this sticky kind of spray that holds your hair in place for hours. My secret weapon for winning this pageant."

"It smells terrible."

"It doesn't matter how it *smells*, dearie. The judges aren't going to smell you. It's all about how it makes you *look*."

They need to be back at Convention Hall in less than two hours. Betty managed to get back in time to spend the afternoon with her family, walking the Boardwalk—Ricky displeased it was not just the two of them, because with just the two of them his odds of getting unfettered access to sweets is good—and listening to everything going on back in Delaware that she didn't care about when she was there and cares even less about now. Ricky's wrist is in a bandage, but his injury has not stopped him from being as annoying as possible every minute. Her father has lectured her for fifteen minutes about not letting all of this go to her head; her mother has filled in the rest of the time asking questions about everything, in detail. Betty has edited her itinerary of the past week, heavily. Still, she has to admit: she's glad they are here. They are so happy, so proud. She has never been the showy one in the family, the one being bragged about or admired or drawing attention. It feels nice. More than that, actually. It feels . . . vindicating.

Betty drops down onto her bed. She should be checking her dress—so many dresses!—making sure that it is pressed and ready for her harp solo tonight, but she cannot do it, because if she does she must again think about playing in front of all of those people, and the less she thinks about that the better. She looks over at Ciji, now expertly shaping her bangs in a curving S shape, sliding a bobby pin behind her left ear to pull one side back. She wishes she could be more carefree. She remembers standing in her bedroom at home just last week, packing and talking to Patsy, feeling so indifferent and cavalier. And then Griff strutted across the ballroom, looking like a magazine advertisement.

"Your hair looks nice," Betty says.

"Thank you," Ciji says, brushing the ends and shaping them. "I'm going for Linda Darnell in *A Letter to Three Wives*."

"You want the judges to see a girl whose husband just ran off with another woman?"

"I want the judges," Ciji says, brushing from the back, more forcefully now, "to see a movie star."

"So that's it, then? After here—assuming you are not wearing a tiara tomorrow night—you're going to get on a bus or a train and go to Hollywood?"

"I wish," Ciji says, putting the brush down. "But I haven't saved enough lettuce for that."

"You won money last night for the swimsuit competition."

"That's enough to get me a better seat on the train home."

"You'll win more money if you make it to the Top Fifteen."

"Maybe. But I don't think these judges are noticing me. I mean, obviously they're noticing my gams. But I think I was too cranky at the breakfast."

"There's another breakfast tomorrow. You can redeem yourself."

"We'll see. Maybe my Linda Darnell hair will dazzle them to-night in my evening gown. If not, it's back to the hotel."

"The hotel?"

"I told you, didn't I? I work at this fancy hotel in Newport called the Cliff Lawn Manor. Overlooks the bluff right on the sound. Small place, but swanky. All the swells come. So I'll go back there until I can save enough money to head out west. You should visit me sometime."

"I had no idea you were a maid in a hotel."

Ciji's eyes dart upward, staring back at Betty through the reflection in the dressing-table mirror. "Who said anything about being a maid, Delaware? Sheesh! Give a girl a little credit, would you? I happen to work reception. I'm an excellent greeter. That's why I would make a great Miss America. I can smile and nod and make small talk with anybody, no matter how much of a louse they are." She reaches into her purse, extracts a card, and tosses it over at Betty. "Here, take this. It has the number and address of the hotel on it. If you're ever in Newport, look me up."

"How do I know you'll take my call?"

"I answer the phone, sweetheart. I *have* to take your call."

She uncaps her lipstick, begins applying a dark scarlet shade. "By the way, don't think I haven't realized you've completely changed the subject. We were talking about you and Dreamboat. What are you worried about now? Didn't lunch with Mama Bear go well?"

Betty wants to tell Ciji everything—about the intercom, about what she overheard, about Honor McAllister's cryptic manner and Griff's moodiness and Eddie Tate's snooping. Ciji's black-and-white way of seeing things may actually help sort it all out. But it's much too long a story to get into now. And it would probably sound ludicrous, anyway. There's no reason to submerge herself in the drama of it any more than she already has.

"It went just ducky," Betty says, walking over to the settee and kissing Ciji gently on the temple. "You look gorgeous. You're gonna knock 'em dead."

Ciji grabs her arm. "Betty," she says in a tone Betty has not heard in her voice before, "listen to me. I think it's great that you and Griff are having this big romance. Really, I do. It's been fun to see you get so khaki wacky. But remember why you came here. Tomorrow night, whatever happens, this will all be over. You'll be back at college, he'll be here, and, well, romances with lots of miles in between them are tough to keep going, no matter how many love letters you write or boxes of chocolates you get in the mail. I think you've got to be realistic about what's happening. These escorts, honey—they're hired by the hostesses to be nice to us, to pay attention to us. You need to keep your eyes on what your future is really going to look like."

Betty wants to say—no, she wants to scream, actually—*No, you're wrong. Griff loves me and I love him and that's all that matters and we will find a way to be together once all of this is over, no matter what it takes.* But she does not say that, because it is pointless to say that. Ciji's verdict is no doubt Honor McAllister's, too. But it's not the truth. Betty knows it's not the truth. She knows what is in her heart, how big and explosive it is, how she has never felt this way about another living person in her entire life. And she knows what is inside Griff's — sensitive, plaintive Griff, who is suffering from a condition not of his own making, one she is certain her love and care can cure.

So instead Betty gently places a hand on Ciji's cheek and smiles. "Don't worry, Rhode Island. I know what I'm doing."

❧

The aria seems endless, a barreling cyclone of notes whirling about the stage, the shriek of a wounded animal masquerading as opera. Miss New Mexico thrusts her gloved arms out with suitable brio at every high note, butchering Bizet with certainty. Betty knows very little about opera but a fair amount about music, and she knows this is a bad representation of the former that contains very little of the latter. Is this really the best New Mexico could find?

She fiddles with her pearls, staring out from the wings, her ice-blue satin gown feeling tighter by the second. She takes a deep breath, the latest in a series of long, gulping intakes of air she is attempting to employ to calm herself down. Polite applause. Mercifully, the aria has ended.

"Miss New Mexico, Cecelia Marie Kihm!" Bob Russell thunders, as Cecelia, basking in the applause and, evidently, a fair amount of delusion, gathers her flowered skirt with two hands and scurries off the stage. Betty has not spent much time speaking with Cecelia but seems to recall a brief conversation where she learned the girl's main ambition was to one day move to Tucson. And of course there have been those rumors about Cecelia and that hotel busboy, caught somewhere near the phone bank in the Marlborough-Blenheim. Betty has made a point not to engage in any idle gossip about the other girls. She is only too aware of what is probably being said about her.

Seventeen girls will perform their talents tonight on this, the last night that will determine the Top Fifteen at tomorrow night's pageant. Cecelia was ninth; Betty is tenth. "And now," Russell continues, "for our next talent performance, we will be treated to a solo on the harp of Alphonse Hasselmans's beautiful composition 'La Source, Opus 44,' courtesy of the musical talents of . . . Miss Delaware, Betty Jane Welch!"

The imposing gilt Lyon & Healy harp has been wheeled onto the center of the stage, and as Betty walks toward it accompanied by cursory if underwhelming applause, she keeps her eyes fixed upon the strings, fighting the urge to scan the audience for faces: Griff's, her parents'. The stage lights are white-hot and harsh, much brighter, Betty thinks, than they were for her swimsuit and evening gown preliminaries. For the best. They keep her sealed in a bubble, where she can see nothing but the harp, hear nothing but the notes.

She had debated performing something more contemporary, a tune the audience would have known, but in the end selected "La Source" because of both its difficulty and its lyricism. As she takes her seat on the bench and smooths her gown about her, she tilts back the harp and squares her shoulders. Belying its romantic appearance, the harp is an awkward, monstrous instrument. One wrong stroke and the harp will buzz, like an alarm; one misplaced foot on any of its seven pedals and you risk an even more horrible sound, something akin to a trombone being played underwater.

For the next three and a half minutes, Betty surrenders herself to Hasselmans's lilting lullaby and dives into its colors, her eight fingers—for one does not use the pinky in harp—gently gliding up and down over the wire strings and the nylon strings and the cat-gut strings, her feet deftly moving among the pedals. She uses the occasional nail to add drama, the "plink effect," as her harp teacher, Mrs. Friel, used to call it. As the melody fills

Betty's ears, everything else recesses into the background: Griff, the pageant, her family, Delaware, Towson. It is simply her and the harp, alone in a room with twelve thousand spectators she blissfully cannot see. Indeed she sees only the strings, spidery fingers crawling swiftly and precisely, then faster, faster, bursting with the occasional crescendo of urgency, her head at points lolling into the melody. She works her way from the bottom up, closer, closer to the top of the harp, her hands extracting the sweet high notes that conclude the composition, before she extends her right knuckles dramatically all the way back down the instrument one last time, ending with a pronounced pluck with her fourth left finger. She extends her arms, places her palms together to stop the vibration, leans back. The performance is over.

The applause is cacophonous, amplified by the high sloping ceiling and rafters of Convention Hall, and Betty lets out a breath of relief. As she stands and delivers a demure curtsy before the audience, she can make out a woman in the front row near the judges. The woman is the lone person on her feet, clapping her hands wildly above her head, so caught up in her own rapturous approval that her pearls swing slightly about her neck.

It is Lenora Slaughter, mouthing, "Bravo."

Ten

You look like you just stepped out of the pages of *Charm!*"
Patsy practically screams as they saunter the Boardwalk
toward the Million Dollar Pier, onto which her parents and brothers have already vanished.

"Hush!" Betty admonishes. "I'm nervous enough without you
adding to it."

"I can't *believe* I missed it last night!" Patsy continues, stopping briefly to bat her eyelashes at three passing sailors who return
admiring nods as they pass. "If I didn't need the money so bad, I
would have just told Mrs. Fitz that I couldn't work at all. The bus
ride here was awful, by the way. But your mom gave me a very detailed description of your solo. Were you nervous?"

"Positively terrified."

"But you won! You won the talent preliminary! A thousand
smackers! And you're a shoo-in for the Top Fifteen. Everybody
says so."

"I won *a* talent preliminary, one of three, and I am absolutely
not a shoo-in for anything, and absolutely *nobody* says otherwise."

"Well, I say otherwise, and I know a lot about these things, no matter what your snooty roommate might think."

Betty sighs. Patsy came directly to her room this morning after she got off the bus from Delaware, suitcase in tow, not even bothering to check into her room. Betty had suspected that Patsy and Ciji would not become quick friends: Patsy was girlish, a little emotionally immature, and a rabid gossip; Ciji was sophisticated, sarcastic, the girl who knew the things good girls weren't supposed to know. Almost predictably, once they were alone Patsy relayed her opinion that Ciji ("Who has a name like that? It's not even a real name") was nothing but a snob who looked like a trollop; Betty was certain that, when the opportunity arose, Ciji would dismiss Patsy as something akin to an annoying baby sister who should be kept in her room. Or worse.

Patsy spies Betty's brothers in line at the ice cream stand and races ahead, no doubt hoping Mr. Welch will spring for her, too. In some ways Patsy is, truly, so much younger than she, despite how close they are in actual age. Maybe because of how much Betty has grown up in the past week.

She thinks of last night, to Bob Russell dramatically looking at his notecard and reading her name as the night's talent winner. Agog, she couldn't move for a good five seconds. It was one thing to objectively feel you did better on your harp than Miss New Mexico did with that painful aria; it was quite another to have bested fifteen other girls and have sent cranky Miss Slaughter into near delirium. Backstage her father had embraced her tightly, telling her how proud he was. She cannot recall the last time her father has showed her any demonstrative affection.

Miss America does odd things to people.

This morning had been the second of the two breakfasts with the judges, and just as they had earlier in the week, each rotated through the tables, armed with quick questions. Some

jotted notes—interestingly, Earl Wilson, the newspaper columnist, took none—but the entire process seemed far different
this time around. Betty was singled out by several for specific
answers, as were one or two other girls at the table. Others
were virtually ignored. All around the room there was a palpable sense that the judges were narrowing the field right then
and there—and that Betty was very much, to her surprise, in
the race.

I can't become Miss America, she thinks for the hundredth time.
I can't.

Can I?

She clamps down on the thought like it's caught in a bear trap.
Winning Miss America would mean that Griff would, in fact, be
Mr. Miss America. A crown he has been very forthright in telling
her he will not wear.

He wanted to meet her after the breakfast, but there was a rehearsal for tonight's main event. So he is coming to the hotel later
today, before she has to leave for Convention Hall, to give her a
kiss "for luck" and to meet her parents. But what kind of luck does
she need? To win? Or lose? In the crazy event that she wins Miss
America, would he really leave her?

How could he?

Her mother interrupts her thoughts. "I put my foot down and
said no ice cream for anyone until after lunch," she says. "We're
going to properly celebrate the recognition of my daughter's talent.
Then the boys want to go roller skating."

"Didn't Ricky just break his wrist?"

"Boys will be boys, Betty," her mother says as they walk into the
restaurant where Betty's father, brothers, and Patsy are already at
a table, scanning menus. "The sooner you learn that, the better."

❧

She doesn't recognize him at first. In fact, she might not even have noticed him at all, except that he has been staring at her for such a prolonged period of time that she *had* to notice him. He is sitting on a bench on the ocean side of the Boardwalk, ostensibly a place to watch the passersby and the rolling chairs, although in his case there is only one thing that is evidently catching his eye.

Betty turns to her parents, brothers, and Patsy, all giving reviews of lunch (the boys have been talked out of roller skating in favor of a better offer to see the diving-horse girls on the Steel Pier), and mimics fluster. "Oh, I am so silly! I forgot about the check-in! All of the girls are supposed to go to Convention Hall to check in before tonight, and Miss Slaughter will absolutely kill me if I don't get there. I'm so sorry. But it won't take long. I'll meet you all on the Steel Pier. Just go on ahead. I'll be there in fifteen minutes."

"I'll come with you!" Patsy offers enthusiastically.

"Contestants only, Pats. Go on. I'll be right back."

After a few minutes of suitable affirmations and confirmations, the five of them walk northward as Betty feigns rushing down toward Convention Hall. When she is certain they are a block away, she pivots and walks over toward his bench.

Eddie Tate is very much not in his reporter's uniform. Just the opposite. He looks summer dashing, in amber sunglasses, a button-down short-sleeved white shirt, and a belted navy bathing suit that shows off surprisingly muscular legs. He has canvas boat shoes on his feet, and—of course—a newspaper in his hand. He smiles as she approaches.

"That's not even the *Press*. Isn't that the *Bulletin*?"

"I don't need to read the *Press*. I already know what's in it." He squints up at her. "I wasn't sure you would know it was me."

"I try to memorize the features of all of the spies who follow me."

"I'm not a spy. I'm a reporter."

"Is there a difference?"

"Yes. And I'm actually not following you."

"So you being parked here in front of my hotel on what is obviously your day off is strictly coincidence?"

He laughs. "Well, I didn't say that."

"You never say much of anything."

"That's not true."

She takes a seat next to him on the bench, stretches her legs out. At this point she doesn't even care if someone sees her with a reporter. Let them.

"It's the big day," she says. "I'm surprised you are not working."

"It's the big night. I have to be at the hall by six."

"Do they give you a good seat?"

"Right by the runway. Make sure to wave."

"Do you enjoy what you do?"

The question appears to throw him momentarily. "I . . . Yes, I do. I give people the news. It's an important job."

"Miss America is the news?"

"In Atlantic City she damn sure is." He recoils slightly. "Oh, applesauce. Sorry. That was cheap, saying something like that to a girl like you."

Betty smiles, shrugs it off. She doesn't know what she's doing here, talking to him, but she can't seem to make herself get up off the bench to go meet up with her family.

For a minute they sit in silence, just watching the people on the Boardwalk, men in linen jackets and flapping oatmeal trousers escorting women in blouses and peasant skirts into restaurants and shops and candy stores; old men, their skin the color of malt whiskey, pushing other couples in wicker rolling chairs to some appointed destination; gaggles of boys and girls, running past them toward the next amusement pier, the echo of stern remonstrations from their parents never far behind. Betty does not spot a single contestant. She wonders if they are all huddled in their various hotel rooms, testing ten shades of lipstick and frantically rolling and unrolling their hair for a pageant that will not start for hours.

He removes his sunglasses. "Look, I—" He wants to say something, by his tone something serious, but stops himself.

"Yes?"

"Never mind. It's not important."

"How do you know if you don't say it?"

"'Cause I do, that's all. I just hope you know I never meant to dog you or anything. I just think you're special, that's all. I think you deserve the best, Betty, I really do. But I think you already suspected that."

It touches her, in an unexpected way, how he has dropped his mask, is talking to her this way. She instinctively feels how hard it is for him to do it and wants to be respectful of that. "You got me out of a jam when you warned me about the phone call you got, and you really got me out of one when you didn't print any of the things that girl told you over the phone. A girl I know has to be Mary Barbara Adair, by the way."

"A reporter never gives up his sources."

"You don't have to. Anyway, I appreciate that, Eddie. I really do. You could have been really crummy, and you weren't. Thank you."

He nods several times, never looking at her, his eyes staring down at the boards below his feet. "Well, you got a pageant to get ready for, and I got a pageant to get ready for," he says softly. He chuckles. "I bet it takes me longer to get ready than it takes you."

"Beauty requires effort," she says, rising.

His arm shoots out and he grabs her hand. He looks up at her, and for the first time she sees the true depth of his affections, reflected in his pale blue eyes. He looks at her the same way she looks at Griff. "Beauty requires no effort from you," he says. "Good luck tonight, Betty."

"To you, too," she says, and instantly wishes she could take it back, because it makes no sense, and he knows it makes no sense, but she cannot douse this moment with an awkward retraction and rephrasing. So she simply withdraws her hand and begins walking toward the Steel Pier, feeling his eyes following her until she melts into the crowd.

Eleven

Down the runway they swan, fifty-two "of the most beautiful girls in America," Bob Russell says to the frenzied crowd, an estimated twenty-three thousand, twice as many as any of the preliminary rounds, inside Convention Hall. Betty's pupils dilate from all of the photographers' flashbulbs. The girls wear opera gloves past the elbow and identical pink strapless evening gowns with full tulle ball skirts by Everglaze, the official something or other of Miss America. Betty thinks they look like a sea of Glinda the Good Witches.

Betty waves to no one and to everyone, smiling—oh, how glad she will be to be done with the incessant admonitions from everyone to smile, smile, smile!—as she reaches the end of the runway and pivots back toward the stage. She can barely make out the people, people everywhere, packed into the endless rows of seats that stretch all the way to the entrance on the Boardwalk, people elbow to elbow by the runway, people standing in the aisles, people hanging over the railings on the balcony. The noise shakes the building, swirls around the girls like a mist, the clapping and cheering and sign waving and hooting and whistling. And for perhaps the first time this week, Betty thinks not of Griff or of romance, but of trying to memorize this lunacy, to lock away the images in her mind so she can take them out and sort through them later.

Standing backstage with his nerve-racked bevy of contestants, Russell had given them a pep talk: "Remember: Tonight you're not girls from different states. You're performers, actresses. You're models, you're singers, you're entertainers. Girls, show this great city that you're happy American girls, happy to be here in Atlantic City, the city of beautiful girls!"

Eventually Betty finds her place on the stage, off to the right, on the riser in between Miss Vermont and Miss California, and again the crowd erupts as Russell introduces the outgoing Miss America, who emerges from the wings in a ponderous ruffled floral gown that makes her appear as if she has just come out from the shade of a Mexican hacienda. She glides about the stage as if on a giant lazy Susan, waving with the slow, effortless grace of Princess Elizabeth at Buckingham Palace. Russell begins to sing.

> *Let's drink a toast to Miss America,*
> *Let's raise our glasses on high*
> *From coast to coast in this America,*
> *As the sweetheart of the U.S.A. is passing by*

And then the folderol and fuss before the announcement of the Top Fifteen. The National Anthem, the introduction of the judges, more banter from Russell with some of the girls near the front. All the while the fifty-two contestants perch on chairs still as statues, their sunny expressions frozen in place.

And then, finally, it is here.

Bob Russell walks over to the judges' table, retrieves his list. He emphasizes that the names of the Top Fifteen are in no particular order, and the timpani rumbles, and the crowd of twenty-three thousand falls silent. The air is thick, suffocating with nerves and expectancy.

"Our first semifinalist . . . is . . ." Dramatic pause. "Miss South Carolina, Marilyn Hortensia Palma!"

Betty recalls the image of Miss South Carolina in a corner, gossiping about her with Mississippi as she was being admonished by Miss Slaughter. *Well, at least she's pretty, I'll give her that.*

"Miss . . . Chicago!"

"Miss . . . Florida!"

"Miss . . . New York State!"

"Miss . . . Alabama!"

Of course, Betty thinks, politely clapping as Mary Barbara Adair —expressing faux surprise and a healthy dose of false humility, and doing both badly—rises from her chair and scurries from the left of the stage to join the four others near Russell. Betty is more convinced than ever that it was Mary Barbara who dimed her out to Eddie. Not that it matters anymore.

I truly don't care who wins. But I do not want it to be her.

"Miss . . . Virginia!"

Betty begins clapping as if she is rooting for the Phillies, then quickly regains her composure. Adelaide Carson, her spirited—if overly nosey—compatriot in Miss Slaughter's Boardwalk swimsuit ambassador brigade. It's nice to see someone like that in the Top Fifteen.

"Miss . . . California!"

Betty turns to Miss California sitting next to her, places a congratulatory hand on her arm, but the girl does not tarry long enough to accept any goodwill from her fellow contestants. She ignores them all, jumps off of the riser as if it's ablaze.

Witch. I hope you lose.

"Miss . . . Nevada!"

Oh yes, the girl in the evening gown everyone was dying for. And she won Miss Congeniality from the other contestants this morning at the breakfast. Such a nice girl! Logical. Okay, I'll root for you.

"Miss . . . Texas!"

I was wondering when they were going to call her. She's the one everyone thinks is going to win, despite the Scarlett O'Hara gown. Good golly, she's gorgeous. How does she get her hair to shine like that? Somebody told me she uses an egg wash.

"Miss . . . New York City!"

Both New York girls. Wow. Though this girl has a reputation even worse than poor tone-deaf Cecelia Kihm. I wonder if the judges know what she's been up to.

Bob Russell roams the middle of the stage, looking like a lounge singer in his white dinner jacket and black trousers. "That's ten, ladies and gentlemen! Only five spots left for the chance to be Miss America 1950! Your next finalist is . . . Miss Ohio!"

So it turns out the early gossip was correct. People thought she'd make it.

The crowd once again calms down temporarily, waiting for the twelfth name.

"And our next semifinalist is . . . Miss . . . Delaware, Betty Jane Welch!"

Delaware?

Did he just say Delaware?!

Betty cannot see her eyes, but she knows how they must look, grotesque and saucer-like, hiding none of her disbelief.

Great Scott! I made the Top Fifteen!

She feels gloved pats on both arms, pats on her back, and gets pulled into a quick side hug by Miss Vermont, and she can't move, she can't feel her own arms or legs, and she wonders if they are going to have to come up and carry her down off the riser, but there is a gentle nudge at her back from Miss Michigan, and she gets up from her chair and begins walking, slowly, toward the center, nodding and smiling—smiling, smiling!—and trying to make sure her sash does not fall off her shoulder and that she does not faint in front of thousands of people as her stomach flips over and over.

Betty takes her place next to Miss Ohio, who gently grazes her with a cheek kiss, and she continues staring into the bright stage lights, able to see no one but trying to breathe and imagining what her mother must look like at this moment, what her father is saying, what her brothers are doing, out there amid the yelling throng. Poor Patsy must be hoarse from screaming. And Griff. Griff! Griff must be so thrilled for her, so proud of her. She knows he is.

The smiling comes naturally now.

Miss Oklahoma sidles up next to her, squeezing her hand, and Betty realizes that she has missed the last semifinalist announcement. Next, Arizona.

There is only one more girl to be selected to move on. She thinks it must be Minnesota, who won her talent, too. Betty turns her attention back to Bob Russell as he draws out the suspense.

"And our fifteenth semifinalist, and the last girl with a chance to be your new Miss America . . . is . . . Miss Rhode Island, Catherine Grace Moore!"

Ciji. She and Ciji, semifinalists for Miss America.

This is nuts! Betty thinks as her heart explodes with joy, and she watches Ciji walk confidently to the middle of the stage.

Surely it can't get any crazier than this.

❧

In the communal dressing room, Ciji finds Betty and throws her arms around her neck, as if Germany has surrendered all over again. "Delaware, we made it! Can you believe it?! Holy cow!"

"Four minutes, ladies," a hostess announces.

The fifteen girls dash and fumble and squeal their way through their collective change into evening gowns, the first of tonight's competitions. The hostess has gravely announced that any one not ready when the radio broadcast comes out of commercial will be automatically disqualified. No one believes her.

No one's willing to risk it, either.

"Gee willikers, I can't find my shoes!"

"Arizona, could you be a darling and let me have a touch of that lipstick? Mine is terrible under these lights!"

"Zip help, somebody, please!"

Miss Oklahoma wipes lipstick from her teeth with a handkerchief; Miss New York City, the first one dressed, paces the floor as if waiting for a jury verdict. Miss Texas sits serenely on a settee, still in her slip, wanly looking into a compact for confirmation of her beauty, rather than fighting it out elbow to elbow with the other girls in front of the big mirror. It's as if the whole thing is a foregone conclusion, and she's just trying to visualize how the crown is going to look with her hair.

"Betty!" Adelaide Carson, Miss Virginia, sidles up beside her, a trail of red taffeta following, and embraces her. "I'm so glad you made it!"

"Oh, Addie, isn't this simply a blast? I never even fantasized about what this would be like, because it never occurred to me in a million years I'd be here."

"Me neither. I think most of us felt that way," Adelaide says, before shooting a side-eye to Texas and California, now exchanging fake pleasantries as Texas shimmies into her voluminous gown. "Of course, some of the girls in here think they've already won."

"They probably have," Betty says, pulling yet another set of satin gloves up her arms. "Oh, fiddlesticks to all that! Let's just go out and play dress-up and have a hoot!"

The hostess, louder now. "Thirty seconds, ladies!"

And so they line up in alphabetical order by state, Mary Barbara at the front, Adelaide at the rear, to be judged for their appearance in evening gowns. Betty has never experienced a sensation like this in her entire life.

"I think I'm going to topple over, right here on the spot," Miss Chicago whispers back to her.

"Don't worry, I'll catch you," Betty replies. "Assuming I don't hit the floor first."

Bob Russell's voice echoes in the distance from the front of the stage. "And our first contestant in evening gown: Miss Alabama, Mary Barbara Adair!"

❧

And off they go, round and round, a carousel of distinctly American femininity, the only thing missing the lilting melody of the calliope. First in evening gowns, floating down the runway to polite applause and the occasional catcall, each girl carrying a bouquet and trying to sneak a glimpse toward the seating section where her family is stowed, unable to make out anything but shadowy figures. Then the first half of the remaining thirty-seven girls is called out for a final "presentation," followed by the bathing suit competition —Betty silently says a prayer of thanks to Jesus for giving her the willpower to eschew the coffee roll she was craving this morning —and then more banter from Bob Russell, then the second half of the non-semifinalists comes out to take their final bows. Betty sits next to Ciji in the dressing room, waiting for their respective turns at talent. Mary Barbara's aria from *La Traviata* was, Betty must admit, far superior to poor Miss New Mexico's Bizet last night, although Betty still does not understand the pairing of this with Mary Barbara's showing afterward of several ceramic vases she has made. Arizona has also finished her talent, a demanding, dramatic piano concerto Betty recalls from the preliminaries.

"So, whaddya think?" Ciji whispers.

"About what?"

"About the Top Five! Who do you think's going to make it?"

Mary Barbara glances over, delivers a look that is simultaneously withering and sanctimonious. It's as if she's just discovered two filthy urchins from the local orphanage hiding backstage.

"I hope not her," Betty replies.

"Yeah, I already know that. So does she, no doubt. Hey, maybe *we* will!"

"Don't be silly. You might, but my road stops here. Half of these people are going to be asleep during my talent. Who wants to hear a dull harp solo?"

"You won your prelim! And Miss Slaughter went cuckoo for it. You said so yourself."

"Miss Slaughter is an old fuddy-duddy from Florida."

"Who do you think's judging this thing? Most of those judges probably have records by Margaret Truman at home."

"Margaret Truman doesn't have any records."

"You know what I mean. C'mon, tell me. I think it's going to be Texas, definitely."

Betty nods. "Definitely."

"I saw New York State's talent. She went on right before me the other night. The girl can twirl a baton, I'll tell you that. She won her prelim, too, and the crowd went loony. So I think her, too."

"That's two."

"Hmm. It's tough, because the only girls in this fifteen who were at my breakfast table were Chicago, who was a chattering mess, and Oklahoma. And I don't remember *her* saying anything to the judges at all. I don't know. You can't rule out our friend Mary Barbara over there, though. She may be a fake, but she's gorgeous."

"Ugh. I cannot imagine having to congratulate her if she becomes Miss America. But I agree with you about Texas. I think it's going to be her, California—are you hearing her song right now? She's pretty nifty. New York State, Virginia—because I am rooting for Adelaide—and . . . Rhode Island."

Ciji nudges her with her shoulder. "Oh, Delaware. I love it when you talk sweet to me."

They sit, looking mischievously at each other, as the applause in the hall swells once more, signaling the end of Miss California's kicky rendition of "(I'm in Love with) A Wonderful Guy" from the new musical *South Pacific*. Across the room, Miss Chicago rises with her book—she's doing a dramatic reading of poetry by Elizabeth Barrett Browning—and strolls purposefully toward the stage.

❧

Back in their matching Everglaze gowns, the fifteen semifinalists stand ramrod straight, lined up, glove to glove, like a collection of porcelain dolls standing on a little girl's bedroom shelf. The evening gown contest is over, the swimsuit contest is over, the talent contest is over—Betty feels she didn't render Hasselmans as well tonight, but lets it go—and now the divertissement is done (an adorable six-year-old playing Chopin) and the Miss Congeniality award has been formally presented—how giggly and lovely Miss Nevada looked when they announced her for the audience!—and it is time to learn the identities of the final five girls who will compete for Miss America 1950.

"I know all of these ladies must be very, very anxious," Bob Russell says, holding the card with the names of the finalists in his hand. He saunters down the line and stops in front of Miss New York State. "How are you feeling right about now, sweetheart?"

"I don't know. Am I still breathing?" she replies, setting off laughter in the audience.

"Hang in there, girls! Well, the time has come, ladies and gen-

tlemen," he says, turning back to the crowd. "In no particular order . . . your first finalist for the title of Miss America 1950 . . .
is . . . Miss Alabama, Mary Barbara Adair!"

Mary Barbara steps forward, waving to the crowd as the bois-
terous Alabama contingent engages in a collective and suitably
earsplitting rebel yell. Betty closes her eyes. *What are these judges
thinking? She's a bad apple if ever there was one.*

"Our next finalist . . . Miss South Carolina, Marilyn Hortensia
Palma!"

The South, rising again. Betty exhales. *Three more to go. Three
more to go.*

"And your next lovely young lady who still has a chance at being
America's queen is . . . Miss Arizona, Lydia Ann Fraser!"

*A breathtaking rendition of Tchaikovsky's jaunty Piano Concerto
no. 1 in B-flat Minor. Very difficult to play something that quickly. I'm
glad the judges noticed.*

"Your fourth finalist for the title of Miss America . . . is . . . Miss
Texas, Eleanor Patricia Wyatt!"

*I knew it! I knew it. We all knew it. She's going to win. She's going
to win. Oh, please, let her win over that terrible Mary Barbara.*

"And this is it, ladies and gentlemen. The name of our last finalist for the title of Miss America 1950. And she is . . ."

Miss Florida clutches Betty's hand tightly. Betty instinctively
lifts her chin up, silently rooting for Ciji.

Catherine Grace Moore! Say it! Catherine Grace Moore!

". . . Miss Delaware, Betty Jane Welch!"

Oh my God. Oh my God.

Oh. My. God.

She does not swear, does not ever take the Lord's name in vain
—her parents have been very vigilant on this point her entire childhood—but the only thing Betty can hear inside her head right now

is herself screaming, over and over, *Oh my God!* As she untangles from embraces from Chicago and Florida on either side, she steps toward the front of the stage, daring to sneak a glance sideways down at Ciji, who is crying, her white-gloved hands alternating between covering her mouth and clapping.

Betty feels like she is moving slowly, so very slowly, as if her feet were trudging through a vat of glue, but in a few seconds she is in her place in line, next to the gorgeous and formidable Eleanor Wyatt, Miss Texas, who takes her hand with a grip equal to Miss Florida's and whispers, in the twangiest whisper Betty has ever heard, "We made it!"

And as the spotlights swirl down from the rafters and the crowd whistles and cheers and screams, Betty looks out. And for the briefest of seconds the spotlight catches him, twenty rows back on the right, and Betty feels her face burst into a brilliant, genuine beam as she captures the image of tuxedoed Griffin McAllister on his feet, hands above his head, clapping for his favorite finalist for Miss America.

His warning is forgotten, her nerves are forgotten, everything she said or has done or wished or hoped or worried about this week is forgotten, as Betty stands under the hot, shining white lights and thinks, for the very first time, about what it would truly be like to be Miss America.

❧

"How can you stay so calm?" Lydia Fraser, Miss Arizona, asks Betty as they wait in a small anteroom backstage. The door is closed, and it is now just the four of them, along with a mousy hostess named Geraldine, each waiting for her turn to answer the "personality" question that will determine which of them ends up with the crown. Mary Barbara is first, already onstage, and Betty

has little doubt she is well on her way through a monologue about how surprised and humbled she is to be here and all sorts of other steaming horse manure shoveled onto the judges.

"I'm actually scared to death," Betty replies. "I never considered I might make it this far."

"Well, I certainly did, and it's much worse than I ever dreamed of," Marilyn Palma, Miss South Carolina, interjects in her ladylike southern lilt. "What I wouldn't give for a shot of whiskey right now."

Geraldine arches a penciled brow but says nothing.

"I'd settle for a smoke right now," Lydia says, shaking her body, trying to expel the nerves.

"I don't know what y'all are fussin' about." Eleanor Wyatt, the ever-statuesque Miss Texas, crosses her legs idly, no small feat in a gown that looks like it came straight from Marie Antoinette's closet. "I mean, somebody's gotta win. It might as well be one of us."

"I think you really mean it might as well be *you*," Lydia says, laughing.

"Well, that tiara *would* look so good with my coloring . . ."

There is a knock at the door; Lydia is summoned. There is cheering in the distance. They will all be asked the same final question. Betty wonders how well Mary Barbara answered. She pictures her, answer completed, now standing on the stage, looking to see how the four who follow her fare and secretly hoping each and every one of them spouts incomprehensible gibberish.

"Well, it's just us three now, chickadees," Eleanor says. "The two southern girls and the girl from the smallest state."

"Actually, Rhode Island is technically smaller," Betty interjects. "But Delaware was the very first state."

"Well, good for *yeeewwww*," Eleanor says. "You sound like you're ripe and ready to give an answer to those judges. Of course," she says airily, standing up, "I get to go last. That's the advantage of being from a state that starts with a T."

"I guess you're lucky Miss Wyoming didn't make the top five," Marilyn says.

"Honey, did you see her? Or West Virginia, or Wisconsin? Oh no, darlin', I had my eyes on those girls from the start, just because of this moment right here. I wasn't worried at all. *At all.* I've seen prettier faces at the rodeo. And I don't mean in the stands, neither." She rustles toward the mirror, analyzes her reflection.

"I think that's rather unkind, Eleanor," Marilyn says. Betty looks over at Marilyn's face, serene and placid, and can easily picture her in the crown and sash. Despite Betty's grudge about her gossiping with Mississippi, there is something intrinsically regal and lady-like about Marilyn. She seems gracious and genteel in a magnolia-scented way that she suspects both Mary Barbara and Eleanor can imitate but not intuit.

Eleanor takes a seat in front of the mirror, begins brushing the back of her hair. "Didn't mean any offense," she says. "I do apologize."

Marilyn is about to say something when the door opens again, and Betty rises. As she gathers her skirt and walks through the doorway back toward the stage, she can barely make out Geraldine whispering, "Good luck, dear."

❧

Betty has not been this close to Bob Russell the entire week, save for a brief moment when she collected her talent trophy during her preliminary. But now she stands, desperately trying not to fidget, desperately trying to appear easygoing and relaxed, as if she were stationed by the refreshment table at a lazy summer picnic. Inside a hot current roars through her body, like a downed electric wire hissing and flailing about a shallow pool of rainwater. It is terribly warm under the lights, but she feels clammy, as if she might begin shivering. Several times this week, she has noted how she has never experienced such nerves before. Now she knows that, in this moment, she has surpassed all of those occasions.

"Miss Delaware," Bob says, "everybody here wants to know: How are you feeling right about now?"

"Oh, just fine, thank you, Mr. Russell," Betty says. "Just another dull Saturday night."

The audience laughs. Betty feels some of the tension dissipate from her aching shoulders.

"Well, if this is a dull Saturday night for you, I need to get to Delaware pronto!" Bob says. More laughs, a smattering of applause. "Seriously now, though. I'm going to ask you the same question I am asking the other four finalists. You will have thirty seconds to answer. If you go over your time, you will hear this sound"—a pleasant bell tings. "Please direct your comments to the judges." He flips up his card, begins reading. "Miss Delaware, please tell us: What person or event has impressed you most since you've been here in Atlantic City?"

Betty's thoughts whisk together as Russell thrusts the microphone at her face. But there is no time to ponder the best answer. The best answer, she decides, is simply the one she feels is true. "I would have to say," she begins, squaring herself slightly, "that the person who has impressed me the most during my stay here in Atlantic City has been my escort, Mr. Griffin McAllister. As you know, all fifty-two of us were assigned young men from the area to keep us company during this week away from our homes and families. Many of us were justifiably nervous about this prospect, because so many of our young men are held suspect in their motives. But the care, warmth, and generosity of spirit I received from this noble gentleman did more than simply allow me to pass the time here comfortably. You know, this week has been all about us girls. But Mr. McAllister has reminded me that a most elusive quality

—gallantry—is still very much alive in our often-maligned young American men."

The bell tings.

The cheering is quick and thunderous, and as Betty scans the shadows and shapes of the audience beyond the klieg lights, she thinks she sees several people actually on their feet. As Bob Russell thanks her and waves her over to her spot next to Lydia, Betty meets Mary Barbara's dead-eyed stare. *I have no idea what answer she gave,* Betty thinks, *but now I know that it wasn't as good as mine.*

Marilyn Palma, the pride of South Carolina, sweeps onto the stage and in her answer talks about the warmth and welcoming spirit of the people of Atlantic City.

Finally it is time for Eleanor Wyatt, Miss Texas, who makes an entrance befitting the belle of the county. She listens intently to Russell's question.

"Oh, Mr. Russell! What a wonderful thing to ask!"

It's an old pageant trick, Betty knows. You buy time to think with a bridge sentence before actually answering.

"Well, I would have to say that the event that has impressed me most this week has been our two breakfasts with the judges," Eleanor continues. "Their probing questions and interest in our lives and goals were not simply conversation, but, I feel, a way for all of us who have competed for the title of Miss America to examine ourselves inside, to dig deep down and to ask ourselves how we might do better to be of the utmost service to our God and our country. Thank you."

Wow, Betty thinks.

As the judges converge to tabulate the final scores, Russell announces a list of dignitaries in the audience—Mayor Bernard Samuel of Philadelphia receives a disproportionately loud welcome—before introducing, for the final time, Miss America 1949, who glides down the runway to suitable fanfare, her ermine-trimmed cape trailing majestically behind her. As she returns to the stage, Betty stands squarely in the middle of the five finalists, and watches as Russell retrieves the notecard with their fate. She wants to see a friendly face — Griff, her mother, Ciji — but keeps her eyes trained on the host, takes the hands of Lydia Fraser and Marilyn Palma, standing on either side, in hers.

And waits.

"Ladies and gentlemen, I have here the final results of this year's Miss America Pageant," Russell bellows like a carnival barker, upping the suspense. "We shall start with the fourth runner-up, who is . . . Miss South Carolina, Marilyn Hortensia Palma!"

A hand squeeze and Marilyn leaves for the middle of the stage, where a page hands her a bouquet of roses and then hustles her off to the side. If she's wildly disappointed, she masks it superbly.

"Your third runner-up in this year's contest is . . . Miss Arizona, Lydia Ann Fraser!"

Betty puts an awkward arm around Lydia, but the poor girl has already been swamped in a hug from Mary Barbara, who grabs her by the shoulders and bellows, "You did graaayyyt!"

Heaven help us.

With only three of them left, Betty and Mary Barbara are forced to join hands. Mary Barbara's smile is so tight, she looks as if her face might crack. Betty is in the midst of calculating how much scholarship money she will receive for third place when Bob Russell's rich voice interrupts her thoughts. "And now, the third runner-up . . . Miss Alabama, Mary Barbara Adair!"

As a clearly dazed Mary Barbara drifts aimlessly toward the front of the stage and her bouquet of consolation roses, reality slaps Betty square in the face. She is one of the last two girls standing. It is her and Eleanor Wyatt. She wonders if people can discern her utter bewilderment. She feels Eleanor turned toward her, their two gloved hands now intertwined, Eleanor's head bowed in silent prayer, as a furious buzzing roars through Betty's ears.

Sweet Jesus.

Russell squares himself, as if he's about to deliver a knockout punch or launch into a Broadway opening number. "And now here we are, the moment we've all been waiting for. Ladies and gentlemen: Your new Miss America 1950 is . . . !"

A thousand sounds—whooshing air, papers rustling, random whistling, heavy breathing, frantic whispering—sough around Betty's head. Though she is struck by how quiet the auditorium of twenty-three thousand people is in this one moment. In this unexpected, crazy, heart-pounding moment.

And then it comes.

". . . MISS DELAWARE, BETTY JANE WELCH!"

It all collapses on top of her: Eleanor Wyatt, pulling her into a sobbing bear hug of both congratulations and bitter disappointment; a gentle push at her lower back from persons unknown guiding her toward the middle of the stage; Eleanor vaporizing off to the side; the outgoing titleholder placing the dark sash across her chest blaring: MISS AMERICA. The cape sliding onto her shoulders. The crown being pinned to the top of her head. The hysterical explosion of noise.

I've done it.

I've won Miss America.

I'm Miss America!

Joe Frasetto, the orchestra conductor, swings his baton, and a reprise of "A Toast to Miss America" fills the hall, and Betty goes staggering down the runway, Miss America's runway, her runway, and as tears of joy and exhilaration and relief begin to leak down her cheeks, she smiles—Smile! Smile!—and turns to the left, and turns to the right, and the flashbulbs go off, and she waves, and she thinks to herself, *This is the most amazing moment of my life.*

Twelve

*T*oo much. *Too much noise,* too much shouting in her ears, too many flashbulbs going off, blinding her in place. And too many people, pawing at her, clawing at her, spinning her this way, turning her that way, talking to her, barking over to her, waving to her, screaming her name. In the fleeting moments where she has indulged in the covert daydream of mulling what it would be like to win Miss America, nothing she conjured matched this.

She has stood before the members of the press, answered a few questions, endured the taking of what seems to have been a thousand pictures, and is now at this moment being hustled down some dim corridor in the bowels of Convention Hall. She desperately needs a few moments alone to gather herself, but she is told there is no time, just one more thing and then we can do that, just this and then that and then this. Miss Slaughter, silent and mirthless, marches ahead of her like a prison matron jangling her keys, about to lock her away in a cell.

And isn't she?

Who are all of these women now surrounding her, whispering

instructions in her ear, holding her cape, scribbling notes in various small leather-bound books? She looks ahead, where Mr. Haverstick now walks in lockstep with Miss Slaughter. She overhears the two of them talking about her schedule, her travel. About her life, which they now own for the next twelve months.

They had brought her family backstage to see her, and she had collapsed into her mother's arms, crying like a four-year-old who'd skinned her knee, all of the anxiety and pressure and sensory overload spilling out in one spontaneous burst. Her mother had admirably struck the right balance of being overjoyed and soothing, stroking her hair like she had when Betty was a little girl, telling her what a marvelous thing she'd accomplished, how proud they all were. But it was not enough. Not nearly enough. Before Betty even knew what was happening, her family had been shuffled away, waving to her as they backed out, her brothers yelling silly, juvenile epithets.

Where is Griff? I want to see Griff.

Miss Slaughter abruptly pivots, and the whole ersatz parade comes to a sudden halt. "We traditionally have the new Miss America give the *Press* an exclusive interview for ten minutes before we go on to the ball, so they can make their deadline for the morning paper," she says. "So we're going to have you sit briefly with their reporter. I have details to attend to, so I will be going directly to the Steel Pier, but Mr. Haverstick will remain and escort you to the Coronation Ball. Do you have any questions, dear?"

A thousand.

Miss Slaughter places a light hand on Betty's forearm, tries to summon something akin to maternal regard. "Now, Betty, please do not worry. I know how overwhelming all of this must seem right now. I can assure you it's perfectly normal. We've had girls who've practically needed smelling salts after they've won. It's all going to be fine, you'll see. You don't have to fret about a thing. You are about to embark on the most exciting year of your life. Now," she says, "let's see that happy smile!"

Another year of smiling edicts.

Betty does as she's told. The crown is tight and digs into the sides of her head, which now throbs. They turn into a meeting room, and there at a table sits Eddie Tate, looking exceptionally dapper in what is surely his best navy suit and silver tie, his note-book already flipped open. He stands up, extends his hand. "Miss Welch," he says with a formality that might suggest they were meeting for the very first time. "My sincere congratulations to you."

She shakes his hand, thanks him, searches his face for camara-derie but finds only perfunctory expectancy. As she sits, out of the corner of her eye she sees Mr. Haverstick, puffing out his chest like a rooster, surveying the two of them, and she understands. *Eddie is trying to protect me. He doesn't want anyone at the pageant to think I really know him.* Miss Slaughter and her hens disperse amid suit-able fluttering; it's just Betty, Eddie, and Mr. Haverstick.

"So . . ." Eddie says, picking up his pen, "I'll ask you the ques-tion everyone in America wants to ask: How does it feel to be the new Miss America?"

She can answer many things, but she knows she cannot answer with the truth. "Surprising," she says. *At least somewhat truthful.*

But perhaps what is most surprising, to her at least, is how quickly she is able to muster the proper answers, bland and pre-dictable platitudes that have Mr. Haverstick beaming, about how she is looking forward to her year of service, how she hopes she can inspire other young women, how grateful and honored and humbled she is to be given this title, how she hopes to become worthy of the other women who have held it before her.

She does not mean a word of it.

She manages to say one thing that is 100 percent true, which is that she is extremely happy to have won this much scholarship money, which might allow her to now go on to pursue a master's degree if she so chooses. Eddie dutifully scribbles it all down. With every question, she wishes he would drop his mask of professional indifference, see her as she is on the inside, a knot of nerves and doubts, and to speak comfort to her, to be the Eddie from the Boardwalk today, the Eddie she knows cares about Betty the girl, not Betty the Miss America. But he cannot, and she knows he will not.

Mr. Haverstick places a firm hand on Eddie's shoulder. "I think you should have enough now, Mr. Tate," he says in his FDR tone. "We must be getting the queen to her subjects."

A quiver drops down her spine. He can't really have just said that, without any trace of the ironic.

"Of course," Eddie says, closing his notebook. "Well, thank you, Miss Welch, and best of luck to you."

"Thank you, Mr. Tate," she says, as tears suddenly spring to her eyes. "I'll need it."

As he exits, Betty turns to Mr. Haverstick. "I am so very sorry to be a bother, Mr. Haverstick, but might I trouble you for a glass of water before we go?"

"Of course, my dear." He looks around. "Oh my, I think all of the ladies have already gone over. Let me see what I can find. You just stay here for a moment and rest yourself. I'll be right back."

Betty slumps back into her chair. She removes the crown, which catches on her hair. "Owwww!"

"Careful, careful!"

Eddie, suddenly back, hovering over her, carefully plucking away myriad strands, smoothing them back in place as Betty finally dislodges the crown and slides it onto the table. She gently brushes his hand away, begins matting down her hair. "I've got it. Thank you," she says quietly.

"Forgot my hat," he says sheepishly, reaching over to pick up his navy fedora on an opposite chair. He twirls it around in his hands. "They left you all alone?"

"Mr. Haverstick is getting me some water." She smiles. "I'm sorry I couldn't give you more quotable answers. I guess not much has changed since our first meeting."

"I wouldn't say that." His gaze bores into her, and the intensity makes her lower her eyes. "Besides," he says, "everybody just wants to see the pictures, anyway."

She looks up at him plaintively. "Oh, Eddie. How did this happen?"

"You were the obvious choice. Everybody seemed to know that but you."

Her face falls.

"Hey, hey! You've just been crowned the most beautiful girl in America! You should be happy. You deserve it. You do."

"It's just a lot to take in," she whispers. "All of these people everywhere, and . . . I feel . . . alone."

He flings his hat onto the table, bends over, and tilts up her chin with his hand. "You're not alone, Betty Jane Welch. You're . . . I mean, you're . . . sensational."

And then his face comes closer, and she can feel his breath on her, and he kisses her—softly, so softly, his lips buttery and gentle—and for a moment she forgets herself, places a hand on his cheek, surrenders to his affection and warmth.

Footsteps approaching.

She pushes him away just before Park Haverstick enters the room, holding a glass of cold water.

His eyes narrow. "Mr. Tate? May I ask what you're doing here? Your interview was concluded."

Eddie quickly wipes his lip with the back of his hand, swipes his fedora off the table. "Just came back to retrieve my hat. My apologies, Mr. Haverstick." He brushes by the scowling pageant president, turns briefly in the doorway to look at her. Betty can clearly see the sorrow in his eyes as he wordlessly mouths, "Not alone," before he vanishes.

❧

Patsy is being Patsy, whirling around the room like a belly dancer, and it's worsening the headache that immediately started up again after Betty had to place the crown back on her head. She is in yet another side room, this one off of the Steel Pier ballroom, and it is packed with people: her family, pageant folk, her state pageant folk (one of whom, a shrill, beak-nosed woman named Phyllis, keeps shrieking, in the most offensive decibels possible, "It's just so crazy!"), and most of all Patsy, who has been peppering her with questions more probing than Eddie Tate has ever queried. In the distance Betty can hear the lilting melodies of an orchestra, the din of conversation, everyone waiting for her.

"It'll be just a few more minutes, dear," a hostess says. "Is there anything I can get for you?"

Yes, you can get me out of here. Just for a minute. I need to find someplace to be alone. To breathe.

"I need to use the powder room. Can you take me?"

"I'll take you!" Patsy says.

"I'm sorry, but an official hostess must accompany Miss America at all times," the woman says, appropriately beatific. She turns to Betty. "Of course, Miss Welch. Just follow me."

Her departure sets off a chain reaction of concern, as the hostess assures everyone that Betty is simply going for a minute to freshen up. Betty pictures the year ahead, being surrounded by a phalanx of hovering hostesses, like Queen Victoria and her court. How will she be able to see Griff, kept under lock and key like this? Surely other girls before her have had boyfriends, perhaps even a fiancé. There must be some provision made.

123

As they reach the powder room, Betty feels a tap on her shoulder, turns to see . . . Ciji.

"They let you out of the cage so soon!" Ciji says, hugging her. "I'm so glad I got to see you before they whisk you away for good!"

The hostess purses her lips in disapproval, interjects that time is pressing and that they must be "getting on." *Getting on? Who says "getting on"?*

Betty seizes the moment. "I am so sorry, but would it be all right if Miss Moore accompanies me in? It's just that we were roommates for the week, and this is the only time we'll be able to say goodbye, and it would mean so very much to me if you could extend me this kindness."

The hostess hesitates, emphasizing the irregularity of all of this. She takes a look behind them, confirming the all-clear. "All right, but do be quick about it," she says. Betty and Ciji sweep into the ladies' lounge, quickly closing the door.

Ciji shakes her head. "Well, you've really done it this time, Delaware. I have to say, I am impressed. Did you see the look on Mary Barbara's face?! It was almost as good as the one Eleanor Wyatt had when they announced her as the first runner-up! We've won the Civil War yet again!"

Betty laughs. And then, out of nowhere, cries. And cries.

"Hey, hey, hey," Ciji says, folding her into an embrace. "What's all this?"

"It's too much, Ciji. I know you were always admonishing me when I said I wasn't going to win, and it turned out you were right to. Because I am completely unprepared for this."

"Honey, anyone would be. One minute you're playing your harp, the next you've got a million people pulling at you. But it's just for the moment. It'll all die down soon enough. You should be enjoying this! You've earned it. They could not have picked a prettier, nicer, more deserving girl. You're just overwhelmed, is all. But this is a happy night. This is *your* night. You need to go out there and enjoy it, so you can tell your grandchildren about this."

Betty swallows, nods. "Yes. Of course. Of course, you're right." She takes Ciji's handkerchief, dabs her eyes, blows her nose. "Have you seen Griff?"

"I have," Ciji says with a smile. "He's here, he looks dandy as all get-out, and I am sure he cannot wait to take you in his arms and dance with you."

"Okay. Okay," Betty says, visibly trying to calm herself. *Griff is here. Ciji is here. My family is here. Even crazy Patsy is here. People who care about me are here, and this is for me, this is to celebrate something I have done, the beginning of a marvelous journey.*

She takes Ciji's hand. "Thank you for being my friend," she says hoarsely, trying not to cry again.

Ciji's eyes shine as she gives Betty one big, final hug. "I will always be your friend, Delaware, the girl you can call in the middle of the night to rally the troops. Tell you what: We'll have a code. You'll say, 'Joan of Arc, I need you,' and I'll be there."

Thirteen

It feels like her wedding. She walks onto the polished wooden floor of the Marine Ballroom on the Steel Pier, looks at the pennants crisscrossing the ceiling, the orchestra in the front, the throngs on either side, applauding and beaming at her, and she thinks that this is how it must feel to be a bride, to draw the attention of everyone around you as you make your first grand entrance as Mrs. Whoever. But she is not Mrs. Whoever. She is Miss America.

Mr. Haverstick, proud as a grandfather escorting his granddaughter into her debutante ball, guides her toward the front, where she will mercifully not have to speak, and Betty struggles with the slow pace of the procession, making sure she turns left, then right, then left again, when all she wants is to see Griff, to feel love and reassurance. The scepter is slippery and ridiculous in the crook of her right arm, and her feet and back ache, like she's spent the day hoeing potatoes.

When they reach the front, she still has not seen him, though she spies Honor McAllister, standing off to the side with the other hostesses, resplendent as always in a sleek crepe silver dinner dress with matching turban.

Where is he?

"Ladies and gentlemen," Bob Russell is saying—where did *he* come from?—"it gives me great pleasure to introduce our guest of honor, and your new Miss America 1950, Betty Jane Welch!"

More applause, as Betty gently curtsies like a member of the seventeenth-century nobility being presented at court. *Perhaps this will be fun,* she thinks. *It's like getting to play dress-up for an entire year.*

And then a burst of something—bright, luminescent, euphoric —seizes her. She is Miss America. She has bested thousands of girls from around the country who entered local pageants and state pageants and this pageant. She has won enough scholarship money to study whatever she wishes, however she wishes. She will have a year of exciting travel, get to see the entire country, meet new and interesting people. And she will have Griff. Surely his reservations must have dissipated in the thrill of watching her achievement. She will write Griff and call Griff to tell him everything that is happening, and he will come and meet her along the way, share in her adventure. It is the chance of a lifetime, and she has done nothing up until now but surrender to doubt and anxiety. For the first time, she sees the opportunity. She has changed more this week than she ever imagined she could. Who will she be a year from now? The thought thrills her and, for the first time, fills her with excitement.

I'm Miss America!

Mr. Haverstick is now talking, thanking endless benefactors and sponsors and volunteers and Bob Russell and the orchestra leader—everyone, it appears, except the laundresses and janitors, and they might well be next. His droning allows Betty some time to covertly scan the crowd for Griff, but still she cannot find him. Though she does spy Patsy, jumping up and down like a kangaroo, waving from her position next to her parents. And there, toward the back, leaning against a pillar, Eddie Tate, his arms folded across his chest, his expression inscrutable.

The microphone is back in Bob Russell's hands, as he asks the assembled to sit. "And now, a wonderful tradition here at the Miss America Pageant. Our newly crowned queen will dance with her pageant escort for this week, Mr. John Griffin McAllister."

The crowd hushes, and suddenly he appears. Griff, so striking in his black tuxedo that Betty actually feels her knees buckle. As he comes closer, extending his hand to her, she searches his eyes but finds nothing to access. She looks and looks, cannot discern anything locked beyond his benign Mona Lisa smile.

As the orchestra strikes up the first chords of "The Miss America Waltz"—a lilting tune Strauss might have written—Griff takes Betty into his arms, and they begin a slow, circular motion around the vast dance floor, every eye upon them. His eyes remain squarely focused over her shoulder. At one point she moves her head to block his sightline. Nothing. A ball of anxiety expands in her stomach, like a milk spill oozing out in every direction on the kitchen floor.

She smiles too brightly, trying to hide her yearning. "You're being very ungallant, Mr. McAllister. You haven't even congratulated me."

His eyes finally meet hers, and the chill in them jolts her even further. "You're right. My apologies. Congratulations, Betty. Truly. I'm sure you're going to be a wonderful Miss America."

Calm. Stay calm. "It's been the craziest week of my life. I could never express how much it's meant to me to have you here to support me through it."

"Well, that's what the escort is supposed to do. I'm glad you enjoyed the experience."

The waltz continues, but she knows it will not continue forever. Even as they glide in circles around the floor, she feels him slipping away. Waltzing right out of her life.

She fights the panic manifesting itself, doubling, then doubling again and again. "It sounds like you're saying goodbye."

He looks directly into her eyes, and for the first time the mask slips, just a little. There is a hardened determination in his face, but at the edges she can make out other emotions: regret, longing. Love. He loves her. She knows he loves her.

"I told you when we were on the beach, Betty," he says. "I told you I couldn't be Miss America's boyfriend, and why. You said you understood."

"I never said I understood!" she says, in a whisper so laced with urgency, she's afraid she has been overheard. She works ferociously to keep a placid appearance, even as her insides begin to crumble. "I . . . I love you, Griff," she says, almost unable to get the words out. "I love you with all of my heart. I know you feel the same way. A girl knows something like that. Please tell me this is not the end. You . . . you can't mean it. You simply can't."

The music stops.

There is polite applause, and for a moment it is simply Betty Jane Welch and John Griffin McAllister, standing in the middle of the Steel Pier ballroom, looking into each other's eyes, the world outside of their ethereal bubble oblivious to everything transpiring between them. He folds her into a short, stiff embrace.

"I'm so very sorry, Betty, truly I am," he whispers into her ear. "But I can't. I wish you every happiness."

With one deft movement, he takes her hand and kisses it through her glove. And then he is gone, retreating gallantly off the dance floor and into the crowd, as Betty is once again retrieved by jowly Mr. Haverstick, who doesn't notice the tears now streaming down the face of his newly crowned Miss America 1950.

❧

"*So we'll be on* the beach at nine," Lenora Slaughter is saying, balancing a slim black binder on her lap, "and the good news is that the water should actually be temperate. We've had years where girls have almost caught pneumonia from having to splash around in the morning surf in the middle of September. But it's a tradition, and the photographers come from all over for it, and those photos will appear all over the world."

She peruses several papers, penning notes in various margins, as a phalanx of hostesses dash about, packing trunks, ironing, barking orders into the suite telephone by the bed. "Then, we'll be back here for you to change—we have that navy suit for her, don't we, Lois? Do make sure it's pressed—then we go on to the Brighton for your farewell press conference. This will be a bit longer than tonight's, since the boys have more time to meet deadline. But no pictures. We have to be on the train to New York at twelve thirty; we have coffee with the New York pageant people at four, and then a cocktail reception and dinner with some of our national advertisers at seven at the Plaza. Monday morning we have your wardrobe fittings with Everglaze—they're giving you an entire new wardrobe! Isn't that exciting?—and, oh dear, I forgot. We'll have to sneak in a radio interview or two somewhere along the way—Katherine, have we heard anything from Barry Gray's people? Do check in with them, will you? And then we have tea with Earl Wilson, which is something of a tradition, but one we must adhere to, and then . . ."

Betty sits in a plush armchair, still in her gown. The crown and sash have been dutifully removed by someone, locked away for safekeeping. The scepter and cape, she has been told, do not travel with her. She is in the "royal suite" at the Claridge, reserved each year for the winner, and it is indeed sumptuous, a warren of tasteful rooms dutifully appointed with the right amount of art, mahogany tables, fluffy towels, and cut crystal. Betty can hear Miss Slaughter talking, but it is simply noise, infernal static that says nothing and means nothing. Betty says nothing herself. She simply sits and stares out of the windows, able to neither see nor hear the ocean below in the midnight darkness.

Miss Slaughter's hand touches her shoulder and Betty looks up. "Please don't feel frightened, my dear. It's a busy schedule, but it calms down considerably after the first week, when we get you on the road out to the Midwest. Have you ever been to that part of the country? Very beautiful, and the people, so lovely! They are going to adore you, and you them. And don't worry—we'll try to wedge a breakfast in with your parents and brothers tomorrow before they return to Delaware. And of course you will have Maude here"— she points to a stocky woman of about sixty, wearing a plain brown dress and thick square-toed leather shoes—"as your chaperone for the next few weeks. Perhaps we can convince your mother to join you for a few days somewhere along the way, for a little touch of home, yes?" She straightens up, clasps her hands in front of her. "Do you have any questions, dear?"

Just one. How do I get out of this?

"No, I understand," Betty says quietly, enveloping herself in her good-girl shell like it's a cocoon. "I'm just rather tired."

"Of course you are! You must be ready to fall over, and we must be up promptly at six thirty to get your hair and makeup ready for the beach. Just remember that Maude will be right next door if you need anything. Now get some rest and I will see you in the morning." She leans back over, clasps Betty by the chin. "You are going to be a marvelous Miss America, Betty. You'll see."

And with that she departs, marshaling her flock and shooing them all out of the suite, until the door finally closes and it is just Betty, still immobilized in her chair—her throne, as it were—the bitter reality of her new life slowly seeping through her pores, like a virus. And to think she had almost convinced herself this would be fun. She will have no say over anything for the next year: what she wears, what she eats, who she sees, what she says, when she sleeps, when she sees her family. Miss Slaughter thinks she can allow Betty home for the day for Thanksgiving but cannot promise Christmas. There is simply too much to do.

She gets up, wriggles out of the gown while still standing in the living room, letting it drop into a sad heap of satin and crinoline. She begins taking the pins out of her hair, feeling it fall, one section at a time, around her face.

I had it. I had the real prize. I had Griff. I had love. Someone I loved, who loved me. And he told me he couldn't do this, but I didn't listen, because I didn't believe it would ever happen. And now I'm trapped in this prison, this jail that will move from state to state, to school gymnasiums and city halls and pep rallies and car dealerships, for the next year. And by then it will be too late. Griff will have found someone new. I'll have lost him forever.

She looks around the room, hoping to discover a decanter full of liquor. But of course there is none. Miss America does not imbibe alcohol. Miss America does not do anything impure or impolite or human. She is a marionette, dancing for the crowd.

Betty removes her shoes, tosses them atop the quickly wrinkling dress on the floor, heads to the bedroom. It's like she is underwater. She cannot remember ever being this tired.

She puts on the hotel bathrobe, still in her slip, garter, and stockings, and slides onto the bed. She wants to turn out the lights, to sleep, and to wake up in Delaware, to wake up in June, before her mother has baked her a lemon cake, before she has come to Atlantic City and met John Griffin McAllister.

She wants to go numb, to not feel anything.

The tears bubble up once again, and this time, in the safety of her aloneness, they spiral into sobs, heaving, gulping, gasping, moaning cries of despair so violent they shake her body as it contracts and folds, as if trying to make her disappear. *I can't do this,* she thinks. *I can't do this. I can't do without him. I can't give up the man I know I'm meant to marry. I'll regret it for the rest of my life.*

Oh, what am I going to do?

It takes twenty minutes for the tears to first subside, twenty minutes for the answer, obvious and as clear as a fine spring afternoon, to come to her. At the twenty-first minute, she reaches for the phone by the bed.

Fourteen

Weekes' Tavern is a nondescript lounge at the corner of Baltic and Illinois — Ciji still can't shake the feeling that she is constantly hopscotching about a Monopoly board — that looks like an igloo with glass block windows. Jerry — she mercifully has trained herself not to refer to him as the Mole in his presence — holds the door for her as she steps inside. It's almost two in the morning and she knows she looks a fright, but desperate times call for desperate measures and all of that. She has repeated it more than once tonight, and there is little doubt circumstances may be even more dire than merely desperate.

She almost hung up when she got the call after midnight. The voice on the other end was unrecognizable, a mix of weeping and wailing fit for a war hero's funeral. It took her ten minutes just to calm Betty down enough to get the pieces of the story out. Griff had ended everything, right there on the Marine Ballroom dance floor. The cad. Listening to Betty's longing and sorrow, her pleading to help find Griff, Ciji felt fury froth in her blood. With one part of her brain she'd listened to Betty lament; with the other she'd fantasized about socking Griff right in the kisser. What kind of buffoon was he, anyway? Poor him, having to date the girl who was just anointed America's princess. Men!

The bar is dim but not as enveloped in darkness as the last two. They'd been to two of Griff's other haunts, the Around-the-World Room at the President and the Torch Club—thank God boys, when thrown together, talk of nothing but sports and booze, or she wouldn't have known any of this—and now were at the last. If he wasn't here, there was only one other option, which was to drive to Longport, wake up the entire McAllister household, and hope that Griff was there, already in bed. But that risks having Griff's mother call Miss Slaughter. And that will not do.

"There," Jerry says, touching her arm and nodding toward the end of the bar.

And indeed, there he is, his bow tie undone, his shirt open, sitting alone and sipping something brown. "Wait here for a minute," Ciji says. "I think it'll go better if I talk to him alone. But stay close. If he blows a fuse, I'll give you a signal."

She walks down the length of the long bar, slides onto the stool next to him. As she places her bag on the bar, he glances at her briefly, then stops the second time.

"Yeah, it's me, Romeo," she says. "I had a heck of a time finding you."

He looks away, takes another sip of his drink. Scotch. The good stuff. "You shouldn't have bothered. I'd like to be alone."

She nods to the bartender, orders a sloe gin fizz. This is one thing she has come to love about Atlantic City—that a woman can sit at the bar and order a drink and no one blinks an eye. She loathes "ladies' entrance" signs, their unspoken implication that women are far too delicate, too sensitive, to have the right to sit at the bar and get as good and scrooched as any unshaven lout sitting on either side. When she gets to Hollywood, she's drinking wherever she damn well pleases.

"We've got a problem, you and me, Griff," she says as the bartender deposits her drink. "Betty's a complete wreck. But of course I'm sure you already knew that, given you're the heel who's put her in this state."

He says nothing, then, "She'll be okay. She's better off."

"Well, that's rich. What? So you don't care about her 'cause now she's got a bunch of rhinestones for a hat? This was all a big game for you this week, your Boardwalk strolls and beach picnics and moony dinners and bouquets of sunflowers? It was all a lie?"

His jaw hardens. "Of course not."

"Then what is all this hooey about? Griff, you have no idea the shape she's in. I'm afraid she might do something . . . terrible."

For the first time, his face registers something other than self-pity. Alarm.

"Wh-what do you mean? She wouldn't hurt herself! Tell me that's not what you mean."

Success. Ciji clamps down on his arm, trying to close the deal. "Griff, listen to me: That girl loves you something awful. And I believe you love her, too. Now she says she doesn't want to be Miss America, which is just crackers. A big part of that is you, yes, but it's also that she's just a girl from Delaware who never thought this would happen to her, and now she's looking at a year away from her family and her friends and she's scared out of her wits. And the only person who can possibly understand, who can help, has gone cold on her. You need to help her. You're the only one. There's no way she can get through this year as Miss America without you."

He looks at her wordlessly for what seems like minutes. She can almost see him arguing with himself inside. "Please, Griff. Just try. If you really ever cared about her, please try."

His features soften, the film over his eyes lifts. "I do care about her. Deeply. You've got to believe me."

"I'm not the one you need to convince. You've got to come with me right now. Right now, Griff! We haven't much time."

They slide off their stools as Griff tosses some bills on the bar. "But . . . how can I see her? I know how this works. There's no way they'll let me near her room."

Ciji is already in front of him, signaling Jerry as she darts toward the door. "With Ciji," she says over her shoulder, "there's always a way."

❧

When Betty flings open the door and sees him standing there, she freezes.

He's here. He's really here.

"Oh, Griff, my darling!" she exclaims, lassoing her arms around his neck, pulling him into a suffocating clinch. He kisses her fervidly before they both feel a shove from behind.

"Let's take it inside, kids," Ciji says, hustling the three of them into the room and quickly closing the door, "before the pageant police come and bust up the party."

"Betty, I don't know—"

"Uh-uh!" Ciji interjects. "No talking until I'm gone. Okay, you two, I've done my part. But I am not risking my hard-earned scholarship money by staying to listen to this episode of *Life Can Be Beautiful* and having a hostess find me in here. I've got to get back to my hotel."

"Oh, Ciji," Betty says, stepping forward to hug her. "How can I ever thank you?"

"Don't you remember? I'm Joan of Arc. Just be happy, Delaware. You deserve it." She takes Betty by the shoulders. "Now talk it all out, but make sure to get some shuteye. Tomorrow is a long day, and you've got to be in the surf in the morning. I'll see you there."

Betty smiles. *No, you won't,* she thinks.

"Yes, ma'am. You've been an angel. I'll never forget it."

Afterward, Griff takes Betty by the hand, follows her into the living room, flinging his hat onto the table as he topples with her onto the couch. He withdraws a silver flask from his jacket pocket. "Want some?" he asks.

"As a matter of fact," she says, "I do."

She takes a swig, choking softly from the earthy bite of the whiskey, hands the flask back to him. "How did you manage to get up here, anyway?"

"Jerry helped us a bit."

"The Mole?"

"Don't call him that. It's ungenerous."

"Sorry. How did he help?"

"He walked into the lobby first, went to the front desk and up to the night manager, started asking him a bunch of questions about nothing. Ciji and I came in a few seconds later, pretending we were a married couple. I even had her wear my class ring backwards so it looked like a wedding band. And while the manager was busy dealing with Jerry, we sailed right on by to the elevators."

"I'm sure you two made a very convincing young married couple to the elevator operator."

"Well, she *is* an actress." They both smile. It feels good to smile, to not be twisted and tortured with emotion. To pretend the last six hours have not happened.

"Betty, I—"

"Don't, Griff, please don't say another word," she says, practically diving into his lap. "Not yet. There's—there's something you must know. I . . . I love you. And I know I told you that tonight, but you don't understand. I love you so much, so much that it hurts all over inside. The thought of being without you, even for a day, it's just unbearable. I know what you said and I just never imagined I would win, that was all, so I didn't really think about it, and then there was all of this craziness and I got swept away by it. But I'm here now, sweetie, I'm here and I'm not letting you go ever again. I can't. You must see, you must. I don't want to be Miss America. I only want to be with you."

He touches her face with his thumb, wipes away her falling tears. "Betty, you can't just walk away from all of this. And I would never ask you to. It would be terribly unfair. You've worked so hard—"

"But that's just the thing, I haven't worked at all. Don't you see? I never wanted any of this! I did it to appease my mother!" She tells him about how she was counting the days until Atlantic City was behind her and then she met him, marvelous him, and everything changed. How she doesn't care about her parents or the pageant, any of it. Only him. "Oh, Griff, please. Please tell me we can be together. Take me home and let's forget all of it."

"You don't understand. They'll never let you do that, Betty. And neither will my mother, for that matter. You signed a contract. It's legal. You work for them for the next year. They'll take everything from you: your scholarship money, they might even take you to court."

She drops her head onto his chest, threads her fingers tightly into his. For a while they simply sit in silence, wrapped in each other. "Can't we just go somewhere?" she whispers finally, in the plaintive voice of a little girl. "Just for a little while? I can't breathe. I just need to get out of Atlantic City. Let's go somewhere. Some-place where they can't find us. We don't have to go forever, just until we can figure everything out. Together."

"It would mean an enormous scandal."

"I don't care."

"You really mean that?" His voice is grave, serious.

"I do." She looks up at him, the longing pooling in her eyes. "Will you help me?"

His face is a plane of shifting shadows: indecision, fear, passion, protectiveness, determination, then back again. His brain is on overdrive, which he knows is risky. It's when trouble happens. He thinks back to two nights ago, the terrible voices screaming at him . . . He knew that the stress of being Miss America's beau would bring them back on a regular basis. But what if she is not Miss America after all? He strokes her hair. He does love her. So very much. He mulls telling her the truth. Doesn't she have a right to know his secret? He suspects she does. And yet he cannot bring himself to mar this image she has of him, this perfect, unspoiled love she feels. "I love you so much, Betty."

"Then help me," she says, leaning up and kissing him fully on the mouth. He leans into her and this time the kiss goes deeper, smoldering then fiery, then ferocious, animalistic. She wants him to devour her, to engulf her, to mesh their souls, to leave nothing behind. She slides the undone bow tie dangling from his neck, drops it onto the carpet, then begins slowly unbuttoning his shirt, sliding her right hand over his smooth chest. She feels the labor of his breathing, can make out the unvarnished lust in his eyes, now unlocked, set free. His left hand is on her, gliding up her slip underneath the robe, his right fingers sliding underneath her bra, circling her nipple. She gasps, and he tilts his chin up slightly, just away from her face, teasing her, wordlessly asking her to submit to her own desire.

"Take me to bed," she whispers.

"Are you certain?"

She does not recognize herself: not her voice, not her thoughts, not her commands. She doesn't know this girl now taking control of her body. She only knows what she wants in this moment, and that she must have it. "Now. Please, Griff. I need you now. All of you."

He swoops her up in one seamless motion, the belt of her robe cascading to the floor, and once again locks his lips atop hers as he carries her into the bedroom.

❧

In the milky predawn light, the sky is a swirling mix of pastels: blue, pink, purple, lavender. Griff awakens first, his arm still around her. He squints at the bedside alarm clock, tries to make out the time. Five twenty? He knows the hostess will be in at seven, maybe even earlier, to get Betty up and dressed for her appointment with the photographers, frolicking in the surf.

He disengages from their entanglement, quickly dresses.

I should leave. I should just write a note and leave her. It's the right thing to do. She doesn't mean what she was saying. Doesn't understand what she's giving up.

Doesn't know the truth.

But then he looks at her, her angelic face resting on the pillow, and he knows he cannot abandon her again. If she has changed her mind, sees life differently in the light of day, so be it. But he loves her. He needs her, as much as she needs him. Maybe more. He wonders, selfishly, if she and her love could be the tonic he has been searching for all of these years, the remedy to what ails him. He feels strong now, in control, his head quiet. How can he ruin not only her happiness but what may be his only chance at his own?

He kneels by her side of the bed, gently nudges her awake. "Hi de ho, my love. Good morning."

It takes her a minute to snap out of the haze of slumber. She reaches out, caresses his cheek. "My prince," she says.

He kisses her palm. "It's time, Betty. It's very early, but the hostess will be in soon to get you and then our chance is lost. If you want to do this, you have to decide for sure now. And if you do, you need to truly understand what it is you're doing. What you're giving up."

"But I'm not giving anything up," she says. "I'm gaining everything." The conviction in her voice is as clear as a classroom bell. "But where can we go?"

His face beams. "Somewhere they'll never look for us."

Fifteen

If she is admitting it—and she isn't, to anyone—Ciji is here only half for Betty's benefit and half for her own. She does want to be supportive and, perhaps more than that, to find out how the summit with Griff turned out in the wee small hours of the morning. A clandestine meeting of lovers, secretly arranged in the middle of the night, in the penthouse of a seaside hotel—it was like a dime novel. And since she was the one who'd made it happen, she figured she had as much of a right as anybody to find out how it had all turned out. Though how she will ever get Betty alone long enough to tell her anything is a pickle.

The other half of her motivation for hauling herself out of bed and walking down to the Claridge at this ungodly early hour on Sunday morning, she knows, is selfish, common, and more than a bit calculating. She justifies it by saying that her counsel to Betty all during the week surely contributed to her victory last night. And so if she is quoted as Betty's roommate for the week, what harm can come of it? And if one of the photographers, tired of snapping pictures of Betty frolicking in the surf, decides a nice portrait of

Ciji, her best contestant pal, would make a nice augment to his story, what could be the harm? So she has spiffed up just in case, in a white dress embellished with olive French embroidery, with of course matching suede and mesh peep-toes and a beret with a cocarde. She is ready for her close-up.

She sits in an armchair in the lobby of the Claridge, spies two contestants—she thinks one of them is Pennsylvania—walking out, accompanied by their parents and bellmen wheeling what appears to be an obscene number of suitcases. Back to real life for all of them. Except, of course, for one of them.

Where is she? Ciji wonders, glancing toward the cluster of photographers there to follow Betty and her various handlers as they trek down to the beach.

She spies Miss Slaughter, obviously flustered, waving her hands by the elevator bank, and gets up and creeps closer, trying to figure out what's going on. She stops a few yards away, pretends to examine a vase holding a huge potted fern, which now partially obscures her.

"... don't understand. Where is Maude? They were supposed to be down fifteen minutes ago. Grady, can you please tell me what's going on? The photographers are waiting!"

"I'm sorry, Miss Slaughter, but neither Mrs. Hodges nor Miss Welch is answering her phone. We've sent Georgette and Lois up to find out what's keeping them."

Miss Slaughter unloads another dump truck's worth of invective, which all seems to come back to how she has to do everything herself if she wants it done at all. She is in the midst of a fresh batch of nattering when the elevator doors open and a mousy, heavyset woman walks out, a look of panic plastered on her ruddy face. Ciji recognizes her: Maude Hodges, the pageant hostess who is to accompany Betty through the first leg of her tour as Miss America.

Maude begins jabbering as the pageant officials all close in, making it difficult for Ciji to hear what's being said. She inches closer.

". . . no sign of her. Most of her clothes are still in the room, but it's an awful mess. Her gown is in a heap in the middle of the sitting room. Very untidy, very unlike Miss Welch. And I found a gentleman's flask behind one of the sofa cushions. I think someone may have broken into the room!"

"There is no sign of Miss Welch, anywhere?" Miss Slaughter, looking ashen.

"No!" Maude is becoming hysterical, her voice piercing. "I think something terrible may have happened to her! We must contact the police at once!"

Ciji dashes back down the hall, pauses to catch her breath against a lobby pillar. *Oh Lord. What's happened?* She flips through the possibilities. Betty decided to run off with Griff. She was so distraught at losing him, but to do something that rash? It isn't like her at all. And hadn't she told Ciji just a few hours ago that she would see her for the splash in the ocean at nine? That left the other possibility: Griff had taken her against her will. But why? *He* was the one who had broken it off with Betty at the ball. Did something change, something happen between them that convinced him he had to have Betty solely for himself?

What if she's in danger? What if I've done something terrible?

She peers back down toward the elevators, now a hive of activity. Ciji can see two hotel security officers conferring with Miss Slaughter. Surely the police are on their way. It won't be long before the news spills out all over the Boardwalk: Miss America is missing!

She should tell them. Of course, her scholarship will be lost. She may even be charged as an accessory if it turns out Griff has abducted Betty, and, however unwittingly, she helped him do it.

Dammit, Delaware, you and your midnight phone call!

She needs time to consider her options. Perhaps the police will find Betty within the hour—and if that happens, what has she achieved by throwing away her scholarship? A wave of nausea roils through her.

I need to go somewhere and figure out what to do.

She takes in another deep breath, strides confidently toward the Boardwalk doors of the Claridge.

She's about to push through when she feels a hand on her arm.

"Hold on there, Miss Rhode Island." Eddie Tate, the *Press* reporter. "Not so fast."

❧

He is not sure what wakes him: the commotion outside or the voices inside.

His dream that being with her might cure him seems to be over before it has even had a chance to blossom into form. Griff looks over at Betty, curled up underneath the blanket on the floor of the boat. Oh, to be able to sleep so soundly.

The voices grow louder. They tell him all sorts of things—that Betty is bad, that the FBI is watching them through the decal on the port side, that there is a shark sent by a Nazi regime in exile that carries a bomb in its teeth, and which will swim up in five minutes to destroy them—and he closes his eyes, accesses his exercises. Does he have time to get back to Longport to get his medicine? He shouldn't go without it. But how can he go home?

The boat bobs gently in the water. The sun is bright overhead, morning in full bloom. He opens his eyes, looks at his watch. Just after ten. His bones feel heavy, sore. How long have they slept? Not long. He is supposed to make sure he gets enough sleep. He must make sure of it going forward.

He'd dashed down the hallway of the top floor of the Claridge, entering the fire stairs and flying down the twenty-four flights as quickly as his feet would take him, the small bag she had hastily packed swinging in his right hand the entire way down. She would be coming behind him in a few moments, but it would certainly take her longer to descend all the way to the ground floor. Which gave him enough time to retrieve his car, circle around to the back of the hotel, and whisk her away.

He'd worn his fedora so low on his brow, in case he found company on the stairs, that he could barely see where he was going. But everything had gone shockingly smooth. He'd wheeled into the loading dock, deserted at daybreak on Sunday, and found her waiting and ready, a silk head scarf around her head, dark sunglasses hiding her eyes. They'd driven straight for the marina, where he'd quickly dashed in to the men's changing room to retrieve fresh clothes from his locker, and they'd clambered into his boat just as the sun was rising. Safely away from any prying eyes, they'd moored two hundred yards off of Steel Pier—just a pleasure boat resting in the ocean on a sunny September day—allowing themselves to at last plummet into the safety of slumber.

He is halfway out of his tuxedo when her eyes flutter open. Betty stares at him a moment, his features momentarily obscured by the sun, and hoods her eyes to get a better look at him. He is on his knees, smiling down at her. He wears no shirt, shoes, or socks, only his formal black pants.

"You caught me," he says, smiling. "I was changing."

"Then it seems I awoke at exactly the right moment," she says.

"You're rather feisty for a girl who's just run away."

"I'm a girl who's free." She rises to her elbows. "What time is it?"

"After ten. We need to go soon."

"I'm just so very tired. And hungry."

"I know. We'll stop somewhere."

"Where are we?"

"Still moored off of the Steel Pier. But there seems to be a lot of activity on the Boardwalk. I think our secret's out."

A flash of worry sweeps across her face. "Do you think they know we're here?"

"No. They'd already have the beach patrol out to get us if they did. We're lucky the weather's so on the beam. This boat looks like a thousand other pleasure boats out on the water. But we haven't much time. My parents will be looking for me soon."

"They're probably frantic. I'm sorry."

"Now don't go into a decline. They probably think I stayed with a friend last night. I told them I might. They won't expect me until dinner. And by then—"

"By then?"

"We'll be gone." He stares at her gravely. "That is, if you still want to go. This is it, Betty. This is your last chance to change your mind. I'll take you back. We can fix things in a jiffy. You can still be Miss America if you want to."

Her eyes are steely, brimming with resolve. "I only want to be with you."

He slides over to her, takes her hand in his. He turns it over. "You cut yourself."

She nods. "I was in such a rush throwing those few things together, I grabbed my razor by the top. I had tissue around it for a while."

He leans down, kisses her wound, takes her hand in his own. "But what about your *family*, Betty? They're probably already worried sick about you. You didn't even leave a note."

"I'll get a message to them, somehow. For now I just want us to get as far away from Atlantic City as we can."

He smiles, bends down to kiss her softly. "You're a helluva girl, you know that, Betty Jane Welch?" He swivels into a sitting position, begins unbuckling his trousers. "Now turn the other way. I need to finish getting changed."

"Why? I saw everything last night."

"It was dark and you saw nothin' last night. The next time is going to be slower, more . . . romantic."

"Last night *was* romantic."

"You know what I mean. Romantic like you deserve. Now c'mon."

She flips onto the opposite side, listens as he slips into a fresh shirt and pants. When he's finished, he slides back next to her, pulling the blanket over both of them as he spoons her. "We can only do this for two minutes," he whispers, "then we have to go to the car and get out of here."

She takes his right arm, wraps it tightly around her. "Where are we going?"

"New York. I have a friend who'll put us up for a little while until we figure out what to do. It's a city of eight million people. No one will find us."

She caresses his arm, plays with the soft hairs. She has just done the most rash, outrageous, un-Betty thing in her entire life. She should feel terrified, apprehensive, subsumed in doubt and regret. And yet she has never felt happier, more joyful, more . . . loved. More alive. "I just need to make one change to the plan," she says.

"What's that?"

She pulls him tighter. "I need three minutes."

Sixteen

Eddie scoops up the remnants of his eggs with his piece of rye toast, seemingly ravenous. Ciji sips her coffee, studying him over the rim of the cup. *How did I get myself in the middle of this mess?* she muses. She wonders whether he can read her mind. You never knew with reporters.

They're in a back booth inside Lou's, a delicatessen in Ventnor, the next town over from Atlantic City; the waitress spent a good two minutes trying to talk Ciji into pancakes, to no avail. Ciji only agreed to come with Eddie because she was afraid a confrontation would attract attention in the Claridge lobby, and the last thing she needed right now was a horde of newspaper men following her down the Boardwalk, barking questions about Betty and where she might be. She just wants to go home to Newport, get back behind the desk at the Cliff Lawn, figure out how much cash she needs to add to her scholarship money before she can get on a train for the West Coast.

"You should really eat something," he says, pushing the plate away. "The food here is pretty good."

"I'm not hungry."

"I'll bet."

"Look. It's like I told you on the ride over. I don't know anything. I don't know where she went. I don't know if someone took her."

"You mean you don't know whether she's with Griffin McAllister willingly or unwillingly."

"How do you know they're even together?"

"Because nobody's seen him since he left the Steel Pier ballroom. Although I suspect if we hit enough of the bars around town, eventually someone's going to remember seeing him. And who he was there with. That's if the cops don't already know."

She folds her hands on the table, looks him square in the eye. "What exactly is it you want from me, Mr. Tate?"

"What any reporter wants. The story."

"I have no story to offer. Now if you will kindly take me back to my hotel, I need to check out. I have to be on a train at four."

"And I have to tell you that train is going to leave without you. Because I guarantee you that at this very moment there are two detectives from Atlantic County who are sitting in the lobby of the Chalfonte-Haddon Hall, waiting for you to come back."

She says nothing, looks at her hands.

"The *Press* is putting out a special afternoon edition. It's been a few years since we've done that. V-J Day, I think. You know what the headline's going to say? 'MISS AMERICA MISSING.' And underneath: 'Newly crowned beauty queen feared kidnapped.'" He leans across the table. "That kind of thing sells papers. But you and me, we know that's not the real story, is it, Miss Moore?"

"If that's the theory, why aren't you out there trying to find her?"

"I am." He eyes her evenly. "It's time for the truth, Miss Moore. I know she's with him. The question is, was it her choice or not?"

"What would make you believe he would have taken her against her will?"

"Because I was one of the last people to be alone with her before she disappeared. And she seemed . . . vulnerable."

"What do you mean?"

So he tells her: about the stilted interview in the room at Convention Hall after the pageant, about forgetting his hat and going back to retrieve it, about how anxious Betty appeared.

He leaves out the kiss.

"She'd just won Miss America, for Pete's sake," Ciji remarks, buying time as she debates what, if anything, to tell him. "Of course she was going to be a bit flustered."

"You were her roommate—"

"For a total of six days. We were hardly sisters."

"You knew she was keen on McAllister."

"So did you." She catches the mild look of surprise in his eyes. "You want honesty, Mr. Tate, how about you go first? Your interest in this story isn't strictly professional, is it?"

He leans back in the booth. "They should have picked you, Miss Moore. Miss America would have been a lot more than a once-a-year story if they had."

She has to tell him something. And it has to be truthful—she can't afford to tell lies, have her stories inconsistent between him and the police, who will surely question her. It won't be long—hours, a day at most—before somebody talks to the bartender at Weekes' Tavern, knows that she tracked down Griff, arranged the reunion. She pictures her scholarship, floating away with the evening tide.

"Betty called me late. She was extremely upset. Griff had broken it off right there at the ball. She begged me to go find him, talk to him."

She swears she sees relief sweep briefly across his eyes. "Why did he break it off?" he asks.

"He'd evidently told her earlier that if she won he was taking off. He didn't want to be known as Miss America's boyfriend."

"Well, that's ironic. Because that's exactly what every paper in town is calling him. Go on."

Ciji talks about tracking him down, bringing him back to the Claridge. She does not mention Jerry. There is no way the bartender will remember him, and there is no point getting him into hot water for doing something chivalrous and noble, if, in retrospect, extremely misguided.

"You took Griff to Betty's room?"

"No," she blurts out, before she even has a chance to think about it. But it appears she has already thought about it. Her last hope of retaining the scholarship money is to end her involvement in the Claridge lobby. The night desk clerk will not remember her and Griff breezing by as Jerry asked his inane questions to give them cover. Though he may remember Jerry's prominent mole. She can't think about that now. Some risks you've got to take.

She squares her shoulders. "I left Griff in the lobby, suggested he call up to Betty's room and arrange for her to come down so they could talk. Then I left. I had done my duty."

"And you just wandered back to your hotel, unescorted, in the middle of the night?"

"It's the Boardwalk, not the slums, Mr. Tate. I am perfectly capable of walking a few blocks in the moonlight by myself." He mulls this for a moment as the waitress clears the dishes, slaps the check down on the table. "Now, you are finished with your meal, and I have answered your questions," Ciji says. "I would like you to drive me back to my hotel. Or else I will have the cashier phone for a taxi."

"All right, Miss Moore. I'll take you back to Atlantic City. But I just have one more question, off the record. I give you my word

I won't print any of what you're about to tell me. But I need to know: Do you think Betty went with Griffin McAllister of her own accord?"

Ciji thinks about it for a minute, verbalizing, for the first time, the argument she has been having with herself since she overheard Miss Slaughter in the Claridge lobby. "She told me she would see me this morning, and I believed her," she says. "But she was also cuckoo for him. And if he was adamant about only wanting her if she was not Miss America . . . I don't know. As I said, we were roommates for six days. But you get to know a girl when you live with her in one room and go through something like this together. She didn't strike me as the kind of girl who would have just ditched her family, left her clothes, not even left a note. It just doesn't seem like . . . Betty."

"But now," she says, "I'm not sure I knew her at all."

❧

Honor McAllister paces the living room of her soigné Longport home like a caged animal. Still in her aqua quilted bed jacket and flowing pajama pants, she takes another drag on her cigarette to calm her nerves. Her husband is with his golf foursome, no doubt merrily chipping somewhere off of the eighth fairway at this very moment, oblivious. Which is for the best. He is weak and feckless in the face of these types of things. Actually, in the face of everything.

The two men sitting in her living room, looking at her stonily as she continues her uncontrollable walking side to side, are jotting notes in their respective pads. Honor notices belatedly that the burly one has tracked in mud on his shoes.

She has more pressing problems.

"We should have a good head start on the police," she says finally, "because they are not equipped for this kind of situation, and there are all sorts of rules and regulations that have to be accorded before anyone in law enforcement actually does anything. Those men are not nimble. If the FBI gets involved that may change, but it will take a day or two before that would happen, I think. They will also assume that they went south, because Delaware is south of Atlantic City, but I know my son and he will go to a city where he knows people—either Philadelphia or maybe Newark: he has a cousin there. He was briefly a student at NYU, so there may be someone there. Unless, of course, they go to a place where she has acquaintances. But I don't think so. Griff will want to be comfortable with his own friends. I've given you the list. You'll have to find the addresses for the ones I don't have. You have his license plate and make of car, his picture. And of course hers will be all over every newspaper in the country by tonight."

She takes a final drag, stubs out the cigarette in a ceramic ashtray on a side table. "I cannot emphasize strongly enough how imperative it is that you find them before the authorities do. Are there any final questions?"

The slender one speaks up. "I understand you don't want the cops involved. But what if we find him and he won't come with us willingly? What do you want us to do?"

He's right. Griff will not go with them willingly. Far from it. Especially if he's . . . She presses her eyes shut, blocks the memory of the last time—that last, awful, horrible time, two years ago, when she was faced with a son she didn't even recognize. "When you find him," she says carefully, "and I am paying you handsomely to make sure you do—you are to call me immediately with your location. Once I know where they are, I can decide on the best way to proceed."

"We can take him," the burly one says, "if that's what you want. We know how to do it."

She might consider it if he were alone, even as the memory of

seeing him strung up like a prize steer two years ago rushes back
to her, slices her through the heart. But there is Betty to consider.
Betty's presence complicates things. Especially since she is clearly
the reason he has done this in the first place. "No. My son is . . .
unwell. And delicate. He needs to be handled carefully in a situation such as this."

The two men give each other a tacit side-eye. They know the
code.

God help this kid if the cops find him first.

❧

The first thing they have to do when they reach New York, he figures, is ditch the car.

Reeve will be able to help. Maybe he has a car to swap or knows
someone who does. Reeve knows all sorts of shifty folk. Griff's
automobile — technically, it's his father's automobile — is a brand-
new black Mercury two-door coupe, the latest in a long line of
trinkets and toys his mother has badgered his father into buying for
him under the guise of keeping him calm and happy, of keeping the
voices out of his head.

The voices do not care what he's driving.

They'll switch cars in New York, hunker down with Reeve until
they can figure out where to go next. His mother thinks she knows
all of his friends, all about his life. But she never met Reeve during
Griff's ill-advised turn as a student at NYU; he was the replace-
ment roommate for a guy who ended up transferring. Which means
she'll have no idea where they are. And neither will anyone else.

Griff has taken the back roads, zigzagging through the thicket
of the Pine Barrens as they head north. He looks over at Betty,
sleeping in the passenger seat, her head rocking in concert with
the hum of the engine. He looks at his watch. Four o'clock. They

156

should stop somewhere, pick up something to eat. But he'll need to go in, bring it back to the car. God knows Betty's disappearance is probably already big news. He thinks of her parents, no doubt worried out of their minds. He wishes he'd thought of making Betty write a note. Maybe they can get to a pay phone, call them, tell them she's okay.

He tries to think of the last time he did anything this brash, this brazen. He has always been impulsive, even as a child. But aside from his episodes — which were not his fault — he has never been the kind of guy who went off half-cocked. He has always enjoyed a good time, but he's not the type to pull anything like this. But then, he loves her. He thinks he loved her from the moment she threw his penny into the wishing well. It feels so good to love someone. The girls he's known in Atlantic City have been nice, fun, but more often than not also deadly dull. He has only felt this way about one other person in his life.

Helen.

I can't think about her right now. I need to think about Betty. Betty is here.

Betty has spirit, verve. She won the title every girl in America dreams of, then discarded it for him. For him! Their love is stronger than anything he could have imagined. She is not Helen. She is better than Helen. Much, much better.

Betty can silence the voices. The two of them just need to find a place to let their love grow in peace.

A little music for the ride. He clicks on the radio, careful not to make it too loud; he doesn't want to wake her. It's hard to find a signal in the depths of the more than million acres of towering trees and brush that make up the Pine Barrens. He remembers the legend of the Jersey Devil, the spawn of a witch named Mother Leeds, who in the 1700s was born as her thirteenth child, fathered by the devil himself. Folklore said that the child soon developed hooves and wings and roamed the Pine Barrens in bloodthirsty search for victims to terrorize and feast upon.

Just let him try to come for us. Because nothing in the world can hurt me today.

Still nothing but static. He fiddles with the dial some more. A faint melody of Tommy Dorsey underneath the crackling. More turning back and forth, searching for anything clear. Finally, a male voice, talking about the weather. He goes on to deliver the news that the Yankees have routed the Washington Senators, 20–5; the Senators set a record for bases on balls in the third inning. The Reds have won the first game of their doubleheader against the Dodgers and are on their way to taking both, Stan Musial continuing his home-run streak.

"And now we return to our top story of the day: the stunning disappearance of the newly crowned Miss America in Atlantic City. Authorities are still trying to sort out what has happened to Delaware beauty Betty Jane Welch, who was toasted at a ball in her honor on the Steel Pier last night after she won the coveted title but has not been seen since. Atlantic County detectives have asked for assistance from other local police forces to locate Miss Welch, who vanished from her suite at the Claridge Hotel sometime between last night and this morning, when officials became alarmed after she failed to appear for the winner's traditional splash in the ocean for news photographers. No other details have yet been released about her possible whereabouts, or the circumstances surrounding her disappearance. But county sheriff William T. Mackey told reporters this morning that, and I quote, 'No stone will be unturned until we find this young lady and bring her abductors to justice.' Stay tuned for more details on this story as they develop—"

He snaps off the radio.

Kidnapped. They think I kidnapped her.

How could he have been so stupid? He knew the pageant people would look for them; that Betty's parents and certainly his own
would be livid. But the police? He should have known. Betty left
no note. She packed almost nothing. The room was in complete
disarray. No one knows that he had broken it off at the ball, that
Betty was disconsolate, that she had decided that she wanted out
of the whole Miss America mess.

But Ciji does. Won't Ciji tell them? But then, what can she
tell them? She only knows that Betty and he were reunited at the
hotel. She may guess that Betty left willingly, but she can't swear
to it. And she may say nothing. Saying anything can only implicate
her in their escape.

He hears the rumbling inside his head; wishes and wills it away,
but he knows it's useless. Softly, softly, then a bit louder they come,
seeping into his brain like invaders pouring over the castle walls,
until their noise is so loud, he feels like he is going to explode, right
there inside the car. He begins muttering, talking back to them,
trying to reason with them, answer them, explain to them, but it is
not enough. It is never enough.

"Stop it!" he screams.

Betty startles awake, grabs ahold of him. "What is it?" she yells,
looking out the windshield, trying to make sense of what's happening.

He pulls over near a thicket of towering green pines, cuts the
engine. "I'm . . . I'm sorry, baby. I just need to take a break, that's
all. I think we need to get something to eat."

"Okay," she says, rubbing his arm. "Poor baby. I wish I knew how
to drive."

"No, I'm fine. We'll just stop somewhere and pick up some
food."

"Are you sure that's it? Is there something else wrong?"

"No, baby. Don't worry," he says, leaning over and kissing her. He's relieved she cannot hear the voices inside his head.

She's evil, Voltaire says.

She is out to get you. You need to get her first, the grandfather one adds.

Why can't you see what she is doing to you? She is the ghost of Helen, haunting you, says the angry woman, interrupting. She always interrupts.

Get away from her! screams the shrew. *Get away now!*

Seventeen

etty peers down onto Twenty-First Street. It's what one would expect on a mid-September day in New York: three girls playing hopscotch, a group of boys immersed in a raucous game of stickball at the end near Eighth Avenue. Two plumbers walk slowly down the stoop diagonally across the street; a woman in a cloth coat and a blue felt hat clutches a grocery sack with both hands, walks purposefully in the other direction, toward Seventh.

She has been to New York only twice: in 1939, for the World's Fair in Flushing Meadow, and in the summer of 1943, a girls' day for just her and her mother, to have tea at the Plaza and see *Oklahoma!* at the St. James. Betty sang "Many a New Day" incessantly for weeks after.

She thinks about her mother, how worried she must be.

"You're never gonna settle into life on the run if you're always this jumpy," comes the voice from the kitchen.

Betty lets the shade fall back. "I'm not jumpy," she says defensively. "And I am not on the run."

He walks out of the galley kitchen into the living room, wiping his hands on a dish towel. He wears only a white-ribbed A-shirt and a pair of pants. He is always walking around the apartment barely dressed, and it unnerves her. But it is his apartment. She can hardly object.

Reeve Spencer is short, at least compared to Griff—he can't be more than five-seven, she imagines—and wiry, a young man with an English name and Italian looks, including a head of bristly black hair, like a particularly hirsute porcupine. He has a lithe, toned physique that suggests he has at some point intersected with athletics, physical labor, or fortunate genetics. His teeth are too big for his mouth and are just crooked enough to give him a permanent look of disinterested insolence, like a grown-up Bowery Boy; his eyes are blue and ceaselessly mocking. Since she and Griff got here just over a week ago, she has been on edge any time she and Reeve have been alone. There is something faintly subversive and unkind in his overall demeanor—he has an awful and juvenile sense of humor. Yesterday he was in near hysterics reading aloud from some vulgar comic book.

"You don't like me very much, do you?" he asks her, shoving the dishtowel into the back of his waistband.

No. I don't. "I'm sorry if you've found me unfriendly," she says. "It certainly hasn't been my intent. I can assure you that both Griff and I are very appreciative of everything you've done for us." The answer a Miss America contestant would give.

She wishes Griff had picked another friend—any friend—with whom to seek safe haven. There is something unctuous about Reeve that unsettles her. Worse yet, she is certain that he knows it.

"I'm gonna fix us a little drink," he says, circling back to the kitchen.

She begins to object but stops, settles onto the living room chair. Maybe it will help. They won't be here forever, but for now they are, in fact, very much here. Griff has spent the last week drawing in a copybook, making all sorts of grand plans for them, like a bank robber mapping out the location of the vault and the proper escape route. Betty finally managed to peek inside the book last night while Griff was in the bathroom and found nothing but slashing lines, circles, odd symbols. She is either in the hands of a genius who has his own symbolic language, or she is in the hands of a madman.

She presses her eyes closed.

Who am I?

More than once since getting to New York, she has awoken disoriented, unable to find her life in her first few moments of consciousness. Nine days ago she was the toast of the nation, the girl every girl wanted to be. And then she threw it away like a day-old newspaper. Sometimes she expects regret to rush in, but it never does; she knows now that she was not meant to be Miss America. In her quest to be the good daughter, she had ignored the woman she was meant to become.

And now she had found her.

The first few days in New York had been as romantic as their escape, filled with adrenaline and backstreet romance. He would dash out and bring back all sorts of foreign foods—how she had, to his delight, practically gobbled down that delicious Cuban sandwich! The daybed in the living room was cramped, but each night they fell asleep in each other's arms, safe in their mutual company and affection. She thought often of his confession of his medical condition that day on the jetty in Longport, worried about triggering it back through the stress of their adventure. But he had seemed more himself these past few days than ever before, almost buoyant in the shared view of a new life they would discover together. Their lovemaking, carefully plotted after Reeve left for work in the morning, had provoked a physicality in her that made her blush. She lived for his touch, his gaze, his mouth, for his body, tight and taut like ship rope, melding into her softness and curves.

Reeve hands her a tumbler with whiskey. He takes a seat on the daybed, clinks their glasses. "Here's looking up your old ad-dress."

So witty.

She takes a sip, fights the choking. Betty has never understood the allure of whiskey to men. She wonders if it is simply another test of virility, like chopping wood or fathering children.

"So," Reeve says, crossing his ankles on the coffee table, "how much has Griff told you about his brief college days here in New York?" His tone carries the unmistakable timbre of *If you only knew.*

"Enough," she lies. She does not want to hear stories about Griff. She takes another swig of the whiskey.

"I doubt that," he says, breaking out into his sickening grin. "I know one thing: the Griff McAllister you know sure as hell ain't the one I know."

A well-timed key in the door. Griff walks in, carrying a paper bag, tosses his hat onto the table as he leans down to kiss her. "How's my girl today?"

"Getting more stir-crazy by the minute. I need to get back *outside,* Griff. I've been out precisely twice since we arrived. I can't stay locked in here like Rapunzel every day."

He plops down, throws an arm around her as he squeezes into the armchair with her. "Whiskey? Boy, you do need to get out."

"Indeed."

"Got a surprise for you. Reach into my breast pocket."

Betty feels heavy paper. Tickets. She plucks them out. Two tickets to tomorrow night's performance of *Miss Liberty* at the Imperial Theatre. "Oh, Griff! Griff! We're going to a play? How thrilling!"

"And dinner beforehand, at some cozy little place. It's time we started to live a little."

Reeve looks on, quietly assessing them. He swirls the whiskey in his glass, gulps the remainder down. "Well, nice to see the love-birds nesting so sweetly. I gotta go get washed up."

As Reeve heads to the bathroom, Griff leans down to Betty, pecks her softly on the lips. "I bought you something else, too," he says, reaching for the sack.

"Oh no, Griff, you mustn't!" He's already bought her two dresses since they've been here, his apology for not allowing her to properly pack. But they do not have unlimited money. Betty has a total of eleven dollars in her purse.

He extracts the contents, and Betty's eyes narrow. "Is that what I think it is?" she asks.

"It is, my pet," he answers. "It's the new you."

❧

She doesn't want Griff to go.

"But, honey, you know I have to," he says, sliding his jacket on. "I finally got a cat to switch cars with me. He's getting the best part of the deal, of course—I mean, a new Mercury for a '45 Fleetline—but then we can finally get out of here."

"Where are we going?"

"That's the beautiful part," he says, kissing her forehead. "Any-where we want."

"We don't have enough money."

"Why are you being a wet noodle all of a sudden? Huh? What's gotten into you, baby?"

I don't want to be alone in this apartment with that creep Reeve. I miss my family. I need to know where all of this is headed.

"Nothing, nothing," she says. "You did send that letter, right? I would hate to think of my parents back in Delaware worrying about me, wondering what's happened. It wouldn't be fair."

"Sure, honey, sure. Don't worry. We'll get settled somewhere, and I'll get a good job. By then those Miss America folks will have moved on from all of this, and we can write your folks back again and tell them where we are. We'll throw a big party!" He takes her in his arms, nestles her head in his chest. "That's what you want, isn't it? You still want us to be together, right?"

There is a faint desperation in his voice that sends the hairs on the back of her neck upright. She loves him. It is exactly what she wants.

Isn't it?

"Of course," she whispers. "Of course it is."

He takes her chin in his hand, bends down to kiss her softly. "Have I told you how beautiful you look?"

"Yes," she says, smiling. "But some things bear repeating."

"You look even prettier as a brunette."

She has never considered dyeing her hair. She'd known a few classmates at Towson who had, but hair coloring was the pastime of mousy-haired girls who'd always longed to be willowy blondes. Dyeing your head black was something old women did to swat away hair now the color of steel wool. Looking into the mirror last night, after she'd rinsed the last of the henna, she hadn't recognized herself. Which was, of course, exactly the reason Griff had insisted. If Betty wanted more freedom to move about the city, she needed to not look like Betty Jane Welch at all. And tonight is her reward: dinner and a play.

A few minutes after Griff leaves, the bedroom door opens. Reeve drifts into the kitchen, scratching his head, seemingly willing himself awake. He wears only pajama bottoms.

"Any coffee left?" he asks sleepily.

"Yes," Betty answers crisply, settling down onto the daybed with a copy of *McCall's*. Griff has been bringing her magazines to pass the time—she knows he is withholding newspapers, and why. God knows what's being said about her. "Aren't you going to be late for work?"

He pours himself a cup, shuffles into the living room. "Nobody notices if I'm late," he says, plopping into the chair. "Actually, nobody notices me at all."

"Well, you must do okay for yourself, to afford an apartment in Manhattan."

"Parents who are swells, sweetie. Same as Griff. And it ain't like I'm living on Park Avenue."

She flips through the magazine aggressively, looking for something to distract her. She's been trying to be nicer, more conversational with Reeve. Griff has pointed out, more than once, that it is Reeve who is doing them the good deed. She knows Griff's right. And yet Reeve's smirking demeanor does nothing but leave her cold every time they are in a room together. Once they get the new car, they can leave Reeve and his persiflage behind.

"I think they're gonna make me work late again tonight," he says, "those no-good sons of bitches."

Thank God. She is about to inquire what it is he does, exactly —he works in an office somewhere in Midtown, that much she knows—but then decides against it. She's done her duty, made polite conversation. She doesn't want to encourage any more of it than is absolutely necessary.

"You know, you're not at all like the girls Griff usually goes for," he says, throwing his legs over the arm of the chair. He takes another sip of the coffee. She can feel his gaze zeroing in on her, studying her.

"I have to say, when we were at NYU, he was a regular Rubirosa. He was the only guy I knew who could unhook a bra with one hand." Reeve's eyes bore into the side of her face. She refuses to look at him, to give him any validation of her own discomfort. If this is the worst she will endure to procure lasting happiness, it's a small price. "You're being very quiet," he says. "I'm sorry: have I shocked you?"

"On the contrary," Betty replies, casually turning the page of the magazine, "I confess I haven't been listening. I'm quite engrossed in my article."

"You're pretty as a brunette."

She says nothing.

He rises from the chair, walks to stand next to her as she sits on the daybed. He reaches out to touch her hair. She flinches, moves her head away. "Very pretty," he whispers. "Griff's a lucky guy. I gotta hand it to him. The man who got Miss America to run away with him."

He stands for another uncomfortable moment, looking down at her as he sips his cooling coffee. She keeps her eyes glued to the page, reads the same sentence over and over as adrenaline spreads inside, like an oozing blob. She can hear his breathing, smell the musk of him. It takes all of her resolve to sit immobile, express laxity. She must speak to Griff when he gets back. Forget the play. They have to leave, now. She cannot spend another night in this apartment with Reeve Spencer and his oily, menacing manner. "You're going to be quite late," she says softly under her breath, but loud enough for him to hear her.

He estimates her, then takes a step back. "Right you are," he says.

Reeve pads down the hall toward the bedroom, talking to himself, but this time loud enough for her to hear him. "Yeah, that Griff sure is a lucky guy. Too bad he's so fucked in the head."

❧

The knocking wakes her up.

Her mind clears gradually from the nap, like walking through an old attic, clearing cobwebs with your hand. For a moment she's disoriented. She props up on an elbow on the daybed, listening.

Tap tap tap.

No question. At the door of the apartment.

She bolts up.

Don't move! she commands herself. Terrible images flood her brain: the police, guns drawn, ready to escort her to a waiting car, photographers outside, waiting to capture an image of the disgraced Miss America.

Get ahold of yourself! You're not a criminal. Listen. Think!

A pause. Then again. *Tap tap tap.* Not a proper knocking, certainly not the urgent pounding one would expect from people in authority. Betty rises gingerly from the daybed, steps over the magazine that dropped onto the floor after she fell asleep. She creeps over toward the door.

"Hey, lady!" A voice, outside. Pitched but small. A child's. "C'mon! I know you're in there! Open up! I got a message for ya!"

She checks the chain across the door. Secure. Griff has been fanatical about his instructions to never answer the door, under any circumstances. Betty hesitates, and the tapping resumes. Clearly the boy is not going to leave.

Betty cracks the door open. "What do you want?" she whispers, careful not to fully show her face. She can see the boy is short, stout, with big brown eyes. He can't be more than ten.

"Finally! Sheesh! You're lucky he paid me to deliver this. Here!" The boy thrusts an envelope through the crack. It goes sailing onto the floor behind her, like an errant paper airplane. The boy rumbles down the stairs. She hears coins jingling in his pocket as he disappears, no doubt headed somewhere for ice cream paid for by his newfound wages.

Betty slams the door shut, turns the deadbolt, reflexively double-checks it.

She kneels to retrieve the unmarked white envelope, furtively tears it open.

She recognizes the handwriting at once—it's not the first note of its kind.

I KNOW YOU'RE IN THERE. MEET ME AT ADDRESS BELOW TODAY AT 3 OR I TELL THE WORLD WHERE YOU ARE.

Eighteen

The Nautilus is a seafood restaurant two blocks away on West Twenty-Third Street that touts its soft-shell crabs and offers a daily lunch special between eleven and three for $1.25. Eddie sits in a back booth, a piping cup of coffee in hand, a copy of the *New York Daily Mirror* on the table, paying no particular attention to either. With his little round glasses and gray blazer, he could pass for a graduate student. Only he is not a graduate student. He is a man with her life in his hands.

She scoots in, nods affirmatively when the waitress asks if she wants coffee. It feels like an eternity as the cup is filled. Betty unknots her head scarf, removes her sunglasses.

"A brunette," he says dryly. "That'll throw 'em off the scent."

"It's worked so far."

"Yeah, I can see things are going great." He slides the newspaper aside, reaches over to cover her hand in his. She retracts, like she's just been bitten. "Please don't."

He bows his head, his hand vanishing underneath the table as she takes a sip of the still-too-hot coffee. He doesn't seem to know what to do now, so he picks up his own cup, does the same. The silence is excruciating, like listening to a telephone ringing and no one picks it up.

"I could lose my job over this," he says finally.

"Over what?"

He looks at her, incredulous. "Over the fact that I am sitting on the biggest story not just in Atlantic City, but maybe in the entire country, and I am not telling my editors about it. In case you've forgotten, I am a newspaper reporter, Betty."

"Shhh!" she hisses, louder than she intends. Her eyes dart around the restaurant, shifty, like a thief's. "Don't say my name out loud. For Christ's sake."

"'For Christ's sake'? A week on the run and you're already swearing?"

She eyes him evenly. Whatever happens, she needs him on her side.

"I'm sorry. As you might imagine, I have been under a tremendous amount of strain. I'm just trying to . . . figure everything out."

"There's nothing to figure out. You need to come home."

"I can't."

"Why?"

"Why haven't you told anyone where I am?"

He leans back. "You know why. Or have you forgotten our last meeting, in the interview room after you won?"

There is nothing in that for her. "How did you find me?"

He deflates, issues a weary sigh. "I repeat: I'm a reporter. And a good one. Especially when I feel I understand the person I'm writing about."

"Eddie," she says softly. "I am so very sorry you are mixed up in any of this, and that I may be jeopardizing your job. I would never do anything to hurt you. You've been a good friend to me."

Hurt falls over his eyes like a pall. "That's all I am to you? A friend?"

Yes, she thinks. He is handsome, and there is no mistaking that he cares for her deeply. She knows little of the world of journalism, but she is not naïve enough not to know the risk he is taking by tracking her down and not telling his superiors. If someone else finds her and gets the story, and his bosses at the *Press* find out, his job is over. His career is probably over. You only do something like this for someone you love. She wishes she could love him back. How much easier that would be, to fall into his arms, to have him lead her back to the car, to go back to Delaware, forget any of this ever happened. But she, too, knows what love is. She loves Griff with all her heart. He's ill, fragile. He loves her and he needs her, and he did all of this for *her.* She cannot abandon him. She won't.

But she needs to buy time. So she looks Eddie squarely in the eye and says, "For now."

He blows out some air—whether in relief or frustration, she can't be sure. "You need to come back with me. I'll be able to smooth all of this out with the authorities, and I'll tell your story more sympathetically than any of the other mooks trying to find you will. I am your best shot at staying out of jail, Betty."

"Jail!"

His turn to look around. Two men three booths away glance over, then return to their argument about the Giants. "Careful."

"What do you mean," she utters in a panicked murmur, "jail?"

"There's a warrant out for Griff's arrest. Kidnapping is a federal offense."

"He didn't kidnap me!"

"They don't know that. You left half of your belongings, including your cosmetics, in the hotel room. It was clear you'd either been hustled out or taken out. There was blood on the carpet."

"I cut myself grabbing my razor." She studies his expression. "How did *you* know that I wasn't kidnapped?"

"I'm still not sure you haven't been."

"You sent me that note when you knew Griff was out. So obviously you've been here for a little while. And you didn't go to the police." She sinks back into the booth. "You knew. You knew I came here willingly."

"I wasn't certain. But I surmised it was likely, yes."

She looks down into her coffee cup, slowly putting the pieces together. "You spoke to Ciji."

He nods. "I spoke to Ciji. Not that she said much. I'm sure she told the police even less. I got a feeling she was unsure she had done the right thing by tracking Griff down for you."

"Even so, this doesn't make sense. I sent my parents a letter. I explained everything."

"Betty, I can assure you your parents never got any letter from you. They are sick with worry, wondering if you're even alive."

The news lands like a punch. Her poor parents, picturing her dead, lying somewhere by the side of the road. How did they not get the letter? *Griff.* He was supposed to mail it. Clearly he hadn't.

But why?

"This is all a colossal mistake," Betty says. "I'll explain it to everybody."

"It's not that simple, Betty. You can't just phone your family and say, 'Sorry for the mix-up.' The car Griff took technically belongs to his father. That's theft. And Griff took some money from his dad's locker at the marina. Old Man McAllister is hopping mad. He's pressed charges. If you tell them you were not forced into this, you could go down with him as an accomplice. Think about your family, Betty. Think about your *life.*"

She shakes her head. "No, no. There is no way that Honor

McAllister would allow her husband to press charges against her own son. She loves Griff more than anything in the world."

"She doesn't have much say in the matter. Rumor has it she's hired her own muscle to find you two. She's far more desperate than anyone to find Griff."

"Of course she is. He's her son."

"That isn't why."

His cat-and-mouse game is growing irksome. "Then why?"

"Griff is sick, Betty. Seriously sick."

"I know."

His eyes narrow. "You know? You know *what*, exactly?"

"He has a nervous condition. It's under control. He's good when he's with me. He just needs some medicine, that's all. He's out getting it now, as a matter of fact." She doesn't know why she's lying. "He just needs his medicine to keep calm. Stress triggers his ailment, and as I said, this has all been very stressful."

He reaches across the table, puts both of his hands atop hers. She tries to pull away again, but he is surprisingly strong, pins them to the tabletop.

"Betty, listen to me very carefully. Griff does not suffer from some mild nervous condition. He's extremely ill. He could be dangerous. He suffers from something called schizophrenia. Do you know what that is?"

She's heard of it, vaguely. "Not precisely."

"It's a serious mental disorder. Griff was diagnosed as an adolescent. He even had electroshock treatments for it a few years ago. It's why he had to drop out of NYU; there was some incident with a girl there. He's capable of wild mood swings and extreme paranoia. He sometimes hears voices in his head saying all sorts of terrible things. He doesn't always have a firm grip on reality."

With one violent jolt, she manages to tug her hands away. "You're making this up. I've been with Griff for over a week. He's perfectly fine. He hasn't shown a single symptom of anything being wrong. You're just trying to frighten me."

"No, I'm not. I wouldn't do that. I care too much about . . ." He trails off. "Schizophrenics can have extended periods where they show no outward signs of turmoil, even as their brain is attacking them with all sorts of delusions and commands. But the one part Griff was honest about was his need to avoid stress. It can trigger manic outbursts. And let's face facts, Betty: this is a stressful situation you've gotten yourself into. He could snap at any moment. You have to trust me. I deal in facts."

"How did you find out these particular 'facts'?"

"I spoke to his mother."

Betty tries to picture it, Eddie Tate in his hand-me-down sports jacket and crooked tie, sitting in front of a silver tea service in Honor McAllister's bay-front living room as she calmly explained that her son, her pride and joy, was a lunatic. Betty remembers the intercom connected to Griff's bedroom, Honor soothing him.

"She would never talk about Griff in such a way."

"She's his *mother*, Betty. Do you honestly think she would be hiring detectives to find him if he'd just gone off for a fling with some girl?"

Betty looks at him archly.

"I'm sorry. That was a crummy thing to say."

"Yes. It was."

"I'm only saying that she's trying to save his life. And she knows that the longer he is away from his doctors and his family, the more likely it is that he is going to hurt himself or people around him. I need you to understand the fix you're in. I can't let you go back to him."

A thought enters Betty's mind. "Does she know where you are?"

He looks her dead in the eye. "Nobody knows where I am. Or where you are. Yet."

"The police won't find us."

"I did."

"You're smarter," she says. "And you know . . . me . . . in a way they do not."

Something flashes in his eyes. As long as he has hopes that his feelings may be reciprocated at some juncture, he won't divulge her secret. She's sure of it.

The waitress comes, refills their cups. Betty glances at her watch. This is taking too long. Griff will be back soon. He'll go cock-eyed if he walks back into the apartment and she's not there.

"I have to go," she says.

"I won't let you."

And he won't. She can see the determination etched in his baby face. She has to buy more time. "I don't want anything bad to happen to him," she says deliberately, thinking out her argument as she enumerates it. "If he's as volatile as you say he is, then he could do anything if he finds out I've gone. I can't have that on my conscience, Eddie. I could never live with myself if something awful happened to him or anyone around him because of what he did for me. Something I asked him to do."

"Only because he didn't have the guts to be Miss America's boyfriend."

"You're being peevish."

He says nothing. His face is impassive, unreadable. "What are you suggesting, exactly?"

"I need to go back and get him to come *with* me. With us. Quietly. Reasonably."

"You'll never get him to do it."

"I got him to slip me out of Atlantic City without anyone knowing," she says curtly. "You'd be surprised what I can get him to do."

"So, what? You're just going to go back and say, 'Hey, Griff, let's take a walk'? And then we all get on the train at Pennsylvania Station?"

"Something like that, yes. We're supposed to go out tonight, in fact. And he doesn't know you're here. That anyone knows where we are." It's her turn to put her hand atop his. "I just need a few days. To talk to him, to get him to come around. I can do it, I promise. A few days, Eddie. That's all I'm asking for. Four days. Five at most."

"I'll give you thirty-six hours." He pulls out a pen, writes down an address. "This is the hotel where I'm staying. If I don't hear from you by midnight tomorrow, I'm coming to get you. And if you're gone, the whole tawdry story goes on the front page, his sick mind and all. Don't cross me, Betty."

Ten minutes later she is out on the street, headscarf tied firmly back around her head, sunglasses firmly in place. They'll go to the play tonight; they'll have a wonderful date, like the ones they had in Atlantic City. She'll find an opening, a way to get Griff to see they have to go back. She must.

Betty barely notices when she bumps shoulders with the man hurrying up Eighth Avenue, does not register his mumbled "Pardon me" as she keeps going her way and he keeps ambling along his.

She does not catch the look of grim satisfaction on his face as he turns up Twenty-Third Street, thinking to himself, *Yup. It's definitely her.*

❧

She allows herself this.

They stroll down Forty-Fourth Street, like any carefree couple on any carefree evening, the brisk autumn air bringing their arms even closer around each other. Griff has bought her a new Scottish tweed jacket, and after properly admonishing him for spending

178

money they do not have, she slipped it on, luxuriating in its beauty. Now they have just come from dinner, barbecued ribs at Embers on East Fifty-Fourth, he gleefully drowning their meal with hot sauce, she protesting in defense of her delicate stomach. Betty has never had beer before, was delighted by its acrid bitterness as it washed down the ribs. She has also never eaten at ten thirty at night — *Ten thirty! For dinner!* — but he insisted they eat after the play, that it would be fun to sit and dine late like regular New Yorkers. It is the kind of night that couples newly in love get to experience. She does not know how many more she will get to experience.

It is the first time since leaving Atlantic City that she has not been nervous out in public, looking over her shoulder. When they exited the apartment, she snuck a quick glance around, expecting to spy Eddie lurking in a doorway. But there was nothing but what one would expect on a Manhattan side street: people coming home, people going out, taxicabs honking, a giddy Labrador retriever galloping ahead of its master, a colored man playing a saxophone through one of the open windows. It was amazing how safe a big, bustling city could make you feel.

The walk home is long, the air crisp and delicious. "Tomorrow," he says.

"Tomorrow?"

"Tomorrow I go to pick up the car. Our new car. The guy couldn't find the papers, not that I should have been surprised by that."

She looks up at him, takes in his new face: he hasn't shaved since they got to New York, and depending on the light, his short, scruffy beard gives him the look of either a young literature professor or an anarchist. He's taken to wearing black-framed eyeglasses he really doesn't need, but which he feels help keep him disguised, part of their effort to hide in plain sight. Indeed, with his altered countenance and her new dark wavy hair, anyone who had snapped a photo of them the day before the pageant and then taken another today would be shocked to have them identified as the same people.

Not for the first time tonight, a question intervenes.

How can you be dangerous?

She considers Eddie's warning. Schizophrenia? How could Griff be suffering so and show no outward signs of it? There have been times he has been quiet, withdrawn, going back to when they first met in Atlantic City. Wasn't he moody the night they met, muttering at the bar? But then something had shifted, a light had come on. They'd gone to Captain Starn's, and he'd eaten that monstrous meal, and they'd flirted over the table, and she'd sent the penny splashing into the wishing well. How long ago it all seemed.

If it is a condition wrought by stress, certainly this week would have been enough to bring it on in full. And yet here they are, two young people in love, walking through a gentle mist that has begun to coat the streets of New York, giggling about everything and nothing.

She has twenty-four hours to convince him to give up their plans and return to Atlantic City, or else suffer a monstrous scandal that will lead the authorities right to them and consume every front page in the country. Either way, their escape from reality is coming to an end. Which she worries may actually be the thing that does, in fact, make him sick.

She wishes to preserve this for as long as she can, even as the ticking of the clock in her head grows louder by the hour, counting down the time until her bargain with Eddie must be kept. And it must be. Betty knows that it must be, just as, deep down, she has always known that this adventure could not last forever. Adventures never do.

Betty leans into Griff. "Darling, I wanted to talk to you about something—"

"Look up," he says, turning them around.

She glances up at him, follows his sightline.

They have arrived at the west side corner of Broadway and For-ty-Fourth, in the heart of Times Square. On the other side of the street is a twenty-seven-foot-high sign trumpeting: BOND. Under-neath it is a running electric scroll of the headlines—"United Na-tions Headquarters to Be Dedicated," blares one—and under that is more neon signage, declaring: TWO TROUSER SUITS. There is a huge waterfall behind it, and on either side seven-story-tall statues of a man and a woman, acting as bookends. A giant clock above the waterfall declares, "Every hour 3,490 people buy at Bond." The building practically vibrates from all of the flashing lights.

"This place, Betty, this city!" Griff exclaims. "I mean, look at it! You come here and you never know what you're going to see, what you're going to do next." He turns to her. "Like this."

His kiss is lingering and powerful, a kiss that attacks the senses. She is at once ravenous, for the touch of him, the smell of him, the taste of him. She puts her left hand behind his neck, pulls him in, as if by sheer force the two of them can meld into one person.

When they finally break, she is almost dizzy. Griff takes her hands in his. And then, with the spinning playground of Times Square behind him, drops to his knee.

"Betty Jane Welch, my love, my heart," he says, with a look in his eyes so pure, so vulnerable, that it brings her to tears. "Will you marry me?"

Nineteen

etty can hear Griff humming in the bathtub. It is the most relaxed he's seemed since they left Atlantic City. Sun slants in through the window shades as she makes up the day-bed. Reeve has already mercifully left for work. Griff mentioned at dinner last night that Reeve was wondering "when he was getting his apartment back." To which Betty wanted to respond, *Not soon enough*.

Perhaps she should be more kind, she considers, as she fluffs the pillows. After all, Reeve did take them in. And surely it has been trying, having two additional people—fugitives, no less—underfoot the moment you wake up and the moment you come home from work, in a tiny one-bedroom walkup in Chelsea. Before they go they need to give him something—a bottle of bourbon, a carton of cigarettes.

For they are leaving tonight. This afternoon Griff will drop off their Mercury, now parked in some secret location only he knows, and trade it for the Fleetline, and off they go. To Buffalo—they are literally shuffling off to Buffalo. Griff has a friend there who can give him work in his dairy, which Griff has tried to convince Betty —and, she suspects, also himself—is just the same as working in a nursery. What was it he said? "It's all nature." Perhaps that is enough. She tunes back into his humming, tries to discern the song. "Sugar Moon"?

Betty steps into the bathroom, pulls the towel from the rack. "You need to get out of there before you turn into a prune."

He reaches out. "Or maybe you should just come in." He starts tugging her toward the tub.

"Griffin McAllister, if you get me soaking wet in this dress . . . Don't you dare!"

He stops tugging but doesn't let go. "You make me so happy, Betty. So incredibly happy. You know that, don't you?"

She kneels down by the tub, kisses him softly. "I do. I feel so blessed to have found you."

"So you don't regret it? Giving up being Miss America, all of it?"

"Of course not. Not for a minute." She sighs, looks away.

"But?"

She cannot stop thinking about her family never getting her letter. She's tried to argue with herself that it might have been lost in the mail. She does not want to admit the likelier scenario: that Griff lied to her about sending it.

"Today is September twenty-first," she whispers.

He caresses her hand. "What's September twenty-first?"

"It's Ricky's birthday. He's eleven today. And not only am I not there, but the whole day is probably being overshadowed by the fact that I am not there. I know we did what we had to. I do. But our families, Griff. They're paying a price for it. It makes me sad."

"It's not like you're never going to see your family again, Betty. We talked about this. We just need—"

"To go back when everything's settled. I know, I know. But when will that be? How long? What are we waiting for, exactly? We'll go to Buffalo, save some money. But I need to know when this is all going to end. I can't live like this indefinitely. I want to go home; I want my family to know you." Fresh tears come. "I want to plan my wedding."

"Oh, baby . . . baby," he says, sitting upright in the tub and taking her into his slippery arms. His beard tickles her cheek. "I'm sorry. I know it's been hard. But it's temporary. And we've had fun, haven't we? I did this all for you, you remember? You asked me to do this."

She nods over his shoulder. He's right. She did. Though he seems to have forgotten that it was his decision to break her heart at the Steel Pier ball that started this snowball down the slope. What might have happened if he hadn't?

There is no time for that now. "Yes. Yes, I did." She breaks from his embrace. "Yes, of course. I'm sorry. I'm just being silly. I'll . . . I'll go make us some breakfast while you get dressed."

Betty closes the door behind her, hears the gentle splash of the water a few seconds later, the sounds of him stepping out of the tub, vigorously drying himself. She walks to the kitchen, retrieves half a cantaloupe from the icebox.

He did this for her. When he told her he had a plan, she had not asked a single question about what it was. What right did she have to ask him to give it all up now? To possibly go to prison? It would be easier to negotiate from afar, to grease the wheels, call his family, negotiate a return. To have time. Except they are out of time.

Eddie Tate is expecting them tonight at his hotel. And if they don't show, the jig will be up. It will be worse. So much worse.

She thinks again of Ricky, his birthday ruined due to her selfishness. And what of Simon, Patsy, her parents? Was her father walking around the bank, seeing nothing but serious faces pitying the father of the kidnapped Miss America? And her mother. Her mother, no doubt now avoided by the Junior League, whispered about as she passes through every market and shop, worrying about her every night, wondering if she's safe, with no one to tell her otherwise. How much worse will it be when Betty finally does come home, when she has to face the truth of her own deception and its consequences? When she is unmasked not as the kidnapped Miss America but merely the wayward one, plastered with a scarlet letter her mother will wear with her for the rest of her life?

The consequences of her actions collapse on top of her with the weight of a building being demolished. She slumps against the kitchen counter, begins sobbing.

What have I done?

She can no longer outrun the truth. They cannot go to Buffalo. They can't go anywhere but home. She must call her family, tell them where she is, beg their forgiveness, hope that their collective relief will be enough to mitigate the pain she's caused them. She must get Griff to phone his mother, tell her the truth, tell her they are coming back to sort it all out, how sorry they both are. She will call Eddie. He'll be sympathetic, tell a measured story, lay the groundwork for emerging from whatever legal entanglements they face. A narrative begins to form in her head, of being overwhelmed by the entire week in Atlantic City, of feeling trapped, of reacting badly. Betty will explain that she dragged Griff into it. That he only did what he did out of love, a sense of duty to her, and because she begged him to.

It's been less than two weeks, not months. The damage is reversible.

It's a plan, and the thought of it steadies her. She slices the cantaloupe, puts in two slices of bread for toast. She hears Griff getting dressed in the bedroom, the humming now turned to whistling.

I need to tell him, she decides. *I need to tell him now.*

❧

She has dithered for the last hour. How to do it? Was it better to be sitting at the breakfast table, calmly broach the idea, as if it were nothing more than discussing what to do that afternoon? Or was it likely to be more palatable in a closer, more intimate repose, the two of them lying together on the daybed, engaging in midmorning pillow talk?

Betty watches him gulp the last of his orange juice, push back from the table. "I should get going soon. I said I would be there sometime around noon to swap the cars. It's better if we leave after dark." He meets her stare. "Sugar? What's wrong?"

She takes a deep breath. "I need to talk to you about something very important."

His look telegraphs confusion rather than expectancy.

"Sweetheart," she begins, in a voice that registers somewhere between a plea and a warning, the kind you might give to a child who was drifting into the deep end of a swimming pool, "I have to ask you something: Did you really mail that letter to my family?"

His face darkens. "Why would you ask me that?"

"Because I need to know. And I need to know the truth, Griff. Did you post the letter? Just please be honest with me. I promise I won't be cross."

She can see him thinking.

"Baby, I couldn't. Don't you see? It would have had a postmark on it. They would have found us right away. We needed that time. For us. But now, now we'll go to Buffalo, and you can call them as soon as we get there, I promise."

She pictures her mother sitting at their kitchen table at this very moment, wringing a dishtowel in her hands, crying. "My parents, Griff. My *mother*. We've been gone almost two weeks! Do you have any idea how devastated they must be, what I've put them through? My brother—"

"You said you wouldn't be cross! And . . . and we talked about this." His voice climbs, cracks like an adolescent boy's. "Honey, we went over all of this. And remember, this was all your idea—"

"You need to stop saying that!" She leaps up from the table. "It's horribly unfair. Yes, I asked you to get me out of being Miss America, that's true. I accept that. But I only *had* to do that because I loved you, because you told me you wouldn't be with me unless I *wasn't* Miss America. I . . . I didn't know . . . it would be like this. I can't live like this. I miss my family, my life." She scurries around the table, drops to her knees before him. "I'm not blaming you, my dearest, I swear to you I'm not. I feel like the luckiest girl in the world. I want to be your wife; I want us to grow old together. It's just that things are clearer now. We can't stay engulfed in the shadows."

"We'll go to Buffalo—"

"No, no. No. Listen to me. We can't go to Buffalo. You mustn't be afraid. We'll go back, and I will explain everything. And then we can start making our plans together. Make sure you're well."

Instantly, she wants to take it back. But it is too late.

His hands are quick, darting down and grabbing her roughly by the arms, lifting her up as he rises from his chair. "*What* did you say?"

"You said you couldn't be under stress. I only meant—"

"Who have you been talking to? Who? Who?!"

"No one, I promise. Stop. Griff, you're hurting me!"

He pushes her away, stalks into the living room. She looks on as he paces, over and over, over and over, clutching his head. His lips are moving, faster now, the muttering audible but unintelligible. There is a look on his face, a slow, frightening devolution, as if his senses are melting right before her eyes. An expression takes over, a look she has never before seen, not on him, not on anyone. The remnants of the cantaloupe rumble in her stomach, threaten to rise into her throat.

She startles backwards against the kitchen counter as he grabs a table lamp and flings it against the exposed brick wall, where it shatters into pieces. His face is wild, feral, painted in hues of anguish. He reaches for the floor lamp.

"No!" she screams.

Betty dashes into the living room, flings her arms around him. "Darling, no! No! The police will come! We can't have that. We can't have that. I'm sorry. I'm sorry!"

His chest heaves and she pulls him closer. *If I can just calm him down,* she thinks. *If I can just calm him down.*

Okay, okay. We can do this. He's not moving. We can do this.

Then he staggers away from her, like a drunkard trying to find his way home. He collapses onto the daybed, throws his head into his hands. "You don't understand, you don't understand . . ." He's crying, gulping for air.

She creeps over to the daybed, slowly sits down next to him, starts lightly rubbing his back. "What, darling? What is it I don't understand? I'm listening. I love you, I'm here, I'm listening."

He looks at her, tears now streaming down his cheeks, disappearing into his short beard. "You don't hear them, do you?"

"Hear what?"

"The voices."

Betty indeed hears something—the echo of Eddie Tate. *He hears voices in his head. He doesn't have a firm grip on reality.*

"They're so loud sometimes," he continues. "You can't understand how loud they are. It's not my fault God speaks to me like this. The Devil doesn't like it. And then he gets angry. So very angry. And the voices start yelling at me, all at once. Why? Why do they pick me for their battles? Why can't they just leave me alone?"

"Honey," she says, with as much equanimity as she can summon, "what are the voices saying to you? What do they want?"

"Lots of things."

"So they are speaking to you right now?"

"Yes."

"Both of them?"

"There's not just two!" he screams, hopping up from the daybed, running about the room, flailing his arms. "You don't understand! No one understands! Don't you see? There's four main ones. But there can be hundreds! Hundreds! I've been chosen. I didn't ask to be chosen. Why was I chosen?" He turns back, registers the fear in her eyes. "Doll baby," he says, sliding on his knees toward her on the hardwood floor. A piece of the broken lamp slices his trouser leg; a small circle of blood begins to form on his right knee.

"You're hurt," Betty says.

"You have to help me. You're the only thing that keeps them quiet. When I met you . . ." He trails off.

"What, Griff? What about when we met?"

"Do you remember the moment we met?"

Of course she does. His sauntering across the ballroom floor, her breathlessness at his beauty. Two weeks ago. It feels like a hundred years. "Of course."

"That moment . . . that was like a veil lifting. It was . . . liberating. Because for the first time in my life, my heart was in charge, not my head. You make me better. You heal me. I can make it. I know I can, as long as you're there with me. But not if we go back. We can't go back. Not yet. She'll—"

"She'll? She'll what, Griff? Who? Your mother?"

He nods, almost imperceptibly. She can barely hear his voice. "She'll put me back there. They'll hook me up to all of those wires." He looks at her, his eyes pooled and vulnerable, in his softest whisper issuing a deafening plea for understanding.

For love.

Betty takes his hands in hers, interlacing their fingers together as tight as a knot. She cannot say anything except the truth.

"I am going to take care of you, sweetheart," she says, bending down and kissing his forehead. "I promise."

❧

Honor McAllister dials the number.

"I got your message," she says when he picks up. "You're certain it was her."

"Positive. I wasn't sure at first: she's dyed her hair black. It makes her look completely different. But I followed her to a restaurant. She met some guy there."

"My son?"

"No."

"Then who?"

"You hired us to find her, I found her. You want me to look up everyone she interacts with, that's gonna cost extra."

His impertinence irritates her, but she has little leverage. For God's sake, the FBI was out looking for Betty—allegedly—and yet Honor's own private detective had found her first. Whatever his lack of manners, his reputation as being the best around was clearly not hyperbole.

"So what about my son? Have you seen him?"

"Not yet. But he's gotta be in this apartment. I mean, obviously they don't go out much, and I can't be across the street twenty-four hours. You didn't want to hire any extra help here."

She exhales coolly. It had been her idea for the two of them to split up, to cover more ground. Now the skinny one was God knows where. She couldn't risk losing this chance by waiting for him to get to New York.

Because she knew what Griffin was like in the middle of one of his episodes. There was no telling what he'd do if he thought there were a bunch of brutes outside his door, waiting to drag him back to Longport. Or somewhere worse. He would never come peacefully, and she needed him, more than anything, to come peacefully. There was only one possible way that was going to occur.

She'd already wasted so much time, investing in wild-goose chases with Griffin's known friends and acquaintances up and down the Eastern Seaboard. The big detective had finally gone to NYU, found out who had roomed with him that one semester. *Reeve Spencer*. Now they had his address in Chelsea—and, more important, Griffin and Betty.

And oh, Betty. Pretty, kind, well-mannered Betty, who had stunned everyone by winning the Miss America title for Delaware. And all of these tabloids with their ridiculous headlines, fed by that incompetent Atlantic City police force, which couldn't find sand. Kidnapped! Griffin, a kidnapper! The very idea was ludicrous. He was ill, yes. He occasionally had . . . unseemly thoughts, which needed to be controlled. But he would never have taken her against her will. It wasn't his nature, nor the nature of his illness. Everyone thought that schizophrenics were these wild creatures, spinning in every direction. Griffin was nothing like that. He was gentle, well-mannered, loving. He fought to live every single day. The only thing he needed was simple: to avoid stress.

Honor recalls that horrible night a few years ago, of getting the telephone call from the office at NYU, of rushing up to New York and having to admit him to Bellevue to avoid the police, everything that came after. *I cannot put him through that again.*

I cannot put myself through that again.

Yet here they were. He was on the run with the abdicated Miss America. So many questions, all unanswerable: Why did she have to win? Honor remembers going to Miss Slaughter, suggesting, in a very banal, backhanded manner, that it might be best if Griffin was paired with a girl with little prospect of earning the title. Miss Delaware? Miss Delaware sounded divine. The state had not sent a contestant in five years!

It was all her fault. But what was done was done. There was only one thing to do now. Get to Griffin before anyone else.

"My driver is on his way here," she tells the detective. "We should be in Manhattan by dinnertime. Make sure you sustain surveillance of the apartment until I arrive. I mean it—no cigarette runs. Pee in your pants if you have to. But you are not to let your eyes off of that apartment. We'll pull up to you on Twenty-First Street and you can get in, and then we can discuss the best method for retrieving my son."

"And the girl? We retrieving her, too?"

"We shall see," Honor McAllister replies icily. "Griffin is my priority."

She is not a religious woman by nature—she attends the Episcopal Church of the Redeemer every week because her husband and her community expect her to, but she finds little comfort in the words and rituals of the church. She has learned, in the most brutal way possible, the value of dealing with hard truth, with coping with life as it is, not as you wish it to be.

But it does not stop her from placing her palms face-down on the secretary, turning her eyes to the ceiling.

Please, dear God, she prays, *don't let this be another Helen Stevens.*

❧

Betty wakes first, momentarily disoriented. They're on the daybed, the late afternoon September sun tinting the living room shades a deep gold. She is lying behind Griff, her arm around him, protective, like a mother with her sleeping child. They're in their clothes, no shoes. *That's right.* She'd removed his shoes, then her own, convinced him to lie down with her, "just for a few minutes," until they'd both drifted into the shallow, medicinal sleep that always follows emotional tumult.

She remains still for a moment, watching his shoulders slowly rise, up, down, up, down, tracking his steady breathing. Her darling love, betrayed by a mind that won't let him rest. And now she has awoken the beast inside him, sent him spiraling downward.

Betty creeps slowly away from the daybed, grabs her shoes, scurries off into the bedroom. *I need to think.*

But what is there to think about it? The answer is clear, even if it smacks of betrayal. She loves him. But when you love someone, you do what is best for them, what they need, even if they themselves cannot see it. But she sees it. She must.

Over the next two hours, she goes over everything: every option, every misstep she's made, and how to correct it. A plan takes final shape in her head. She hears Griff stirring in the living room. She plasters a knowing smile on her face and walks back in, sits down beside his stretched-out form.

"Do you feel any better?" she asks, stroking his hair. "Can I fix you something to eat?"

His eyes flutter, as if he's trying to concentrate. "What time is it?"

Betty glances at the clock hanging in the kitchen. "Almost six."

Griff jerks up, rubs his face awake. "Dang! I gotta blow. I'm really late. I need to get the cars swapped if we're going to get out of here tonight."

We're not going anywhere, Betty thinks.

"Of course. Is there anything you need to bring with you?"

He looks up at her. "Yes. You."

"Me? That doesn't seem wise, Griff. It's one thing to go out after dark; it's another to risk being seen together during the day."

"I'm afraid, Betty. I'm afraid if I go out, you won't be here when I get back. I'm sorry about before. I just feel like I can't . . . breathe. It'll be better when we get to Buffalo. You'll still come with me, won't you? You won't leave me?"

193

His face is that of a five-year-old, panicked at his father going off to war. "No, Griff, I won't leave you alone, I swear," she says, noting her own parsing and hoping he does not. "I told you I would take care of you, and I am going to do that. I give you my word."

Seemingly mollified, he dips his head onto her shoulder. "Okay, then," he says.

"Okay, then."

When the door to the apartment closes fifteen minutes later, Griff en route to their car and the swap, Betty looks back at the clock. How long before he gets back? It's hard to say—she has no idea where in the city the exchange of vehicles is happening, if license plates need to be interchanged. But it can't be less than an hour. Hopefully an hour is all she needs.

Betty rushes to the telephone, jerks up the receiver, and dials the operator. "Long-distance operator, please," she commands, counting the interminable seconds until a second nasally voice pipes onto the line. "Yes, I need to make a collect call to the McAllister residence on Amherst Avenue, in Longport, New Jersey."

"Who may I say is calling?"

Betty clears her throat. "Betty."

It takes five maddening minutes for the call to be put through. Betty is about to jump out of her own skin when she hears the operator asking for the charges to be accepted by the answering party, hears a tentative feminine "yes" in the distance.

"Hello? Hello?" Betty practically shouts into the receiver. "Are you there?"

"Betty? Betty?! Is it really you? Jeepers!"

Martha, Griff's sister.

"Yes, Martha, it's me. Listen—"

"Where are you? Are you all right? Is Griff okay? Everyone is just—"

"Martha, listen! I don't have much time. You must listen carefully. I need you to get a message to your mother. We're in New York. She needs to come. I'll give you the address."

A pause. "She already has it."

Betty feels her stomach plunge. "She . . . she does? She knows where we are?"

"Yes. She hired some private investigators to find you. She's on her way up there right now."

Betty takes another glance at the clock. "When did she leave?"

"I'm not sure—she was gone when I got home a half hour ago. She just left me a note telling me she was going to New York to get Griff and everything was going to be fine and to tell Daddy when he gets home that she'd call him later."

So Honor was alone. That was good. Griff would be better if his mother came alone. He does not like his father, does not trust him, rarely speaks of him. But this also means Honor McAllister may be knocking on the apartment door at any moment. There is no time to spare.

"All right, then. That's good news."

"He didn't do it, did he? He didn't really kidnap you? I mean, good golly, he couldn't do a thing like that. I keep telling all the kids at school that Griff could never do such a thing."

How young Martha sounds. She cannot be more than four or five years younger than Betty herself, but it's a testament to how many years have passed in Betty's soul these past two weeks. She feels like an old woman inside, already weary of the world. Poor Martha. Another in a long line of Betty's victims. "No, Martha, he didn't. Everything is going to be fine." She can hear the girl's relief on the other end. "Now I must go. But we'll be home soon." They're about to hang up when a thought zips across Betty's mind. "Martha, I need you to do something for me. It's rather important. I need you to get a message to my family in Delaware that I am all right, that we spoke, and that I'll be home in a day or two and will explain everything. Can you do that for me? I'll give you the number."

Martha dutifully writes it down, swears she will dispatch the task, like a Girl Scout pledging a service oath. Betty puts her finger down in the cradle, waits for a new dial tone. She swings the dial once again, pulls out the piece of paper Eddie gave her. "Yes, I'd like to be connected to the Hotel Chesterfield on Forty-Ninth Street, please."

It takes a few minutes before the hotel switchboard patches her through to Eddie's room. The phone rings. *Ring. Ring. Ring.* A hotel operator comes back on the line. "I'm sorry, miss, but your party doesn't seem to be answering. May I take a message for the front desk?"

"Yes, please," Betty replies. "Tell Mr. Tate that . . . Miss Betty called. That she'd like him to meet her at this address at his earliest convenience." She gives Reeve's address, has the operator read it back to her.

She hangs up the phone. Honor will come, soothe him, calm him. Perhaps she has medicine with her. Eddie will get her message, arrive and help, organize, protect her from what will surely be Honor's rightful wrath. Griff will be horribly upset at first, but it will be temporary. In the end, this is what's best. She knows it.

Betty bends underneath the daybed, slides out her suitcase, and starts packing.

Twenty

"Well. *What do we* have here?"

Betty whirls around. How did she not hear Reeve come in? She has been so intent on her packing that she never noticed the advancing shadows of night, his key in the door. He stands in front of her breathing heavily, as if he's just run down the block. His eyes are glassy, unfocused. As he ambles toward her, the smell intensifies: whiskey, on his breath, oozing out of his pores. She has no idea how much he's drunk, but she knows it's a lot.

"I'm packing," she replies, trying to stay casual, airy, as if she's just bumped into the landlady in the hall and shared that she's off to the washateria. She will be so relieved to be rid of Reeve, to leave New York, to go home and put this mess of her own creation behind her. "Griff is out getting the car. We're leaving."

"Mmm. That's good." Reeve walks over slowly and plops down on the daybed, watching her through his haze.

Fold, smooth, place. Fold, smooth, place. Betty strains not to make eye contact, to focus on her task, and appear carefree as she does it. "I'm sure you'll be happy to be rid of us. You've been very kind to take us in for so long."

He tilts his head. "You think so?"

Betty meets his stare, despite her better instincts. "Of course. It was very generous. We both very much appreciate it." She tries to will Griff back, wonders how close Honor is to the city. She has spent days in silent panic, flinching at any motion at the door, and now prays for someone to walk through it.

Fold, smooth, place.

Reeve slides onto one elbow. "I'm a little drunk."

"Tough day?"

"You might say that. I got fired."

She stops folding. "What? Why?"

"Because they're sons of bitches, that's why." The words are labored but surprisingly clear. He's neither mildly intoxicated nor falling-down drunk, but rather lolling somewhere in between. "Coming off a toot," as her mother used to wearily describe her uncle Leonard. The face of her mother again leaps into her consciousness, and Betty is unprepared for the impact. How worried she must have been all of this time. How stupid, how selfish Betty has been.

Reeve spies her glassy look. "Oh, don't cry for me, baby," he says, reaching up with his left hand and lightly brushing her cheek with the backs of his fingers. "I'll be okay. Ol' Reeve always knows how to get himself right again."

She shakes him off, snaps the lid of the case shut. There's more to pack—Griff has some clothes hanging in Reeve's bedroom—but they can wait. Or they can leave them. Betty only wants someone, anyone, to come.

Why is no one coming?

Reeve springs up from the daybed, his face suddenly inches from hers. "You sort of owe me, you know," he says.

She doesn't respond, externally at least, even as dread seizes her insides. She wonders if he's one of those people who can smell others' fear.

"I saved you and your sweetie, hid you, gave you a place to sleep, *to make love all day* . . . And what do I have to show for it? Tell me! Huh? What?"

It's foolish to engage. But she's too scared of what will happen if she doesn't. Better to keep him talking.

"You have been very good to us, Reeve, as I said. We appreciate it. We were going to take you to dinner. But now we have to leave sooner than we expected. But I promise, we'll find a way to properly show our gratitude."

He leans closer, whispers in her ear. "I know a way you can show your gratitude. Right now."

The breathy malevolence in his voice strikes her like a body blow. Betty turns, grabs her coat from the back of the kitchen chair, swipes her bag off the table. "I need to go out for a bit, buy some things for the trip."

Before she can reach the door, Reeve bolts up, blocking her path, surprisingly agile for someone so intoxicated. "I just told you I lost my job today," he says, his stare accusing, steely. "And now you're all bad business."

Betty is paralyzed.

"I need to use the bathroom," is all she says.

Before she can get to the safety of the locked door of the bathroom, he lunges, grabs her roughly by the arms. "That can wait," he whispers urgently, and now his mouth is on hers, on her cheek, on her earlobe, on her neck, his lips brittle and chapped, his tongue dry and acrid, slithering around her face and clavicle. She struggles to break free of his grip, but even drunk he is strong, determination turning his hands into vises. "Stop!" Her head thrashes about on her neck, trying to avoid his mouth. "Reeve, let go! You're hurting me!"

"No, baby, no, Reeve will make you feel good. So, *so good*," he says, pushing her toward the bedroom.

She forces her body to relax into his hold, feels Reeve's arms loosen their grip just a bit in response. She even manages a soft moan, as if she's enjoying this.

He never sees her elbow coming until it's already slamming into his rib cage.

Reeve cries out, his arms instinctively flying to his side as Betty unlocks from his grasp, pushes him out of her path as she flies toward the apartment door.

He crashes onto his knees, extends his body, and flings his right hand out, catches her ankle and yanks. Off balance, she careens into the chair by the desk, which topples over, sending her tumbling down onto the floor. Her body lands with a bruising thud onto the hardwood; her elbow is bleeding. She writhes around on her stomach, like a rattlesnake escaping a trap, kicking her left leg violently to try to dislodge his grip. But instead he uses the hand he has around her ankle as a pulley, drawing himself closer, until he is on top of her, pinning her stomach to the floor.

In one muscular swoop, he pulls her up to him by the torso, both of them now on their knees. "Oh, a fighter. I like that. I bet Griff does, too. You want to play, girlie?" he whispers, his breath bitter and sour. "'Cause I'm the best player there is."

He scrambles to his feet, drags her upward, backing her toward the bedroom once more. He spins her around, falls on top of her on the messy unmade bed, jackknifing his knees between her legs, prying them open, trapping her right arm behind her head as she frantically beats on his chest with her left.

His movements are precise, almost militaristic. And the thought comes to her.

He's done this before.

She feels the fingers of his right hand spidering up her leg, unhooking her stocking. They continue up their path, marching toward her corselet, probing, insistent. When he thrusts into her with his middle finger, she arches her back in pain.

Her head explodes in terror and shame so loud that she cannot even hear herself screaming.

"Get off me! Get . . . off . . . me! No! No! Don't!!!"

With her free hand, she claws at him with all of her remaining strength. She manages to poke him right in the eye.

He yells out in pain, relaxes his body for a moment, and in the few seconds she's bought, Betty manages to wriggle out from underneath him. But just as her feet hit the bedroom floor, he pulls her back violently onto the bed. His voice is low, dripping with evil. "A real spitfire, ain't you? Miss America! Ha! You want Griff, do you, baby? You want good ole, sensitive, happy Griff? You're a dope, you know that? 'Cause you know who can't *ever* be right again? Griff. Griff has some serious problems there, cookie. As crooked as a corkscrew, that one. You think you're the first girl he's got all moony? Ask him about Helen Stevens. She was cuckoo for him, too. Ask him what happened to *her*."

His lips clamp back down roughly on hers, and she tries to bite him, but he is too strong, deceptively strong for a man so lean and angular, and as Betty thrashes around, he seems to almost anticipate her choreography, to be one step ahead, to have his cracked lips ready to cover hers at any angle. She hears the zipper of his pants almost as if the sound were coming from afar, somewhere in the distance, not here, on top of her, and she feels his thickness pressed against her—insistent, monstrous—and in the few seconds where she is able to speak, she begs him not to do this, begs him to stop, begs and protests and screams, speaking softly, then screaming in hysteria, but she's trapped, immobilized. She cannot prevent this from happening, and it is this, the knowing what is coming, the knowing that she is helpless and alone and that he is going to take what he wants, and that she will live with the damage from it for the rest of her life, that sends the gasps and gulping sobs choking inside her throat, the tears running like rivulets down her inflamed cheeks.

And then he cries out, in a voice she at first mistakes for passionate release. But when she dares to open her eyes again to look at his face, poised above hers, she sees his eyes rolling, like a penny circling down the drain, and she feels his body slack, his arms going limp, and as she seizes the opportunity to push him away, slide from underneath him, his body slumps off the bed, crumpling into a heap on the bedroom floor.

And that is when Betty realizes that there is blood on her arm, and on her dress, and a trail, brown-red like dark Georgia clay, leading to the floor, where it has begun to pool around Reeve's head. And then she screams.

There is a gaping wound on the side of his head, the blood oozing out, matting his hair, funneling into his ear canal. But his eyes remain open, unblinking.

She hears a heavy object clunk onto the bedroom floor, sees the heavy glass ashtray, now covered in Reeve's blood and lying a few feet away from his body. Griff stands before her, reaches down for her, pulls her to him. His right hand is also covered in his friend's blood, which smears the back of her dress as she folds herself into his embrace. And then the room is suddenly quiet, so very, very quiet, and the only thing Betty can hear is the collective heaving of their mutual breathing, staggered and furious. Her body shudders violently, erupting in spasms, as if an Arctic chill has just whistled through the window. She can't catch her breath. Griff kisses her temple, draws her tighter into his arms.

"It's okay, honey, it's okay. It's all over now," he finally whispers, and she does not believe him, for she knows it is not over.

It is only just beginning.

I'm in a nightmare.

❧

Griff escorts her shaking form into the living room, washes his hands in the sink, reaches for the suitcase and places it by the door. He pours her a glass of bourbon, hands it to her. "Here, sip this. Stay out of the bedroom," he commands. "I just have to get a few things in the closet and then we can leave."

Betty grabs him. "What do you mean? Griff, we can't go anywhere. We must call the police!"

He looks at her as though she's just suggested that they jump from the roof. "Police! Police? Are you mad? Betty, there's a dead man in the next room! A man I killed! They'll lock me away forever!"

"No, my darling, they won't! You were defending me. They'll understand. I'll explain everything, about how Reeve attacked me and you came in and saved my life. Everyone will know you did it to protect me."

Griff handles her roughly by the arm, shoves her down onto the daybed before kneeling before her. His brow sweats. There's a petrified glaze over his eyes. "Betty, listen to me. They already think I kidnapped you—"

"But that's not tr—"

"Betty! Please! Listen to me! You *have* to listen to me. They are never going to believe us. They will insist I took you, I hid you. They'll say Reeve was blackmailing me, threatening to go to the police or the press and expose us, so I killed him. That's the story they're going to believe, because that's the story that fits.

They won't care about what truly happened. They'll turn you against me."

"I could never turn against you."

His face turns hard, as if he's just been told very bad news. "That's not true. You already have."

Her heart nearly stops. *Eddie. Does he know? Does he know she called home?*

Betty searches his eyes for clues. Nothing. "I don't know what you mean."

"Yes, you do. They've told me you do. They've told me all along that I couldn't trust you. But I did, because I loved you."

"Griff, what are you talking about? Who is telling you such things? I do love you! More than anything! Which is why we have to go to the police, to explain everything. This has to stop!" She grabs his arms, tries to break through. "Please, Griff, I'm begging you!"

She starts to get up from the daybed, reaches for the phone, but he pulls her back down, shaking her. "I'm not going back, do you hear me? We can't go back now. I've just committed murder."

"It was self-defense—"

"It was *murder!* They'll ask why didn't I just pull him off you, why didn't I just sock him in the nose? Why did I have to grab the ashtray, use it like a baseball bat to his head?"

The prick of truth pierces her. *Yes, they will ask that,* she thinks. But she cannot will herself to say aloud what comes into her head next.

Why didn't you?

Griff takes her back in his arms, still kneeling. Betty fights the urge to stiffen, to push him away.

"Honey bear," he whispers into her ear, stroking her hair now, "I was just so crazy when I saw what he was doing, that's all. I couldn't think straight. I didn't even know it was happening. It was just instinct, was all. I had to make him stop, right then, right there. I had to make sure he couldn't hurt you anymore. So I grabbed the ashtray . . ." She tunes out the rest. She doesn't need to hear it.

Because it's all coming together now, the visual of Griff walking into the apartment, hearing her struggle in the bedroom, rushing in, and seeing what was happening. But instead of doing what any other person would do — grabbing Reeve by the shoulders, pulling him off, wrestling him over, knocking him out — Griff had found a weapon and, with one, precise, fatal blow, killed his college roommate by crushing his skull.

Almost as if he'd been waiting for the chance.

Betty tries to push the idea away. Impossible. There was no way Griff could have known Reeve would attack her, and certainly no way he could have timed it perfectly to fatally intervene. But his instinct. His instinct had not been to rescue.

His instinct had been to kill.

Betty steps out of her thoughts, sees Griff now pacing about the room, babbling, as if he's arguing a legal case in front of a jury. Who is he speaking to? She knows who he is speaking to. Them.

She wants to go home. She must concentrate on that. Getting home.

Griff retrieves her new coat. "We have to go, right now," he says, holding it out for her. "C'mon, Betty! Put the coat on!"

"The rest of your clothes —"

"There's no time for that now." He puts on his hat, rams his hands into his coat pockets. She hears the jingle of keys. When his right hand emerges, he's holding a gun.

Betty gasps. "Where did you get that?"

"Never mind where I got it. We need to protect ourselves. People are after us."

How could you have been so stupid? So blind? Everyone warned you he was ill. But you were so very certain that your love was the cure. And now here you stand, in the middle of a crime scene, with a boy you don't recognize anymore. A boy with a gun, who hears voices, who is leaving, and is not leaving without you. Who else is going to end up hurt—or dead?

Knocking at the door. Betty jumps.

She looks to Griff, his hand still holding the gun. Neither of them move.

"Griffin! Griffin, dearest, it's Mother."

Honor. Here.

"Griffin, I know you and Betty are in there. You must let me in. I'm alone, I promise you. I just want to help you, darling. I'm here now. It's all going to be all right. Open the door."

Griff silently lunges over to Betty's side, clamps his hand down over her mouth. The gun in his hand is not pointed at her, but she feels it nonetheless, pressed up against her thigh.

"Not a word," he whispers.

Twenty-one

The cab drops Eddie at the corner of Twenty-First and Seventh. He doesn't want to spook Griff by being seen getting out right in front of the apartment building in the middle of the block.

His stomach churns, as if it's ingested a meal comprised of sour ingredients. He tries to dismiss it as natural, a result of the stress he's put himself under by allowing things to get this far. But even as he strolls in an overly casual manner down the sidewalk of Twenty-First Street, he knows he is lying to himself. This feeling is not new. It is not due to his career or what may or may not happen to it. It is because he is seeing her again, this girl who has bewitched him as none other has, with her grit and gumption, all wrapped up in the prettiest wrapping paper. This girl he must admit he loves, and who may never love him back.

Damn you, Betty Jane Welch.

He had been at the barber. The barber! Of all the places, that's where he was when she called the hotel, left her cryptic message. Would Edward R. Murrow miss a message for a haircut? He imagines what will happen if his editor finds out what he's been up to, what he hasn't been reporting. He'll be cleaning out his desk within the hour, lucky to land at the weekly *Ocean City Sentinel,* writing obituaries.

He is nearing the entrance to the building when its glass front door swings open. He stops, melts back into the shadows under a tree, out of the glow of the streetlamp.

Honor McAllister is leaving. She gingerly grabs the railing with a gloved hand and proceeds carefully down the front steps, the shiny patent-leather handbag on her right forearm swinging back and forth with each alighting. She seems overly coiffed for such a grubby street, in an ink-blue dress with a fluffy silver fox collar, pearls on her wrist and throat. Her hat, blue velvet, is artfully tilted, with a natty plume spraying outward. If he didn't know better, Eddie would swear she was on her way to dinner at '21.'

For the first time he notices the car, a dark blue late-model Hudson, idling in front of the building. Honor leans into the passenger side window, utters something to the driver and a thick-set man in the front passenger seat, then opens the rear passenger door and slips inside. Eddie looks back up at the building. So she's in on this, too? Betty was paranoid about being discovered; she certainly would have mentioned Honor being here. No. Honor must have found them on her own. If he could find Betty and Griff, it was perfectly reasonable that private detectives with access to the resources purchased with the McAllister checkbook could find them, too.

Eddie leans back against the tree, tries to piece together what's going on. Is Honor waiting for them to come out, to take them back with her to Atlantic City? He notices the driver has cut the Hudson's engine. No. They're waiting. Maybe Betty and Griff are out.

Or already gone.

Why wasn't he in his room to get her call?

Why does it matter?

He doesn't want it to. He has fought them, these aimless, fiery feelings. And yet — what was the Emily Dickinson quote? "The Heart wants what it wants — or else it does not care." What a great, sensitive guy he was — able to quote a poet! And yet what was the point? In high school he fell hard and fast for willowy June Price, only to watch her saunter off into the arms of the football team's running back. Now this, falling for a beauty queen. Twenty-four and already a master in the art of unrequited love.

A half hour passes before the door to the apartment building swings open again. Betty comes out first, Griff right behind, as he hustles them both down the steps. Instinctively, Eddie takes a step forward. The doors of the Hudson fly open, Honor McAllister and her two dark-suited compatriots scrambling onto the sidewalk. "Griff! Darling! It's Mother! Wait! Wait!"

Griff has no intention of waiting. He and Betty take off running down the block, until they stop at a parked Fleetline and separate, Griff tumbling into the driver's side and firing up the ignition. Honor and the men carom back into their own sedan, which roars to life. Wherever Griff and Betty are going, they aren't going alone, whether they like it or not.

Betty grabs the handle of the Fleetline's passenger door.

And that's when it happens.

She glimpses back up Twenty-First Street and spots him, now standing in the lachrymose orange hue of the streetlight. Their eyes meet for the briefest of instants, locking together in understanding.

Hers simply say, *I have to.*

And like a summer storm she's gone, into the car, which screams away from the curb toward Eighth Avenue, turning wildly at the corner, vanished in a cloud of gray exhaust. The Hudson zips down the street seconds later, makes its own turn, chasing the country's most talked-about couple through the streets of New York.

Eddie stands, still as a statue, looking down at his shadow on the sidewalk. He doesn't even register the young couple now passing by him, giggling and snuggling, probably on their way to dinner, does not see the woman approaching from the other direction, the metal cart she pulls behind her brimming with a sack of cleaning supplies. He can only stare at the shadow, at the shape of his fedora at the top, the shoulders, the straight lines of his silhouette that end at his feet. *This is what I am to her,* he thinks. *A shadow.*

Their eyes met for only seconds, but he could see what was in hers. He wonders if she could see what was in his. That she had made her final choice, and that he had accepted it.

Enough.

Eddie pivots away from his sidewalk shadow, begins to head east toward Seventh Avenue.

He is less than twenty feet from the corner when he stops, looks up at the night sky. He turns around, heads back toward the apartment.

If you can't get the girl, he tells himself, *you might as well get the story.*

❧

He has buzzed at least five times. No answer.

Eddie checks the name again, which is ludicrous, because he's already checked the name thrice. Third down on the left: R. SPENCER.

It had been surprisingly easy finding him: while the Atlantic City detectives — and, presumably, those hired by Honor McAllister — had spent their days asking around the nursery and the bars and the beaches about Griff's friends and contacts, trying to find out who might help him and Betty escape, Eddie had gone straight to NYU. He knew from experience that there was no one more likely to help you out in a jam than a buddy you'd lived with in college. College was the first place you were away from everything —your high school friends, your family, most specifically your parents. You shared secrets and rites of passage with your college roommate that you didn't with anyone else. It hadn't taken Eddie long to figure out that Griffin McAllister had been something of a loner during his years in high school. He'd originally enrolled at the elite Lawrenceville School in the middle of the state, only to last less than a year and finish his education at the decidedly less posh Atlantic City High School. Same thing in college: Accepted into NYU, lasted less than a year. But at NYU he'd had a roommate who'd quickly left, replaced by a new one: Reeve Spencer, a skinny prankster who'd grown up north of Albany and who was now an apprentice at a Midtown bank, handling mortgage applications. Reeve and Griff had been written up more than once for their behavior at NYU—including twice for public drunkenness. It was only natural, Eddie thought, that Griff would come to New York after fleeing Atlantic City with Betty. The city offered peerless terrain for disappearing.

Perhaps if his newspaper career ends because of all of this, he can apply to become a detective. No doubt it pays better. And actually gets you dates.

Eddie mulls whether to just begin randomly buzzing residents, see if anyone will let him in, when the inside door opens and a man of about thirty-five breezes past. Eddie catches the door with his foot, swings it open, and walks inside, up the three flights to Reeve's apartment. Is this how Honor had gotten in? He suspects not. People like her merely open their wallets to get someone to let them in.

He is about to rap on Reeve's door but stops. It's ajar.

Eddie pushes it with his finger, listening to its slow, moaning creak, steps inside. "Hello? Hello? Reeve Spencer? Is anyone here?"

The door to the apartment opens onto a small galley kitchen, its harsh overhead light illuminating a few glasses sitting downturned on a dishtowel by the sink. Eddie walks into the dark living room. Pieces of a broken lamp lie scattered on the floor.

He pivots back to the kitchen, which has an alcove opposite where there is a small desk. The desk chair had been flipped on its side; Eddie can see one of its sides has splintered. He inspects the floor. Blood, small droplets all over the place. A few specks on the wall.

His pulse speeds up.

He can make out the light coming from the open crack of the bedroom door at the end of the hall, past the bathroom on the right. He steps carefully toward it, listening intently for movement, sound, anything. There is nothing but eerie silence. He pokes the door, watches it slowly swing open.

Eddie has never laid eyes on a dead man before—his branch of the Tates does not believe in open caskets, no matter what the other English do—but he knows, instantly, that Reeve Spencer is dead. His body lies crumpled on the floor by the bed, torso now mired in a sticky, burgundy pool of blood. His head has been bashed in. His open eyes stare at nothing. A blood-soaked ashtray sits on the floor a few feet away.

Eddie bolts from the room, fights the retching rising in his throat. He pictures it: Reeve and Griff arguing, Griff reaching for the ashtray. But why? How could you justify that? Griff was tall, muscular. He had at least thirty pounds and six inches on Reeve.

This was not self-defense. This was murder.

Unless.

Eddie closes his eyes at the thought.

What if it wasn't Griff who killed Reeve?

Twenty-two

From the passenger seat, Betty cannot get a clear look into the rearview. But as they zigzag through the streets of Manhattan, she can see enough to know that the Hudson, with Honor McAllister inside it, is still in striking distance behind them.

Griff has raced up Eighth Avenue, banking a sudden, hard right turn at Thirtieth Street, almost mowing down three people crossing. A block up, a right on Seventh Avenue, another few blocks, left on Twenty-Sixth, then up to Fifth Avenue, and so it's gone for the last twenty minutes, literally getting nowhere fast. He's sailed through at least two red lights, horns blaring from all sides in protest. Betty keeps her ever-whitening knuckles gripped to the passenger door. She's afraid to utter a sound, to distract him. It is astonishing, she thinks, that a police car has not pulled them over. She worries what will happen if it does. If this is his reaction to being cornered by his own mother, there is no telling what it might be if surrounded by the cops.

How did she let it come to this, to a car chase through the streets of Manhattan? She had a plan. Then Reeve had come home and torn it asunder. How could she possibly explain what had happened now? Who would ever believe her?

They'd stood in the apartment, silent as the grave, as Honor had kept up her incessant knocking and inquiries, determined to be let in, assured they were inside. And then, after minutes that felt like hours, she had suddenly left, her heels clicking as she descended the marble staircase of the apartment building, until they heard the interior door swing open, and then the fainter, muffled sound of her going down the outside front steps.

Griff had relaxed his hold on her. "She'll be outside, waiting for us," he said.

Betty had not been able to get her mind off the gun. As long as it was her and Griff alone, she had a chance to calm him down, to cut through the voices and their fog of paranoia. But the gun. It was one thing to be a man who was under tremendous stress and having it manifest in crazy ways. It was quite another to be that man and to be carrying a loaded weapon.

I have to get the gun.

His hand was in his coat pocket, and though she couldn't tell for sure, she was confident that he still had his right hand firmly around the grip. Her mind had been whirling with schemes and diversions to get him to take off the coat when he'd suddenly turned to her and said, "We'll have to make a run for it."

Instinctively her eyes had darted around the room, high, low, and sideways, as if some sort of magic alternative was going to present itself. "I . . . I don't know if that's a good idea, my darling," she eked out. "I am sure the authorities are downstairs with your mother. We'll be walking right into a brigade of police." *Which might not be the worst thing,* she thought. *As long as I can get him to go down without the gun.* Because if they walked outside, and there *were* policemen to greet them . . . there would be no way to know what Griff would do. He'd already killed a man today. In those first moments after Honor left, his expression had seemed wild, untamed. There was just too much risk going out now, when they didn't know what was on the other side of the door. She had to convince him to stay, to settle down. Maybe she could go out alone first, assess the situation, talk to Honor, develop the right plan.

Oh, why hadn't Eddie come?

Griff had begun stalking around the apartment, throwing more things in the suitcase Betty had started to pack earlier. He was suddenly oddly calm and workmanlike, as if he were late for a train and needed to focus in order to allow enough time to make it to the station. "No, that isn't how Mother operates," he'd said flatly, wadding a white shirt into a ball and stuffing it in. "The only thing she's truly afraid of is scandal. Believe me, I would know: I've caused enough of it. She would never involve the police. Though I am sure she's not alone."

Betty watched him work, fascinated and unsettled by the spooky calm now draped over him like a shroud. "You think your father is here, too?"

Griff scoffed. "Dear old dad? Ha! No sir. He lost interest in me years ago, when the doctors first diagnosed my 'problem.' Besides, he'd never take a day off from the nursery. That's the child he really cares about."

"I am sure he cares about you. And Martha."

He straightened up, took a minute to consider this. "Martha. Yes, maybe. She's pretty and bright and in many ways like a younger version of Mother, before all of the bitterness and social rivalry set in. Martha's a good egg."

Betty was about to tell him she'd spoken to Martha today but stopped herself. Even an innocent phone call could seem like a betrayal, like it was Betty who had tipped off Honor where they were, drawn her to their doorstep. She had to make sure she stayed on his good side.

"Even if you're right," Betty had said, trying to sound breezy, "your mother is formidable. If she has anyone with her, they are not likely going to let us simply walk past them out into the evening air."

He nodded, almost imperceptibly. He circled around the dark living room, sidling up next to the window and peering down onto the street. "So predictable," he said.

"What?"

"A Hudson is parked right in front of the building. I can make out two guys in the front. She's got to be in the back."

She didn't know why, but Betty glanced toward the light streaming from the bedroom, thought of Reeve on the floor. A dead man in the rear, a mother on a mission of salvation out front. To her, the choice was obvious. If Honor had come without the authorities —and it appeared she had—she was their best, and only, option.

"I could go down and speak to her—"

"Shhhh! Quiet! I can't hear my own thoughts with all of you talking!"

With all of you talking.

What were the voices telling him now?

Betty reached for her coat. "I'm going to go down and explain—"

Griff had charged from the living room wall and intercepted her, backed her up against the anteroom wall by the door. "No! No. No." Each "no" became calmer, flatter, like a punctured tire slowly deflating. He kissed her, hard, his lips hungrily parting hers. His cheek was next to hers, his mouth on her ear, her neck. "I love you. I love you so much, Betty. Everything I have done I have done for you. You know that, don't you?"

She encircled his shoulders, for the briefest of seconds considered trying to reach into his coat pocket. "Of course I do, my darling. Of course I do. You've done so much for me. Let me do this for you."

"I'm not ready," he said, his eyes moist and full, boring into hers, his voice an exigent moan. "We have to get away. Go somewhere where we can be alone, like we planned. They'll never understand. They'll find . . . him . . ."

Betty pulled him closer. "All right, dearest. I understand. We'll go. The car is just down the street. We'll be down the stairs and in it before they even know it's us."

❧

The car banks another hard right turn, jolting Betty out of the memory. Where were they now? A big street. Back on Eighth Avenue? No. Farther west. The West Side Elevated Highway.

"Where are we going?" Betty asks, daring to turn and look out of the rear window. Various cars behind them. She can't be sure if the Hudson is still one of them. "I think we may have lost them."

"No, we haven't."

Griff presses his foot to the floor of the Fleetline, dodges in between two cars in the left lane, then back to the right, then again, crossing and crossing back, trying to evade the accelerating Hudson, which drops out of view, then back, then out, then back. "This silly car," Griff says. "If we'd kept the Mercury, we'd have ditched them at Twenty-Third."

At the very last minute, Griff jerks the wheel all the way to the right, sending the Fleetline skidding across two lanes of traffic, barreling toward the exit at Seventy-Second Street. Betty closes her eyes, waiting for impact—with a wall, with another vehicle, with something—but the only sound is that of a crash behind them, a small explosion of twisting metal and shattered glass as the Hudson's driver loses control of his car, sending it careening into the right-side barrier of the highway. Betty jerks back just in time to see the Hudson spin completely around, its front now partially blocking the right lane of oncoming traffic, where a speeding Packard tries to veer to its left at the last minute but cannot make it. The two cars collide, the impact spinning the beleaguered Hudson back into the right direction, but wedging it between the barrier on the right and the now-smoking, battered wreckage of the Packard on the left.

Betty whirls back to Griff. "Griff, please, we have to go back! Your mother may be badly hurt!"

Griff shifts the clutch, his eyes never leaving the road. He keeps driving, as if they were out on a pleasure tour on any Wednesday night.

After several minutes, they safely blend in with the traffic on the Henry Hudson Parkway. Griff reaches into his jacket pocket, extracts a cigarette. "You know what that road used to be called in the old days, before they built the West Side Elevated?" he finally asks, his lips encircling the cigarette.

Betty shakes her head.

He flicks his lighter, leans the cigarette into its jumping flame.

"Death Avenue," he says.

❧

"Kansas."

Betty startles awake at the sudden sound of his voice. How long has she been asleep? It seems like each one of her limbs weighs a hundred pounds; her brain feels fogged over. So much to process. Too much. It's just all become too much.

She shakes her head to clear the cobwebs, checks the landscape outside her window. It's Thursday, by the look of the light sometime in the relatively early morning. After evading Honor, they'd parked somewhere late last night, immediately fallen asleep. She's frightfully hungry.

They're now on some winding country road, trees on either side, the occasional cottage-type house popping up, mailboxes and newspaper boxes lined up like toy soldiers. Where are they? She has no idea what direction they were headed when they left New York. North, she thinks. She wonders if the police have found Reeve's body yet, if they are on this very road, looking for them. But she and Griff are in someone else's car, and even they don't know where they are going. Or maybe now they do.

"Kansas?" she finally utters aloud. "That's where we're going?"

"It's as good a place as any."

Betty tenses up again. It was one thing to escape to New York, to catch their collective breath. It is quite another to take off for the Midwest, especially after leaving a dead body in their wake. "Who do you know in Kansas?"

"Not a soul," he says nonchalantly, as if he's reporting tomorrow's weather on WDEL radio. Perhaps this is all part of his illness, this veneer of nonchalance he takes on and off like a Halloween costume. It's what bubbles underneath the costume that has her still gripping the door handle as if she's dangling from a window ledge twenty stories up. "We need to get as far as we can from all of that craziness in New York," he continues. "I was a fool to take us there. But that's all behind us now."

"But what will we do in Kansas? We know no one. People will be looking for us. We must almost be out of money."

He shakes his head softly, like a father losing patience with a child begging for an advance on her allowance. "Nobody is going to look for us in Kansas. That's the point."

Buffalo. Now Kansas. And then what? she wants to scream. *We buy a farm? We change our names to Ted and Ida and hoe potatoes?*

No. No no no no no.

She searches the dewy countryside for answers. She needs a new plan, now.

She must get them somewhere they can hunker down undiscovered but where she can access help to get them back to reality.

To get the gun out of his pocket, the voices out of his head, the cavalry to come in and sort out the mess they've made without anyone going to jail or getting hurt. Or anyone else dying. She has gotten them into this mess; it is up to her to get them out. She goes back to the night she won, lying in the bed with him, her head on his chest, begging him: *Let's go somewhere. Someplace where they can't find us.*

There is nothing for them in the Midwest. They can't go south —he'll be panicked at the thought of crossing back through New Jersey. North. What's north? Upstate New York. Connecticut.

Rhode Island.

Betty turns back to him. "Baby," she says, in almost a purr, "I'm starving."

They stop at a diner called the Lucky something, Betty couldn't make out the sign right away as they pulled into the gravel lot— and take a back booth. It's a little after eight in the morning, yet there are only a few stragglers in here, most perched at the counter, sipping bad coffee and eating eggs. Betty adjusts her hat, which itches but which she cannot take off. Her hair is a fright. Ciji will be able to fix it.

Ciji. How did she not think of Ciji sooner? As she flips through the menu, the new plan begins to crystallize in her head: they will go to Newport, to the hotel where Ciji works. She will find a place to stash them. Then she will somehow get Ciji alone, confess everything. Perhaps Ciji can get her hands on a sleeping aid, which Betty can crush up and use to drug Griff into peaceful slumber. She'll steal the gun, have Ciji get rid of it. Then she can call Martha, find out how Honor fared in the accident, arrange for help to come and retrieve them without alerting the authorities. They'll go back to Atlantic City. Surely the McAllisters will find a lawyer to explain everything? Griff will get to a hospital, away from the police. And Betty will go where she should have stayed all along: home.

She exhales, mulls the potential comfort of pancakes. It's a blueprint. Not bad for being composed within half an hour. It's simple, and it won't take long to execute. They just have to get to Rhode Island.

A bolt of doubt slams her in the stomach. What if Ciji isn't there? She doesn't even remember the name of the hotel. *Don't I have a card somewhere?* What if Ciji has taken her pageant money and already left for Hollywood? God couldn't be that cruel. Could He?

She can't risk it. She has to call first, make sure the plan gets underway before they show up. Her eyes flicker up over her menu on to Griff, who is softly humming. A man who a little over twelve hours ago killed another man in cold blood, who left his mother possibly dead in a car wreck behind him, who is on the run with a girl he's known less than three weeks in God Knows Where, sitting at a diner, and he's . . . humming.

Betty Welch, we jumped into the deep end of the ocean without a life preserver.

Ciji would have to deliver one. She had to. It was the only chance they had to get out of this madness without any more collateral damage.

"Poached eggs, bacon, hash browns," Griff says, "with a few slices of toast, or maybe a corn muffin."

Keep it light. Keep it fun. "You're even more ravenous than I," she says.

"What about you? What are you in the mood for?"

If you only knew. "French toast with lots of butter and maple syrup," she says nonchalantly. "And no stealing from my plate, either. You'll have enough food of your own."

He smiles, reaches his hand across the table. For a moment

it's just the two of them, back at Captain Starn's. Then a pang of memory. The next morning she met Eddie. Where was he now? The look on his face, standing in the light of the streetlamp. Confused. Disappointed. Heartbroken. Her intentions had been pure. Truly. If he had just gotten her message in time, they might be on their way back home right now. Reeve might even still be alive. But there is no escaping how callous she has been with Eddie's fragile, open heart.

There is no time for any more recriminations.

The waitress, a bony woman wearing a name tag that says SHIRLEY, fills their coffee cups, jots down their order. "So I've been thinking about Kansas," Betty says.

"Oh?" Griff replies, splashing sugar into the cup.

"It's awfully far, honey. The amount of gas we'd need alone . . . and what if the car breaks down and we're in the middle of nowhere? I'm worried we'll run out of money. And I don't like the thought of going somewhere where we have no one to help us."

"You mean like Reeve helped us?" He says this stoically, his eyes still staring into the milky coffee he stirs.

"You didn't know Reeve as well as you thought you did."

"I wasn't going to ask," he says, "but what happened back there?"

Betty feels a flame of indignation rise up through her chest. "I don't want to talk about it. And this certainly isn't the time or place to discuss it."

"We're in the back of a diner in the boondocks. It's the perfect place to discuss it." For some unknown reason, he clangs his spoon on the side of his saucer. Betty wonders if one of his voices is telling him to. The voices, the voices. She is both glad she herself cannot hear them and at the same time terrified that she cannot hear what they are saying inside the soupy mess inside his brain. "Attacking a woman like that," he continues, "that doesn't seem like the Reeve I know. Knew."

She knows she shouldn't say it, but she has to. "Are you imply-
ing I somehow . . . *encouraged* him to try to rape me?" He eyes her
evenly, and she feels her blood starting to boil. But she must sup-
press. Immediately. She cannot allow her emotions to get the best
of her. Especially anger. Anger would be the worst possible element
in this equation.

She is surprised how easily she is able to manufacture tears.
Perhaps they come quickly, she thinks, because she has not allowed herself to ponder the horror of what might have happened
if Griff had not come into the room. "I've never been so afraid of
anyone in my life," she says faintly.

He reaches back across the table. "I'm sorry, angel. I'm being a
knucklehead."

Shirley the waitress brings the food — the French toast smells
heavenly — and as Griff forks a heaping serving of his bacon and
poached eggs, Betty goes on offense. It is a peculiar trait of his,
though certainly not his oddest, as she has learned in the most unpleasant manner, that he has a fanatical aversion to uttering a word
with his mouth full, under any circumstances. "I think we should
go to Rhode Island," she says.

He chews thoughtfully, takes a bite of toast, swallows. "Ciji."

"Ciji."

She pours out a stream of syrup over her breakfast. From
across the diner, they might be a couple discussing the best
route to a friend's birthday party. Griff's eyes search the air above
her head, as if the correct answer is floating there, scrawled
in an air balloon, like in a newspaper comic strip. He nods.
"Maybe."

"We know we can trust her. She has been a terrific gal — to both
of us. She runs a hotel" — not quite true, but close enough — "and
she can stash us somewhere inside it easily, with no fuss and with
no one asking who we are. We wouldn't even have to pay for it. We

can take our time, get cleaned up, figure out what to do next, with no pressure. It's perfect."

He scoops up another helping of his eggs, chews them like a Guernsey. It has all come down to this—the fork in the road literally tied to the fork in his hand. If he agrees, there is the chance to avoid disaster. If he doesn't, she has no idea what to do. He's the one with the car keys. And the gun.

"It's a good idea," he pronounces finally.

She revels the doughy sweetness of her French toast. Her appetite returns with a fury, and soon she's stuffing her mouth like a child. They'll go to Rhode Island. This ordeal will finally be over.

It is this thought that's pleasantly wafting through her head as she sees the policeman walk through the front door, whispering something to Shirley before heading straight toward their table.

Twenty-three

*C*iji *has errands to run* but cannot remember a single one of them. She simply ambles about Bellevue Avenue, trying to look like she knows where she's going, when in truth she has no idea about anything at the moment.

Mr. Clifford, the manager of Newport Florists, brushes by her carrying a large bouquet of cymbidiums and tulips, odd blooms for this time of year, but florists always seem to know how to get flowers mere mortals cannot. "Oh, hello, Catherine," he says, in the courtly manner that has made him the preeminent purveyor of flora to every socialite in Newport. His eyes narrow, his brows two bushy haystacks above them. "Are you quite well, dear? You seem like you have the weight of the world on your shoulders."

Ciji tosses out her best faux smile, the one that greets hotel guests when she is tired and cranky and doesn't care a whit about the extra pillows they request, the one that got her to the Top Fifteen at the Miss America Pageant. Mr. Clifford likes it when young ladies flirt. It's how you get better flowers. "Not at all, sir," she replies. "Just distracted by this lovely fall weather. And, of course, such a handsome man walking the streets."

"Such a charmer. I still cannot believe they did not crown *you* in Atlantic City."

"I tried very hard to get you named a judge but, alas, was unsuccessful."

"Have you heard any more about the girl who won, the one who vanished? I haven't read much about it lately."

Ciji looks casually around the street, as if suddenly searching for an address. "No, not a word. I confess I haven't been paying very close attention."

He seems puzzled. "Didn't I read in some account that she was your roommate?"

"Yes, but we were always so scheduled, so busy, there wasn't much time to form friendships, I'm afraid. The whole thing's dizzy, if you ask me. I only know I was done for when it was all finally over." She glances over his shoulder, waves to someone who isn't there. "I have to run. But I'll see you Saturday."

"Bright and early. A lot of work to do. Goodbye, Catherine dear."

She roams the streets, picks up a few items at Downing Brothers pharmacy, makes a quick deposit at Newport National Bank on Washington Square, remembers that she has an order to retrieve at William Covell—housekeeping needs two new mops. The stop she'd really like to make is on Broadway, to Rex Liquor Store. Never mind that it is the middle of the morning. She is in desperate need of a stiff drink.

It has been only two hours since the front desk phone rang and Ciji casually picked it up, as she did dozens of times a day. "Good morning, Cliff Lawn Manor. This is Catherine. How many I assist you?"

There'd been a pause, so pronounced that Ciji had almost hung up. "I'm looking for Joan of Arc," came the barely audible reply.

You'll say, "Joan of Arc, I need you," and I'll be there. Always.

"Betty?!" Ciji had whispered, clutching the phone tightly to her ear. Instinctively her eyes had darted around the reception area, as if secret agents might be eavesdropping. "Where *are* you? Are you all right?"

"Yes. But I need your help."

Ciji was still attempting to get her bearings, grappling with the fact that it was Betty on the other end of the line. "My God! What happened—"

"There's no time for that now. I'll explain later. But I need you to do something for me. Has anyone been in contact with you, looking for me? For us?"

"Us? Griff is with you?"

"Ciji, please! Has anyone been poking around there, asking you questions?"

It had been hard to hear her. There was static on the line, maybe wind. Betty had sounded like she was outside, maybe inside a telephone booth by the side of the road. "No. A local detective came by early on, the first week you were gone, asked me some routine questions. I think the Atlantic City cops had asked him to. And I had a call from some private dick working for Griff's mother. And of course reporters. But nothing since then. Betty, where have you *been?* Your parents are worried sick."

Ciji absorbed the silence from the other end of the line. She thought she heard Betty choke out a sob. "Betty? Are you still there?"

"I'm here," Betty replied weakly. "I'm almost out of change. Listen to me: I need you to do something for me. We're coming to Newport. We'll be there tomorrow sometime, probably later in the evening. I don't want to risk arriving during the day. I need you to find us a place to stay. Just for a day or two. Just until I can figure things out."

"Figure *what* out? Betty, do you realize how many people are looking for you? I—"

"Ciji! I'm begging you. You're my only hope to get out of this mess. You don't know what's gone on. You were my friend in Atlantic City, and I need you to be my friend now. I'm sorry for getting you into all of this, going back to asking you to find Griff that night. Truly I am. But I desperately need your help. I don't know what he'll do . . ." She trails off. Ciji can make it out more clearly now. Sniffling, the onset of tears.

"Sweetie, of course I'll help. But shouldn't we call the police?"

"No. You can't. You have to promise you won't tell anyone I've contacted you or that we're on our way there. Promise me."

"All right, all right. I promise. I promise. But you need to tell me something first: Are you really okay? Has he . . . hurt you?"

Betty cleared her throat, regained her composure. "I'm fine. Really, I am. I just need a place to get to so I can undo all of this in a way where no one gets hurt. Will you help me?"

Ciji had looked up at the ceiling, wondering how much she would come to regret the only answer she could possibly give. She spied a middle-aged couple through the window, walking up toward the front door, the man carrying a large brown suitcase. "I will do whatever I can," she told Betty. "I'm working tomorrow from nine on. Call me and let me know what time you think you're going to get here, and I can arrange to meet you somewhere and get you settled."

Another pause. "I . . . I can't thank you enough."

"Joan of Arc," Ciji replied. "Always here."

She steps out of the recollection, walks purposefully down the street en route to William Covell and the mops. She has no idea where Betty has been the past two weeks, or what to do now that she's headed here. *Do I really want to get mixed up in all of this?*

Do I really have a choice?

228

The responsibility of hiding Betty and Griff weighs on her with each passing step, like she's walking in leg irons. *What if something goes horribly wrong? What if they've been up to no good since they've disappeared, and I'm dragged into it?* She pictures Miss Slaughter marching into a courtroom in her pearls and heavy leather shoes, loudly telling a judge that Ciji's scholarship has been revoked, that it's perfectly fine to lock her up and throw away the key for harboring a fugitive. She'll be run out of Newport, shunned by Hollywood, her dreams evaporated in a cloud of scandal.

She wonders if she's doing the right thing by not calling the police. How does she not know that Griff was standing right at Betty's side, listening to every word, scripting her entreaty as he pressed a knife to her throat?

I need advice, she thinks, smiling and nodding at two women she knows by sight at church as they pass her. But she has promised not to utter a word to anyone.

Unless . . .

She stops dead, pretends to look in the window of Joseph's Beauty Salon, surveying the women gabbing under the dryers. The place will be a madhouse in two days, when every matron in town comes in to pretty up for the Masquerade Ball.

She has given Betty her word to tell no one of her plans, but she cannot keep it. He won't betray her, she's sure of it. She just has to find his business card, fish it out from the bottom of the bag she was carrying that day at the Claridge, now shoved onto the back of a shelf in her bedroom.

Even Joan of Arc didn't fight alone.

She begins walking again, faster now, each minute suddenly more precious. *Joan stood up, did the right thing,* she thinks.

And they burned her at the stake for it.

❧

At noon the following day, Ciji walks back into the hotel, exhausted. The meeting at the Hotel Viking with the Preservation Society has dragged on for hours, a round robin of seating charts, décor quibbling, tangents about the latest grand mansion being sold for taxes, gossip about whether Mrs. Peyton van Rensselaer really had snubbed Mrs. Armando Canizares, the wife of the naval attaché of the Mexican embassy, during a particularly feisty round of bridge two days earlier. Mrs. Benjamin Franklin Fitch, the chair of this year's Masquerade Ball, tried in vain to keep order but found herself swept away with the chattering tide, until she, too, was submerged in the minutiae of the foibles and fallacies of what was left of Newport's gilded class, covering everything from whether it was too late in the season for pastel tablecloths to whether Barbara Hutton's diffident RSVP ("I shall make every endeavor to join you") could somehow be solidified into a firm vote of attendance—preferably with husband number four, Prince Igor Troubetzkoy, in tow.

How the relatively modest—by Newport standards, anyway—Cliff Lawn Manor had managed to get itself selected as the site of this year's ball remained a mystery. Somehow, the dowagers and their assorted ladies in waiting had deigned that the idea of a sprawling tent over the back lawn, with its soft slope down to the Cliff Walk and the sea below, would provide the perfect tableau for the fete. Ciji had come back from Atlantic City to find herself thrown into the hurly-burly of preparations, along with every other breathing staff member on the property. While hardly in charge, she had managed to amass enough responsibility to wake up each morning with a low hum of anxiety rippling through her. As the reigning Miss Rhode Island, she warranted a kind of respect from her superiors, who were planning to show her off during the ball to the guests, the way one might ask partygoers to pet the family's new dachshund.

Not that she had the time or the energy to worry about any of that. As she walked through the calling room, past the parlor on the left and the dining room on the right, she bore left to the sitting room, its fireplace already cheerfully ablaze despite the mild temperatures outside. Guests loved seeing the fire crackling every day, even if it made the place feel like a gentlemen's bathhouse.

Cliff Lawn Manor sat on six prime Newport acres, an ivy-covered, gothic reminder of the legacy of the great summer "cottages" that had helped define Newport as one of the great American playgrounds of the rich. A *Wuthering Heights*–style estate, it had originally been built for a New York congressman and his wife —an Astor—in 1873 and had hosted guests ranging from Henry Wadsworth Longfellow to Teddy Roosevelt. It had been sold in the early 1940s, changing hands seemingly every year—a girl's school one year, a naval officers' retreat the next—until a fire in 1944 did in the third floor. It had now been reimagined as a thirty-room hotel, where on certain days at the front desk you could find yourself greeted by Miss Catherine Grace Moore, beauty queen and aspiring movie star.

It was a modest hotel by anyone's standards. But its location on a picturesque, if not particularly steep, cliff, and the curving walkway that ran to its left all the way around to some of the grandest estates in town, ending at Doris Duke's kingly Rough Point, imbued it with a rustic élan it would not have otherwise possessed.

Mrs. Hensley, the brisk head of housekeeping, intercepts Ciji as she makes her way toward the kitchen to retrieve a Coke.

"Your young man is on the back porch," Mrs. Hensley says disapprovingly, because Mrs. Hensley says everything—whether it is "Good morning" or "The oatmeal was particularly hearty this morning"—disapprovingly, and especially so if there is a young man involved. Ciji has often wondered what it must be like to go through life possessing no talent for expression other than the scowl.

"Thank you, Mrs. Hensley."

The housekeeper issues a soft harrumph and flits away, assuredly to share a confidence with one of the maids about how Ciji has hastily arranged a room for the young man now waiting for her, no doubt to begin some questionable assignation that will disparage the reputation of the hotel and everyone in it. She can cackle like a hen. Ciji doesn't care.

He'd come.

When she pushes through the screen door to the back porch, littered with scattered fallen leaves in hues of chocolate and orange and yellow and stubbornly hanging-on green—it is virtually impossible to keep up with them this time of year—his back is to her. He wears a tan gabardine jacket and casual light wool trousers, no hat, his blond hair Brylcreemed to a shine. He stands at the far end of the porch, surveying the calm blue water that shimmers in the autumn sun.

He can hear her approaching—she sees him turn his head slightly, catch her out of the corner of his eye—but he doesn't turn around. As she draws closer, he says, "I had no idea it was so beautiful here. You live by an ocean you think nothing could be sweeter, but this . . ."

She follows his sightline. "Yes. It never grows old."

Eddie Tate pivots around, and for a few seconds they look at each other, sharing a "How did we get in this fix?" expression, both of them seeming to fight bursting into inappropriate laughter at the absurdity of it all. He steps forward and embraces her, not because he wants to or she wants to, but because it seems like what the situation calls for. "Thank you for coming," she whispers.

He shrugs. "A free train ticket to Providence, a fancy car picks me up and takes me to Newport," he says. "Hell, before all of this, I'd never been out of Jersey."

"Where do they think you are, your bosses at the paper?"

"I don't imagine they much care. They canned me yesterday."

Ciji instinctively gasps, quickly scans his face in the hope he's joking. When she'd called the newspaper office, they had simply said he wasn't in, given her his home number. "Why?"

"Well, you can't really disappear for a few days and promise your editors you're going to deliver the goods on the biggest story going and then come back . . ." He struggles to finish the sentence. "With nothing."

"You *knew* where she was?"

"More than that. I met with her. In New York. She and Griff were hiding out in the apartment of a college friend of his. She promised me she'd come home with me as long as I made sure Griff wasn't hurt. He's not well, you know."

"Not well . . . how?"

So he tells her: the truth about Griff's condition, about his meeting with the now raven-haired Betty at the restaurant, about finding Reeve's dead body in the apartment after watching Betty get in the car and speed off, Griff's mother right behind them. Ciji's hands fly to her face. "I know, I know," he says. "It gets worse."

"How much worse?"

"Well, I decided to cash in right then and there. Walk away— from her, from the story, all of it. The girl's done nothing but twist me up sideways and back around again since the day I laid eyes on her. Which is your fault, by the way. Do you remember, that morning after the photo shoot of all the girls on the Boardwalk? You said to me, 'Oh, you've got to interview my roommate, Miss Delaware. She's a pistol.' She sure was."

"None of us could have guessed what would happen."

He sighs wearily. "That's for sure."

"You said it gets worse?"

He leans back against the railing, folds his arms, as if trying to decide either how much to tell her, how to couch it, or both. "Look, I don't know what happened in that apartment. But once

Griff and Betty took off, Honor and her two goons took off right after them. I had no idea how it turned out until I got back to Atlantic City. Before they fired me, one of the reporters told me that Honor's car had been in a bad wreck on the West Side Elevated. Evidently Griff must have ditched them off one of the exits and her car crashed into the rail."

Oh, Betty. What are you doing? "Christopher Columbus," Ciji exclaims. "Was she badly hurt?"

"Just pretty banged up, from what I could gather. She may have broken a bone in her foot. I think the driver took the worst of it — I heard his hand went through the windshield. Guy in the front passenger seat fractured a rib or two."

"I haven't read a word about any of this."

"It's a car accident in New York. They happen every day. I don't think anybody's pieced it together yet. I'm sure Honor invented a whopper of a story about why she was in New York and why the car crashed. Though how she explained away the detective in the front seat, I don't know."

"She's still protecting him. After everything."

He shrugs. "She's his mother."

"And Reeve's death? That hasn't been reported, either? How?"

He stares back out at the water again. He's silent for longer than he needs to be to answer such a simple question. Finally, he says softly, "Perhaps they don't know he's dead yet."

She feels her blood freeze. "You mean . . . you didn't call the police? You just . . . left him there?"

He shakes his head, as if willing absolution. "I needed it to be *over*, don't you understand? She's . . . I mean . . . I lost my *job* over her. I will have killed my career if it ever gets out I sat on this story instead of telling it to the world. She doesn't love me. She loves him, no matter what he is or what he's done, how sick he is in the head. And I couldn't bear it any longer. And I didn't want to know—" He can't make the words come.

"If she'd done it." Ciji rests against the railing, so they are now shoulder to shoulder, facing opposite directions. "You can't honestly believe she's capable of murder."

"I didn't think she was capable of abdicating Miss America," he says. "But she did. The fact she got into that car with Griff, when she had a clear path of escape, opens it all up to question. I mean, I was standing less than half a block away from her. She could have run."

"And let a mentally unbalanced man get behind the wheel, with his mother in pursuit behind him? If anything happened to Griff, Betty wouldn't have been able to live with herself. She feels responsible for all of this."

"She shouldn't. She— It doesn't matter."

"I think it matters to you a great deal."

"I wish it didn't."

"I know. Honestly, I wasn't even sure you'd agree to come."

He scoffs. "Funny. Me neither."

"So why did you?"

There is no mistaking the pain in his eyes: deep, raw, exposed. A little boy's brand of wounding. Ciji is certain she has never loved anyone the way Eddie loves Betty. Looking at him, she is equally certain she never wants to. She possesses neither the bravery nor the optimism to forge such a feeling for a man.

He smiles resignedly. "The heart wants what it wants."

Twenty-four

Her neck aches. Everything aches. Her arms, her legs, her back, her head. Her dress looks like an unmade bed. She's now slept in the car for two straight nights, the last curled up like a kitten on the back seat, repeatedly trying and failing to get comfortable against the hard leather. Griff had simply slinked down in the front seat, tilted his fedora over his eyes, and conked out, the voices inside his head blissfully gone silent. Or so she'd hoped.

He hadn't mentioned them of late, and Betty hadn't asked. She was too fearful of what they were saying. There had been times since she discovered the truth about him that she had looked over and forgotten he was suffering, become delightedly unaware, once again, that there was anything amiss at all. But then she'd see it — a twitch of the eye, a faraway look, a nervous gesture — and she'd remember that deep inside his brain there was a war going on.

Had he sat there with her during that first dinner at Captain Starn's, listening to these voices as he blithely sipped his martini? Had they been yelling at him as he'd leaned over in the shadows that night on the Boardwalk, taken her into his arms and kissed her as if he were going into battle? She has lost any sense of what is real anymore. If she thinks about what is real, she must think about the consequences of what she's done, and she cannot afford the recriminations that will come if she does. She has to get Griff to Newport, find a way to get him help, and get it all done before anyone links them to Reeve. It may already be too late. But she must try. She owes it to him to try.

"Look," Betty says, pointing to a big blue metal sign on the right that says: WELCOME TO RHODE ISLAND, THE OCEAN STATE. "We're here."

"A bit of a ways to go before we get to Newport," Griff replies. He seems almost merry, as if they're headed to a long-overdue holiday with friends.

She catches glimpses of her own reflection as they wind their way north. She looks tired. Bluish dark circles have formed under her eyes; her hair is a black, untamed haystack. She attempts to smooth it down in spots but quickly gives up the ghost. She's always liked that metaphor, wonders where it comes from. *It's fitting. I certainly feel like a ghost.*

She rests her head back on the seat, succumbing to the rhythmic rumble of the car. Her mind is a jumble of puzzle pieces — images of her mother making lemon cake in their kitchen, waiting for Betty to walk back through the front door; of Miss Slaughter, huffing down the Boardwalk trailed by nervous men in suits, trying to salvage the image of her pageant; of Griff's gun. She's lost track of it, thinks he must be constantly switching where he keeps it. She likes to consider that perhaps he has thrown it away but knows that cannot be true. When the image of Reeve, lying in a pool of blood on the bedroom floor, takes its turn on the kaleidoscope that plays through her head, she shuts it down. Some houses on Memory Lane need not be visited.

Betty thinks back to yesterday morning, to the cop walking slowly toward them inside the diner, the strenuous effort she'd had to make to appear stolid. With each of his approaching steps, she'd zoomed right to the worst—being escorted out of the diner, a thousand flashbulbs exploding at the disgraced Miss America. Griff behind her, screaming and attempting to shake off the escorting officers, his internal voices at full throttle. It had unfurled like a ten-second newsreel before a movie showing.

"Is that your Fleetline out in the parking lot?" the cop had asked Griff. He had the mailbox build and beefy hands one would expect of a policeman, but his face seemed soft, delicate, almost feminine, as if the wrong head had been placed on his body.

"Yes, sir," Griff had replied, and then picked up a slice of bacon and shoved it into his mouth, as if the question had been asked and answered and that was that. Betty had studied him like one does a particularly exotic zoo animal. She wondered if the voices were telling him what to say, how to act. This was now her default: everything was about the voices.

"Your brake lights are on," the cop said curtly, clearly annoyed either by Griff's lack of suitable apprehension at being questioned by an officer of the law or by his insouciant reaction to the cop's kindness for coming into the diner and pointing this out. Betty had quietly let out a long, hearty exhalation, even as she continued to wipe her clammy hands against the sides of her dress under the table.

Griff looked up, smiled. "Why, thank you, Officer . . ." He squinted at the cop's lapel. ". . . Staiber. I do appreciate you letting me know." He stood, extended his hand. "I'll take care of it."

Patrolman Staiber, seemingly mollified, shook Griff's hand and wished them both a good day before heading back to the counter for a cup of coffee and some harmless flirting with Shirley the waitress. "I thought the jig was up," Betty whispered.

"You worry too much," Griff had said, and then returned to the last of his eggs.

The memory fades as Betty feels her body slacken, dovetail into the rocking of the car. She dozes off once more until she feels his tapping on her forearm. "Bett, wake up, honey," Griff says, pointing to the looming, multi-gabled mansion in front of them. "We're here."

❧

Ciji almost hadn't recognized them. Betty seemed skeletal, as if she had just emerged from the shadows of Ravensbrück rather than New York; her drab, wrinkled dress hung around her frame limply, like it was too tired not to slouch. Her hair was a disaster, dark and wild, which only made her skin, which had been like porcelain the night she won the crown, now seem chalky and gray. Purplish circles framed her eyes.

And Griff. The mustache and scraggly beard had transformed him from movie idol into someone who looked like a young, angry Russian history professor. Ciji couldn't tell whether she had been influenced by Eddie's revelations yesterday, but to her he seemed shifty, bordering on paranoid.

She leads them up the flights of narrow, winding servants' stairs in the back of the hotel until they reach a tiny attic of a room at the end of the hall. Betty goes to the window, which looks out onto the rear lawn below and where workers scurry about, laying out thick bolts of canvas. The room is stuffy and horrifically small—it can't measure more than nine-by-eight—and boasts only a single bed in a metal frame, a floor lamp, and a small wooden nightstand with a ceramic bowl and pitcher. "I'm sorry I couldn't do better," Ciji says. "But I needed somewhere you wouldn't be seen. It's the best I could manage."

"It's perfect," Betty says, arms crossed, eyes still fixed outside. Her monotone matches her appearance: tired, flat, defeated.

"We truly appreciate everything you are doing for us," Griff says. "And, of course, the money."

The money? Ciji turns expectantly as Betty jerks around from the window. "Darling, let's not discuss such things when we've only just arrived," Betty says. "We don't want to be rude when Ciji is showing us such kindness."

Ciji picks up the cue. "Don't be silly, Betty." She turns to Griff. "I'm happy to help. It's just that I can't get any money until the bank opens again on Monday. But that will give you two some time to relax a little bit, to regain your strength before you begin on the next leg of your journey."

Griff takes her hand. "This is very generous of you."

"Not at all. Now I think we should let the driver rest a bit, and I will take Betty down to my suite for her much-deserved bath."

Griff appears suddenly stricken. "Oh, no, no. I don't think that's a good idea. It's important . . . that we stay together."

"Griff honey, you're exhausted," Betty says. "You need to sleep. And I'm only going one floor down. I'll be back in half an hour. And look at me!" She grabs lumps of hair in each hand. "I'm a mess. Please, my darling. I need to sit in a nice hot tub and wash away the road. You go lie down. All right?"

Ciji drinks in the scene. *And I thought I was the actress.*

Griff's eyes begin shifting around the room. "They're listening."

Betty takes him by the shoulders, leads him slowly onto the bed. She practically unfolds him, stretching his body out, gently removing his shoes, whispering to him the entire time. Finally she leans over, kisses him tenderly on the lips. She turns to Ciji. "What room are we going to?"

They're listening? Ciji says nothing for a few seconds, wondering whether she is supposed to lie. "It's my room," she says finally. It is not her room—it is the staff room, kept for those who fall ill or who need a place to sleep in case of car trouble or inclement weather. But today it's her room. "From the front desk, you turn left and go down the hall, and it's the last door on the left."

"Now there, you see?" Betty says. "You know exactly where we'll be. But, Griff, you must promise not to come down unless it's absolutely an emergency. We wouldn't want our plans to go awry, would we?" She says it like a grandmother admonishing a little boy not to get out of bed on Christmas Eve and risk running into Santa.

He reaches up, brushes her cheek with the back of his hand. "Okay, then," he says. "I suppose I *am* tired." There is no more talk of anyone listening.

❧

The bath was heavenly. Hot, soapy, Betty blissfully alone in the bubbly suds, not having to think of anything beyond her taut muscles unwinding into the water. Ciji had whisked away her rumpled clothes to be laundered, after Betty had stripped naked right there in front of her, something Betty would have never considered during their week together at the pageant. The tenets of survival easily vanquish those of modesty and ceremony. Ciji left her an outfit to wear, a navy blue and white polka dot wool crepe day dress with a Queen Anne neckline and a gathered waist panel, along with a white cashmere cardigan sweater. Eyeing Betty's dainty feet, Ciji had warned her that the navy peep-toe heels might be a tad roomy, so she'd left tissues to stuff into the backs just in case.

Betty knew that Ciji had a thousand questions, but Betty had pleaded putting off answering until she could at least look and feel like a normal human being again. Brushing her now-dark hair in the mirror, she studies her own reflection, wondering if there are any traces left of the naïve girl who traded her life for a slice of lemon cake all of those months ago. She tries not to think of her family, wondering where she is now, why she's done what she's done. She feels assuaged in the belief that Martha has gotten a message to them. For now, that must be enough.

Betty gathers up the towels from the floor and tosses them into the nearby laundry bin, checks to make sure she still has the key to the room. She'll dash down the hall toward the sitting area, then make the quick left toward the interior servants' stairs.

But when she emerges from the hall, she finds herself momentarily turned around: are the stairs she needs these to the right, then? Or are they down a little bit, on the left? The ground floor is a warren of well-appointed drawing rooms, mercifully deserted save for one young couple, deep in conversation, having tea near a front window. As Betty tries to get her bearings, she feels a presence slide behind her.

"Hello."

Eddie Tate's pale blue eyes are as piercing as ever.

"So nice to see you," he says, taking advantage of his sneak attack and quickly guiding her by the arm toward the back door of the hotel. "I think it's high time we caught up, don't you?"

Twenty-five

*B**etty cannot decide** whether or not to keep the cardigan on. At times, when the sun is shining down on them as they stroll the Cliff Walk, she feels unbearably warm; then, as soon as she starts to remove the sweater, some clouds pass overhead, the temperature plummets the way it only does in New England, and she finds herself buttoning it back up. It's fitting. During her entire relationship with Eddie, she has run hot and cold.

She'd protested that it was risky for her to go waltzing out in public. He was unmoved. "You owe me one walk," he'd said.

He was right about that.

His hair, a throwback to her own former shade and perfectly parted to the side, flits about his face in wisps as the wind whips off the water. Combined with his dark sunglasses and form-fitting knit shirt, it all combines to give him a more rugged, masculine appearance than she would have thought him capable of.

They pass the great back lawn of the hotel on the right, where dozens of workers hammer and lift and carry ropes and long metal poles and more bolts of pale yellow-and-white-striped canvas. "I wonder what all of this is about," Betty says.

Eddie stops. "Tomorrow night. It's the big Masquerade Ball for the Preservation Society. Ciji says the Ocean House was pretty peeved they weren't selected. I think everyone was worried that if the weather was bad the Cliff Lawn couldn't pull it off, using a big circus tent. But it seems like it's all going to come together."

An elderly French-speaking couple passes them. Betty laughs. "You never stop being a reporter."

He thinks about his own career, now in ruins. "Sometimes I do." He reaches into his pocket, extracts a fresh newspaper clipping. "News from the home front. I thought you'd be interested."

Betty unfolds it, begins reading.

NEW MISS AMERICA TO BE CROWNED IN A.C.
Betty Jane Welch "left of her own free will," officials declare

By Charles Kaisinger
Press Staff Writer

ATLANTIC CITY—Officials at the Miss America Pageant announced last night that they will crown Miss Texas, Eleanor Patricia Wyatt, the first runner-up in this year's contest, as the new Miss America. The move will officially strip the title from Betty Jane Welch of Delaware, who vanished the night of her crowning, reportedly in the company of her pageant escort, Mr. John Griffin McAllister of Longport.

Miss Welch's disappearance set off a frenzy of searches by law enforcement for clues to her whereabouts, and wild speculation that she had been kidnapped by Mr. McAllister or other parties. But yesterday pageant officials confirmed reports that Miss Welch had recently contacted Mr. McAllister's sister, Martha, and through her relayed a message to her family in Delaware that she was well and had not been taken against her will. Interviewed by authorities, Miss McAllister—whose mother, socialite Honor McAllister, was recently involved in a car crash in New York City but is now recovering—said that Miss Welch had telephoned her yesterday and stated emphatically that she was not under duress and had left Atlantic City with Mr. McAllister of her own accord.

As a result of these new facts, Atlantic City police have closed the case and stopped searching for the fly-the-coop lovebirds, whose whereabouts remain unknown. Pageant director Lenora Slaughter said a formal crowning of Miss Wyatt will occur this Saturday at the Traymore Hotel, followed by a small reception for honored guests. "We are happy to put this unpleasant chapter behind us," Miss Slaughter said in a brief statement to reporters. "We are confident that Eleanor will represent the finest traditions of Miss America for her year of service."

Miss Welch's win will be expunged from pageant records. Miss Slaughter declined to say whether the pageant would seek compensatory damages from Miss Welch, if and when she surfaces, for her abdication. "At this moment we would like to concentrate on the future, not the past," she said.

Thank God for Martha. My parents know I'm safe. This is one step closer to all being over. Betty turns to him. "Well, at least they've stopped looking for us."

"The Atlantic City cops, anyway." Eddie conjures an image of his last day in the office, packing his desk as his coworkers tried not to look, except of course for that chucklehead Chick Kaisinger. He'd been panting like a German shepherd to take over the missing Miss America story since it began.

"How come you didn't write the story?" Betty asks.

He shrugs. "On a different beat now."

They begin walking again, away from the cacophony of the workmen and the rising tent. "I didn't think I would ever see you again," she says finally.

"Were you hoping you wouldn't?"

"I know you must be sore. But I did call. I did. I left a message at your hotel. You were just . . . too late."

"Yeah, well, I'm sorry about that. I didn't realize I was going to miss the murder."

He wants to stuff it back into his mouth, like eating a piece of paper. She stops dead in her tracks.

"That was cheap. And unworthy of you."

"A man is dead, Betty."

"You don't understand."

"So help me understand."

Betty folds her arms, walks slightly ahead of him. "You went into the apartment."

"Yes."

"Why?"

"I was chasing a story."

"Which you didn't write." They walk a bit farther in silence, until she finally asks, "Why are you here?"

"Ciji asked me to come."

"You didn't come for Ciji."

"Do you love him?" he blurts out. It is the question he does not want answered, because as long as it isn't answered, declaratively, plainspokenly, then his mind still contains room to be unencumbered, to host fantasies that he cannot let go of, no matter how hard he tries. But he must have the answer. He must.

"I don't want to, if you can believe that."

They are silent for seconds that tick by like hours, both of them now looking out at the placid, rippling water, the spray from the whitecaps mixing into the breeze. "I fell in love," she says finally. "I won't apologize for that. It was real and true, and I had never been that happy in my entire life. I didn't know the world could look like that, could smell like that. He told me I was the world to him. You have to understand what that does to a girl when she hears that."

"The world," Eddie says, "until you won Miss America."

"Until I won Miss America," she repeats. "I mean, I can't say I wasn't warned. He told me straightaway that he was not going to be Miss America's boyfriend. That the stress of it would prove too much. And I didn't care, because it never occurred to me that I could actually be Miss America. And even after I won, I didn't think about it. I just thought it was something he'd said, that when he saw me—"

"Like I saw you."

She nods. "Like you saw me. Yes. The truth is I wanted him to look at me the way you did after you came back to retrieve your hat."

"So you were kissing some image of him, then? Not me?"

She takes a deep breath in. "No. I certainly knew it was you."

"And yet you're still in love with him."

"It's more fraught than that. I owe him."

"For what? For being your escort for a week?" His tone is sardonic, laced with a virulent jealousy that makes him ugly. He hates himself for it.

Betty wants to see his eyes, but his sunglasses obscure them. Instead he keeps looking off intently at the sun-dappled water, as if he's trying to catch the end of a yachting race in the distance.

"Griff made his position perfectly clear right off the shake: I ignored his concern, and I swept away the warning signs of his illness because they didn't fit in with the summer romance I was having. And then, to make things all the worse, when he simply kept his word by breaking things off, I not only had Ciji track him down, but I begged him to take me away, to let us go someplace, just the two of us. He did everything I asked. And now, because of that—because of my selfish actions—his sickness has become much more grave, and his judgment's impaired, and Reeve is dead, and the scandal grows bigger by the day. And all of it is my fault, don't you understand? I can't just toss him aside now, discard him like some old garment that no longer fits. It's not who I am. Surely you see that."

So Griff killed Reeve.

Eddie ponders her words, feels his heart constricting as silence descends once more, like a curtain coming down between them. For a while the only sounds are those of idle conversations that grow louder and then softer as people pass, and the gentle ripple of the breakers.

"So we walk him down to the police, all of us. We tell the truth—"

"It's not that simple."

"It is that simple. It's the only thing that makes sense, to stop this madness."

"He has a gun."

"What?"

"He has a gun. I don't know where he got it, and it doesn't matter. But he has it. I've seen it. Only he keeps changing where he keeps it."

"Did you look for it? When he was sleeping?"

"I can't risk that. If he were to wake and find me snooping . . .

I don't know what he might do. That's why we have to handle this very, very carefully. He's . . . fragile."

"Fragile? When are you going to finally start using the right word? He's sick in the head. He needs help. Medical help. His mother—"

Betty zips back to the newspaper clipping, the report of Honor's accident. "How is she? Do you know?"

He reports what he told Ciji, registers her visible relief. "Too bad Reeve Spencer didn't fare quite as well," he says.

She nods, almost imperceptibly. "It wasn't what you think."

"Then tell me what it was."

So she does. The telephone calls to him and to Griff's sister, her plan to coax Griff out, to come home. How Reeve had come back early, circled her like a panther, attacked her, pinned her to the bed. "He did it to save me."

"I doubt that's how the cops will see it."

"What do you mean?"

"Betty, don't be daft. Griff is what, six-one, six-two? Reeve didn't look big at all. They're going to wonder why he didn't just pull Reeve off you, pummel him, toss him into the next room. But instead he picked up a heavy object and bashed his head in. That's third-degree murder, Betty. Maybe even second. Manslaughter at the very least. And then there's the fact you two fled the scene. You'll be lucky not to go down with him."

"Do the police know?"

He shifts uncomfortably, kicks a pebble in the path. "Not yet."

"So no one even knows we were there," she says. "Except Honor. And . . . you."

He nods. "And me." He stops, turns back to the water, because he cannot bear to look at her as he says what he must say. "I love you, Betty. I have from the moment I laid eyes on you in that swimsuit that first day on the Boardwalk. But I cannot—I will not—be an accomplice to a murder. I'm already in this thing deep enough as it is. I've already lost too much. And for . . . for . . . what?" He fights it, this slow crumpling in his face, and he is silently grateful she cannot *see* his face, spy the tears forming in his eyes.

She turns his shoulders back to her. "For me, Eddie," she says, gently removing the sunglasses. She takes his face into her palm, caresses his cheek. "You did it for me."

She does not see the figure standing by the window of the room under the gable three stories up, looking down at them with dead, dispassionate eyes. Does not see Griff's mouth settle into a long, grim line, as the voices again rise up and deafen him from the inside.

❧

Chick Kaisinger pulls into the parking lot of the diner, his sore back twitching like a son of a bitch. He's never taken his temperamental Plymouth this far on the road. He just hopes it's hale enough to make the trip all the way back to Jersey.

He sidles up to the counter, hops onto a stool. "Coffee?" the waitress asks.

"Yes, please," he says. "I'm looking for Shirley."

The waitress points to her name tag. "You found her," she says, sliding over the sugar and creamer.

Chick retrieves his press badge, slides it onto the counter. "Chick Kaisinger, of the *Atlantic City Press*. We spoke on the phone?"

She gives it a cursory glance. "Oh, yeah," she says. "You called about that Miss America who's on the lam."

Indeed he had. He'd gotten a tip that the New York cops had found a dead body in Chelsea of a guy who used to be Griffin McAllister's old roommate in college. Then the news of Mrs. McAllister's accident northbound on the WSE had come in. It was too much to be coincidental. Were Betty and Griff heading north? Hadn't Betty roomed with a girl from one of the New England states?

Chick had spent the better part of yesterday mapping out the most logical route from New York to Newport, then calling every diner and gas station between the two, hoping to confirm a sighting of Griff and Betty. And then, yesterday, pay dirt. Shirley, the waitress at the Lucky Strike diner. He'd win a Pulitzer for sure.

"Is this the couple you saw in here yesterday?" He plunks down a photo of Betty and Griff, dancing at the Miss America Ball on the Steel Pier.

Shirley scrunches her face. "I dunno. Could be. The girl in here was a brunette. And he had a beard and a mustache, kinda scruffy-like. Didn't you say on the phone there was some kind of reward?"

"I said I'd be happy to give you a bonus if your information was copacetic."

Shirley picks up the photo, studies it more closely. "Yeah, I mean, she looks a lot different. It's the hair. It's not done like it is here, and like I said, it's almost black now. But that's him. I remember he sat there slap-happy, eating his eggs and toast."

"Did they say where they were going?"

She shrugs. "I don't ask a lot of questions after 'Whaddya having, folks?'"

Chick throws a fin onto the counter, tips his hat.

I knew it! They're in Newport, he thinks as he jumps back into the Plymouth. *And I'm going to tell the whole world.*

Twenty-six

ry it on. I bet you'll look very dashing."

Betty extends her arm, holds the hanger with the Colonial costume up so she can assess it better. The coat is brocaded, a bright canary yellow—admittedly no one's best color—but the ruffled shirt gives it a certain historical panache. There are pale beige breeches, and, on the dresser, some white hose and a pair of buckled black shoes, along with a tricorn hat and a mask.

"I'll do it later," Griff mutters absently, sitting with his legs folded on the bed, as if in an Indian prayer, eyes still fixed on the window. He looks waxy, sallow, gaunt. His nap seems to have had little restorative effect. Ciji has procured an electric razor, and Betty hopes that Griff will feel better when he's able to trim the wildness of his hair and beard, able to look into a mirror and see more of himself staring back.

He's been unusually quiet since she returned from her bath and unscheduled stroll with Eddie. In these last few days, Griff has materialized in two shapes: normal, the confident, handsome young man she met in Atlantic City; and shifty, the tortured soul fighting his demons. But this one — this wan, vacant Griff — this is new. He unsettles her even more than the latter.

"I can't wait to see what Ciji found for *me* to wear," Betty says too enthusiastically, like a schoolteacher attempting to rally her pupils for a math lesson. "We're going to be the most swell couple there."

He finally breaks his gaze from the window, turns to her. "I still don't understand why we're going. It seems awfully risky, when we've spent all of this time trying to stay out of sight."

An excellent point, she thinks. One she cannot easily refute. On her way back in, Eddie had said cryptically, "Ciji and I are working out a way to get Griff the help he needs without anyone knowing, and without risking anyone's safety. So whatever directions you get from her, even if they seem cockamamie, follow them. You have to trust us, Betty."

She knows he's right, that he's been right about more than this. So when she entered the tiny room and saw the Colonial garb hanging on the back of the door, she'd rushed to read the note Ciji had left:

> *You two have been cooped up so long, and we are hosting this big costume ball tomorrow night. I am getting outfits for you both; this is Griff's. You can wear your masks and roam about, and no one will be the wiser. Please accept this invitation as my way of giving you some joy during your trying journey of the last few weeks. Love, Ciji*

There is certainly more behind the invitation than respite. But what? She has to trust them. And so she has spent the last ten minutes cheerleading for Griff, doing everything but a cartwheel across the room to get him enthused about the ball. Even if it indeed does not make any sense as to why two people hiding out in the attic of the servants' wing would suddenly roam the grounds in period costume amid hundreds of people.

Betty hangs the outfit back up, slides onto the bed, and places her arms around him. "You'll feel better after a bath," she says.

"I washed up in the basin."

He smells of strong lye soap and mint. "You don't want to show me how spiffy you're going to look in your Colonial best?"

He tilts his chin up. "You really want to see me in this, I see."

She grins, thrilled by his sudden animation. "Yes!"

"Hmm." He hops off the bed, strips off his shirt. In the bright light of day, his weight loss is noticeable. But looking at him, at the fine, sinewy lines of his torso, she can still feel her breath shorten, feel the flicker of her own desire, even now, even after everything. "I guess I have to take these off, too," he says, unzipping his pants and stepping out of them. Then he unexpectedly tugs down his drawers, stands by the bed completely nude.

His eyes are piercing. She holds them in her own, despite the fact she wants to look away, she most desperately wants to look away, but something tells her urgently that she mustn't, that this is a test and that she must pass it. So she stays frozen in place, casually resting on one arm on the bed, laid out in her borrowed polka dot dress like a calendar pinup, and he continues staring down at her, unflinching. Trying to decipher what's lurking behind his gaze has become an impossible task, for only he can hear the commands barking inside his head. But still she tries, studies his eyes, glassy and impassive and . . . something else, something she faintly recognizes but cannot identify right away.

"You used to like seeing me like this," he says softly.

She intakes a small breath through her teeth. "I still do."

"Do you?"

"I'm the girl who accepted your marriage proposal in Times

Square three nights ago." It stuns her how easily the words come, words she doesn't mean. When did she become this person, this girl of the cool lie? Sometime after taking off her tiara and sash and throwing them away. She thinks of the artless, trusting girl sitting in her mother's kitchen, how gullible she'd been, packing up her crepe and taffeta and dismissing everything at every turn as yet another silly adventure, as if life were a game played in the penny arcade. She remembers hearing stories during the war, stories she wasn't quite old enough to comprehend, about women in Europe, the things they'd done, the tactics they'd resorted to in order to survive. She looks at his face and she knows she loves him, knows part of her always will. But their road together is coming to an end. A casualty of a different kind of war.

"Come here, my darling," she says, patting the bed, and he does, and as he climbs on top of her, she runs her hands lightly up and down his body, feeling him thicken and harden, hearing his breath grow short as he kisses her neck, her ear. He reaches under her dress, explores her with his fingers, and she arches her back, cries out softly as his finger plunges inside her. "Oh, Griff," she says, "I love you." She means it and yet she does not, wants him and yet does not. She knows that this may be the last time they ever make love. She wants it to matter, to signify something, to mark something, and so she kisses him, hard, their mouths wet and ferocious on each other. And she finds that she suddenly needs this as much as he, that she needs to remind herself of what this was all for, what her heart fought so hard to attain, even if the battle has already been lost.

He undresses her slowly, achingly. He slips the panties from underneath her, hikes up her skirt, pulls her off the bed just long enough to lift the dress above her head and toss it onto the floor. He unhooks her bra, discards it, and now the two of them lie naked, bodies rubbing together, Betty reaching for him, wanting him inside her, but he resists, teases her nipples with his tongue, makes her wait. The frottage builds and builds, and he can feel the friction, can see what it is doing to her body from the inside out, until finally she reaches her hands above her head, grabs hold of the iron slats of the headboard as if clinging to a life raft as she topples over the edge of her own desire.

For a moment he considers simply falling over to the side, of having the act finish right then and there, but he knows she will not allow this, that she will want him to climax, to feel she has given him what he has given her.

But she has not given him what he has given her. He can see that now, even as he guides himself inside her, feels her breath catch again in his ear as he moves rhythmically back and forth. He buries his face in her shoulder, her arms tightly encircling his back, and yet they will not even allow him this. They give sound to her betrayal, now not the competing voices of argument but of one damning verdict.

She doesn't love you! She is making a fool of you! Why can you not see it?

Where is the gun? Where is the gun?

They're all laughing at you. Look to the window! They're all there, looking in on you, laughing at you!

There is a microphone in the basin, recording every movement, every thought. They know everything you do. They're waiting, waiting to put you away, just like your mother did. Is that what you want?

Where is the gun? Get the gun!

Look at her, writhing underneath you. She's a whore. A dirty whore! You watched her get all moony over that reporter. She loves him, not you. Can't you see him? He's floating right above your head, looking down at you from the ceiling, joking about you!

You must get the gun.

Save us.
Kill them all.

❧

The knock at the door elbows her out of shallow sleep.

Betty springs up in the bed, her breasts exposed as the sheet falls to her waist. Griff is on his side, facing her. His eyes are open, unblinking. She shivers, as if a bitter cold wind has just blown through the room.

Another knock, louder this time. A whisper. "Betty, open up." Ciji.

"One minute," Betty replies as she reaches over the side of the bed, retrieves her clothes scrunched up on the floor. She shimmies into them quickly, trying in vain to smooth out the dress, even as she feels Griff's eyes following her around the room like a prison guard. His passivity, the cool detachment during their lovemaking, rattles her. She wants to both know what he's thinking and not know at all.

"Coming," Betty says in the direction of the door, hustling over and undoing the latch. Ciji steps in, takes in Betty's disheveled appearance, Griff's bare torso tangled up in the sheets. "I see," is all she says. "So sorry to . . . interrupt. But I'm afraid it's time for Betty's fitting."

"My? . . . Oh, right. The costume."

Griff sits up, suddenly alert, like a sculpture suddenly magically animated to life. "You're leaving me again?" he asks tremulously.

Betty turns to him, gestures Ciji to button her up the back. "You know how it is, darling," she says. "I can't just slip into some breeches like you boys. Ciji has arranged this lovely gown for me to wear tomorrow night, and I have to go try it on, get it pinned so that it will fit."

"I don't want to go anymore. We're not going to go."

Without turning around, Betty can register the alarm in Ciji's eyes. She does not know why she and Griff must attend this ball, but she knows there is a reason. A good one.

"All right, honey," Betty says slowly, walking over and sitting at the bottom of the bed. "If you don't want to go, we don't have to go."

Griff looks at her for several seconds, then over to Ciji, who stands perfectly still. "I'm sorry," Griff says to her. "I know you went to a lot of trouble to get these getups for us and to get us in. But I just don't think it's a good idea. We only came here to get money."

"Griff!" Betty says.

"No, it's fine," Ciji says. "I appreciate your candor, Griff. Betty has told me about your need for funds, and of course I am happy to help you. But as I said earlier, there's no way I can get to the bank today. There's too much to do for the ball, and I'm already taking a risk stealing these few moments here with you. But I can get you the money on Monday morning, and you can be on your way."

Betty frowns. "We're being terribly rude, Griff. Ciji has done nothing but help us, going back to the night of the pageant. We wouldn't be together if not for her. I don't understand." She feels like she is playing a game of chess in the pitch-dark, carefully moving a rook across the board, a bishop diagonally, with no idea where her opponent's pieces are approaching in return. "These past few days have just been so very trying and . . . upsetting." A Reeve reference, to bolster her argument. "I just wanted us to have one nice evening before we go back onto the road. I didn't think it was so much to ask."

He says nothing for a little while, simply looks back to the window. Finally he says flatly, "A fitting, then? Now?"

Betty and Ciji exchange furtive looks. "Yes," Ciji says. "It won't take long."

Betty reaches over to the table and grabs her hairbrush. "You can come if you'd like," she says airily, and she knows without even looking over that Ciji must be in open panic, that this is not at all part of the plan, whatever the plan is, but she needs to say it, needs to show Griff that nothing untoward is happening behind his back, even if it is.

There is always more spirit in attack than in defense.

"No, I think I will stay here," he says. "You go on. I'll be surprised when I see you in your lovely dress."

Awkward quiet descends. It's like all sides have agreed to a peace treaty that none believe will hold.

"Thank you for not being a crumb," Betty says, leaning over and kissing him. "I'll be back in a jiffy."

"I can come back with some food for you while they're pinning the dress," Ciji says. "Some goo and the moo sound good?"

"Oh, pancakes," Betty echoes. "That does sound delicious."

He hates this, the way they're talking to him, as if he's a five-year-old about to devolve into a tantrum if he doesn't get his way, as if he must be constantly monitored and mollified. Something isn't right, he knows it isn't right, but he needs time, time alone to go back to sleep, to quiet the voices and just rest. Then he can decide what to do. "It does," he says.

"Then I guess it's all peachy," Ciji says. "C'mon, Betty. The seamstress is waiting and she's got other dresses to hem."

Griff waits for a few minutes, making sure they've gone, then gets up, pads around to the other side of the bed, where the floor lamp stands. He moves it, drops down to his haunches. He pries the loose floorboard, wiggling it a bit this way, then that, until it finally pops up. He lifts it and reaches down into the black hole beneath, until he feels the beaded grip of the Browning. He retrieves the gun, studies it, the way he used to study the rare flowers they would sometimes get in the nursery. He thinks of the sunflowers, his special signature flower; remembers the day he stood on the muggy Boardwalk as Betty's float drifted by, how proud he was of his excellent aim in sending the sunflower arcing onto her platform. *Why couldn't it be like that again? How had it all gotten ruined?*

But it had been ruined.

He replaces the floorboard, slides the lamp back over to cover it, then picks up the Browning again. It feels heavy, significant in his hand. He crawls back into bed on his side, the gun still in his hand as it slides under the pillow. There is much to be done. It's time to rest.

❧

"I cannot believe you."

They are twisting down the servants' stairs of the Cliff Lawn, Betty trying to keep up with Ciji, who wants to stay quiet, to stay focused on the task at hand, but now finds that she cannot.

Betty catches up to her on the landing. "What do you mean? What are you talking about?"

Ciji checks to make sure no one's in earshot. "I mean you sleeping with Griff," she hisses. "I mean, really, Betty. In the middle of all of this? With his . . . state? And this is what's important to you, a romp in the hay with a psycho?"

"Hush!" Betty's eyes blaze back at her. "Don't you dare call him that! Do you hear me? I don't care what you're doing for us. You have no right to use such language!"

"Well, I'd be careful if I were you, dearie. Eddie and I are the only two people who stand between you and disaster."

"I didn't ask you to bring Eddie here."

"No, you asked me to help you. Which I am doing. Now: Do you want my help or not? Because if you don't, you and lover boy up there can just pack up and move on, and you can figure a way out of this mess all on your own. In case you haven't noticed, I've got four hundred people coming for dinner tomorrow night."

A young maid comes up the staircase, brushes by them; Betty tilts her head downward, a reflex she's picked up ever since leaving Atlantic City. Never let anyone see your face, remember your features.

Betty slides her hand down Ciji's arm until she finds her hand, knots their fingers tightly together. "I'm sorry. I'm so very sorry," she whispers. "I'm so torn, can't you see? There are these moments when I still think he's still in there, the boy I fell in love with on the Boardwalk. And then it's not just about getting him safe, in ending this in a way where no one gets hurt. Sometimes I look at him and I wonder . . . I wonder if I can reach him. If I can . . ."

"Cure him?"

"I'm not that much of a pistol to believe that."

"Listen to me, Delaware. We've been through a lot together in a very short period of time. We can't quit on each other now. But I need you to trust me. You asked me to get you out of this pickle, and I'm gonna try. But I can't do it if you muck up the works by going soft. You know Griff needs help. You owe it to him to put your own feelings aside and make sure he gets it."

Betty hugs her. "How did *you* not win Miss America?"

"That damned harp. Gets 'em every time."

A few minutes later they are in the calling room, waiting by the door. Guests and workers mill about, immersed in the anticipation and frenzy surrounding tomorrow's ball. Betty feels exposed, being out in the open like this, where anyone can see her, identify her. "Why are we here?" she murmurs. "Where is the seamstress?"

Ciji points outside. "You have a more pressing appointment. The brown sedan. Just run out and get in the back. He knows where to take you."

"What? I don't underst—"

Ciji shoves her out the door. "Now!"

The sedan soon pulls out of the carport and onto Memorial Boulevard, Betty in the back seat.

Twenty minutes later the car turns right onto a long gravel drive that leads to the front of a sweeping sea captain's house with weathered brown shaker shingles and a porch extending all the way around to the rear. A bulky man in a black suit walks gingerly down the front steps, opens her door. She thinks she recognizes him but can't recall from where. She alights, falls in step behind him.

They walk slowly down a long hardwood hall lined with appropriate art: oil paintings of dunes and oceans, a larger one of a whaling captain, photographs of beaches. Their footsteps echo through the hall ominously, like those of a prisoner being led to the courtroom to hear the verdict.

He steps aside, ushers her into a drawing room that overlooks the water. There is a hearty blaze crackling in the fireplace, and a long figure sitting at the end of a large tufted sofa, sipping a cognac.

"Ah, Betty," Honor McAllister says. "We are reunited at last."

Twenty-seven

B *etty sits in an armchair,* balancing a Wedgwood teacup on her lap, cautiously eyeing Griff's mother across from her. She is expecting wrath, knows she deserves it, but something in her has toughened up in these past few weeks, changed her, probably forever. And so she holds the cold eye contact, watches impassively as Honor daintily sips her cognac, shifting ever so slightly on the sofa. A walking stick is propped over to the side, a gilded accessory no doubt necessary to help her walk on her in-jured foot. It only adds to her general grand dame–ness.

Betty decides at last to jump in, get it over with. "Mrs. McAllis-ter, I know you must have questions, so many, many questions. And I am sure you are quite cross with me, for making all this muddle."

Honor arches an eyebrow. "Muddle! Is that what you call it, dear? You undersell yourself."

"I never thought things would—"

"Do you know who Margaret Gorman is?"

Betty stops, thrown by Honor's sinister serenity. "No, I cannot say that I do."

"She was the very first Miss America, almost thirty years ago now. A slight thing she was. Fifteen years old! On the day they went to tell her she had been selected as Miss Washington, D.C., they found her lying on her stomach in a dusty old park, shooting marbles. Isn't that enchanting?"

Betty sits motionless as her tea turns cold.

"Such wonderful girls we've had over the years. Pat Donnelly— Jack Warner personally offered her a contract at Warner Brothers. He thought she could be the next Ann Sheridan. And Jo Dennison, Jean Bartel. Even Bess Myerson was a delightful queen, once everyone got past her being a Jew. Somehow, the pageant has always managed to correctly identify the right young woman to lead us. To inspire the country."

Betty places her teacup on the side table. "I owe you an apology, Mrs. McAllister, and I extend it to you with a full heart. But I am not going to sit here and—"

"Quiet." It is not a request.

Betty feels her hackles rise but says nothing. She silently curses Ciji.

Honor stands, struggling for a moment to maintain her balance. She reaches for the walking stick, begins to make a slow circle around the room. "Griffin was always an impetuous little boy. I always knew he was different, in that manner all mothers know their children. Martha is studious, a good observer of things. But Griffin . . . he always seemed off somewhere, slightly out of reach. Even as a child.

"He was eight years old when he first told me about the voices. I thought he simply had an overactive imagination. I often wonder about that, about whether I could have made a difference had I taken it all more seriously straightaway. But as a parent one cannot flagellate oneself over every past ill-advised decision. It serves no point.

"By the time he reached puberty, Griffin was having these terrible delusions. Paranoia. The wireless was emitting brain-controlling waves. His teachers were plotting to kill him. We even had to fire the gardener because Griffin was convinced he was a Nazi spy who was going to burn down the house and take us all to Germany as prisoners. We tried everything. Or at least I did. My husband was not a man equipped to deal with . . . such deficiencies. I tried my best for Griffin, not only for his sake but also because I needed to protect Martha. It was very difficult for her, explaining away Griffin's odd behavior. I fear she lost a good part of her girlhood to it.

"And then things leveled out, as they might say. He seemed better, more like a steady young man. He loved the nursery, threw himself into learning all about the flowers and the plants. He was outgoing and convivial with the hotel managers. I cannot express how relieved I was. The doctors warned me that his condition was not cured, that it would never be cured, that the best we could hope for was that it would abate for periods, that the symptoms would fade, like scars. But I was convinced they were wrong. Once we got him home from Lawrenceville, he blossomed. He filled out, so strong and handsome, joined the rowing team. Being on the water had a very calming effect, so we bought a motorboat." She shoots over a scathing stare. "Your getaway vehicle."

She keeps circling, as if giving a lecture in a great college hall. "He was the beau every girl in Atlantic City wanted. After a time I began to have periods where I even forgot he'd ever been ill at all.

"He graduated high school, wanted to go to NYU. I was terribly nervous having him that far away, because his experience at boarding school had been brief and difficult, and because New York is such an unruly place. I knew Griffin needed order, quiet. I begged him to go to the University of Pennsylvania, where he would be closer to home. But he wore me down, because that's what sons do: they wear their poor mothers down.

"We didn't know Reeve — he was not Griffin's original roommate — but Griffin told us about his family: mill owners, from upstate New York. Good people. I assumed — incorrectly, it turned out — that he would be a good influence on Griffin. The boys seemed to get along and lived in an apartment near Washington Square. I tried to assuage my nerves as best I could. But it didn't take long for my worst fears to become realized. Griff met a girl. Her name was Helen Stevens."

Helen Stevens. Betty's mind boomerangs back to that horrible day in the apartment in New York, to Reeve's ominous warning: *Ask him about Helen Stevens. She was cuckoo for him, too. Ask him what happened to* her.

Honor meanders to the fireplace, stares intently into the flames, lost in her recollections. "Poor Helen. A nice little girl, actually. Bright, sunny. But a bit of a flibbertigibbet. She and Griffin were quite the pair for a while. He brought her to Longport for a weekend to meet us. She seemed very smitten with him, and he simply *adored* her. But she was young, and when you're young life seems endless, and there is always a better possibility somewhere ahead, and so after a few months she told Griffin she'd met someone else and she wished him well and that was to be that. Those things happen in first love. But not to Griffin. He was heartbroken. But more than that, he was triggered. His illness roared back almost instantly, like a forest fire being sparked. Of course, I had no idea any of this was happening — he was in New York, and I was a hundred miles away. But then he phoned, and the moment I heard his voice I knew. I knew."

She comes back to the sofa, settles wearily back onto the cushions. "He didn't mean to do it, you see. You have to understand that. That's not who he is. He's not violent. The voices may sometimes suggest such things, but he's never acted on them. Instead he gets flummoxed, confused, suspicious. It takes him out of balance.

"He went to her apartment, begged her to take him back. She refused, and from what I can gather was rather cold about it. Everyone paints boys as the unfeeling cads, but I've been around enough young ladies to know they can be equally cruel and careless in matters of the heart. I don't know. Perhaps she'd simply had enough by that point. After all, she didn't know about his condition. Neither did Reeve. Another error I made." She smiles ruefully. "So many."

Betty leans forward. "What happened? To Helen?"

"Griffin was agitated, began arguing with the voices aloud. I'm sure by now you've unfortunately witnessed one of his episodes. They can be quite terrifying. Helen became frightened, ran for the door. Griffin attempted to intercept her, and in the altercation she fell backward. Her head hit the corner of a glass coffee table. It was an accident. A horrible, horrible accident." She pinches between her eyes. "It was a disaster, as you might imagine."

"She died?"

Honor nods, almost imperceptibly.

"But it was an accident."

"It seemed very unlikely that the Stevens family would see it that way. And Griffin was in a very bad way. It took some doing to clean it all up."

Doing. Betty knows what this means in the world of people like the McAllisters. Payoffs. Bribes.

"We became much more aggressive in getting Griffin help," Honor continues. "There was so much gossip on the campus. We pulled him out of the university, brought him home. We tried medications, therapies, counseling. My husband wanted to put him away. But I knew he was still here — my little boy was still here. We put him through electroshock treatments, which I can tell you is the worst thing a mother can ever see her son endure. But I was desperate. I did it because I wanted him well, I wanted him . . . back. A doctor we knew began prescribing lithium, which helped enormously. He told us we just had to have Griffin avoid stress. So we eased him back into the family business. We installed an intercom system in the house so we could hear him when he was out of sight. And it was working. He was getting better."

"And then he met me."

"And then he met you," she answers mournfully. "Feisty Miss Delaware."

"Mrs. McAllister, I am so, so very sorry." Betty has more she needs to say, but the words are caught, trapped in the emotion now clogged in her throat.

"There is neither the time nor the luxury for blame, Betty. I bear the responsibility for all of this as much as you. Now we must fix it. We need to get him to a hospital, where he can be properly treated."

"How can we do that? He almost ran you off the road in New York. He's not going to go with you peacefully."

"There is a method. But before we get to that, I must insist on knowing one detail: which is exactly what happened to Reeve Spencer in that apartment."

So she knows that Reeve is dead. Of course she knows.

Betty explains it all. Through the entire recitation, Honor's expression remains staid, implacable, as if she's listening to a report on the nursery's third-quarter sales. If she's shocked or alarmed by any of Betty's lurid tale, she doesn't show it.

Honor rings a bell on the end table, and soon the burly man comes back through the door. "Bring the car around. It's time to return Miss Welch to the hotel."

Betty rises. She feels clumsy, like a gawky teenager trying to decide whether she should hug her forbidding aunt before departing.

"Sam will return you to the Cliff Lawn. He'll give you the dress for your costume tomorrow night. After all, this was supposed to be your fitting." She rises slowly from the couch. "Miss Moore will fill you in on the details."

Ciji. Ciji and Eddie and Honor, all of them. What a peculiar image, of the three of them together crafting a plan to mop up her mess. "How can you be sure this will work?"

"Because, despite everything, there is one thing I know for certain," Honor McAllister says. "And that is that my son loves you."

❧

Chick Kaisinger is wired; he has driven from the diner without making a single stop. Now he strolls through the front door of the Cliff Lawn, takes in the surroundings. The foyer is a handsome mix of dark woods, tapestries, and Edwardian furnishings, all set on an ornate floral area rug, the wood underneath a weathered pine. A small circular mahogany table sits in the center, a spray of artfully arranged hydrangeas springing from a pale green porcelain vase. There is a small silver tray as well, a nod to the space's former use as "the calling room" of the house, even if no one comes to call anymore.

He pulls out his notebook, begins scribbling down descriptions. You never know when the desk is going to want a few fancy details to fluff up a piece. He's surveying a gilt-framed oil portrait of an aristocratic-looking bearded gentleman in an ascot and waistcoat, hanging against the striped wallpaper, when a voice behind interrupts.

"John Winthrop Chanler," the voice says. Chick turns to see an officious woman in a light wool skirt suit and unadorned white blouse. Her hair is dark brown, pulled back from her face in a bun so tight it looks like it might provoke a headache. She carries a clipboard against her body and has the erect posture and faintly dour look of a Depression schoolmistress. "I see you are carrying a notebook. May I assist you with information about the hotel?"

He reaches into his breast pocket, flashes his badge, with PRESS in big block letters across the top, then quickly puts it back. He doesn't need her to read the fine print, see the words *Atlantic City Press* at the bottom. "Chick Kaisinger," he says, extending his hand. "I'm a writer for *Holiday* magazine. Up here doing a story on great New England hotels. Somebody gave me the dope on this place. Said it was really the cat's meow."

He can't tell what's impressed her more: that he's an alleged writer for *Holiday* magazine or that the hotel's reputation is so keen. She visibly brightens, her smile a tattered row of small, coffee-stained teeth. "Well, I can see you are well informed. Mr. Chanler was a well-respected congressman who built this mansion for himself and his wife as a summer residence in the 1870s. She was, of course, the former Margaret Astor Ward, the great-granddaughter of John Jacob Astor."

Chick makes some nonsensical notations on his pad. He couldn't give a hoot about some old congressman and his rich wife. But he cares very much about this woman, who he suspects knows everything that goes on in the hotel. Her type always does. "Can I get your name, for the story?" he asks earnestly. "Uh, Miss . . . ?"

"Mrs. Hensley. Eugenia Hensley. I'm the head housekeeper here at the Cliff Lawn. My family has been in Newport for generations."

"You don't say," Chick says. Scribble, scribble. Chick points toward the back windows, past which the billowing tent is now up, some of the side flaps fluttering in the wind as various men in gray overalls and sweat-stained T-shirts secure them to wooden stakes. "And what's going on out there?"

"Oh! Yes, we're very proud to be the host hotel for the Preservation Society Masquerade Ball tomorrow evening. It's the highlight of the season. Anyone who is anyone in Newport society will be here."

"That sounds like a lot to get off the ground," Chick says. "You must have a great staff here."

"The finest."

Chick puts on his best "searching for a memory" face, chews his pencil thoughtfully for a few seconds. "Hey, didn't I hear somewhere that Miss Rhode Island works here? She must have every man clobbered."

Mrs. Henley's face melts back into its *American Gothic* blankness. "Miss Catherine Moore, yes," she says, suddenly checking the cuffs of her jacket. "But of course we have many, many fine people working here."

"But not everybody's Miss Rhode Island," Chick says, grinning.

"Mercifully, they are not."

"Is she around, by any chance? It would be great to get a quote from her for the story."

Mrs. Hensley delivers a cursory look into the other rooms. "I don't see her. She's been disappearing a bit of late." She looks at Chick regretfully. "I shouldn't have said such a thing. Please don't write that."

"No problem," Chick says, making a pronounced slash in his notebook. Mrs. Hensley relaxes visibly. He adds, "I wouldn't want to upset the person who is obviously the one who makes this place run shipshape."

She colors slightly. "Well, you are kind. I wouldn't quite put it that way—"

"But back to Miss Moore. I mean, it doesn't seem fair that she gets to just vanish whenever she feels like it. I mean, just between us." He smiles again, and she returns it. He is not a handsome man, not dashing in even the most elastic definition of the term, but he has always been good with women like this, the invisible ones, the ones who are the play's scenery, not its stars.

"Well, I probably shouldn't be saying this," Mrs. Hensley says conspiratorially, "but she does have a young man visiting. They seem to be spending quite a bit of time together. I think that has a lot to do with it. You know how young people can be."

Griffin McAllister. He knew it! But where is Betty? Has Griff ditched her somewhere along the road, come to Newport to bebop with the best friend? This story was getting better every minute. "Well, ain't that just the floy floy," he says, shaking his head. "She's off having a romance and you're left with the work. That's applesauce."

Mrs. Hensley's eyes open wider. He's hooked his fish. "Actually," she whispers, "I believe the young man is out on the back porch. I saw him walk out just a few moments ago."

Chick's heart speeds up a couple beats. He's got to be careful. He can't risk spooking McAllister, blowing his cover. And his camera's still in the car. If he can get pictures, he'll have the biggest story in the country. Goodbye, Atlantic City. Hello, New York.

"Good to know, Mrs. H. You've sure been swell to help me out like this." He looks around. "I don't want to keep you from your duties. But who do I talk to about getting a press pass for tomorrow night? I think it would be great for my story to get some details about the big party."

"Oh, no trouble. Just ask for me when you arrive. Seven sharp!"

"I'll be here," he says with a wink.

She drifts off, floating on the cloud of her sensuous new identity as informant. As soon as she disappears from view, Chick beelines for the back of the hotel, peering through the windows onto the porch. A few couples sit in variously grouped white wicker chairs, drinking cool beverages; a grandmother, a younger woman, and two small girls daintily sip tea at the far right end. Chick cracks open the rear door, looks all the way down to the left, and sees a young man standing, both hands leaning on the railing, as if he's catching his breath after finishing a long race. It takes a minute for Chick to process.

Eddie Tate.

Chick quickly dodges back inside, and the door slams, causing him to retreat even more quickly, back into the safety of the calling room. What the hell was Tate doing here? He wasn't even on the payroll anymore.

Chick curses himself. *Damn!* Tate has beat him to the story. No doubt he's got the exclusive. That's why he let them can him. He's got Betty and Griff, is getting the whole sordid tale, no doubt selling it for big moolah to the *Herald-Tribune* or the *Times.* Maybe even *Time* or *Life.* He'll be a star, the next Sevareid.

Well, we'll see about that, pal, Chick muses, hustling out the door. *Because nobody's scooping ole Chick Kaisinger this time.*

Twenty-eight

*I*n they pour, *the elegant,* the wealthy, the diffident, the scandalous, the dull, the dutiful, the beautiful, and the merely filthy rich. Newport was founded as a haven for those fleeing religious persecution and was now, in one of its more ebbing periods, primarily known as a rowdy navy town, teeming with too many bored, obstreperous sailors looking for too much stimulation. The America's Cup race, once a stalwart attraction, was suspended several years ago. Indeed, the grandeur of Newport's gilded age seems long past—even Gladys Vanderbilt gave up the Breakers just last year, leasing it to the Preservation Society for a dollar.

Ciji stands, in her plain black Maggy Rouff evening gown a stark contrast to the women in their costumes—the dresses of courtesans and Colonial dames, flappers and southern belles. Seventy-eight-year-old Miss Amy Varnum of the Garden Club of Newport, not particularly known for her boldness of attire, has nonetheless arrived in a gentleman's tuxedo, complete with top hat, cane, and patent leather spats, telling various astonished guests she is paying homage to Marlene Dietrich and that, if she consumes a few glasses of champagne, she might later be persuaded to belt out a chorus of "The Boys in the Back Room" with the orchestra.

The Countess de Rougemont has come from La Forge Cottage. Mrs. Vanderbilt has not come (and neither has the mercurial Barbara Hutton), but the Van Rensselaers are here, as are the Auchinclosses, the Bruguieres, the LeRoys, the Gambrills, the Drexels, and a plethora of Adamses. Of course no one has quite managed the entrance of Doris Duke, who arrived perched atop a baby elephant, which clomped right down the Cliff Walk to the edge of the tent, where it dutifully bowed to allow its mistress—clad in Persian silk pajamas and holding an ornate mink mask on a stick made of glittering rhinestones and a cluster of peacock feathers—to dismount. Ciji thinks about what it must be like to have a life where your daily thoughts revolve only around where you are to travel and what you will wear to do it. She wonders if she will ever realize her dream of going to Hollywood, get to find out for herself.

She takes a spin around the cavernous tent, which has three Swarovski crystal chandeliers strung up on the inside, a larger one in the middle, two smaller versions spaced north and south. A few couples are already on the dance floor, circling around as the Alexander Haas Orchestra—in from New York just this morning and now dressed in their fine scarlet, gold-braided uniforms—plays a catchy rendition of Vaughn Monroe's "Ballerina." The air is fogged with the scent of expensive perfume and Mr. Clifford's award-winning white and cream tea roses, which swirl up in a sea of delicate greenery from the crystal centerpieces on the forty tables. Each table is set for ten, and they gleam with heavy bone-white china trimmed in gold, augmented by gold-plated dinner forks and salad forks and shrimp forks and soup spoons and sherbet spoons and coffee spoons and dinner knives and butter knives. Water goblets reflect the light with the same sparkle as that from the diamonds and rubies and emeralds on the throats, wrists, and fingers of the masked women who now glide through the room as if they were skating across Corcoran's Pond.

"It's magnificent. You've done a terrific job."

Eddie stands behind her. He's dressed in an ill-fitting, slightly musty tuxedo, old livery she dug out from the hotel basement. Her efforts to procure a costume for Griff left her no time to think about one for him. Eddie's mask is also too big, covering three-quarters of his face. He looks like Claude Rains in *The Phantom of the Opera*.

"I can't take credit for it," she says, surveying the room. She returns the polite wave of a masked older gentleman she doesn't recognize. "Mrs. Hensley and the staff were the ones who really did the work. But it should raise a nice amount of dough."

"You look very beautiful."

"If that were my only concern."

"This is going to work."

"How can you be so sure?"

"Because it's a very, very simple plan with very few elements. Everyone in the hotel is out here. Betty and Griff come down from their quarters, in costume, to a virtually empty building. Betty makes an 'impulsive' decision to take Griff out the front door so they can be alone outside for a few moments. We're waiting out front with Honor and her goons. We shove him in the car, they take off, it's over."

"He still has a gun."

"But we have the element of surprise." He exhales. "And chloroform."

Ciji shakes her head. "How did this happen?"

"Your roommate," he says mournfully, "picked the wrong guy."

A couple dressed as Henry VIII and Anne Boleyn commands the floor with an artful, amorous tango to "El Choclo." Ciji eyes

Mrs. Hensley in the distance, barking instructions to two suitably terrified busboys.

"I hope she appreciates what we're doing for her," Ciji says.

"Me, too."

"You've checked? Her highness is out front in the car?"

"Parked right by the side of the hotel." Eddie takes another glance around. "Mutt's in the car with her. Where's Jeff?"

Ciji nods slightly to the far right corner of the tent. "Big guy in the white dinner jacket and black mask. Holding the tumbler of whiskey."

Eddie watches a waiter carrying hors d'oeuvres pass them with a polished silver tray stocked with canapés. The orchestra has moved on to a string-heavy arrangement of "So in Love" from *Kiss Me Kate*. He smiles at the irony. "When are they due down?"

Ciji checks her watch. "Fifteen minutes. I wanted to make sure all of the guests were here so we wouldn't have company out front." Everyone — save for Doris Duke, of course — is being shuttled directly from the car park around to the tent. But there is still the risk of a random straggler coming upon them as they nab Griff. It can't be helped. If worse comes to worst, she'll explain that one of the guests has fallen ill and is being taken to the hospital.

Eddie glances around. "Well, I better try to blend into the woodwork, even if I do look like Jeeves."

Ciji smiles faintly. "I'm sorry. It was the best I could do."

"It's a humdinger." He takes her hand and squeezes it. "I'll meet you out front in fifteen minutes."

❧

"Well," Betty says, taking a slow turn around. "How do I look?"

Her insides are jelly. No, worse than that. Lava. She thought she could never feel more anxiety than she had standing on the

277

stage next to Eleanor Wyatt, waiting to hear the announcement of the new Miss America. But her life was not hanging in the balance that night. Tonight, it is.

Her costume is a plain cotton dress with a lace-decorated bodice and a bright yellow satin ribbon at the waist, with a skirt that flares out to the floor. A matching mobcap covers her dark hair. She is modeling the outfit for Griff, projecting an outward buoyant image at complete odds with the nervy mess on the inside. He sits glumly on the bed, holding his tricorn hat in his hands, barely looking at her.

She stops. "Griff, you're supposed to say how lovely I look."

"You look lovely," he says in monotone.

Betty spies the clock on the bed table. They need to go down.

"I think you look quite dashing. It's time to go, sweetheart. Ciji is waiting for us. It's going to be such fun. We deserve a nice night out." She walks over, drops before him, kisses him lightly, is encouraged that he seems to respond. "Please."

They creep down the back staircase, and as they near the ground floor, the din of conversation and orchestra music grows louder. Griff brightens at the noise. "It sounds quite peppy," he says.

This is it.

Betty turns to him, takes both hands in hers. "The hotel is empty," she says devilishly. "C'mon, let's go explore a bit while we can. I'm dying to see what the hotel looks like all decorated in the front." Her heart hammers inside her chest.

Griff's eyes remain fixed toward the back. "No, no. This is risky enough. Let's just go to the party. We need to blend in with the crowd."

"Oh, please, darling, please? Just for a moment. I just want to see—"

He jerks his hands from hers. "Do as you please. I told you I'm not going. They don't want me to go."

They don't want me to go.

Betty absorbs the dark clouds in his eyes. She risks a furtive look toward the front. She thought she would be strong enough to mollify him. But she will never be strong enough to mollify the voices.

"All right, Griff. All right. We'll go out to the party."

❧

Eddie checks his watch again. He walks back into the hotel.

Ciji is standing behind the front desk, fiddling with papers. "They're late," Eddie says.

"I know." She checks the clock again. Twelve past. "Let's just give them a few more minutes. Maybe he's —"

"Crazy?"

"Eddie."

"There's something wrong, Ciji. I can feel it. Can't you? And I can't keep Honor in the car much longer. She's going to insist on coming in here and retrieving him herself if they don't show up soon."

"Okay,".Ciji says. "I'll go find them. Wait here."

❧

Chick curses himself. He couldn't be more conspicuous if he tried. Every reporter here has to wear a badge that says PRESS pinned to his lapel. Worse yet, he wasn't allowed to bring in his camera from the trunk; turns out the jerks from the *Newport Daily News* have exclusive rights to photograph the party. But, Mrs. Hensley has assured him, she can put him in touch with their photographer for any photos he might need for his *Holiday* magazine feature.

Swell.

He stalks the perimeter of the tent, looking for Tate, but with every guy in kooky duds, it's impossible to even narrow the field. Is that him, standing over there in the English duke's costume, talking to the woman who looks like Maid Marian? Or is he the guy by the huge silver punch bowl who looks like General Grant?

I gotta make sure I see him before he sees me.

He feels naked, exposed without his fedora to cover his eyes, but all these other jokers doffed theirs, and he couldn't be the only one inside the tent wearing one. He finds a large potted fern in the tent's corner, darts behind it. He scans the crowd for several more minutes before his eyes home in on a couple on the other side of the dance floor. The girl is dressed as some sort of Colonial wife, maybe Abigail Adams or something. Next to her is a tall man wearing what looks like some sort of Colonial regimental outfit, complete with a tricorn hat. He sports a light mustache and beard.

It could be them, he thinks.

And then he spies Catherine Moore, rushing in from the left, approaching them. She stops, makes polite chitchat with the couple for a few minutes. Chick feels his pulse begin to race. He takes a few steps forward, tries to manage a better sightline. *Is it . . . ?*

He catches Catherine leaning in, whispering something to the woman, then brightly bidding the couple goodbye as she scurries away. The woman she was speaking to turns to her male companion and smiles. She turns back toward the dance floor just long enough for Chick to now see her clearly, and even hidden beneath her white mask he knows it. He recalls a picture of her on the runway, waving to the throng inside Convention Hall, the tiara on her head, and that smile—that indelible, original smile.

Holy Christ. It's her. It's Betty Jane Welch.

Betty and Griff McAllister, right here, right under everyone's noses. Chick wills himself to stay calm, stay smart. If only he had his camera! No one is going to believe it without a photo, or want it without a photo.

I gotta get the picture.

He takes a big step back, ensuring he's once again adequately camouflaged by the potted foliage and passing patrons. He peruses the perimeter of the tent, looks for the seams, where the flaps have been lashed with heavy ropes tied to stakes in the ground outside. That's his ticket. All he has to do is go get the camera, sneak around to the back of the tent, undo one of the rope knots, and slip in between the seam closest to Betty and Griff. Catch them off guard, snap the picture. Then run like hell.

Chick stuffs his notebook into his pocket and strolls out of the tent.

Twenty-nine

*B*etty *tries not to fidget,* to appear what she is supposed to be, a party guest enjoying herself here, inside Newport's *l'affaire sociale de l'année.* Instead she is simply a hopeless tangle of tension and doubts and regrets. And she is exhausted. She cannot ever remember being this tired, of just wanting to go to sleep and never wake up.

Ciji has walked her through the plan. When she first heard it, Betty thought it was ludicrous, something Nancy Drew, George, and Bess would have concocted in a story called *The Disappearance at Cliff Lawn Manor.* But it had one thing going for it: it was simple. That is, it was. Until Griff had decided not to do the one thing she had needed him to do.

It is now on to Plan B, which Ciji has hastily whispered in her ear not five minutes ago.

Betty will keep glancing over to the far side of the tent, where Eddie stands nursing a drink, until Eddie gives her the signal that they're ready. Betty will tell Griff she must go back into the hotel to use the lavatory. He will, of course, insist on accompanying her.

So she will calmly take his arm, exit the tent. Eddie will discreetly follow. Honor's muscle will be waiting right outside, silently subdue Griff with the chloroform, and with Eddie's assistance they'll put Griff in the back seat of the car. It's more public, riskier with people coming in and out. But they're out of options. Anyone approaches, then Ciji goes back to the original plan: they are helping a partygoer who has imbibed a bit too much champagne. Honor drives Griff off to a private hospital for treatment. And Betty goes home, at last.

What if Griff pulls out his gun? She must hope the element of surprise will prevent it.

Betty takes Griff's arm, places it around her. He is jumpy, sullen, his momentary interest in the music and frivolity dissipated. She glances over at Eddie, waiting for the nod that tells her it's time to go. It seems like hours are passing. It's all taking too long.

I just need this all to be over.

❧

Chick carries the Hawkeye by his side, and if it were just the boxy camera, he'd be on Easy Street. But the flash attached is big and bulbous, and Chick knows he has no shot at getting a decent frame without one. So he has to risk it, hope that the shadows offer enough cover, that the flow of party guests and general gaiety provide enough diversions so that he can get to the rear of the tent undetected.

He creeps along the Cliff Walk, passes the left side of the buzzing circus-size tent, listens to the laughter and exclamations and music and clinking of glasses. His eyes roam, shift, circle, trying to spy the slightest sign of a wrench in his plan. *I'm so close to getting the biggest story of my life. I'm so close.*

He darts off the walkway to the right, dashes across the lawn lugging his heavy camera, hunched and quick, like he's running underneath helicopter blades. Once he reaches the back of the tent, he crouches down, like he's in a battlefield bunker, stops to catch his breath. He's got to give up those damn Old Gold cigarettes.

Chick glances farther up the lawn, spies a few men enjoying cigars in the night air near the back entrance of the hotel. They shouldn't be a problem. By the time they figure out what's going on, he'll be in his car. Out of the corner of his eye, he spies a lone figure—a man—walking down the Cliff Walk.

He's gotta move. Now.

Chick scurries around to the other side of the tent, hastily begins untying two of the ropes securing the flaps together. The first comes apart fairly quickly. But the second is knotted more tightly, and as he sits on his haunches, camera at his side, he struggles to undo it.

Damn it!

Rustling. Is someone coming across the lawn?

The knot finally loosens, and he grabs at it, quickly pulls the flaps apart. He picks up the Hawkeye and charges into the side of the tent, right behind Betty and Griff.

"Say cheese, Betty!" he thunders, and as Betty and Griff spin around in stunned surprise, Chick Kaisinger begins clicking his camera, the flashbulb blinding them as assorted guests look over, curious about the unfolding scene.

He's gotten off three, maybe four frames when he feels a hand at the back of his collar, jerking him off balance. He whirls around, still holding the camera, and sees sheer fury in Eddie Tate's eyes.

Chick never sees the punch coming, just feels the spray of blood explode from his nose and onto the expensive dresses of two nearby matrons, who howl in horror.

A few male guests charge in to break up the ruckus just as Eddie rips the camera out of Chick's hands, raises it, and smashes it onto the dance floor. The orchestra stops, women start screaming, men yell, swarms of costumed guests descend on the scene from every direction. A thickset man dressed as a sea captain grabs Eddie from behind, barks, "Easy there, fella!" Chick is on the ground, frantically searching for his handkerchief to staunch the bleeding.

All the while Betty has been frozen, trying to sort out the bedlam erupting around her. She spies Ciji, both hands holding up her gown, furiously charging over from the far end of the tent toward them, then spins back to see Eddie being roughhoused. Instinctively she cries out, "Eddie! No, no!"

Griff's hand clenches her arm with the force of a leg iron.

His eyes whirl about the room as the voices explode.

They're coming for you. Look at them coming!

They're going to strap you back onto that table and throw the switch.

They want to kill you. All of them. They're all in on it.

He looks over at Betty, disbelieving.

Her! It's her! She's leading them!

"How could you?" he asks.

"Darling, I don't know who that man with the camera is! I—"

He jerks her to him, circles his arm tightly around her waist as more guests pour in around them to check out all of the commotion. "We're leaving," he whispers.

She shakes her head. "No, Griff, no . . ."

As he forcefully backs them away from the tumult, he removes the gun from the back of his waistband, throws his hand inside his jacket, the barrel now pointed directly at her. "Don't make me do it, Betty. I don't want to. But I will."

"Griff, please! I'm begging you!"

Griff glares over at Eddie, who is trying to extricate himself from the grip of the sea captain. Griff recognizes him. The guy Betty was hugging by the water. "Or maybe I should just point this at your friend over there."

"No!" she screams, but in the chaos her protest goes unheard. "All right, Griff, all right. Let's just stay calm. We'll go. Just you and me."

A bunch of older gentlemen have now removed their masks and are barking questions, demanding an explanation, as their flustered wives attend to the two hysterical women with the bloodstained clothing. The orchestra conductor, momentarily befuddled by the hubbub, commands his musicians to their feet and strikes up a muscular version of "The Merry Widow Waltz" in an effort to restore civility. Mrs. Hensley flies about like a squawking blackbird, ordering ice, towels, first aid. Ciji tries to elbow her way through the thickening throng to reach Betty and Griff. In all of the chaos, she momentarily loses sight of them.

When her view finally clears, they're gone.

❧

Betty's body floods with panic as Griff prods her through the open flap in the tent, then hurries them down the rear slope of the lawn toward the Cliff Walk. The moon-washed water of the Sound ripples in the moonlight, and Betty wonders if this expanse of beauty is the last thing she will ever see. An image of her mother, doubled over in grief, rams into her brain, and the brute force of it almost knocks her over. She barks out a keening sob.

They reach the Cliff Walk by the slope that curves down twenty feet to the water and rocks below. It is not an imposing cliff, like those of Amalfi or Moher or Malta or the imaginations of the Brontës. It is quieter, more expansive, more horizontal in scope. On another night, in another moment, it is a place for possibility and romance. But it is not another night. It is now, where her world has come crashing down from every corner.

"You're right," Griff says, his chest heaving, the gun now out, pointed directly at her. "You told me all along she was bad, she was out to get me, she was lying. Why didn't I listen to you? Why do I not listen to you?!"

He's answering the voices out loud.

He's gone.

Betty takes a small step toward him, then jumps back as he waves the gun wildly in her direction. "Griff, you *must* listen to me. The voices, they aren't real. I am real. *We* are real. You must believe me, you must fight back—"

"Shut up! Shut up! You were going to betray me! You just wanted your picture in a magazine! You were going to leave me there, run away with that other man, weren't you? Just go! Just leave me! Admit it! Admit it!"

"Griff, I don't even know—"

He steadies the gun, points it right at her. "You *knew his name!*"

Her knees fail her, and in a combination of fatigue and despair she collapses onto the Walk, mewling, too tired to think anymore, too tired to fight. Regret swamps and drowns her. "Oh, Griff, my sweet Griff . . ." she whispers, clutching at herself in grief—for what she's done, for this illness she has awakened that now roars inside of him, for the suffering she's caused with her selfishness.

And then another voice, calm, steady, from farther down the Walk, growing slightly louder. "Griffin," it says slowly, almost trance-like. "Griffin, it's Mother, sweetheart. Mother's here. Don't be afraid. It's going to be all right now."

Griff turns and cocks the gun, directs it toward his own mother, who now stands regally a few yards away, leaning on her walking stick. But it is his voice—suddenly equally calm, strong, clear, dispassionate—that terrifies Betty more than anything. "Not another step, Mother. I mean it."

"Griffin, I need to talk to you. Just you and I. Let Betty go, and we'll talk all of this through, sort all of it out. All of this unpleasantness is past now. I've come to take you home, to get you well again."

Ciji drifts up a few feet behind Honor. She says nothing, but her eyes confess their own abject fear.

"Stand back!" Griff yells out. "You, too!" he says, pointing to Ciji. "Nobody takes another step, or—"

He doesn't need to finish the sentence. Honor and Ciji freeze.

For a while the only sounds are the whistle of the breeze coming off the water and the waves gently washing up on the rocks below. In the distance there is the lilting music of the orchestra, the din of the party once again building inside the tent. The show always goes on.

Betty remains on her knees, trying to catch her breath, willing herself to summon something inside she doesn't even know if she possesses. Her breath is shallow, staccato, as she gazes out onto the Sound. *I have to do something. I got us all into this. I have to try to get us out. I owe it to them.*

She looks up at Griff, his face a twisted map of torture and anguish. She can see his lips moving, rapidly muttering responses to the voices.

I owe it to him.

"Do you know the moment I fell in love with you?" she asks.

"Be quiet," he snaps, but there is something, a yearning, in his voice that reveals him, that says, *Tell me.*

"It was that first night we met," she says, staring up at him, her eyes shining. "That night we first met, and you whisked me away from the horrible mixer for the contestants and we went to the restaurant and you ate half the menu and I had to eat a lousy shrimp cocktail. Do you remember?"

Griff keeps babbling to himself, keeps the gun aloft, though it seems to be getting heavier in his hand, painstakingly lowering, half inch by half inch. He does not respond to her. But he does not tell her to stop talking, either.

"That's when you told me about the sunflowers, and how they

can only go to very special girls. And I so wanted to be your special girl. I could feel myself falling in love, right there sitting at the table, looking into your eyes. You were the most charming boy I'd ever met."

A tear splashes down his cheek.

"You felt it, too. At least I hoped you did. I think that's why I ended up winning Miss America, you see: because I didn't care about it. I was relaxed, I was me, I came out of my shell that week with you, I found the girl hiding inside, the girl you brought out with your heart. And she was spunky and high-spirited, and she sat at a nightclub and listened to the boy she loved sing her a song he wrote just for her. Do you remember it?" She begins singing. "'*I was searching, for so long . . . though I kinda didn't even really know it . . .*'"

She crosses both her hands over her heart. "I've made mistakes, my darling. And you got hurt in the process, and I am so, so very sorry for that. You can't imagine how sorry I am. Because the only thing I have ever wanted—the thing I wished for when I sent that penny into the wishing well outside the restaurant—was for you to love me. You must believe me. You must!"

Griff remains still, begins sobbing. Whispers, "Oh, Betty . . ."

It is Ciji who spies him first, emerging out of the shadows behind Griff and Betty.

Eddie.

He moves furtively, skulking up from behind.

One step. Stop.

Three more steps. Stop.

Honor sees him, too, but her face betrays nothing. Her eyes remain squarely fixed on her son. She is trying to reach him as she has always strived to reach him, her little boy lost, scared and alone in a horrible and confusing world of angry noise.

"My sweet son, you're not alone," Honor says, once more taking slow, cautious steps toward him. "Give Mother the gun, sweetheart." She extends her hand out, reaches toward him. She is now only a few feet away.

And this is when it happens.

This is when Griff attempts to shake out the voices, shake away his tears, and in the process from the corner of his eye he catches sight of the figure behind him, spies Eddie Tate running at full bore toward him, about to pounce, as Honor rushes in from the front, hands outstretched, reaching out for the barrel of the revolver.

"Betrayed," Griff whispers, as Betty shrieks "No!!" from her knees.

And Eddie is just a bit too late, because before he can get to him, Griffin McAllister raises his gun, points it directly at his mother, and pulls the trigger.

Thirty

April 1950

he car hums through the thicket of towering trees on the other side; the road seems to stretch forever, one long line going on and on toward the horizon. Her eyes feel heavy, both from the length of the trip—she alighted from a two-hour bus ride, only to walk through the bus terminal, push out onto the sidewalk, and open the passenger door of a sedan and settle in for another long journey—and from the gravity of the last six months. Betty thought once she left Newport it would be over. It wasn't.

The irony had been that the ridiculous plan had almost worked. Almost.

If only Betty could have pleaded a bit longer. If only Eddie had leapt a second sooner.

If only Betty had defied her mother and never entered Miss Delaware, almost a year ago now.

She had looked on, powerless and aghast, as Griff had aimed the Browning at his mother and fired. It wasn't for several minutes before she realized that Honor had moved—either flinched or been pushed by Ciji, she still wasn't certain—just inches enough to the left so that the bullet rocketed into her shoulder rather than her heart. She left her feet from the force of the shot, tumbling backwards onto the Cliff Walk as Betty screamed and Ciji screamed and Eddie tackled Griff to the ground a few seconds too late, the gun skittering across the Walk and down the cliff side.

So many people. Hotel guests, curious partygoers, Mrs. Hensley, Honor's driver. The police were on the scene instantly, the price of splashing blood onto the expensive gowns of two socialites. That was the problem with the rich: when they are compromised or inconvenienced, they instantly telephone the police. Then came the medics and the Newport city detectives, astonished to find out they had America's most famous missing couple in their midst. And then there had been Chick Kaisinger, who through his bandaged nose had managed to dictate a story to the *Atlantic City Press* that was soon racing its way across the wire services. The jig was up.

Honor had been taken away by ambulance to the hospital, leaving a helpless Betty to try to ensure that Griff was not lost in the chaos. It was Eddie who had come to her rescue, as he had so many times in the previous weeks, explaining Griff's condition and getting him whisked away in his own ambulance before any ravenous reporters had been able to feast.

She'd spent the night at police headquarters, saying little, sitting in a small windowless room wrapped in a blanket, waiting for judgment. It came the next morning when her parents had arrived, their joint expression one of relief and fury. Her father had taken control, hired an attorney to represent her as they attempted to sort out the whole sordid mess. Her mother had appeared stricken, her thin pink lips set tightly above her rock-set jaw, a veil of bitter disappointment draped across her eyes like a lace curtain. Life would churn slowly onward, never as good as it was or should have been, Betty's disgrace a stain on the family that would fade but never quite be scrubbed out.

The FBI had come, two detectives from Atlantic City had come, and Honor McAllister's private detectives had given statements. It had taken days—and, Betty suspects, significant money from her father to various parties, none of it recorded—to unravel it all. The subsequent press accounts had been lurid, and that was with most of the details still kept under wraps. At least Miss Slaughter had not come. That might have been enough to end Betty for certain.

They'd indeed given her title to Eleanor Wyatt, Miss Texas, who said all of the appropriate things about wanting to be an example to young women around the country. A twelve-minute press conference was held where Betty's name was mentioned only once, by a *Philadelphia Evening Bulletin* reporter who was quickly hustled out onto the street for violating Miss Slaughter's command about inquiring about She Who Must Never Be Mentioned Again.

Betty understood. What she could not understand was the relentlessness of the newsmen, their fedoras tilted up on their foreheads like baseball caps, who had sat parked outside her house, day after day, week after week, yelling at her through the dining room windows, who dropped off disingenuous letters and cards promising that they only wanted to get the story right, that America's readers had a right to know how she was and that she had some sort of moral duty to tell them. That by betraying their trust the night she won Miss America, she now owed them repentant piety and moral rectitude in return.

And where were her friends? Ciji had sent a few letters from California, where Hollywood had been piqued by her supporting role in the real-life drama. Betty had felt too depressed, and too guilty, to reply. Patsy had drifted away, miffed about being kept afar from the spectacle. There was no way Betty could return to Towson, walk the campus as every head turned, every mouth whispered. Her brothers had been, bless them, surprisingly protective of her, as if she were made of glass. But the house was now a prison. This was her first day out in months.

And who would offer her sympathy? Who wanted to hear how she had suffered? How she had almost been raped in New York, had slowly discovered she had put her trust in a young man battling demons the naked eye could not see? That would have to wait for another hour, another day. Today was about closing the door on all of this for good. For making amends. For letting go.

The car turns left onto a long drive, slows as it approaches the guard at the front gate. Betty cannot look at the guard, so she keeps her eyes peeled out the passenger window, gazing over the trees and flowers everywhere, her sight inching up the lush front lawn that lies beyond the tall metal fence to the imposing white columned building beyond.

It's in the thicket of rural Burlington County, just over an hour from Longport, so it will be uncomplicated for his family to visit him, which fills Betty with an undeserved sense of relief, like the thief who is grateful that the bank has stepped in to make full restitution to his victims. She wonders how often they will visit, how much they can bear. How much she has caused them to bear.

Honor was in the hospital for a little over a week. The bullet had missed a vital artery by inches; she'd had additional injury to her damaged foot from the fall. But she has recovered, the way such steely roses do, though the scar that counts—the one on her heart —is the one that will never evanesce.

Betty wrote Honor three times asking for permission to see him and got no reply. The last letter contained outright begging. By that time Betty had little regard for her own pride. How could she? She knew nothing except that she had to see him again. And then finally she had received a letter from Martha, explaining all that had happened in these last few months, and as Betty went paragraph by paragraph through the prose, standing in her bedroom, she had felt herself falling, as if she were sinking in quicksand. She had pressed her back against the bedroom wall and actually slid to the floor, a bit at a time, as she read Martha's explanation, written in her girlish, overly round script, and absorbed the reality of the ghastly bargain Honor had struck with the authorities to ensure that Griff was not sent to prison. "We are sustained by the knowledge that his acute suffering has come to an end, and he can live his remaining days in peace, surrounded by beauty and nature and those who can give him the care he needs." Poor Martha, robbed of her own days in peace. It would only be a matter of time before she, too, despised Betty, resented her for all of it.

The gate opens and the car slowly winds its way up the pebbly drive, the only sounds the crunching of the tires, the sweet singing of blue jays in the just-budding trees. It stops in front of the white marble steps that lead into the place. She's worn her Sunday best: a green crepe afternoon dress with embroidered detailing, with a light off-white coat with raglan leg-of-mutton sleeves. She had debated the hat for an hour—a braided snood, to show modesty and contrition, or the matching hat made of light green netting and large fabric roses, to show effort? In the end she chose the hat. Her hair is back to its natural strawberry blond shade. She has color on her lips, blush on her cheeks, Shalimar on her neck and wrists. She wants to look nice when she sees him. She owes him that.

She takes a deep breath, steps out of the car, prays that the knots in her stomach will unfurl as she walks inside.

❧

She follows the well-starched nurse down a corridor that seems to stretch for miles. Amid the drab off-white and gray surroundings,

Betty suddenly feels showy and self-conscious, like she's worn a gown to a backyard picnic.

They push through a set of double doors that lead to a garden in the back, a pleasant space marked by brick paths that bifurcate another large, lush lawn. Several other nurses sit with patients, and as Betty passes them, she notices a towheaded boy of about twelve, who sits at a table rolling a marble inside a large metal mixing bowl, over and over and over. He looks up and their eyes meet briefly, but his look is hollow, faraway, as if he is looking at something a great distance behind her.

Betty and the nurse finally turn into a small glen with a gently tinkling fountain, where Betty glimpses the form of a lone young man, his back to her, sitting on an ornate white metal settee.

"There he is," the nurse says impassively. "Remember, you've only been approved for fifteen minutes. I'll be back to pick you up. Dennis over there will be watching in case you need help." She points to a lithe young orderly in a white shirt and matching pants, standing sentry about twenty feet away, his look bored, like his only thought is how much he's dying for a smoke.

Betty cannot move. She insisted on coming here. And now that she is here, her feet feel like they're made of cement, planted in this garden like a statue of Venus. She finally walks toward him, gently, timidly, like Dorothy first approaching the wizard. She wills herself on, remonstrating her own recalcitrance.

She turns to the left, decides it's better to approach from the empty side of the settee. She's afraid of seeing the damage too close.

From the side he looks much the same — even remarkably well, one might say. His hair is longer now, no doubt on Honor's orders, so that the surgical scars are not visible. But his face is clean shaven, his skin bright and clear. His profile remains intact, striking and Roman, the face of a god. He wears a loose, blousy shirt and matching oversize pants; there is a pair of leather slippers on his bare feet. His hands remain fixed in his lap, and even as she draws near, enters his sightline from the side, he never looks over, never acknowledges anyone is there.

Betty gingerly takes a seat on the other end of the settee. "Griff," she says, "Griff, it's Betty." She wants to touch him, to take his hand in her own. It isn't permitted.

He remains still for a full minute, so long that she is about to address him again when he slowly turns his face in her direction.

It's the eyes. Dead, horrible, unblinking. He might as well be a mannequin, staring vacantly out of the window of John Wanamaker. He says nothing.

"Griff, it's Betty," she tries again, a bit louder this time, almost beseeching, trying to excavate a trace of the young man she knew.

The young man she destroyed.

"I've come from Delaware to see you. I . . . I wanted to bring you a present, some of those butterscotch candies you like, but they wouldn't allow me to. I've been thinking of you so often, hoping you're well. I only found out just a few weeks ago you were here."

He says nothing but does not turn away. Which forces Betty to do so instead. "It's rather gay here," she says, taking in the grounds. "Very green and bright and wide."

In her letter, Martha had warned her. But how could Betty have foreseen this? She bites her lower lip, fights tears as she fishes through her bag for a handkerchief.

"Pretty," he says finally. She pivots around, looks again for something in his eyes, something . . . there.

"You're pretty," he repeats, slowly, wondrously.

"Thank you, Griff," Betty says. She dares to lean a bit closer, her eyes searching his face for something to hold on to. "Griff, do you know who I am?"

A barely discernible smile forms at the edge of his mouth, the mouth she had kissed, so many times, passionately and hungrily, on the Boardwalk, on the beach, on the daybed in New York, the mouth that had told her he had a plan, that it was all going to be okay, until it wasn't okay at all. "Pretty," he repeats. And for the first time she hears his voice, hears it as it is, not as it was. It is the timbre and diction of a four-year-old. The ensuing years and all of their many complications and demons, removed by the surgeon's scalpel.

Betty stands, tosses the handkerchief back into her clutch and closes it. Griff looks back out to the meadow, as if she is merely a shadow that has briefly passed over and is now gone. She dares to bend over and place a gentle hand on his shoulder, kisses him softly on the cheek. "I'm so very sorry, my love. You'll never know how much."

And then she walks away, and as she trudges up the steps and back through the hospital, her pace picks up, more of a stride than a walk, and she feels her face tighten with the bubbling of resolve.

❧

Outside, Eddie leans against the passenger side, arms folded in front of him. Her barreling out of the front door appears to catch him by surprise.

"How did it go?" he asks, walking toward her.

Betty brushes past him, reaches for the car door, then stops.

"It was difficult," she says, turning back to him. Even now, in the mild spring temperatures of April, he is perspiring slightly at the temples, his blond hair matted down at the brim of his fedora. She wonders if he is someone who is simply always warm, even in the coldest of climes. And she wonders what might have happened if she had met him in a different climate, a different city, at a different time, and whether there might have been a different outcome for them if she had. For she knows there is no chance for them now. He has yet to accept it, but he will. He must. "I thank you so much for bringing me, Eddie. You have been so good to me. I don't deserve it."

He looks at her, his eyes baby blue and mirthful, swimming with the love he thinks she can no longer see. "I think you deserve to be happy, Betty."

She leans up, kisses him tenderly on the cheek. It is that kind of day. A day for goodbyes. "Let's go home."

As they pull away, she studies his profile in the driver's seat. She knows she will again break his heart, this time for good. But he will be better for it. He will recover; he will put all of this behind him and marry a nice girl and have nice children. He will have the life he was supposed to have before she showed up on the Boardwalk with her bathing suit and sassy answers, derailing his life. His, and so many others'.

As the car rolls back to Atlantic City, Betty presses her bag closer to her, thinking of her return bus ticket back to Delaware, safely tucked inside. But she will not stay in Delaware, trapped in her parents' house. Their windows of concern are now frosted over, covered by the sheen of stinging disapproval that will last a lifetime.

She will go somewhere where no one knows her. Betty has an aunt in Colorado. *Colorado. That would be fine.* She will bury her past, so deep no one will ever find it. She leans her head back onto the seat, watches her life unfurl inside her head, as if she's turning the pages of a photo album. She will transfer to another college. Change her name, introduce herself everywhere as Jane. She will change her hair, her clothes. Invent an entire new history. She will meet and accept the courtship of a nice, bland, simple young man whose obsessions lay with his hometown baseball team and keeping his whitewall tires pristine, and who has no interest whatsoever in the Miss America Pageant. They will have lovely children and live in a lovely house. And she will never eat another slice of lemon cake for as long as she lives.

Epilogue

His leg aches. It's to be expected, the doctors have told him, especially in rainy weather such as this. And even though he is only twenty-six, this—the dull, twinging stiffness, the occasional jolts of pain like when ice cream hits a sensitive tooth—will be with him until he is an old man, assuming he makes it to be an old man. Once you smash your femur into powder and break three ribs, then throw a blood clot in your lung for good measure, you don't walk away unscarred. Actually, you don't walk anywhere for eight months.

Bron parks the car. He has just started driving again. It feels odd, new. He cannot believe it has been a year since he was last here, walking backwards down the driveway, looking at this house and wondering how he was ever going to convince the old woman inside it to talk to him. And then the car, roaring up seemingly out of nowhere, slamming into him as he feebly threw his arms out at the last minute, as if he were Superman stopping an oncoming train. It was eleven hours before he even woke up, lying in a bed at Bryn Mawr Hospital, his leg in pieces.

He cracks open the car door, grabs the cane from the passenger seat. He hates using it, feels that after all of the physical therapy he has been through, he shouldn't need it anymore, but the doctors have warned that rain is a wild card that will, for now, make it necessary. He worries that she will see him hobbling in and think he is trying to manipulate her, guilt-trip her. Though he suspects she is not a person who is easily influenced by such things. By anything.

She was the one who called the police, ordered the ambulance. He still doesn't know whether she watched the whole mess from behind her curtains, or whether the awful shriek of the crash sent her scurrying to the front door to survey the carnage. Doesn't matter. He was surprised when she sent a card to the hospital. Brief, just signed, "So sorry for your accident. Wishes for a full recovery, Jane Proctor."

He wrote her a month ago, relaying his journey back to health and thanking her for calling 911. He also asked her if he could see her, to talk to her about the story he wants to do about her, about her journey, and why she should trust him to write it. It took him two days to find the right language to imply, but not specifically say, "Look, you owe me." To his surprise she responded a week later, calling his office at six in the morning, when she knew he would not be there to pick up. Her voicemail was crisp, offering this date and time for a meeting, and little else. Though she did make it clear she would agree only to a "conversation," not an interview.

He has brought his digital recorder and notebook just in case, tucked away in his jacket pocket. The last thing he wants is to scare her off.

He rings the bell, and a woman who is not Jane Proctor answers. She is short and squat, in her early fifties, with a wide, pleasant face and short reddish hair, wearing a baggy aqua sweatsuit with running shoes. "Come in, come in," she says. "I'm Karen. I help Mrs. Proctor out a few days a week. Oh Lord, it's really raw out there. Here, let me take your coat."

Bron shakes off the jacket and then follows Karen into a sitting room, where Jane is perched on a petite floral sofa perpendicular to an old stone fireplace. A well-laid fire smokes, sparks, crackles. The room is dim, worn, cozy, like the set of a Christmas special. There is a full tea service and a covered cake dish on the mahogany table in front of the sofa, with two comfortable club chairs in faded yellow upholstery on the other side. Jane is wearing a pale blue blouse with embroidery and dark slacks, a navy cardigan sweater thrown around her shoulders. She carries a slightly royal air, like the matriarch of a political dynasty.

Bron hobbles in with the cane, extends a hand to her. "Thank you so much for having me."

She nods primly, waves him into a chair. "I'm sorry to drag you here in such terrible weather. Did you drive yourself?"

"Yes, yes. Just back behind the wheel. Few weeks now. The leg gets creaky in the rain, but it still works on the gas pedal, thankfully." They make idle chitchat for a few more minutes — his rehab process, the colder-than-normal spring, his neighborhood in Fairmount — as Jane pours the tea, adds lemon for him, cream and sugar for herself. Karen throws another log onto the fire, then disappears.

"Thank you for having me," Bron repeats. He cannot believe how nervous he is. Why is he so nervous? He has interviewed all sorts of people, many of them wary. But in every case there was some crack, some opening, some place to wedge in and pull back the casing, to dig to the person underneath. He looks at Jane Proctor, at her icy hazel eyes, and sees nothing but armor.

It is almost impossible to believe that this woman was once Betty Jane Welch, Miss America 1950, the girl who at nineteen abdicated her title the night she won it; ran off with her boyfriend while being chased by private detectives, the police, and the press; then found herself mixed up in a toxic web of deceit, scandal, and murder that was eventually splashed onto the front page of every newspaper in the country. And then who, perhaps more amazingly, managed to vanish yet again.

Jane gently places her cup and saucer on the table, then leans back into the sofa, eyeing him cautiously. "There is a reason, Mr. McCall, I have never spoken of the events of 1949," she says, slowly, deliberately. Like she's rehearsed. "And that should be obvious. I realize in this age we now live in, where everyone wants to go on the Internet and be as famous or infamous as possible, the notion of wanting to avoid it just as passionately must seem rather strange. Or at least quaint. I was a public figure but for a brief moment in time. And I would very much like to keep it that way."

"But you have such an amazing story to tell," he says. "You must know that. I mean, all of your privacy issues aside, objectively speaking, you must realize that your story is an incredible one."

"My 'story,' as you put it, is that I was a naïve girl of nineteen who got in over her head. I am hardly the first woman to have that in her past, I dare say."

"With all due respect, Mrs. Proctor, that's a rather broad simplification of what happened."

She folds her arms. "What possible benefit—other than that of feathering your own career—can my rehashing all of this possibly hold? News vans outside my door all day and night? Strange people calling? My face plastered on the *Today* show? Tell me: Why on earth would I ever subject myself to that, subject my children and grandchildren to that, relinquish the quiet, orderly life I have spent the last sixty-five years building?"

It is a good question. Actually, it is *the* question. But mercifully he has known it would be coming. A clear and honest answer, he is certain, is his only shot at getting her to lower the emotional draw-bridge she's kept raised for more than half a century.

"I would say only this to you," he replies. "We do not get to de-cide what history is. History decides what history is. And I think we, as a civil society, as a society of people who want to learn where we have been and where we are going, have a duty to record his-tory as it happened, as accurately and comprehensively as possible. Yours has not been recorded at all. It's a hodgepodge of rumor and speculation and some old tabloid headlines aggregated on Wikipe-dia. You are the only person who knows what really happened that fall of 1949."

"And I have some sort of moral duty to share it?"

"You have an opportunity to educate people."

"That's a liberal application of the word 'educate,' Mr. McCall. We are not talking about the details of the Yalta Conference."

He cracks a smile. She is spirited, eloquent, direct, a deft fencer with words and reason. If she were six decades younger he'd be asking her out. He can see what led Griff McAllister to fall for her, to do what he did for her. To literally lose his mind for her. He wishes he could be recording this. It's gold. And all off the record.

He looks at her with a fondness he never expected to feel and hopes she can see that it is organic, genuine, not some act of manu-factured smarminess. "You're right, of course," he says. "It's not the Yalta Conference. But it is a missing chapter in the life and history of an American institution. And I think that's a shame. Will others show up to bother you if you talk to me? Maybe. I can't promise they won't. But I can promise that no one can tell your story more fairly, more honestly, and better than I can. And deep down I think you'd like to tell it, to share it, to help people understand, if not specifically what happened to you, what happens to someone when you are suddenly an ordinary person thrust into extraordinary cir-cumstances. I do believe there is value in that, Mrs. Proctor. I honestly do. But I am not here to badger you into this. For one thing, I suspect you cannot be badgered, by me or anyone else."

She laughs, and it catches him off guard. "My grandchildren," she says quietly, "would disagree."

He nods. "I'm sure. So how about this? How about we just sit, and have a lovely visit, and drink some tea, and enjoy this nice fire."

The room falls silent, the only sounds the snapping and popping of the glowing orange wood, the quarter-hour bong of the grandfather clock in the hall. Her eyes are warm but studying. He can almost hear her weighing sides inside her head. But he remains quiet. If nothing else, this has been a start, the crack, whether anything comes of it or not.

"Pour yourself some more tea," she says, leaning over the table and lifting the cover of the cake plate. A wonderful aroma fills the air, sweet and tart. She cuts a generous slice of the yellow cake, tips it onto a sage green plate, hands it to him with a dessert fork and a linen napkin.

He brings it up to his nostrils, takes in a deep whiff. Lemon. "Smells delicious," he says. "What is it?"

"It," she says, again leaning back into the sofa, slowly crossing her legs, "is where the story starts."

Author's Note

In September 1987 I got my first job in magazine publishing, as a writer at *Atlantic City* magazine, which operated out of a ratty former shoe store on Atlantic Avenue. It was run by a fabulous woman named Frances Freedman, who always wore fur coats draped over her shoulders and who had a mad penchant for tuna salad. Atlantic City in those days was beguiling: casino gambling was less than a decade old, and there was this feeling of expectancy everywhere. And the characters! Donald Trump (and Ivana), Mike Tyson, and Celestine Tate, the woman who played the keyboard with her tongue on the Boardwalk.

During my first week, I was promptly dispatched to see all of the preparations for the upcoming Miss America Pageant at Convention Hall. At one point I ended up alone in the historic arena, so — making sure no one else was around — I snuck a walk down the legendary runway. And it struck me, standing at the runway's terminus, looking around at those thousands of seats, how powerful an experience it must be to actually *win*.

Over the years I wrote several stories about the pageant, one of them centered on a little-known chapter in Miss America history. In 1937, egged on by her girlfriends, seventeen-year-old Bette Cooper had entered a beauty contest at an amusement park in Bertrand Island, New Jersey. She won, finding herself a most unlikely contestant at Miss America that September. Back in those days the pageant assigned each young lady who competed an escort, a young man from one of the area's better families to squire her around for the week. Bette's escort was named Louis Off, a dashing twenty-two-year-old who drove a maroon Buick Special convertible and whose family ran a prominent nursery called Brighton Farms. Bette and Lou fell hard for each other; Lou sent Bette orchids every day. But Lou did not want to be "Mr. Miss America" and told Bette plainly that if she won, their relationship was over. Naïve and love-struck, Bette thought such an outcome impossible.

And then she won.

True to his word, Lou broke off their relationship that very night. (When I interviewed Lou many years later, he told me how much he regretted how he had handled it.) Bette was inconsolable, later calling Lou in the middle of the night. Arriving at her hotel, he asked her if she wanted to get out of being Miss America, and she said yes. With the help of two buddies, he spirited her out of the hotel, into his car, and then into a boat, where they hid moored off of the Steel Pier as a countywide manhunt for the missing beauty queen ensued.

The next day, Lou drove Bette home to northern New Jersey, just as furious pageant officials uncovered their caper. A chilly détente was struck, where Bette agreed to a few appearances as Miss America. Alas, like many summer romances, Bette and Lou's fizzled. The following September, Marilyn Meseke of Ohio was crowned the new Miss America.

The pageant abandoned the escort program.

Each year the Miss America Organization extends an invitation to all of the surviving members who comprise the unique sorority of its former titleholders to come back for the contest. Bette Cooper never accepted. She never spoke about what happened that eventful night. Instead, she retreated to a quiet life as a wife and mother in Connecticut, where as far as I know she still lives, now in her mid-nineties. Piqued by her story, reporters have occasionally tracked her down and knocked on her door, asking to interview her. She's told them all the same thing: "There is no Miss America here."

Though these facts about Bette Cooper inspired this novel, it is important to note that *The Night She Won Miss America* is purely and completely a work of fiction. Betty Jane Welch is a character developed from my own overly active imagination, as are the other characters and dramatic circumstances she encounters. And while several named real-life people make appearances—chief among them pageant director Lenora Slaughter—their words and actions here are strictly fictitious. I only hope this invented narrative proves as entertaining as the strange, scandalous true tale of the apple-cheeked ingénue from New Jersey who, in 1937, changed the course of Miss America forever.

Acknowledgments

The irony of writing a book is that it is a solitary enterprise—you and the blank page—that in the end requires the help of an extraordinary amount of people. My agent, Jane Dystel, was as usual my brassy, sassy advocate. I have been blessed to find in my editor at Houghton Mifflin Harcourt, Nicole Angeloro, a kindred spirit who both shares my unvarnished love of midcentury glamour and who provided incisive direction and deft edits to help polish the narrative.

When it came time to actually write, I discovered a sanctuary in the Martha's Vineyard Writer's Residency at the Noëpe Center for Literary Arts in Edgartown, Massachusetts. I started this book there, and I finished it there. To its director, the elegiac poet Justen Ahren, and its convivial house managers, Jack Sonni and Sean Murphy, I extend my heartfelt appreciation for creating such a welcoming and inspiring space in which to create.

Of course, good historical fiction starts with research, and there was much to undertake with this story. Both Beth Ryan, coordinator at the Atlantic City Historical Museum, and Heather Perez, archivist of the Atlantic City Heritage Collections at the Heston Room in the Atlantic City Free Public Library, were invaluable in guiding me to clippings, letters, menus, memorabilia, and endless spools of microfiche about Miss America and Atlantic City in 1949. I have done my best to stay as true to the feel and traditions of both the pageant and the era as I possibly could, while making creative allowances to advance the story. Any mistakes are completely my own.

Additional thanks go out to Christine Sullivan, the former general manager at the Chanler at Cliff Walk (in 1949 known as Cliff Lawn Manor), in Newport, Rhode Island, who courteously hosted me for several days and replied to my many detailed inquiries about the history of the beautiful property; Bertram Lippincott III, reference librarian and genealogist at the Newport Historical Society Museum & Library, who just might know more about Newport than anyone else alive; harpist extraordinaire Anita Findley, who explained the ins and outs of playing that beautiful instrument; and Dr. Neel Burton, professor of psychiatry at Oxford University and the author of *Living with Schizophrenia,* who not only patiently answered my many questions about the disorder and its manifestations, but also took the time to take me on a lovely walking tour of the private Oxford gardens on that rarest of occasions, a sunny day in England.

Of course, no one understands what it is like to actually *be* Miss America better than the women who have worn the famous tiara. I am forever indebted to the incredibly warm and lovely Bea Waring—the former BeBe Shopp, Miss America 1948—whose recollection of her time at the pageant remains razor-sharp, and who was gracious enough to share her memories with me. My additional gratitude to all of the former Miss Americas whom I have had the pleasure of meeting and interviewing over the years: Phyllis George, Heather French, Kaye Lani Rae Rafko, Kate Shindle,

Donna Axum, Angela Perez Baraquio, Carolyn Sapp, Ericka Dunlap, and Kellye Cash.

Several books assisted my research, chief among them Frank Deford's *There She Is: The Life and Times of Miss America*, which, almost fifty years after its publication, remains the seminal work about the pageant; and also *Miss America: In Pursuit of the Crown*, by Ann-Marie Bivans; *Atlantic City: 125 Years of Ocean Madness*, by Vicki Gold Levi and Lee Eisenberg; *1940s Fashion: The Definitive Sourcebook*, by Emmanuelle Dirix and Charlotte Fiell; and *1940's Style Guide: The Complete Illustrated Guide to 1940's Fashion for Men and Women*, by Debbie Sessions.

And finally some personal *mercis*, to my fellow Miss America–ophile Lisa DePaulo, who shares my obsessive love of the pageant and its colorful history; to Jenny DeMonte, who as the editor of *New Jersey Monthly* in 1994 let me write the story of Bette Cooper, planting the seeds for this book; to my beta readers, Cheryl Della Pietra, Christy Speer Lejeune, and Jean Callahan, who provided thoughtful feedback; and to all of my family and friends, always there to support my storytelling endeavors. And lastly, to my wonderful mom, Eileen, who suitably oohed and aahed over the kooky crayoned stories I whipped up when I was a little boy, and saved each and every one: For all of the years of calls, cards, and the very best hugs—I love you.

A Discussion Guide

1. What does it usually mean when Betty's mother makes her favorite lemon cake? Why has her mother made it this time? Why does Betty agree to join the Miss Delaware pageant even though she claims to have no personal interest in pageantry? Do you think that her choice is a good one? Why or why not?

2. According to the novel, what is the Miss America pageant supposed to represent? Does the pageant and its participants truly live up to this? Explain. Why do you think that the pageant was so well-beloved at that time?

3. What are some of the rules that pageant contestants must follow? Would you say that these rules seem reasonable? What purpose might they serve? Do Betty and the other contestants

follow these rules? If not, which rules do they break and what are the consequences?

4. What are Betty's first impressions of Griff? Would you say that she is able to accurately assess who he is within their first few meetings? Are her first impressions of him correct? What does the book suggest about identity and first impressions?

5. Why do you think that the judges seem interested in Betty even though she expresses minimal interest in the pageant? What makes her stand out from the other young women in the pageant?

6. How does Betty respond to winning the Miss America pageant? What is her time like after being crowned as Miss America? Were you surprised by her reaction? Why does she ultimately decide to take an action that she knows will mean giving up her position and the crown?

7. What is the secret that Griff keeps from Betty? Why do you think that Betty stays with Griff even after she learns of his condition? How does knowing about Griff's condition makes Griff "seem" to her?

8. Who is Eddie Tate and why is he so interested in Betty and her story? Why doesn't Tate report what he finds in Reeve's apartment?

9. Although Ciji ultimately helps Betty, she first denies to others that she and Betty were ever close friends. Why does she do this? Why is Ciji afraid of honoring her promise to come to Betty's aid if Betty needs a "Joan of Arc"?

10. Consider the motif of denial. Which characters in the novel are in denial of something? What do they deny, and what causes them to do this? Do they ever reconcile with what they try to deny? Explain.

11. The book captures the story of an ordinary person changed in an extraordinary moment. What does the book suggest about the impact and legacy of fame? Is fame something that should be sought after? Why or why not?

12. Why does Bron think that Betty should tell her story, even after so many years have passed? How does he try to convince her to do this? Is he successful? Why or why not? What does he tell Betty that he believes about history? Do you agree with him?

13. Through *The Night She Won Miss America* the author creates a portrait of a bygone era. What does the novel reveal about this time period and its culture? Consider language, setting, imagery, and thematic material such as the treatment of social class, race, and gender roles, for example.

14. Reviewers have referred to Callahan's novel as "cinematic." What do you think they mean by this? What cinematic qualities does the book have, and how does the author give the book this quality? What kinds of films would you compare to the novel and why?

15. What were your thoughts and feelings about pageants before reading Callahan's novel? Did the novel change your view of pageantry or the Miss America pageant in any way? If so, what caused you to change your point of view? Discuss.

About the Author

Michael Callahan is a contributing editor at *Vanity Fair* and was formerly a deputy editor at *Town & Country* and *Marie Claire*. He is the author of *Searching for Grace Kelly* (2015) and *The Night She Won Miss America* (2017). His work has also been published in *Elle*, the *New York Times*, the *Hollywood Reporter*, and many other national publications.

Suggestions for Further Reading

Benjamin, Melanie. *The Swans of Fifth Avenue*
Buntin, Julie. *Marlena*
Davis, Fiona. *The Dollhouse*
DiSclafani, Anton. *The After Party*
Hepinstall, Kathy. *The Book of Polly*
Meyers, Randy Susan. *The Widow of Wall Street*
Peterson, Holly. *It Happens in the Hamptons*
Scottoline, Lisa. *One Perfect Lie*
Segal, Francesca. *The Awkward Age*
Shindle, Kate. *Being Miss America: Behind the Rhinestone Curtain*
Williams, Beatriz. *A Hundred Summers*

A Conversation with Michael Callahan

The Night She Won Miss America is "inspired by a true story."
What's the story—and how did you come to learn it?

In 1937, Bette Cooper had been with some girlfriends at a
New Jersey amusement park when they nudged her into entering a
beauty contest being held there; the winner got to compete in Miss
America. She did, and she won. Back in those days, the pageant
assigned each contestant an escort for the week, and Bette fell in
love with hers, a young man named Louis Off. But Lou wanted no
part of being "Miss America's boyfriend," so on the night she won
he cruelly broke things off—years later, when I interviewed him,
he still felt bad for being such a cad—and later that night she
was devastated, and begged him to get her out of it. So he snuck
her out of her hotel, and the next morning all hell broke loose.
Their romance was short-lived, and Bette did, in fact, do some
limited appearances as Miss America. But once her year was over
she never spoke about it again, and in some cases actively denied
she had ever been Miss America. As a writer in Atlantic City in the

late 1980s, I learned the story and eventually wrote a piece about it. I always thought it would make for a great piece of fiction, if you took the bones and then turned it into a real soapy story, about a Miss America who takes off the night she wins to parts unknown.

Miss America seems almost anachronistic in modern society. To what do you attribute her longevity?

It's hard to believe that in a few years Miss America will be one hundred years old. But the princess ideal is something all girls grow up with, even today. And we never had royalty in this country. There is still something fizzy about crowns and capes. And remember that Miss America is our longest-running reality show: you take a group, whittle them down little by little, until a winner emerges. That's been the template for half of the shows on television this century.

A lot of feminists and others say Miss America is long past her due date.

I don't subscribe to that. Must everything in society be discarded a year later, like the latest iPhone? We think young women who pole-dance to earn college tuition are owning their sexuality and showing their grit. And yet, a young woman who enters a contest to earn scholarship money by playing the oboe and wearing a bathing suit is somehow setting women back a century. You can't applaud women like Lady Gaga, Katy Perry, and Miley Cyrus, who put out hyper-sexualized content in the name of female empowerment, and then throw brickbats at Miss America. It's unfair.

You seem very attached to Miss America. Where does that come from?

Well, I've interviewed and met almost a dozen Miss Americas

over the last thirty years, and I have been to more than my share of pageants, so I feel an emotional attachment. At the very first pageant I attended, in 1987, I sat by chance with Miss Michigan's family. Miss Michigan won the title that year. It was insanity. I got completely swept up in it. I just love Americana, and you can't get more Americana than this contest.

This book, like your last, Searching for Grace Kelly, *is set in mid-century America. Why do you love this period?*

I think because while there was a lot wrong with America then, particularly in the area of civil rights, women's rights, and race, there was also a lot right. People dressed well, people had manners, there were civics and respect and a cultural belief in American exceptionalism. I just find it so glamorous. I gobbled up every episode of *Mad Men*.

How did you research this novel?

Well, I obviously had written a lot about the pageant over the years, so I knew where the resources would be and how to curate them. I found some terrific researchers in Atlantic City who were enormously helpful, and BeBe Shopp, Miss America 1948, spent a good deal of time with me on the phone, which was just the best thing ever. The research was pretty exhaustive, taking me from Atlantic City to New York to Newport, Rhode Island, and even to Oxford, England. But I love research, because historical fiction is like a big puzzle you have to put together. And I really wanted people to feel like they were there in 1949, and to do that I needed the details. I pulled old menus, old postcards, and old ads. So, for example, the pageant judges in the book are the very same ones who judged the pageant in 1949, and the host was that host, and that was the program itinerary, and even the talents are representative of the talents that year. I took some liberties for the story—for example, the escort program, which is how Miss Delaware Betty Jane Welch meets Griffin McAllister in my novel—was abandoned after the Bette Cooper incident in 1937. But it's still part of the Miss America legacy.

Given that this novel and your first are about young women in mid-century America, how are they different?

Searching for Grace Kelly was more of a character portrait, of three young women who became unlikely friends because of this hotel they all lived in in 1955. *The Night She Won Miss America* is more of a caper, a yarn; I think it has a bit more gallop in the narrative, especially once Betty Jane Welch runs off with Griff. The pacing was more of a challenge here, because of all the moving parts. But it was mad fun to write.